"I thought it would be trite and magnificent," Dick Gibson laments.

Like *The Great Gatsby,* he wants life to live up to myth. An itinerant early media man, he travels across the country working for dozens of small-town radio stations. He is the perpetual apprentice, whetting his skills and adopting names and accents to suit geography. Stanley Elkin captures the essence of the man and the time. His "prose is alive, with its wealth of detail and specifically American metaphors," says *The Library Journal,* "and the surreal elements are tightly controlled," with "brilliant sequences . . . compulsively readable and exhilarating."

Novels by Stanley Elkin

A Bad Man
Boswell
Criers and Kibitzers, Kibitzers and Criers
The Dick Gibson Show
The Living End

Published by
WARNER BOOKS

Stanley Elkin

The Dick Gibson Show

WARNER BOOKS

A Warner Communications Company

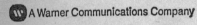

To

Jack Eigen: WMAQ
Jerry Williams: WBZ
Long John Nebel: WNBC
Joe Gearing: WJAS
Bill Barker: KOA
Ira Blue: KFRC
Jean Shepherd: WOR
Barry Gray: WMCA
Jack McKinney: WCAU
Joan Elkin: WIFE

I would like to thank the Rockefeller Foundation
for its generous financial assistance
while I was writing this novel.

Part I

1

When Dick Gibson was a little boy he was not Dick Gibson. And he could get Omaha, could get Detroit, could get Memphis; New Orleans he could get. And once—it was not a particularly clear or cold night; for that matter it may even have rained earlier—he got Seattle, Washington. He listened almost until sign-off, hoping that the staff announcer would say something about the wattage put out by the station. Then, after the midnight news but before the amen of the sermonette, the station faded irrecoverably. He'd learned never to fool with the dial, that it did no good when a signal waned to reclaim it with some careful, surgical twist a half-dozen kilocycles to the right or left. It was best to wait through the babble and static for the return of the electronic tide. Often it would come, renewed for its haitus, its cosmic romp and drift, strongly present again after its mysterious trip to the universe. This time it didn't.

11

He did not hear that particular station again until he was a part-time staff announcer in Butte, Montana, a kid who in those days—it was his first job—liked to doll up his speech and introduce into its already bygone mid-Atlantic base—Tex Ellery he called himself—some heroic man's man drawl, a quality of bright bandanna, checked wool shirt and sheepskin coat—a crackling, youthful noise, courteous and ma'aming, but cautious and deceptively slow in another, knowing register: last to draw, first to shoot. He had not yet learned the good announcer's trick of distance, his way with a mile, the sense he gave of the alien, of the Southerner come north, the Northerner dropped south, sliding subtly into regionalism only during the commercial, not presuming to persume to direct, but doing all commanding and urging and wheedling in a sort of moral blackface, deferentially one of them only when the chips were down and money passed.

He heard the station again in Butte, Montana. He was sitting miles out, in the transmitter shack where he sometimes doubled as engineer. He had just done his sleepy duty to the dials he did not really understand, uncertainly monitored the audio frequencies and seen to their many-trillioned amplifications. (He did not read the figures themselves, merely the dangerous red margins of the curving dial faces, looking out for the insufficiencies implicit in the needles' steep ascent, the surfeits of their fearful plunges at the other end, alarmed only for their throes, engaged by extremes and compensating by reactions, reining in and pouring it on by turns.) It was a quiet night in an early stormless spring, the stars distinct, the sun spotless. The needles floated easily in their white calm, and he listened to the radio he had brought with him. The other, a speaker permanently tuned to the Butte station, softly played a transcription of dance music. Rotely he turned the dial of his radio, a little bored, too familiar with what he could expect to bring in here, when suddenly, and as clearly as if it were a local station, he heard the old Seattle call letters and remembered at once the evening he had first heard them in bed. Strangely, though he was thousands of miles closer to Seattle than he had been when he had first heard its signal all those years before, the city seemed just as distant, the intervening planes of time undiminished, all imagination's vast, seamless landscapes still between. Excitedly he entered the station's call letters and wave length in the logbook he kept. He listened for the announcer's name and entered that, together with a brief description of the nature of the program. The log, a ringed, black leather looseleaf notebook, was thick with the entries he had made over the years. Arranged alphabetically according to their call letters, the designations seemed more like words to him than sounds or names, the harsh, often vowelless "K" calls and softer "W" calls and "C" for Canada calls and stations in Mexico beginning with "X" like the difficult names of Aztec gods.

When he had made his entry he was momentarily distracted by the low sounds coming out of the speaker mounted above his desk. The music was still playing, but he thought he detected a shift, a sudden soprano sharpness in the mix. He looked nervously at the dials but saw that all the needles still treaded easily in the safe middle depths of their dial faces. He turned up the volume on the speaker and listened. He had a sensitive ear, for the sound of radio some sort of unmusical perfect pitch, and he was certain that the tone quality had changed. Yet the dials, consulted again, registered nothing wrong; as blandly steady as some Greenwich constant, they signified an almost textbook energy. He turned off his radio and tilted his head judiciously toward the sounds that came from the speaker. He looked at the telephone that connected him on a direct line to his station, certain it would ring. Checking the dials a third time—the sound had thickened now, exactly, it occurred to him, like the signal of a station just before it fades—he decided that the trouble must be in the transcription itself.

He picked up on the phone. The studio engineer was already on it. "What's going on?" the man asked.

13

"It's got to be in the transcription. The dials show I'm putting out everything I'm receiving. Get Markham to make an announcement."

"Markham's out," the engineer told him. "The transcription was supposed to run for a half hour. I'm the only one here."

"Well, put on something else. It sounds awful."

"I know. Look, use the standby mike. I'll cut you in from the shack. Open your mike in thirty seconds. I'll have to duck out to the music library and get something. Can you talk for a few minutes?"

"I'll say *some*thing."

He replaced the receiver and rushed to the microphone. It was an ancient thing from the earliest days of broadcasting, an enormous iron web used now only for emergencies, calming alarm at alarm's source with messages of contingency deflected and the handled untoward. It shattered the sudden or extended silences with the hearty good cheer and sweet reason of all backstage coping, by that fact creating a sense of the real silence held off, engaged elsewhere: nothing to worry about while the auxiliary microphone still burned and the staff still lived. The bulletins of reassurance—PLEASE STAND BY; ONE MOMENT PLEASE!—showing that emergency could still be courteous, disaster graceful-spirited. He had first heard them as a child, thrilling to their lesson that help was available. When the film tore or the lines went down there were always calm men to give these signals. In a way, it was what had attracted him to radio: the steady steady-as-she-goes pep talk of trouble shooters who routinized the extraordinary.

He counted to ten and opened his microphone. He heard the needle arm tear across the surface of the transcription, leaving the mounted speaker not dead but crepitant, the mike still open at the station braodcasting the void itself now, amplifying the bristling snap and hiss of the universe. "Please stand by," he announced. But he had forgotten to turn down the speaker and heard his voice bounce back at him, enormous and delayed by a fraction of a fraction of a second. He became confused.

"One moment please," he begged, and again the two voices—the one in his mouth that all his life he would stand behind, his sound but always sent away, forever sacrificed, and the one booming from the speaker—seemed to collide fiercely in midair. It was a phenomenon he had experienced at the studio whenever someone had carelessly left open the door to the engineer's booth, and he knew it could combust in a sudden piercing feedback. But something about the shack's isolation, the idea of his ricocheting voice, its far-flung ventriloquous roundtrip, was exciting to him. Although he still expected momentarily to ignite a shriek as the two voices sparked each other, he began to speak.

"Please stand by," he said again. "One moment please. Please stand by one moment. Stand please. Please, one moment. Please stand one moment." Meanwhile he reached for the control knob on the mounted speaker, found it, and turned the volume all the way down.

Air time was expensive, a queer, infinite vacuum that might be filled with a whisper but always had to be fed with sound. Unthinkingly and forgetting the engineer who waited at the studio, he began to discharge his voice into the vacuum. "A little technical difficulty, pardners. This is your announcer, Tex Ellery, assuring you that it's only some trouble with the ol' transcription. We'll set it all to rights in a minute, folks, and that's a promise. You can bet your boots it is. Meanwhile this is your master of ceremonies, Ted Elson"—it was a slip of the tongue but he liked the sound and repeated it—"Ted Elson out at the transmitter shack just outside beautiful Butte, Montana, promising all his radio friends that something very special's coming up, something they wouldn't want to miss. So stand by and don't touch that dial or you'll be making a mistake. Ma'am, Mom, call the ranch hands in, they'll want to hear this too. Sure as shootin' they will. One moment *puhleeze!*"

He expected to hear the music when the engineer put it on at the station, but he had forgotten that he had turned down the speaker. He figured the man could not find anything suitable and continued to speak, perhaps above the music the engineer may already have put on the turntable. He was no longer nervous and began to enjoy himself, excited by his efficiency and the sense he had of successfully handling an emergency.

"Ted Elmer here, folks. We're just about ready. Meanwhile I thought you'd like to hear this joke." He told them the joke; remembering another story, he told that, and then a third joke and a fourth. He was easy now, elated by the deep-breath risks he took, delighted by the sound of his voice, those swaggered drafts of lung-strut, chug-a-lugging the vacuum itself. Disregarding voice level, he laughed loudly at the punch lines, getting a generous sense of helping his cause and clearing his sinuses, blowing those seats of the crabbed and ordinary skyhigh. As he spoke he fidgeted with the looseleaf notebook he still held, absent-mindedly tearing pages from it and dropping them to the floor as he would the pages of a script.

He spoke until it was time for the next program to go on; then, reluctantly, but with the certainty that they would hear him again this way—he envisaged a magnificent future—he turned his listeners back to the studio.

"This is your host, the inimitable Dick Gibson, signing off for now." (The name had come to him from the air.) *"Take it away, Markham!"*

SOME DEMO'S; FAMOUS FIRSTS:

"Dick Gibson, WLAF, Somerset, Pennsylvania—

"I can tell you this much: I was among the first to hear of Pearl Harbor, to hear of D-Day, to hear FDR died. I knew that Hitler had marched into Russia before the President knew. And Hiroshima—I was one of the first Americans to get the word on that. 'Keep calm,' I said on that fabulous night when Orson Welles scared hell out of the country with his invasion from Mars. 'Stand by please for a bulletin.' You might have heard me say something like that if you lived in Toledo when Eisenhower suffered the first of his heart attacks. Or Winston-Salem the afternoon we made our move in Korea. Of course you'd have

16

to have had certain principles, been out of lock-step with a number of your kind, had this penchant for the rural and off-brand, distrusted, perhaps, the smooth network voices of the East. Maybe you're kind to amateurs. Maybe you're an amateur yourself.

"Not that *I* am. A pro true blue and through and through. As you can tell from all the history I've been in on. It was no fluke that I heard before you did of the birth of that new volcano in Yucatan. Four hundred farmers died. I saw *that* come in over the wire. I chose to sit on it, chose—I remember I was spinning Doris Day's 'It's Magic'—to let the music finish. And then I still didn't say. Chose not only not to say but not even to read it on the late news. I pulled it off the machine and folded it into my pocket and that was that. And if you lived in Pekin, Illinois, in the middle of the summer of 1954 and didn't take a Chicago or St. Louis paper or keep up with the magazines, you still don't know, or know only now. Power. The power of the pro.

"No fluke. All the invasions, surrenders and disasters. No fluke I'm in on the revolutions, those put down as well as those pulled off. That I know bad news first and bear it first, absorbing in split seconds my priority knowledge, adjusting to it, living with it minutes before my countrymen. Oh, the newsrooms, those ticking anterooms of history, where I, the messenger, hang out. Or called by a bell or flashing light to the ticker tape. Oh, those New York and Washington sequences, those graduated two-blink, three-blink, four-blink hitherings! Those ding and ding-dong and ding-dong-ding and *bong-bong-bong-bong* beckonings! Who determines those? Now *there's* a messenger. *There's* power—the kind I had in Pekin when I fished those four hundred Mexican farmers out of my machine, whisked them away and lit a match to them in my room at the Pekin House, singeing them a second time, unsung singed Mexicans. The Yucatan volcano was a four-flasher. Did you know that the atomic bomb—this is interesting—was only a three-flasher? Or that in the whole history of radio there have been just three five-flashers, and no six-flashers yet at all? They say that the end of the world will be only a six-flasher. Shock's rare half-dozens. There's something in that. Please remain calm. Please stand by. Please be easy.

"But maybe you take your assassinations elsewhere. Television, perhaps. Or network radio. Maybe you didn't catch my six-flasher grief when I let go for once—'They shot him. In Dallas. Oh, Christ. Some son of a bitch in Dallas shot him.' I'll tell you something. Mad and stunned as I was, I knew what I was doing. I threw in 'son of a bitch.' I made that part up. Maybe I was anticipating my mention in *Time,* but I threw in 'son of a bitch' for the verisimilitude of the passion. You may have been tuned elsewhere, or speeding out of range with the car radio down the highway. But it's something, I tell you, bearing bad news. It's something, all right.

"And I'll tell you another thing. There are times, watching the mountain outside this studio, staring at it for hours while I spin my records, when I seem to see it go up in flames—the whole mountain, the trees go up and the town come down and the fire fighters on fire, a new Pompeii in Pennsylvania, and me, the stringer getting the word out. The sugary coda sweet in my mouth. 'Dick Gibson—WLAF, Somerset, Pennsylvania.' *That's* the word. *There's* my message.

"People ask how I can sound so sincere on the commercials, as if this were some burning question—*sure, the questions burn, but not the mountains!*—as they'd pry trade secrets from the wrestlers or demand of lawyers how they can defend guilty men. My advice to these folks is relax. Use your grain of salt, everybody. That's what it's for. Please remain calm. Stand by please.

"For a long time these demo's of mine have been the talk of the industry. Well, I'm gutsy, brash, waiting for someone to come along who likes the cut of my jib. My demo's are jib-designed. Collector's items they'll be one day. Because: though hypocrisy can take you far, it can only take you *so* far. When will you station managers realize that? Is there any one of you out there who likes the cut of truth's jib?

"If you want tricks, I can give them to you. Every

18

last trick I know. I have a friend who does a five-minute slot twelve times on weekends for one of the networks. You've heard him. (We say 'heard,' not 'heard of,' in this business.) Who doesn't know that voice today? Only the deaf. (We despise deafness. We'd rather hear a friend has gone blind.) He has this sports news and comment show. (*Sports!* He throws like a girl but he has an athletic voice.) Well, we used to work together on WPMT, Pompton Lakes, New Jersey. It's a resort town, and often there'd be celebrities around from the big hotels, and my friend or I would interview them. One time when I was in the booth before the show I heard the engineer ask for a level. 'Listen, Mr. Thus-and-Such,' my friend was saying, 'my first name's written down here on this piece of paper. Would you mind very much if you called me by it when we talk?' Then, on the air, he would hit the star with the guy's first name, and the star would hit my friend with *his* first name. They could have been the best pals in the world. And you'd be surprised how it worked on the listener's imagination, what it did for the listener's idea of my friend to hear him so intimate with big shots. I tell you that I myself—who knew how it was done—forgot sometimes and found myself wondering about my pal's rich past; I was proud to know such a guy. (But notice how I keep him anonymous here. Not here do I call out that phony's name. 'Mr. X' I call him here, or 'my friend.' How do you like that 'Mr. X', my friend?)

"So I know the shortcuts and the cheats. I'm not old but I've been in the business years. Listen, I've jazzed up my fan mail to impress a station manager. There have been times I've written myself up to a hundred letters a week. Jesus, I'll never forget this—in one batch I once made the mistake of asking for pictures, and the station manager had me make them up and pay for them myself. And one time, at KRJK, Benton, Texas—I was Bobby Spark back then—I organized my own fan club, using the name Debbie Simon as a front. I described the club's activities and made them sound so attractive over the air that before long almost two hundred teen-agers were interested in joining. They wanted to know how they

19

could get in touch with Debbie Simon, and I was really in trouble there for a while. I told them that Debbie had been spending so much time on the fan club that she had been ignoring her schoolwork and her parents had made her drop out of the club until her grades improved. Out of fairness to Debbie all activities of the fan club were suspended, I said, until she could get back into them too. So about a month later some kids wrote in to ask how Debbie was making out in school. For some reason it had become a big thing in Benton, and one day I had to announce that Debbie Simon was sick. Then, the next day, and treating the news just as I would some three- or four-flasher, I waited until I was playing the nation's number one song—which I was sending out to her in her sickbed—and broke in on it to tell them that Debbie's mother had called to tell me her daughter had passed away—with my name on her lips. In large part Debbie's mother blamed herself, I said, for putting too much pressure on her daughter, and making her drop out of the club. Then some sixteen-year-old kid named Stuart Standard called to ask if he could take over the club and continue Debbie's work now that she was gone. I told him he could, and the kids themselves renamed it 'The Debbie Simon Memorial Bobby Spark Fan Club.' Don't tell *me* there's anything wrong with today's teen-agers.

"For the most part, though, I'm above tricks. Instead, I pour myself into these demo's. (But demonstration records are expensive. I pay for the sessions myself, and press up to a hundred at a time. Something had better happen soon, no kidding. Networks and affiliates please note.) What programs these would make! Honeys! I could change America. But what do you need me for to do that, hey you big shots? You do it yourself every thirteen weeks. There are always stars. We breathe in the sky, for god's sake. (Give *me* a crack at the yahoos one time. *I'll* make their tabletalk for them, *I'll* be their household word, my taste as high or low as anyone's in the industry.) But don't contact me unless you've really got something to offer. You've got to put me on a clear channel station and give me a show of my own. The last demo got me this job at WLAF, and here I am doing another demo. Oh yes, big deal—NBC invited me to take their Page exam. For*get* it. (See? See how vulgar?) Look, forget the part about doing my own show. I'm willing to start further down if the station's important enough. I'll do continuity for you, commercials. I won't even insist on a talent fee. Consider my voice. Listen: 'This is WPTA, Hometown, America. Now back to the Baton Twirling Contest.' How do you like that? The voice is young, strong as an ox, flawless, no hoarseness, no crack, educated but not what you could call cultured—four years at the state university, say, or three years in the army as an ROTC lieutenant. I've been blessed, you guys, with my God-given gift of a voice, my voice that's been thirty-one years old for the past decade and won't be thirty-two for another ten years. And where did I grow to manhood? I *defy* you to say. Regionless my placeless vowels, my sourceless consonants. Twangless and drawl-less and nasal-less. And my name: Dick Gibson. (Though thus far I've used it only a few times on the air; I'm still saving it.) Dick Gibson of Nowhere, of Thin Air and the United States of America sky.

"I'll tell you how I came by my interest in radio. It's an interesting story. I'm not just another of your starstruck kids turned artist and sissy from childhood's isolation. You could say, I suppose, that it's actually in my blood. My father was in the point-to-point dot-dash news and private-message market back in the late teens and early twenties during the fabulous wireless/cable wars. He was a personal friend of Dr. Frank Conrad in East Pittsburgh, where KDKA started. My earliest memory is of being with Dad and a bunch of other men crowded around a receiving set to hear the Harding-Cox election returns. November 2, 1920. I was an infant, but I remember everything about it.

" 'Listen to this, son,' my father said, 'and remember all your life that you heard the birth of modern radio.' And I have. I was so impressed that I have.

"'Gentlemen,' Dr. Conrad said, 'this day wireless has come of age.' There were tears in the old man's eyes. He must have suffered plenty to make his dream come true.

"'It's grand, Dr. Conrad,' my father said. 'Let me say that I feel privileged to participate in this historic moment. Congratulations, Doctor.'

"'Thank you,' the great visionary said, 'but any thanks there are must be shared with others, with those workers in the vineyards who are no longer with us, men without whose contributions this great moment would have been achieved—oh yes, it would have come anyway; sometimes it would have come; there is no withstanding the siege of destiny; it would have been achieved, but delayed, the world made to wait. I mean men like Edinburgh University's James Clark Maxwell, who was the first to encounter ether waves as long ago as 1867; forgotten men like Hertz and the naïve Righi who gave us the phrase "magic blue sparks"; men like Onesti and Lodge and the Russian Popoff. To say nothing of the giants—the Marconis and De Forests and Lieutenant Sarnoff?

"'And Dr. Conrad,' my father said.

"'Thank . . .' Dr. Conrad began sweetly. But perhaps something caught in his throat at this moment, or it may be that he was too tired after his heroic efforts to bring this night to pass; or even, simply that by one of fate's tragic twists and ironies Dr. Conrad had voted for Cox—whatever it was he couldn't finish, and the rest of us, the men with him and my father with me in his arms, feeling the old man should be by himself just then, tiptoed softly from the room. I remember as if it were yesterday.

"There you have it. I am marked, historically attached to radio. Thank you for your time. *Dick Gibson, WLAF, Somerset, Pennsylvania.*"

In the first years following his departure from the station in Butte, Montana, he did not again have occasion to use the name. For three months, with WMAR in Marshall, Maine, he was Ellery Loyola. Then, for an even briefer season with KCGN, Butler, Kansas, he was Mar-

22

shall Maine. He replaced an announcer who had been hired by KCMO, Kansas City, to MC a program of dance music originating in the Buhler Hotel there, but the hotel burned down—the program was on the air at the time and the announcer had been instrumental in guiding the dancers to safety—and the man was given his old job back, and Dick became Bud Kanz of KWYL, 1450 on your dial, Hodge, Iowa. By the fall of that same year he had become I. O. Quill, WWD, La Crosse, Wisconsin. He worked for the La Crosse station for a little over a year; then in the next two years he had jobs with five more radio stations.

That he moved about so often in those early years was no proof of his restlessness; rather, it was his way of learning the business. He was your true apprentice—eager, willing, a boy who would chip in for any chore—but all the while he kept a careful accounting and worked with a special sense of his own destiny that converted the difficult into the necessary and created in himself metaphorical notions of money in the bank and bread cast upon the waters—a priggish, squirrelly sense of provision. Even his rooms in those days, those below-stairs cubicles in the homes of widows for whom he shoveled snow and stoked furnaces whose heat never seemed to reach his room, and which were all he could afford on the fifteen- and twenty-dollar-a-week salaries he made, or his rooms in the towns' single hotels, near the railroad stations, bargained for, a rate granted not simply in deference to his extended stay but in recognition of some built-in inferiority, the bed always in a vulnerable position, the room itself in a vulnerable position, over a boiler perhaps, or machinery, or behind the thin wall of the common washroom, or too far from it, or his window just behind the vertical of the hotel's blazing electric sign—there was a room in Kansas where owing to some obscure fire law the bulb in the high ceiling could never be turned off—even these rooms left him (despite the indifferent luke warmth that came from ancient, prototypical radiators) with an impression not of poverty or straitened circumstance, so much as of guaranteeing his life later,

23

discomfit comforting, assuring him of *his* mythic turn, patience not just a virtue but a concomitant of future fame, hard times every success's a priori grist.

The American Dream, he thought, the historic path of all younger sons, unheired and unprovided. The old-time test of princes. "One two three testing," he had said into countless microphones on hundreds of cold winter mornings, sleep still in his eyes, he and the engineer the only ones at the station, and he there first, his key to the place not a privilege but a burden. "One two three testing." And even as he spoke the announcer's ritual words, he suspected the deeper ritual that lay beneath them, confident that a test was indeed being conducted, his entire young manhood one. There were so many jobs—*then;* later he had different reasons—because he insisted on these tests. He built a reputation as a utility man, an all-rounder, and he was never really sure that this didn't harm rather than help him because he was, for many of the 500- and 1000-watt stations for which he worked, a luxury, primed for emergency and special events which rarely, in those uneventful places he served his apprenticeship, occurred. But so set was he on sacrifice, so convinced in his bones of some necessary pay-as-you-go principle, that even an absolute knowledge that his special talents worked against his career would not have altered him. He continued to work in whatever he could of the unusual and by consistently putting himself in the way of opportunity, managed to do everything, discovering in the infinite resources of his voice, in the disparate uses to which it could be put, the various alter egos of human sound.

He was forced by radio to seem always to speak from the frontiers of commitment, always to say his piece as if his piece were all. Emphasis disappeared, for everything, the merest community-service announcement of a church supper and the most thunderous news bulletin, received ultimately the same treatment. With the necessity it imposed to be always talking, singing, selling, to be always speaking at the top of its voice, radio itself became a vessel for collateral truths. He had come to think of the sounds radio made as occurring on a line, picturing speech as a series of evenly sequenced, perfectly matched knots on a string, chatter raised by the complicated equipment to the level of prophecy. Pressured by the collateral quality of the noises he made, it would have been easy to have turned against the noises themselves. Others did. Most announcers he knew were men with an astonishing facility for disengaging themselves from their copy. Many actually made it a point to have their faces laugh while their voices continued to speak seriously. They horsed around—and those who had been in the business longest horsed around the most. He had noted—in New York City he took the same Radio City tour that everyone else did—that even the network people loved to clown, to shock their studio audiences with their studied superiority to the material, creating an anecdote for them to take back to Duluth, giving them all they could of the insider's contempuously lowered guard.

He eschewed their wiseguy character and scorned to duplicate their vicious winks for a deft professional reason of his own. He felt these acrobatics, these defections of the face, took away—however minutely—from the effectiveness of one's delivery, that even such muscular stunts as a mere wink pulled, too, at the vocal chords, puppeteered them. He could hear this. Monitoring his radio in the signal-fortified nights, omnisciently tuning in America, transporting himself with just his fingers five hundred miles north or a thousand east, these lapses were as clear to him as lisps, and he could see in his mind the smug double-dealing of a hundred announcers through their voices in the dark, as if he sat in the control booths watching them. The faculty for belief in the things he was required to say was no greater to him than in the biggest star or the oldest studio hack on the most important network station in America, but he used sincerity to body-build his voice. It would no sooner occur to him to insist on his personality when he was on the air (with the others, he knew, it was a last ditch shriek of their integrity, an effort to write off their disgust) than it would occur to an actor on a stage to answer for himself instead of for

25

the character he played. So, striving for conviction, he became something of a boomer, a hearty herald. (Briefly he was Harold Hearty, WLU, Waverly, Georgia.)

For a time—and he never completely rid himself of this habit—he carried over into his outside life the tones he used on radio, sometimes actually frightening people with his larger-than-life salutations: *"Good* morning there, Mrs. Cubbins! Lou George, WBSF, Kingdom City, Mo., here to see about the *room* you advertised!" Or embarrassing them with the breathy intimacy of his ten-to-midnight "Music for Lovers"; "Haie there, Miss. Bud Kanz. I've got a three o'clock appointment. The doc said he'd—sque*eeeee*ze me in."

Bluffness and sensuousness were not all his range, nor even a significant part of it. If he had to single out a tone which best characterized him in those early years it would have been rather a flat one. And why not? He was chiefly a man speaking to farmers, reading them the weather, telling them the hog and sheep and cattle prices, a harbinger of grain and vegetable conditions—"soybeans" and "rye" and "oats" words in every other sentence out of his mouth. He had learned almost from the outset to avoid folksiness, vaudevillizing their ways. The single time he had tried to appropriate what he took to be their vocabulary, he himself had had to answer the telephone to listen to their offended complaints: "You tell that damn Jew you got down there he'd best not make sport of us. That town bastard don't know piss from cowplop." From then on he spoke to them in flat accents as unnatural to him as dialect, his neutral reading of the daily markets as much a performance as any he had ever attempted.

But it was precisely on stations such as these that he got his best experience and was permitted to exercise his widest range. As soon as it became light—it was as if he could hear the farmers leaving their houses—he was left with their wives. These took, if their husbands didn't, a certain amount of kidding. Not that he tried any more than with the men to pass himself off as a country boy. Instead he went the other way entirely. He felt himself some traveling salesman among them, come to life from a joke. Emphasizing his alienness, his dazed slicker-in-the-sticks incarnation, as if he had just been set down there from Paris or New York, he made all he could of their funny ways. He flattered them with their homespun notion of themselves, never letting them forget their ailing-neighbor-fetched soups and astonishing pies of vegetable and wild fruit, finding his theme in the idea of appetite, exaggerating their capacities, bunyanizing the hunger of their men and selves: "Ladies, I've got a recipe here for a Kansas farm omelet. First, take eight dozen eggs. All right, we'll need some butter in this. Four pounds should do it." Or zeroing in on the quilts he pretended they were always making: "An Easterner came by yesterday, saw one and went blind. What I want to know is how you get any sleep under one of those things. One lady I heard of hung hers to dry out in the henhouse. Those hens laid eggs all night. The rooster came in about midnight, saw it and started to crow. He thought the darn sun had come up."

But he tickled them hardest with his allusions to the wily sex in them, inventing this appetite as he had built on the other, taking his biggest risks here, openly blue, barnyardy, pretending a kind of slicker exhaustion at the thought of their lusty bouts, frankly animalizing them, claiming awe and a ferocious physical respect in the face of their enormous sexual reserves, careful only to specify the essential domesticity of their ardor, its vaguely biblical franchise. (But even this sop shrewdly dispensed with when it came to their daughters, those—as he had it—one-hundred-sixty-two-pound, big-boned killers of traveling men, singing their raucous muliebrity and celebrating their quicksand bodies in which whole male populations had gone down, entire sales forces.) The opportunities were limitless—their alleged floursack underthings another source of his feigned astonishment, imagining for them beneath the hypothetical homespun and supposed calico, hypothetical bodies, heavy toonervaudevillian tons of robust flesh, imperial gallons of breast, the thick, fictive restraining chest bands helpless against such soft erosion. And this was as aboveboard as their concupiscence, for it was all in reference to an exercise-and-reducing show he had talked the station manager into letting him do.

"What? A skinny kid like you? Don't make me laugh."

"What difference does it make how I *look?* I've got a voice like Tarzan. Let me try."

And the man did—on the condition that he stay off the streets and that his audience never be permitted to see him.

He became "Doctor Torso." The voice he created for his new role was extraordinary. Deliberately aged, carefully made to seem just senior to the oldest lady doing the exercises, he sounded like some professional, not a gym teacher but a coach, with all the coach's indifference to the bodily distinctions between male and female—the body, ulteriorly, one big muscle he crooned over in his faintly theatrical telephone operator's diction. Himself sitting perfectly still at the table with the microphone, and, for the sake of the slight strain it gave to his voice, leaning on his elbows, his forehead forward and clamped into the heels of his hands. "With a *one* and a *two* and *three* and a *fower.* A *fiuv* and a *six* and a *seven* and an *eight.*" Then, blowing out his breath to clear the poisons, "All right, ladies. This next exercise is for your sitters. Get right down on the floor, now. Palms spread and about four inches to the side of those thighs we just firmed up so nicely for your hubbies. All right, now those precious legs straight and shut tight. Just like the vaults in the Bank of England." Interrupting himself. "Mrs. Frangnadler"—his imaginary scapegoat, his one-hundred-sixty-two-pound common denominator—"I said *tight.* No cheating on me. Tight together. You don't still have that rash. Tight now, tight. *Squeeze.* Pretend they're the two halves of your purse, and you're in town on a Saturday night, and you've got your egg money in there. Come on, Mrs. Frangnadler, I said tight." Slyly. "Why, if I was a thief I could reach right down in that purse of yours and steal something really valuable. Then what would your husband say? There, that's better. Why, I could hardly

28

get the edge of my knife down there now. Could I, ladies?" Then, pretending that he had turned back to the rest of them, "All right, then, when I start counting I want you to bring up the left thigh high as you can. I want to be able to slip my hand under there. Then down on the even number and bring up the right on the odd. We'll do this ten or twelve times together and then you practice it by yourselves at home. You'll soon feel the difference it makes. And if I know those husbands of yours, they'll feel the difference too. Incidentally, you mothers, start getting your young daughter to do this exercise with you. I pity the traveling man that tries to pinch *her*! All right, that's enough rest period. Ready, begin!"

But the rest periods, of course, were the point of the program; it was what they listened for. All of them relaxing together and him giving them all any of them would ever know of the locker room. They must have thought longingly of the easy sensuality of the city.

Just before he left that station and went on to the next, he announced the official tally—he had had them send in cards—of the weight they had collectively lost. It came to exactly one hundred sixty-two pounds. He always felt as if he had taken one of their women from them.

In lieu of a raise. For though he was a member of AFRA, the small stations he worked for in those days were not required to pay union scale. There were too many graduates of radio schools waiting for jobs. And though the big-city stations wouldn't touch them—back-of-the-matchbook dreamers, bad-complected, imperfectly pitched tenors and forced basses you had to hear just once to know all you ever needed to, not just of the condition of their lungs but of their glamour-caught souls too, their striven-for resonances accusing as fingerprints—small stations depended upon them. With his experience he might already have moved up to any number of stations cuts above the ones he worked. The NBC affiliate in Columbus, Ohio, was looking for someone exactly like himself, and would have paid him twenty-five dollars a week to start and jumped him to thirty dollars at the end of three months. Had he taken such a job, however, he would never have been allowed the liberties he took on the small stations. He was grateful for the temptation, but threw it into the pot with all the rest of the sacrifices he had made—more bread cast upon the waters, further frog years.

So he continued, for a while anyway, as an itinerant, a circuit rider, his colleagues still those same graduates of the radio schools, actual fairies many of them, but fairies of a lower order: penniless, pained fellows who strove for taste and a sense of the finer as they strove to stretch their range and improve their diction.

SOME DEMO'S; FURTHER FAMOUS FIRSTS:

"Dick Gibson, KWGG, Conrad, California. This next number is 'Dick's Demo,' Demonstration Record number twenty-seven, and goes out to all the guys 'n' gals in the industry who hire and fire. This is a take. Take! I am calling you—ooh-ooh-ooh, ooh-ooh-ooh.

"I tell you about the time I worked the newsroom at KROP, Roper, Nebraska? The apprenticeship was on me and I wasn't Dick Gibson yet. I was Marshall Maine, KROP, The Voice of Wheat. Some place that was. The ad I answered in *Broadcasting* said it reached listeners in three states. And so it did. We saturated two counties in northeast Nebraska, and leaped across the Missouri River to the Dell Indian Reservation in South Dakota. Whoever happened to be tuned in along a small rough stretch of Route 33 in western Iowa could also catch us.

"But let me tell you about those two counties. Sylvia Credenza County and Louis Credenza, Senior County. The whole area consisted of eight enormous farms owned by these eight brothers. The Credenza brothers: Louis III, Jim, Felix, Poke, Charley, George, Bill and Lee. That part of the state had been gerrymandered long before, and every two years each county sent a brother to the statehouse in Lincoln. They took turns. I was there during the reign of Charley and Bill.

"The station was a family hobby, sort of a Credenza

30

hookup. Like a party line. They built it in 1935 when reception was still bad in the area and they had nothing else to listen to. Later, when Sioux City, about sixty miles off, put up KSUX, a 5000-watter, reception improved, but the boys had gotten so used to having their own station that they decided to continue it. The funny thing is, none of the brothers enjoyed speaking on the radio themselves. They became self-conscious and would cough and sputter and stammer helplessly whenever, during those biennial political campaigns they put on for each other—brother ran against brother, though only two brothers were nominated from each county and, for all I know, only Credenzas were registered to vote—one of them had to make a speech. So, though they listened constantly to their own station—they had radios mounted on all their tractors and each barn—they never performed on it except during one of those queer campaigns. (I was around during one of them. Lee was running against Jim in Sylvia Credenza County, and Felix was up against George in Louis Credenza, Senior County. It was something, hearing those speeches, each Credenza urging his three constituent Credenza brothers—one the incumbent —to get out and vote. It didn't make any difference, they said, who they voted for. The important thing was that they exercise their ballot.)

"A staff ran the station for them from the beginning. When I was there there were two engineers, two transmitter men and two announcers. We all spelled each other and took turns sleeping in the same bunk beds out at the transmitter shack.

"Surprisingly, we did almost as many commercials as a normal station. With their two votes in the Nebraska legislature, the Credenzas carried a lot of weight with important firms around the state and could always pressure a little business out of them. They even prided themselves on the good job they did for their clients, though almost no one but Credenzas could ever have been listening. One time, when I was really into something and neglected to do a commercial exactly when it was scheduled, I received an angry call from Louis III.

31

" 'Hey you—Marshall Maine. What do you think you're doing down there? The Coca-Cola Bottling Company of Lincoln paid money to have that commercial done at 3:15. That don't mean 3:14 or 3:16 or 3:18 or 3:20. Three-fifteen means 3:15. They picked that time because that's when folks get thirsty and want something cool to swallow. They want their message said right then. You understand me? You think the Coca-Cola Bottling Company of Lincoln wants its message jammed up against the Mutual of Omaha message at 3:23?'

"When people are thinking of their deaths, I thought, when they're thinking of loss of limb, their houses on fire, liability, personal injury. 'No sir,' I said. 'I'm sorry. I was into something.'

" 'Well, you look to your knitting, sonny, or you'll be fast out on your ass of something else.'

" 'Yes, sir,' I said, for the truth is, I liked working there. The apprenticeship was on me, as I say, and I was getting valuable experience.

" 'Call me Lou. You last long enough around here I might be your representative. I expect it'll be me over old Poke in a landslide. In America it don't do to say sir to the man that's your representative.'

"We followed FCC regulations to the letter, and functioned exactly as any station would, with all the ordinary station's customary programming, though with the sense I had of the station and its listeners, the programs seemed experimental to me, as any public activity would seem strange performed in private. I had this notion of command performance and, because of this, a fear of my audience which was unfamiliar to me.

"Yet even granting our ordinary format of music, news, and public service, there was something special about our programs. The Credenzas wanted their tastes catered to. 'A station has to meet the needs of its audience,' Felix Credenza often reminded me. So for Jim, the musical Credenza, we did 'The John Philip Sousa Hour' from eleven to midnight. For Felix and his wife, childless Credenzas who liked to pretend there were kids around the house, we did a children's program with fairy tales and Frank Luther recordings. The most popular program, however, the one that pleased all the Credenzas, was a public service show called 'Know Your County!' It was about—I quote from the introduction—'the living legend of Sylvia Credenza and Louis Credenza, Senior Counties.' What it really was, was the history of the Credenza fámily done in fifteen-minute dramas, the Credenzas themselves putting together the scripts from their memory of family gossip. The program had been on since the station's founding, and everything that had ever happened to the Credenzas had already been aired several times. When they came to the end of the cycle—each one, like the verses in 'This is the house that Jack built,' slightly longer than the last because of the additional increment of history—they simply started all over again. It was the way congregations read the bible.

"Most of the programs I was involved with dealt with the family's founders—Sylvia and Louis Credenza, Senior —and related how they were sweethearts in the old country but couldn't marry because Louis was scheduled to be called up for military service. There were shows about the plots and payoffs that got him smuggled to America. Louis Senior's wanderings in the New World, the letters they exchanged once he was settled in Nebraska, Louis's dreams, Sylvia's misgivings about making the trip, the bad time she had in steerage, her missing her train in Chicago. This last was a milestone in the legend, a sort of Ems telegram approach to history, just that destiny-ridden. For Louis, it seems, had missed *his* train in Omaha. He had intended to surprise Sylvia by meeting her in Union Station and riding back to Nebraska with her, and if the two lovers hadn't *both* missed their trains they would have missed each other, presumably forever. The mutual layover somehow permitted their reunion for all time.

"And what a program *that* was—the reunion. KROP montages. Excerpts from Louis's letters about his dreams. Solemn, forlorn blasts of exodus ship's whistles become Chicago's cheery choo-choo chugs. Then Louis's 'Hello, Sylvia.' And Sylvia's 'It's you, Lou.' It was all down

33

there. I tell you, I embraced myth then—all myth, everybody's, anybody's. To this day I'm a sucker for all primal episode: Bruce Wayne losing his parents and vowing vengeance; Tonto teaming up with the Lone Ranger; Clark Kent chipped out of Kryptonite—whatever.

"Who played Sylvia? Who played Sylvia if there were only the two male announcers? Some Mrs. Credenza, you think? Not at all. Ego like the Credenzas' wouldn't have permitted it. They insisted on themselves being out of it, insisted on the high privilege of others doing it for them, their words in other people's mouths, themselves cozy by their receivers, hearing their own legend. An Indian lady. A squaw did. A chief's old wife. Squaws were brought in for all the female Credenza parts. Credenza legend was the single Dell Reservation industry. The counties had been theirs; the Credenzas had been their enemies, were still their enemies. They loved their grudge, I guess, and thrived—anyone in the studio could see it—on the Credenzas' side of the story, bland with omission, the blandness and good will the givens of the Indians' patient rage. At air time, the old squaw's voice was waverless with Sylvia's youth; it could have been under a spell. It *was* under one. How else could she, who had never heard it, get the precise mix of old country accent and young English? And how did I, who had never heard it either, *know* it was precise? Better, how did she manage the hyperbole? I mean the exact input of glory and meaning with which she iced those pale speeches and which the Credenzas licked up at face value? Why, she *was* an Indian. She had come up on the settlers' wagons, infiltrated Fort Credenza, outwoodsed them, I tell you, crept up on their Credenza souls and last-laughed them to death in some red way the Credenzas never understood or even suspected.

"But I'm getting ahead of myself. My major effort at KROP, what I thought at the time was the most valuable thing I did there experiencewise, grist-for-the-millwise (do you see what I was like back then? how ingenuous my concerns? I had an apprentice's heart; I wanted to learn everything, do everything, conscientiously preparing

34

myself with some self-made, from-the-ground-up vision of the world, assuming the *quid pro quo* and just desert as if they were laws in nature) was the news programming. I had done news before only as a rip-and-reader, pulling the sheets off the teletype seconds before they were scheduled to be read, doing them cold. (And deriving thereby a certain false and snotty confidence, a sort of pride in what I took to be my professionalism. I didn't see that this was the cynic's way, the wiseguy's way.)

"At KROP I became a real newsman for the first time. I still had to depend heavily upon the wire services, but just as the Credenzas were interested in Credenza history, so were they interested in Credenza current events. When I saw a brother and asked 'What's new?' it was as a reporter I asked, and I was required to make a good deal of his answer. 'Flash: Louis Credenza III announced today that the new car he purchased three weeks ago has gone back to the dealer for its one-thousand-mile checkup. "The defective cigarette lighter that came with the car will be replaced for nothing," Mr. Credenza said. This is in accordance with his 20,000-mile guarantee covering parts and labor. . . . Elsewhere in the news, George Credenza, wife of the candidate for state representative from Louis Credenza, Senior County, spoke long distance last night to her sister in Worchester, Massachusetts, Mrs. Lloyd Brossbar, the former Dorothy Kiddons of Rapid City, South Dakota. Mrs. Brossbar is said to have told Mrs. Credenza that the children are well and send their love to their aunt and uncle. KROP has also learned that they thanked them for the chemistry set . . . The 8 P.M. Worcester temperature was sixty-two degrees.'

"It was at KROP that I got to do my first remote, calling in my news over the telephone when I was sent to Lincoln to cover Charley Credenza's maiden speech in the legislature. It was, I recall, a filibuster. No particular issue was at stake, no great principle; Charley just didn't want to give up the floor. They finally had to vote cloture on him—the first time in Nebraska history. I was there. Marshall Maine was there.

"But do you know what the Credenzas liked best?

35

Better even than self-reflexive history or on-the-spot coverage? Human interest. Folksy coda. I scoured the wire services and newspapers to feed their need for anecdote, their love of contretemps and feeling for that long line of the pratfallen—stick-up men who pulled their heists in front of police stations on plainclothesmen, double-parked judges who appeared before themselves on traffic raps, candidates for mayor outpolled by their wives. And when, as it sometimes happened, the news was all hard that day, I made up stories. 'And that would be all the news if it weren't for the fellow in the Pacific Northwest whose wife filed for divorce today; her first, his fifth. This time, however, Leonard Class of Seattle, Washington, may have some difficulty meeting his alimony payments, for Leonard lost his job as well as his wife. The city fathers are just a little upset with Leonard's marital difficulties and have voted to remove him from his position as Director of Seattle's Bureau of Matrimonial Counseling.'

" 'You have a nose for news,' Poke Credenza himself told me after one of these stories. And so I had—a flair for all the trivial lessons of come-uppance, an intuition into the Credenza conscience itself. I fueled their condescension with an endless parade of housewives who won national bake-offs with ready-mixes and firechiefs whose homes burned down. The human comedy, the lofty laugh, a bit of patronage, and no harm done."

Ultimately he went too far, betrayed by the dark side of his professionalism that came to light in northeast Nebraska.

These were heydays. There was Uncle Don and his "That ought to hold the little bastards." Coast to coast, it seemed, in the primest time of that prime time, there were open keys, unthrown switches, bloopers, stoopnagelisms —but diffusing accident, there was form, order, a national sense of the institutional. There was *Allen's Alley, The National Barn Dance, Manhattan Merry-Go-Round, Lux Presents Hollywood, Town Meeting of the Air*. And not even partisan, a wider community than mere *fan*—though these were the days of the signed glossy, of the fifty-cent "family album" of stars—something constitutent almost, franchised. One knew that all America was tuned in. You can see the photographs in the encyclopedia. The family in its cozy parlor. (It is always wintertime in these photographs.) Father in his business clothes, Sis in wools, Mother with a bit of knitting in her lap, the floorlamp behind her right shoulder, the shade slanting the light forthrightly where her book would be if she were reading. The son is stretched out on the floor, belly to carpet, doing his homework. The gothic radio, like a wooden bell, on a table in the corner. They smile or are concerned or absorbed or wistful, as though they hear a song common to each—an anthem perhaps of some country where they had all once lived. The caption explains that this American family, like so many millions of others, is enjoying the jokes of a popular network comedian, or engrossed in the news that will be tomorrow's headlines, or engaged by one of the many fine dramas that may be heard on the radio. And you know that it's no fake, no mere posturing for the photographer, and indeed if you look close you can see that the dial in the radio glows.

There is another photograph above this one. A newscaster sits in his studio behind a big web microphone. In his dark, wide-lapelled suit he looks like a banker, the longitudes of his decency in the dimly perceived pinstripes. He holds his script. You glimpse a thin bracelet of shirtcuff. The "On the Air" sign is still inert, but there is a large-faced wall clock behind him, a thick second hand sweeping toward the landmark at the top of the clock where time begins. He looks toward the control booth at his director. He sits militantly, responsibly urgent—and this is no posture either but the careful, serious alertness of a man pacing himself, as attuned and concentrate as a child waiting to move in under the arc of a jump rope.

Alias Dick Gibson, alias Marshall Maine, alias Tex Ellery, alias a dozen others, knew, knew *then,* blessed by nostalgia as some are blessed with prescience, this steady hindsight that was contemporaneous to him and as involuntary as digestion, that all this was the truth, that those pictures had it right: Americans *were* in their living rooms, before their floorlamps, on their sofas, in their chairs, along their rugs, together in time, united, serene. And so he felt twinges, pins and needles of actual conscience: he needed to join his voice to that important chorus, that lovely a cappella.

He approached Lee, the reasonable Credenza, and spoke to him about it. He said KROP should be no different than other stations.

"I see what you mean. I'll talk it over with the brothers and get back to you," Lee told him.

And then, two weeks after he had first introduced the subject, he received a delegation of Credenzas in the transmitter shack. Surprised by their presence there and to a certain extent intimidated by seeing so many of them gathered at one time—only Charley and Bill, whose legislative duties kept them in Lincoln, did not come—he was at first alarmed, suspecting actual physical attack.

Louis III spoke. "You, Marshall Maine, Lee says you ain't satisfied with the way we do things on our station."

He was prepared to yield at once, to concede to the pressures of what seemed to him their vigilante loomings, when the off-duty transmitter man—one of those tattooed vagrants common in those days, an old navy man, retired possibly, but more probably court-martialed and perhaps even a deserter, one of those thick-veined, long-armed quiet men, someone keeping to himself, soured by a grudge or ruined by a secret—woke up and, seeing the brothers, having less contact with them than Maine—even more of a drifter than Marshall, there less time than him—not knowing who they were, or perhaps suspecting that they had come for him, threw a punch, drew a knife.

"Hold it!" the transmitter man yelled, missing Felix. "No tricks!" he screamed, and turned briefly to Marshall Maine, forming their plan even as he lunged toward the Credenzas. "The Saigon caper, mate," he said, "I take these four, you get them two." At these words—they had barely spoken in the three weeks the man had been at the station—Marshall felt an unaccountable flush of pride.

38

Then Poke poked the transmitter man and the old fellow fell down—collapsed, for all Maine knew, died. Poke's punch had loosened the man's grip on his knife and it flew neatly, almost politely, handle first into Jim Credenza's hand.

Marshall Maine found himself mourning, grieving for a pal. "The Credenza County caper, mate," he said softly. Then, anger at the Credenzas' building on his grief for his new friend, he addressed himself to George and Louis III, the two Credenzas he had been left to handle in the transmitter man's plan. "He thought you—" he protested. "He was only . . . What did you have to hit him for?" The Credenzas looked at him blandly, the transmitter man's four as well as his own two, incapable of understanding friendship's way despite their expertise in family's. Seeing their indifference he reversed himself again, having in the same two minutes found a buddy and lost him, mourned and forgotten him.

Forlorn, he gave in to the Credenzas, putting for good and all their value on things and feeling abashed, exposed, like one caught out in an act of bad taste. Thenceforward, for as long as he remained at the station, Marshall Maine was never again to feel comfortable with any of the other employees, seeing them as the Credenzas saw them—not family, outsiders like himself. And not only not comfortable with them, but actively resenting them, squeamish for the first time in the bunk they shared, fastidious over the common washstand, handling the common soap as if it were tainted, hovering and actually constipate on the seat of the flush toilet the Credenzas had added on in a corner of the transmitter shack. He found himself longing to stretch out luxuriously in Credenza tubs and to sit wholeheartedly, four-squarely, on Credenza-warmed toilets, those fine fleshpots and seats of kinship and power. If he could divorce himself from his colleagues, he felt, he would be that much closer to the Credenzas.

"And that's why I'm such a good radio man. Because there *are* standards, grounds of taste. Because I would rid myself of all dialect and speak only Midwest American Standard, and have a sense of bond, and eschew the private and wild and unacceptable. Because I would throw myself into the melting pot while it's at the very boil and would, if I had the power, pass a law to protect the typical. Because I honor the mass. Because I revere the regular. Because I consent to consensus. Because I would be decent, and decently blind to the differences between appearances and realities and daily pray to keep down those qualities in myself that are suspect or insufficiently public-spirited or divergent from the ideal. Because I would have life like it is on the radio—all comfy and clean and everyone heavily brothered and rich as a Credenza. This is KROP, the Voice of Wheat. Your announcer is Marshall Maine, the Voice of Wheat's Voice, staff announcer for the staff of life. Give us this day our daily bread. Amen."

He tried to explain to the brothers what he had in mind, first apologizing for his apology for the transmitter man, washing his hands of that dirty old seadog and showing them clean to the Credenzas (". . . who didn't care, who hadn't noticed past the time it took Poke to dodge the punch and counter it anything other than the man's otherness, who held in a contempt that could pass for forgiveness *all* otherness, who expected that sort of thing from unbrothers, and not only didn't bother to despise it but did not even bother to distinguish between one sort of otherness—the hostile deserter's—and another—my, Maine's, benign own").

"Never mind that," George Credenza said, "you sometimes get too close to the mike. We hear you breathe."

"You're not always careful with the records. There's some that are scratched," Lee said. "Lift the arm clear when it gets to the end. Use your chamois to wipe them clean."

"Sometimes it's the needle," Louis told him. "Dust it, pull off the crud. That's a thirty-five-buck needle, but it's got to be clean."

"The turntable squeaks. Oil it," Poke ordered.

"When there are storms," Felix said, "make sure the studio clocks are reset correct."

"On 'News, Weather and Sports,' when you give the reports, a death on the highway or damage to crops, get a little chuckle in your voice."

"We don't mean to laugh."

"It ain't no laughing matter."

"But a chuckle, a smile, something to signal it isn't so bad."

"Say the time and temperature twice. I don't always catch it the first time around."

"Now what was it you wanted?" George asked.

"I didn't know you were so disappointed in me," Maine told them dejectedly. "I didn't know you weren't satisfied."

"Who ain't satisfied, Marshall? We're satisfied. We're satisfied fine."

"When we ain't satisfied you'll hear we ain't satisfied."

"We'll haul your ass out of there."

"We'll fire your ass."

"We'll see you never work your ass in this state again."

"That your voice, you take your ass to Iowa or Dakota nearby, croaks at the state line."

"We're satisfied."

Just keep those cards and letters coming in, Marshall Maine thought.

They had intimidated him. Making one kind of metaphor of his ass as he made another. He saw them now as something closer knit even than family, close knit as interest itself, and himself forever absolved of the hope of kinship with them, reduced by his very value to them to something not just expendable should that value wane, but destroyable as a gangster's evidence. The ass they spoke of so dispassionately he came to see as more vital somehow than the heart, not their metaphor for his soul at all, but just their prearranged, priority target, the doomed bridge- and railheads of his being. He would be undone in the behind when the time came, there kicked

41

(they would actually do it), scorned. Destroyed in the ass. They were dark, gigantic generals, booted for business and answerable only to themselves. So he was intimidated, and he knew it. And this is what happened.

For the first time in his life he developed mike fright. Not just that stage-wary fillip of excitement, nor even that panicked realization that one's words are gone, nor yet that temporary, pre-curtain woe in the wings that is often an actor's capital, a signal, like the rich man's haunted look, of money in the bank, of reserves of adrenalin to turn terror—no ordinary, innocent commotion, the heart all thumbs, or momentary inability to function that is only function in the act of sparking. Not mike *fright* at all, really, but some pinched, asbestos quality in himself of unkindling, some odd, aged and deadened dignity. That is, he could speak, could read his scripts and do his commercials, but he had a sense that he was working on slack, a loose-tooth sense of margin. All urgency had gone out of his voice. There was a certain loss of treble, a corresponding increment of heavy bass. It was the voice of a drowned man, slow and waterlogged.

He was forced to make certain changes in his chatter, to bring his talk into accord with the changes in his delivery. Formerly his remarks on introducing a song matched the mood of the song, while filler material provoked an illusion, even at this distance, of KROP's relationship to show business. ("Now, from the sound track of Walt Disney's feature-length animated cartoon, *Snow White and the Seven Dwarfs*, the RKO Studio Orchestra plays the wistful 'Someday My Prince Will Come.' Maestro . . ." "From the hit Broadway show *Showboat* of a few years back, the lovely Miss Helen Morgan sings this show stopper, the haunting 'He's Just My Bill' . . .") With his new constraint, however, words like "sound track," the names of studios, even the titles of films, suddenly made him self-conscious. Catch phrases like "from the motion picture of the same name" caught in his throat. His old attempt to set a human mood—"A romantic confession now, some sweet excuses for a familiar story: 'Those Little White Lies' "—seemed the grossest liberty of all. The idea of setting a mood for the dark-booted Credenzas was blasphemous, a sort of spoken graffiti.

At first he tried simply to announce the title and identify the singer, but the discrepancy between the tunes and his flat statements was even more disturbing to him than his old chatter. As a consequence he began to play a different sort of music altogether, songs that were so familiar they needed no introduction, love songs nominally still, but from a different period, or rather from no period at all, songs that had always existed, in the public domain years, nothing that could ever have connected KROP with show business: "The Old Oaken Bucket," "Alice Blue Gown," "I Wandered Today to the Hill, Maggie." Because they were the sort of songs no crooner anyone had ever heard of was likely to have recorded, he found it difficult to speak the names of the obscure tenors and sopranos who *had* recorded them, the Fred L. Joneses and Olive Patzes and Herbert Randolph Fippses who had cornered the market on this kind of thing. So he said nothing and looked instead for instrumental versions of the recordings, leaving Sylvia and Louis Credenza, Senior Counties on his day off and going down to Lincoln on his own authority to the big radio station there, to speak to the music librarian and offer him money for his discards. At first the man didn't seem to understand what he wanted, until Marshall explained that he did a request show for shut-ins, and invented for him the Sylvia and Louis Credenza, Senior Counties Old People's Home, a place, he said, where the staff used the golden hits of yesteryear as therapy, offering the invalided and senile a musical opportunity to re-court their wives, re-raise their children and re-fight their wars, the idea being, Maine said, not to pull the afflicted (he called them that) from their pasts but to push them back into them.

Together they went into the music library, and there he found a cache of exactly the sort of thing he was looking for: "There'll Be a Hot Time in the Old Town Tonight," played by the Netherlands Deutschgeschreir Orkestra, Jerome Klopf conducting; "I Wish I Was in de Land ob Cotton," sung by the Luftwaffe Sinfonia; Sir Reginald

43

Shoat leading the Edinburgh Festival Orchestra in a Stephen Foster medley. There were also some fine things by the Hotel Brevert-Topeka's Palm Court Band.

"Gee," the librarian said, "I didn't know we had all this stuff."

"Yes," Marshall Maine told him. "These will do."

The man put one of the recordings on the library console. "The quality's not good. This one sounds strained, as if it was transcribed from the short wave."

"Yes," Marshall Maine said, "that's fine. They want that quality—the suggestion of the distant past."

"But they're all instrumentals."

"Yes, that forces them to remember the words."

"Oh, look here, Lily Pons doing 'Funiculi Funicula.'"

"No," Maine said sharply. "But if you had choral groups, I might take some choral groups of the right sort."

"Choral groups?"

"It gives them the sense they're not alone."

So he took back with him a hundred and twelve instrumentals, plus an armful of recordings by a few choral groups—rejecting, for example, Fred Waring and the Pennsylvanians' rendition of "In the Merry, Merry Month of May" in favor of the Utah Military Institute's Marching and Singing Soldiers' version of the same song, and the Brockton Riding Academy Mounted Chorus's "Silver Threads Among the Gold."

Furnished with these he returned to KROP and put them on the air. He could hear through his long afternoon record show the adulterated strains of the vaguely decomposing music he played, performances that the wind might have blown through, or the sea squeezed. Usually he no longer bothered to announce the songs. Remembering the Credenzas' warning, he made sure that no dust stuck to the needle. He oiled the turntable, lifted the tone arm smartly when a record was finished and placed it carefully in the right groove of the next selection. Every few minutes he moved his head a precise seven inches from the microphone and gave the time and temperature

44

twice: "It's two thirty-five. It's two thirty-five. The temperature is fifty-three degrees. It's fifty-three degrees."

He had never been to England and so had never heard the BBC, but he had an impression that this was what it must sound like. He had a sense, too, of service, a special nonprofit feel of a government-managed, tax-based, public utility, as if the story he told the music librarian at the radio station in Lincoln somehow had come true. Giving the time and temperature, he imagined his voice coming out of loudspeakers in the dining halls of prisons or the card rooms of veterans' hospitals. He liked this. In a way—though it had come about in a manner entirely different from the one he had counted on when he had approached the brothers—he felt exactly the responsibility he had hoped to feel.

His nervousness began to relax its hold on him, though he did not tamper with its effects. Now his constraint was designed, a technique, and he acquired still another sense of his professionalism, a wicked inside knowledge of his own manner, the same knowledgeable sensation available, he supposed, to workers on newspapers who see the headlines before they hit the streets—a split-second edge that was all one needed to maintain a notion of his uniqueness and to confirm his closeness to the source of things.

"I had never had it before. But what did I have? What did I have exactly? A knowledge of what time it was and what time it was getting to be? Access to the weather report? The sequence in which the records would be played that afternoon? What I had was inside information about myself, what *I* was going to do, what particular shape my dignity would take next, how much shyness or reserve would be there in the next time signal, what unmood would be provoked by the next unmusic I played."

But that only got him through the afternoons. The music, however transatlantic and anonymous, was the point. He merely served it, bringing it to the turntable like

45

a waiter, his presence hidden in his deference, his shyness only the giver's decent effacement. If it weren't for the music, however, and the time and temperature, he would have been lost, so though the fright did not actually return, it waited for him like that portion of a sick man's day when the temperature climbs and the pain begins.

Doing the news that followed his afternoon record show, for example, and recalling the brothers' insistence that he make more palatable the inevitable reports of accident and sudden death with a deflective cheer—they meant, he supposed, no more than that he lift the pitch of his voice—he felt enormous pressure to oblige, pressure that existed even as he read those stories that had nothing to do with disaster: neutral items about the sale of farms in adjoining counties, or the paving of the dirt road that led to the new dam. He knew what was coming up, and like some unsure singer who knows of a difficult passage later in his song that he has negotiated hit and miss in rehearsal, he could anticipate only those bad places in the road where the car turned over and the children died, and felt his throat begin to constrict, his mouth to dry, his teeth to dry too, like hard foreign objects suddenly in his mouth. So, even as he continued to read the report of the new engine purchased for the volunteer fire department and what the governor said in his address to the Building and Loan convention, he would sound a little hysterical, and once or twice when the time came for him actually to give the damaging bulletin, he lost control entirely. Aiming for the C above high C that was the perfect pitch the Credenzas wanted, the exact and only comforting tone of catastrophe for them, his voice broke, he overshot and gave them not perfect pitch nor even imperfect pitch, but *wild* pitch, shattering the decorous modulations of radio with falsetto, with something close to a real shriek or scream. Someone hearing him might have thought it was *his* child who had burned to a crisp in the fire, *his* wife raped and slain, *his* father struck down by the lightning or fallen into the thresher.

After these performances he waited to hear from some angry Credenza, not even returning to the transmitter

46

shack when his relief man came for fear they would phone the moment he left the station and not wanting to add anything to their already considerable rage should they miss him. So he sat by the telephone to wait for their call.

It didn't come.

Nor did it come the next day or even the next time he lost control of himself and, too keen, keened the ferocious grief of his mistakes. He knew, of course, that he was vulnerable now, that this time he would surely hear from the Credenzas. When he didn't he realized that they were giving him not leeway but rope. He took their unspoken hint and went the other way entirely. To save himself he went the way they had told him not to go. Now when he came to those bulletins he laughed openly: "Early this morning—along the Lake Baxter rim road—a car with two pa-ha ha-hass-engers went out of contro-ho ho—l, and h-hit a t—a tee—a tee hee—tree. The passengers, Ha-ha-ha-rrr— ho ho—ld, Ha-ha rold and Haw-haw Hortense Sn-sn-snick, were be-ha ha-headed." The engineer stared at him. "It's seven minutes after four," he ad-libbed. "It's seven minutes after four."

Still the call did not come. It was clear; they meant him harm. He returned to the shack as soon as he was finished with his shift and asked if there had been any calls for him. The transmitter man did not even look up.

"Have there?"

"The injuns want you to their picnic," the man said.

Still frightened, but made willful by his fear, he determined to force a confrontation, convinced that only through a showdown could he ever hope to negotiate his brotherhood with the Credenzas. He eliminated from his repertoire all those human interest stories they loved, and selected only bad news to read. He gave it euphorically, blithe as Nero. Some Credenza cattle had come down with disease. A few had already died. He gave the news of these fatalities with a chipperness nothing less than ecstatic. He'd heard from one of the hands that when disease had broken out on a ranch he had once worked in Texas, the herd had to be shot. He took this gossip and repeated it over the air. "An undisclosed but reliable source high up in Credenza management," he said, "is already speculating that the entire herd may have to be slaughtered." He added that it was better economics to cut one's losses at once than to drag out hope, meanwhile spending more on feed each day for the sick beasts.

He seized on every rumor available to him—desultory talk among the farmers about the expectation of a severe winter, random chatter of a decline in the price of dairy or a dip in grains—and presented it as the hard inside information of experts. If rye prices were expected to be disappointing, he carefully pointed out that the Credenza interests were heavily overextended in rye. His weather reports were jeremiads. If the sun was shining in northeast Nebraska he found a storm gathering in western Canada and spoke darkly of the prevailing gravity of weatherflow, its southern and easterly shift from its fierce source in the Bering Strait.

The engineers and transmitter men and the other announcer, silent as the Credenzas, pretended to ignore his new antics. He supposed that they were under instruction, that the Credenzas, fearful of tipping their hand, wanted him to continue for a while in his fool's paradise.

"At the time of the tone," he announced on his record show, "it will be three-thirty." Then he coughed brutally into the open mike, dredged up phlegm from deep in his chest, and made the lubricious rattle preparatory to spitting. "It's three-thirty. It's three-thirty."

And often when he played his records now he deliberately kept the key open on his table microphone, thus adding even more hollowness to the already bloated convention-hall vagueness of the music.

Then, almost two weeks to the day since he first began his campaign to get a rise out of the Credenzas—the record on the turntable was "Asleep in the Deep," sung by the South Philadelphia A. C. Girls' Aquacade Chorus and recorded at poolside—he purposely brushed his elbow against the switch on his table mike, and beginning not only in mid-sentence but in mid-syllable so that it seemed accidental, he said in perfectly controlled, conversational speech, as if to a guest with him in the studio, "... rstand that Charley's wife, Grace, and Poke Credenza have been seeing a lot of each other lately. More than it's usual for a brother- and sister-in-law to see each other. More than it's even *legal,* if you know what I mean. Well, what the hell, Charley Credenza's been down at Lincoln with the legislature two months now. Grace told him she couldn't be away from the house that long. Couldn't or wouldn't. Anyway, she's an attractive, healthy woman, even if she is too heavy. Poke likes them big, I guess, though why he didn't marry a large woman in the first place instead of that furled umbrella of a Lucy, I can't say—unless of course the talk is true that he had to. Come to think of it, it might be true at that. That woman has hot pants. Did you see the way she was riding Louis III's right leg at the Fourth of July dance, and how she put her hand on *his* ass? I thought there'd be trouble, but old Poke was making out too good with Grace even to notice. Wait a minute, I've got to take this record off ..." Then, as if he hadn't noticed that the switch was already on, he turned it off and, extending the myth of the accident, spoke into the dead microphone: "That was 'Asleep in the Deep.' We hear now 'Come Josephine in My Flying Machine' in the new instrumental version recorded by the Association of Missouri Underwriters."

He faced the engineer and winked, but couldn't get the man's attention.

He went back to the transmitter shack convinced that at last he'd torn it, and when he got there things *did* seem different.

For one thing the beds were empty. Carpenter, the off-duty engineer, in whose car they had returned to the shack without speaking, hung around only long enough to pick up Mullins, the off-duty transmitter man; then they had gone off to town together. Murtaugh, the other transmitter man, was not by his equipment but had gone out behind the shack to check a guy wire on the tall main transmitter. Alone, the cramped, submariney quarters seemed almost spacious to him. He lay down on his bunk

49

and it occurred to him that except for those few minutes in the outhouse when spurning the new flush toilet he had vainly sought Credenza brotherhood by emerging himself in what he took to be the Credenza smell, despite his knowledge to the contrary—he knew they were only the anonymous and corrupt smells of former staff, an indiscriminate odor that was no longer shit but shit's shit, chemically changed, fermented to something beyond the strongest wine in the world but vineyardy still, acrid and eye-searing, smelling not of the cozy, snuggish intestines at all but of fire, or of sun gas perhaps, if you could get close enough—this was the first time in the months since he had come to work for them that he was by himself, without an engineer, without a bunkmate, without anyone.

Then he heard the radio.

"I knew it was no accident I was alone, that the Credenzas had anticipated me, that plans had been laid in advance, that Carpenter and Mullins now worked as a team, that the Credenzas picked up their check and they rode to town on Credenza gasoline to toast my disaster in Credenza beers. Still in my bunk I looked out the single window at Murtaugh, the transmitter man, squatting on his heels by the base of the antenna fooling with a wire and I thought: you lazy bastard, is that what Credenza (they had become one enormous undifferentiated persona for me now) pays you for? Climb, bastard, decoy me at something better than ground level. Ah, old sealegs, a little at least sweat, please! Make those picturesque adjustments up in the mizzen of that thing. Lazybones, landlubber, less decorousness in your game, if you don't mind. Murtaugh must have been left by him (I meant the Credenza brothers, and the wives and sisters too now) as a sort of staff sentinel and shill, a nice philosophic touch. Can a man fall in the forest if there's no one by to hear him scream?

"I heard the radio and realized that's how it could come, my fate a spot announcement perhaps, or a bulletin, or maybe he would come on the air himself and read out my doom in some Credenza fireside chat: 'We'—

strangely, Credenza, the single merged nemesis did not mean 'we,' he spoke for himself but had slipped royally into the inverted synecdochic—'have not lightly arrived at our decision to speak out this evening. No one not in our situation can know the ponderous personal gloom and wrenching loneliness attendant at these levels of responsibility. It gives us the headache and we would rather be in heaven on a picnic. But despite our hopes for an amelioration of our difficulties and maugre our four times forbearance, those hopes have foundered. Sadly we needs must admit the priority pull of necessity and lay at once the claims of all soft sentiment. We have decided to act—whatever the cost in dashed hopes and even, we may say, lives. No matter that it gives us the headache and we would rather be in heaven on a picnic. We needs must, perhaps, go into a little of the background of the situation. We must needs indeeds lest what is devastating seem harsh.

" 'At the beginning, then, the man that calls himself Marshall Maine . . .' "

Music was coming over the radio. It was *The Children's Hour*. The man who called himself Marshall Maine could not make up his mind whether it was more likely that Credenza would allow the nursery rhyme to finish, or interrupt it, hoping to take him by surprise. The song concluded and Maine thought *now,* but it was only the relief man speaking patronizingly in the voice of Uncle Arnold. He played another nursery rhyme. Then it was time for the relief man to read the bedtime story, and Maine again thought *now,* but except for what Marshall felt to be some strange emphases—the story was "Jack and the Beanstalk" and the relief man's voice was loud when it should have been soft and meek when force was called for—he was permitted to get all the way through it without interruption.

The suspense was terrific. He knew it would come, but he could no longer even hope to anticipate when. It would be random; he could not second-guess it. It was as if they were playing some mortal version of musical chairs with him. As if this were exactly the case he turned away from watching the transmitter man and went to stand by the receiver that couldn't be turned off as long as the station was on the air. It was within a yard of the transmitter man's chair, close by his complicated machinery. He thought that if he heard Credenza's voice he would still have time to rush to the chair before the man could pronounce his doom. Credenza may have permitted him this one hope of forestalling his annihilation, he thought crazily.

"Why did I stand around waiting? Why didn't I just get out? I couldn't. Mullins and Carpenter had taken the car. There were endless empty miles of Sylvia and Louis Credenza, Senior counties to traverse before reaching safety. Why, I would have had to have run out of the effective range of the radio station itself."

He stood there all through *The Children's Hour* and through *The Six O'Clock Round-Up* (thinking he might hear it as a piece of the news itself, announced as something that had already happened; perhaps it would be tacked on at the end, what they meant to do to him one last human-interest story), and through *Dinnertime Melodies till Seven,* and was still standing there during the electrically transcribed *Mormon Tabernacle Hour—Now,* he thought, *now he'll break in, his plans for me a goddamn sacrilege*—and on into the sixth inning of the remote pickup of the charity ballgame between the migrant workers and graduating seniors at the consolidated high school, when something suddenly seemed very wrong indeed.

The migrants were ahead 1–0. The seniors were up with the bases loaded. There was one out. Shippleton, the relief announcer, a man who had been with Credenza for years, was doing the play-by-play. "The tension here," Shippleton was saying, "is terrific. Consolidated High has a good chance to tie it and even to go ahead, and this crowd knows it. Their hopes are on Scholar Joe Niebecker to hit one out of here. (Scholar Joe's the valedictorian and could really make himself a hero if he connects.) Just listen to this crowd. I want you to hear this—" Then came the sound that Shippleton was talking about. Only it wasn't the expected roar at all, just something very faint, something softly liquid, not a roar or a rush but more like a trickle of water in a pipe in a distant corner of the house at night.

Shippleton's gone crazy, Marshall Maine thought. He knew that Credenza, like the parents of the boys themselves, was a strong supporter of the high schoolers, and resented something in the mute underprivilege of the migrant workers as the townies resented their strange rough ways. Did Shippleton mean to be ironic, Maine wondered. What was the point? Appalled, he thought, have *I* inspired him? It was insane. Shippleton was a hack, a safe man. Yet when Niebecker hit into a double play and ended the graduating class's chances in that inning, Shippleton's voice came booming over the speaker in top-heavy decibels. "IT'S A DOUBLE PLAY! THIS INNING IS OVER!" It was exactly like the wrong weight he had given Jack's slow progress past the sleeping giant.

In the last inning, when the kids went ahead and won the game, Shippleton sounded quiet, defeated.

He left the shack to call Murtaugh. The man lay on his back inside the steel ribbing at the base of the antenna, poking a flashlight up at the various angles of the tower and pulling on cables to test their tension.

"Heh, Murtaugh," he shouted, "you can knock that off now. Come here a minute."

The man directed his beam into Marshall's eyes. "What? What is it?"

He thinks it's happened, Marshall Maine thought. Whatever it is, he thinks it's already happened.

"Maybe an emergency," Maine said. "Come inside."

Moving from beneath the steel tent, Murtaugh swore softly.

Marshall Maine stood at the speaker and waited for

him. They had switched back to the studio where the engineer had put on some marches while waiting for Shippleton to return. Maine pointed at the speaker. "Listen," he said.

"For Christ's sake, buddy—"

"Shh," Maine said, *"Listen."*

There was no mistaking it. The values of the music were totally confused. The volume bore no relation to what the band was playing. The sound was completely erratic—now loud and booming where it should have been soft, or so thunderous and distorted where it should merely have swelled that Maine thought the cone of the speaker had ripped. At other times the music was incredibly tinny, as if someone was moving the needle around the record at exactly the right speed but with the power off. Then the sound would settle normally, only to erupt or fade again seconds later. The effect was incoherence, a sort of musical gibberish.

"Hey, that ain't right," the transmitter man said. He went to the control board and examined some dials. He turned a knob experimentally, Maine watching his hand carefully as it reached out for the knob. It *ain't* right, he thought warily. Something's fishy, Murtaugh. You were supposed to be pulling cables, weeding the hardware, planting the tower deep in the garden.

"Something's wrong," the transmitter man said.

"It is," Maine said, and wondered what Credenza was up to, how his ends were served by throwing the transmission out of whack. What did he mean to do, give him the headache?

"Here," Murtaugh said, "when I give the signal, push the amperage on that dial up to eighty. I want to try something."

So, thought Maine. So. Electrocution. It's to be electrocution. Then he understood why Credenza troubled with vagrants, why he kept them around—so they could electrocute the announcers when they got out of line. Maine shook his head and, walking calmly toward the doorway, planted his feet firmly on the rubber welcome mat, grounding himself.

"Come on," the transmitter man said. "Quit fucking off. I'm testing for a short circuit."

"I'm a staff announcer," Maine said simply. "I have nothing to do with the equipment."

"Shit," Murtaugh said. Then, to Maine's surprise, he went through the motions without him, fiddling with knobs and dials, throwing switches and, at one point, actually taking apart a rather complicated piece of machinery with a screwdriver, the best acting Maine had seen him do that evening. When Murtaugh finished he looked up at Maine. "It's at the studio," he said.

"Is it?"

"I've checked everything out. It's at the studio. The only thing it can be is the coil."

Marshall Maine planted himself even more firmly, making himself a dead weight on the doormat. "The coil, is it?" he said.

"The meter's disabled," Murtaugh said. "I'll call the station." He picked up the direct-line telephone and said something to someone at the other end. He waited for a few moments, appearing to listen as the engineer got back to the phone and made his report. The transmitter man nodded. "I didn't either," he said. "No, what's-his-name, the staff announcer told me about it." He put back the phone. "It's the meter, all right," he told Maine. "The needle must have jammed and shorted the coil."

Marshall Maine looked at him.

"That's why it sounds like that," Murtaugh said. He pointed to the loudspeaker. "He's been riding a false gain. There's no equilibrium in the output. He couldn't tell. The needle was just floating free."

"ONE MOMENT PLEASE!" they heard the engineer shout. Then the loudspeaker went dead.

"And he hadn't noticed," Marshall Maine said.

"What's that?"

"He hadn't noticed. That's what he told you before you said, 'I didn't either.' That he hadn't noticed. You hadn't either."

"That's right. Hey, how'd you know that?"

"He hadn't been listening. Only watching the needle."

"That's right. Say, mate, could you hear all that?"

"When I shrieked," Marshall Maine said.

"What's that, fella?"

"Nothing," Marshall Maine said. He stepped off the mat and came back into the shack. He leaned against the equipment. He played his fingers over the dials and stroked the switches. He thrust his hand into the space from which the transmitter man had removed the electric panel which he had taken apart. He picked up one of the loose wires.

"Hey, watch it!" the transmitter man yelled. "You want to get burned?" Murtaugh knocked the wire out of his hand.

"Right," Maine said calmly, grabbing the wire again and picking his teeth with it.

Murtaugh shook his head and started outside with his flashlight. "Call me when it comes back on," he said.

The first time I laughed, Maine thought. When I shrieked that time. That's what jammed it. That's when I tore it. And they hadn't noticed. Not the engineer or the relief engineer, not the transmitter man or the relief transmitter man, not Shippleton, not the Indians—not even Credenza himself. Hell, not even me.

"Because we had all stopped listening.

"And that's why I never heard. Because one by one we had all stopped listening weeks before when I came back from Lincoln with the new records. Because they never heard those other programs. Because without consulting anyone each of them had become bored, without even recognizing the moment when they no longer cared to listen to their own radio station, and without even *deciding* not to, without—my *God,* they must have been bored —it's even being a conscious act on their part, and so there was just this piecemeal tuning me out, just this gradual lapse as one loses by degrees his interest in a particular magazine he subscribes to, just this sluggish wane, just this disaffection, not from my programs alone but from Shippleton's too. They were all *so* bored that it was simply something personal, taking boredom for

56

granted, almost as if it were something in the eye of the beholder with no outside cause at all, just a shift in taste, as one day one discovers that he can no longer eat scrambled eggs. So bored that it was just too trivial to mention to one's brothers, because each made the unconscious assumption that the others still had their appetites intact."

Well, thought Marshall Maine, I'll be. I ran KROP right into the ground. All by myself. *I* did it. Not even my engineer listened to me. Not even my transmitter man with nothing to distract him except the sound of the relief man's snoring. I'll be. It doesn't have a single listener. Not one.

"This is Marshall Maine," he said aloud in the empty shack, "KROP's Voice of the Voice of Wheat. Be still. We interrupt this radio station for a special announcement. Be still."

2

It is not enough to say that he lost his job. Rather, it disappeared—his as well as the jobs of the transmitter men and engineers and the other announcer. Even the radio station disappeared—KROP plowed back under.

As it happened, Dick Gibson was able to take advantage of the Credenza boredom for a few more days. Though now that some of his colleagues had realized what had happened—or soon would—he knew he did not have much time. Once the requisitions were put in to replace the equipment he had damaged, the Credenzas would easily be able to fill in the rest of the story. Meanwhile he worked.

Perhaps it was the knowledge that no one heard him, or perhaps it was to make a sort of amends for his former fear, or simply the hope that if they should tune him in now, at the top of his form, they would forget who it was that had driven them away from their sets in the first place and would place a new and stronger confidence in him. At any rate, using the name Dick Gibson, he spoke during this respite with a silver tongue, lips that were sweeter than wine, a golden throat. He was in a state of grace, of classic second chances. The more it galled him that no one heard him, the better he was. The weather had turned bad and there was a thin film of unseasonable ice along Route 33; yet he hoped that someone passing through might be listening. It could make the difference between one concept of the place and another. Such a stranger might think, for as long as the signal lasted, that he had entered a Shangri-la, crossed a border more telling than the Iowa–Nebraska one, and come into—despite the flatness stretching behind and before him—a sort of valley, still unspoiled, unmarked perhaps on maps. To stay within range of the signal—never strong and now damaged further by the involuntary surges and slackenings of an inconstant electricity—the stranger might slow down (it would have nothing to do with the ice) and Dick would guide him, preserving him on the treacherous road as art preserves, as God does working in mysterious ways. The stranger might even pull over to the side. Dick pictured the fellow, his salesman's wares piled high in the space from which he had removed the back seat, sitting there, his appointments forgotten, time itself forgotten, preoccupied, listening with a recovered wonder unfamiliar since childhood, in a state of grace himself.

No matter. Within four days of discovering the truth he received word from Shippleton that none of their services were required any longer, that the Credenzas had decided to close down the station. That they fixed no blame and were willing to write letters of recommendation for all the staff was evidence that they had not yet figured out what had happened. But Dick knew, if the others didn't, and felt a fondness for his crew, determinedly sentimental on the last morning they were together. (Actually it was the first morning: all six of them were in the shack for the first time, plus Lee Credenza, who had driven over to bring them their last paychecks.) As they packed and made hurried preparations for their exodus, he saw that in emergency each had auxiliary lives which they would now take up. They might have been men who had served

59

with him in a war, or political prisoners given some eleventh-hour reprive and told to leave the country. He saw that he had one of Murtaugh's handkerchiefs and that Shippleton had a pair of his shoes. They re-exchanged combs, ties, books and magazines they had lent each other over the months. Why we've been friends, he thought, amazed, brothers (the six of them only two less than the sum of the Credenzas themselves, and actually equal if you didn't count the Credenzas in Lincoln).

It was Dick, however, who went about taking down their addresses and carefully writing out his own for them. "Of course I won't be there long, but a letter would always be forwarded. I've put down my real name, but here in parenthesis is the name you've known me by. No, keep the scarf. I've got another."

And when the valises were closed and placed beside the bunks while they waited for the taxi that would take them to town, he saw the makeshift essence of their belongings—bandboxes, cardboard grips tied with rope, duffel bags, paper parcels, only one leather suitcase—and was moved by this additional evidence of their gypsy, trouper lot.

And so, still a young man, he started out for home, where they would probably be happy to see him.

It took him months to get there. He found himself explaining this one night, a few years later, to strangers.

"How do you do, ladies and gentlemen, this is Dick 'Pepsodent' Gibson. I'm very happy to be here in Minneapolis tonight. Bob Hope will be with you in a few minutes, but first he's asked me to come out here and talk to you all for a bit. I'm your warmup man. Are you cold, madam? Skinnay Ennis was supposed to do this but he's working out, he's getting in shape for a tug-of war next week against the 142nd Airborne. I won't say Skinnay's team is the underdog, but Frank Sinatra's the anchor man. Frank Sinatra—he was putting one of his songs on the phonograph last night and his hand slipped through the hole in the record. I won't say he's thin, but his mother used to use him to test cakes.

"Listen, Bob asked me to tell you he's got a great show lined up for you tonight. Bob's here, and Frances Langford and Vera Vague—and Frances Langford. Let's see, then there's Skinnay Ennis and his orchestra and Jerry Colonna—and Frances Langford. Frances Langford, I won't say she's pretty but the other day someone told me she looks just like the girl next door and I went out and bought a house. You know who lives next door to me? Vera Vague. Vera Vague—that's Fibber Magee's closet in a girdle. I won't say she's ugly but her beauty mark died of loneliness. I won't say she's unattractive but the St. Paul police saw her crossing Kellogg Boulevard yesterday and put out an all-points alert for a hit-and run driver.

"Now the show's going to begin in about thirty minutes, so if anybody has to cough let him do it now. I tell you what, when I count three everybody cough together. All at once now. All right, are you ready? Let's go. One. Two. *Three.* Cough, everybody. Let's do it again. One. Two. *Three.* Fine, now just once more. One. Two. *Three.* Wonderful. Everybody passes the physical. You've all just been inducted into the United States Army!

"Well, come on now, you don't think *I* tell jokes for a living, do you? This is Dick 'Pepsodent' Gibson. I just warm you up for the star, let you know you're among friends. Bob's show's dependent upon audience reaction and the way we get that—this is inside stuff, folks—is to let you know we're human too. Now that fellow sitting on the stage there is Joe Glober. Joe's Bob's card man. Been with him for years. During the show he's going to hold up a sign that says 'Laugh,' and that cues you to laugh. Joe, hold that sign up for these folks. Not upside *down,* for God's sake. Who hired you, Red Skelton? There, that's better. All right, people, let's hear your laugh. The engineer wants a sound level. Come on, when I say three. One. Two. Two and a half. Two and twenty-one thousand twenty-two thousandths. Three. *Go.* Look at Joe's sign,

Joe's sign. Too soft. This is coast-to-coast. How are they supposed to hear you in Tucson? All right. There were these newlyweds. They go off on their honeymoon. The trains are crowded, so all they can get is an upper berth. It's their first night together and they're in this little upper berth, do you follow? Well, it's pretty crowded up there and they don't want to disturb the other passengers, so the little bride whispers in her husband's ear, 'Sweetheart, when you want to make love just say, "Pass the oranges." That way the other passengers won't know what we're doing. "Pass the oranges." ' So the husband agrees and in five minutes he gets pretty excited and he tells his wife to pass the oranges. Then a little later the wife says, 'Pass the oranges.' Then in twenty minutes the husband says, 'Pass the oranges.' And that's the way it goes all night. Then, just before dawn, after the guy's asked for the oranges about forty times, they hear this voice from the lower berth: 'Lady, will you hand him the god-damned glass carefully this time? The juice keeps dripping in my face.'

"Oh, you liked that one. Did you get a level on that, Mel? Mel Bell, ladies and gentlemen—the engineer. Mel's been with Bob for years.

"So that's the kind of material you people like, is it? Well, you won't hear any stories like that once the show starts. We don't talk dirty mouth around here. Not on your tintype we don't. Not on the Pepsodent Show. Anybody here ever been to Boulder Darn? No, seriously folks, we can make all the jokes we want to about lust. Well, we *can*. What do you think those Frances Langford jokes are all about? And the Vera Vague routines? Why, to hear Bob tell it you'd think Miss Vague was a nymphomaniac or something. You want the inside story? Frances Langford isn't even my type. (Herbie Lauscher, ladies and gentlemen, one of Bob's writers. Been with him for years, years.) And Vera Vague is actually a very lovely person. A real lady. Sinatra weighs as much as I do and last year Jack Benny raised a quarter of a million dollars for United War Relief. Skinnay Ennis spells his name S-k-i-n-n-a-y. He's from down south. They name folks like that down there. Wait till you see him. That's just a joke about his being thin.

"All right?"

"And only the band goes by bus. That's a practical arrangement, a matter of logistics. Mr. Ennis arrives by plane a day before the show. Mr. Hope travels first class but alone. The private life. And it would break your heart to see him come down the ramp from the plane with his coat over his arm and his briefcase in his hand. He brings the script, you see, he carries it with him. And even if some flunky fetches his baggage, why at least Hope has to hand him the claim checks. And most of the time he picks it up himself, if you want to know.

"All right, granted Bob Hope's got a face people recognize. That makes a difference. But what about the others? The poet who carries his bags aboard the train and takes off his coat but doesn't know where to hang it and rolls it up with the manuscript inside, then remembers and removes it, and folds up the coat all over again and puts it down beside him this time because he doesn't want people to see him jump up and down and think he's a hick? What of people in air terminals waiting for connecting flights, passing the time at coffee counters, the sleeve of their trench coats in the puddle of Coca-Cola? What of men on vacation or business in countries where they don't speak the language or know the customs? What of the arrangements men have to make? I'm talking about obtaining rooms and getting your supper sent up. There's no way of greasing all of life, I say.

"Are you warming up? Jacomo Miller, folks, Bob's microphone man for many years. Been with him since he was a kid in fact. This summer the final adoption comes through.

"There's always the tire gone flat in the desert and no air in the spare. This is small time, peanuts, granted, agreed. All I mean to get across is—

"Listen, maybe this will explain what I mean. The guest lecturer for the Men's Auxiliary or the Temple Sisterhood. He's been around the world. He has slides from the upper reaches of the Amazon. Beautiful stuff, no white man's ever gotten this close. The slides are in a black leather case. He's afraid to check them so he takes them aboard the plane with him. But the case is too big. They won't let him put it in the overhead rack, and it doesn't fit comfortably under the seat. Besides, he's uneasy; suppose they hit an air pocket and the case slides forward under someone else's seat? It would be all right in the rack, but the stewardess won't let him put it there. What does she know? Where's *she* been? To Cleveland five hundred times? This guy's been everywhere—the top of the Amazon, the bottom. Still, he has to hold the case on his lap like any salesman with an order pad on his knee. It's different, but who's to know this? *No*body knows. There's this appearance of ordinariness. That's what breaks your heart. You follow? You see? Mel, quick, get a level. No?

"All right, try this . . . Your *father*. Your father goes to Indianapolis to call on a store. He forgets to take his shaving cream, or maybe he's all out of it. Well, he has to make a good appearance. You don't walk up to L. S. Ayers's head buyer with five o'clock shadow. If you've got bad breath you can put something sweet in your mouth, you can hide it, but how do you hide your whiskers? What do you do, throw your hands up over your face? Well, it's Sunday night, and he's got an appointment first thing in the morning. The drugstores don't open till nine or nine thirty. In a town the size of Indianapolis there *could* be some place open all night, even on a Sunday, but it's late. What's he going to do, start looking now? The man's tired, he's had a hard day, it's been a long trip. He goes to bed. The last thing on his mind before he falls asleep is the lousy shaving cream.

"In the morning he unwraps the little soap, the souvenir Ivory with the hotel on the wrapper, and he lathers with that. He rubs his palms furiously to work up the lather. He goes through the whole bar until it's only a tiny sliver. He pats it on his face. He shaves. He cuts himself. That cut, that blood! *That's* what I'm talking about—your daddy bleeding in a stuffy little room in Indianapolis. Where's the dignity? Where's the authority? Do you see? Do you see what I mean? Do you follow? Turn on the applause sign, somebody. Where's Bob's applause sign man? Joe Glober, hold up the 'Laugh' card. Pretend it's applause. No?

"The private life. That everybody has. Being loose in the world. On your own. On mine, Dick Gibson's. 'Pepsodent' is not actually my middle name. This is inside stuff. How much time do we have? Seventeen minutes? Twenty? . . . Marty Milton, ladies and gentlemen, Bob's pre-show time man. How long have *you* been with Bob, Marty?

"I'll tell you what happened to me after I lost my job. I meant to return the twelve or thirteen hundred miles to my home by bus. You'll just have to accept this. It was exciting for me, the most exciting thing that had ever happened. I was in disgrace, you see. In a way. I'd blown it, fucked up, torn it. The shit had hit the fan. I'd lost this job in Nebraska. There's a certain kind of disgrace in declining fortunes. And a certain kind of excitement in disgrace. This was a sort of ill health—an illness of recuperation. Oh, how weak I was, how vulnerable to everything. Dizzy as a lover. My pores were open, goners to drafts. I mean my spirit was such that I could have caught cold or picked up bad germs. Just to stand up straight made me giddy. And young as I was, I had this power of the has-been like a secret weapon. How sweet is weakness! How grand it makes us feel when we *really* feel it, how happy and how solemn! You've seen those men, five months past their heart attacks, making their leaden progress up the stairs, one foot on the next step and the other brought up to join it, a hand on the banister perhaps, and the deep, stately breathing.

"That's how *I* was. And not the least of it was the bus itself. This was a few years ago, before the war. It was still the depression; only the rich traveled by plane and even at that only between coasts. Buses were respectable then. You remember Clark Gable and Claudette Colbert in that movie. But this was my first time on a bus. Before when I had moved about—I was turning myself into a professional and I traveled considerably—I took trains.

65

Well, I was always going to better jobs; people were to meet me. And even if that hadn't been the case I would still have traveled by trains because I associated them with show business . . . The movies did that, the montages. Remember those triumphant tours, hands clapping over the big wheels and the successive signs saying Cleveland and Chicago and Detroit and the last one always New York.

"So there I was on this bus with this incredible ticket they give you like folded scrip—I hope you folks like small talk—and my unfamiliarity with the nooks and crannies of the thing, as if a bus were some queer sort of contraption they didn't have in America. That's *it!* I could have been a foreigner, but a foreigner come from a really major power to some hole-and-corner country where they drink wine with their meals and have no facilities for dry cleaning. My demeanor must have invited hospitality, reminded others I would be taking back my impressions of them. Or maybe it was the weakness I was telling you about. Whatever, several people smiled at me. And one older man actually got up and prepared this empty double seat for me. He raised the window shade and adjusted the footrest. Then he helped me with some of my things, kneeling on the arm of the seat to put them neatly on the rack.

" 'Thank you,' I said, pronouncing my words distinctly. 'You are very *kind* to me.'

"I sat down but the old fellow still stood in the aisle looking at me uncertainly. I smiled at him pleasantly but he seemed troubled. Then, looking away, he spoke to the woman in the seat in front of mine. 'I think he ought to take his coat off. It gets pretty warm once the driver closes the door.'

" 'He'd probably be more comfortable,' she said.

"The man turned back to me and I looked up at him with that curiously alert anxiety people show when others are discussing them. 'Yes?' I asked.

" 'We were thinking you might be too hot in that overcoat once the bus starts,' the man said.

" 'Oh, yes. Thank you.' I started to wriggle out of the

66

coat and the man in the seat behind mine leaned forward to help. 'You are *very* kind to me,' I told him. The old man in the aisle folded the coat carefully and put it in the rack above *his* seat where it would not be crushed by my parcels. 'Thank you,' I said. 'You are *all* very kind to me.' We smiled at each other and nodded, and then the man in the aisle took his seat and I settled in. In a little while the woman in front offered me her newspaper. 'Oh, no,' I said brightly. 'Thank you. I am looking through the *window*.' The woman nodded approvingly and looked where I was looking.

" 'Those are elm trees,' she said.

" 'Oh, yes?'

" '*Elm*,' she said.

" '*Elm*,' I repeated.

"We came to a town and passed a schoolyard where some kids were playing basketball. 'Those boys are playing the game of basketball,' the old man said.

" 'The game of basketball takes much skill,' I told him thoughtfully.

" 'Oh, yes,' he said. 'There are great universities that will pay for his education if the boy is skillful enough.'

" 'Ah.'

" 'They certainly have their energy. I suppose they'd play till the cows came home if no one stopped them.'

" 'With children it is much the same everywhere,' I said.

"We went by an International Harvester agency where the machines were jammed up on the apron outside the store, the great yellow seats on the tractors and harrows like enormous iron catchers' mitts. I looked out the window at everything, the best guest in history. And indeed, after my isolation and dedication of the last years, there *was* something profoundly interesting, astonishing even, about it all. I *might* have been a foreigner, a greenhorn to ordinary life.

"It was necessary for me to change buses in Des Moines, and over coffee in the Post House my new friends scrutinized my tickets and consulted with each other.

" 'His best bet,' one said, 'would be to lay over in Chicago for a night, look around the city tomorrow morning and catch an early afternoon bus out.'

" 'I don't think that's such a good idea,' the man said who had helped me off with my overcoat.

" 'He'd want to see Chicago.'

" 'Of course. But look. He doesn't get in till two-thirty this morning. Then, until he gets his bags and finds a locker where he can check them and looks over the bus schedule and hails a taxi cab it's another forty, forty-five minutes. Then he first has to start looking around for a hotel. It could be four o'clock before he gets into a room. You think he's going to be up to sightseeing in the morning? And even if he *is*, how much can he see in a few hours? No. I say if he wants to look around Chicago, fine, but he should make it a separate trip. Not a lousy layover that don't mean nothing.'

" 'Well, maybe,' the old man said.

" 'What maybe? There's no maybe about it. I'm right and you know it.'

" 'If he doesn't know Chicago it could be very confusing to come in at two-thirty in the morning,' the woman who had offered me her paper said.

"Then the driver called for them to reboard the bus and we all shook hands. The man who had helped with my overcoat paid for my coffee. I went with them to the bus and stood by as they climbed on. 'Everybody is very *kind*,' I said, 'very *friend*ly.'

"The old man was the last to go up the steps. He turned at the top and looked down at me just before the driver pulled the big steel lever that shut the door.

" 'Listen,' he said, 'good luck to you.'

"The old man was an old man, no high priest but a stranger with a good wish no stronger than my own, but it made me uneasy. There's something terrible to have it assumed that one needs luck. And, remember, we were at a crossroads.

"And, indeed, when I returned to the restaurant where none now knew me, my foreignness seemed gone. No longer an object of interest to my fellow passengers, I was

68

just one more weary pilgrim with all the pilgrim's collateral burdens—his sour taste, the beginning of sore throat, a sense of underwear and standing oppressed by his luggage in an open place, feeling the attention divided and a touch of panic.

"Today with an hour to kill in Des Moines I would call up the big radio station, introduce myself and accept whatever professional courtesy was offered. But not then.

"In a few hours I was traveling again, comfortable and safe now that it was dark, snug, aware of the glowing dials on the driver's console, relaxed by the long moist hiss of the tires.

"Somewhere along its route a girl had boarded the bus and sat down beside me. I saw her when I woke. Her eyes were shut but facing my lap. I turned on my haunch and closed my eyes again. I do not like to fall asleep in public because of the erection. I had one now—piss and lust— and I turned away to hide it. Something about my breathing must have put her wise, and I sensed that she too only pretended to sleep. We traveled like this for a time, both of us ever more wakeful. That she had come aboard some time after eleven o'clock from some small town, or even from beside the road perhaps, made her tremendously sexy to me. Somehow, even more than her proximity, her isolation and the lateness of the hour—which suggested that she was in trouble—made her seem available. It excited me that she had seen my hard-on, and our mimed sleep, of course. My God, I don't know what I might have done, but just when I could stand it no longer, just when I was capable of doing something for which they could have thrown me off the bus, just then *her* hand moved, made a suicide leap from its place in her lap to the narrow space between us. No, not a leap; it was one of those great surrenders from an enormous height, this lovely Acapulcan plunge. The edge of her hand grazed my hip as it fell, took a wee nip of my buttock. Ah, I was on fire. Oh, I was hot. From this I took hot heart and turned blindly, still feigning sleep, boldly forcing my erection into her palm.

"She shrieked and slapped me. Was I wrong about

69

her? 'Don't give me that,' I said. I shook her shoulders and pulled her to me and maneuvered the whole works into her hand again. And you know what? She *took* it.

"What a lesson! What a lesson! So much for your timidities and reservations, so much for your doubts and reluctances, your equivocations and hesitancies and shields of decorum more heavy then the world. She held me, I tell you. Then I held her. We grabbed at each other like drowners grasping at spars. (We sparred all right: sparring partners!) But she *had* been sleeping, there was no question about it. It was like something in a charm: one smash of passion and poof went the world. There is more rape than ever gets into the papers, and madness is the common cold of the emotions.

"So we hugged and we kissed. Right there in the bus I put my hands up her skirt and down her panties and in her crotch. We hadn't yet spoken, nor had either of us seen what the other even looked like. She unzipped me and pulled me off and collected my come and patted it on my prick like butter. In the bus. She squeezed it for luck and locked her legs around my hand when I started to withdraw it. These were her first words to me: 'Not so fast, not so fast. Do *me*. Do me or I'll scream again.'

"I did her. I thrummed her parts like rubber bands. Right there in the bus where they could throw you off for lighting a cigarette or talking to the driver. Then, when it was over and I was thinking well now we can relax, she still held on. She did me again and I did her again. Then she started to tell me jokes, and that was the way we traveled through the night—me with my hand in her pants and her playing with my cock and ears and touching my teeth lightly with her fingers so that I could taste my own semen, and telling me jokes. Dumb little jokes like a kid might know, not even dirty, just silly riddles and 'Knock Knock' stories and dopey limericks and one-liners about 'the little moron.' She knew them all and whispered them to me as if they were love words. After a while I thought she might be in show business. I asked her that.

70

"She put her head down shyly, 'I thought that's the way people speak.'

" 'Maybe it is,' I said.

"When it grew light I sat with a newspaper across my lap until my pants dried. I put the paper down and saw that some of the print had come off on my fly. People stopped to read my crotch as they passed by.

" 'We'll get off the bus,' I whispered. 'We'll find a tourist cabin. We'll make love properly. You'll tell me all your best jokes.'

" 'We're miles from anywhere. We have no motorcar.'

" 'Then let it get dark. I can't stand sitting next to you and not being able to touch you.'

" 'Shh.'

" 'I mean it. This daylight is a bad business.'

"We introduced ourselves. 'Marshall Maine,' I told her.

" 'Miriam Desebour,' she said, 'pleased to meet you.'

"Miriam was on her way to a convalescent home in Morristown, New Jersey, where she had taken a job as a practical nurse. I had intended to go home to Pittsburgh, but I went on with Miriam instead. She told her employers we were married, that I had been one of her patients, a sort of invalid who would never recover, and they accepted this.

"Do you know about Morristown? It's a very peculiar place—the languishment capital of America, maybe the world. It's the major industry. There are no famous clinics or hospitals, but there are schools for the deaf and the famous Seeing Eye Institute. There are convalescent homes like the one that hired Miriam, and old people's homes, and a farm for crippled children, and a sort of plantation where the retarded children of the wealthy spend their whole lives. There were people whose plastic surgeons had botched their operations and who felt they were too ugly ever to go home. There were 'training schools' from which few ever graduated, and old gassed soldiers from the First World War. There were other veterans, men who came to Morristown to learn how to

71

use their artificial limbs but never got the hang of it somehow. To my knowledge there were no lepers, but one of the persistent rumors was that a colony of them lived somewhere in the hills around the city. (I think the occasional appearance in the streets of the failed plastic-surgery patients gave rise to these rumors.) Many had lost limbs. There was lameness of all sorts, and it occurred to me that to be without a finger or an arm or a leg was a stunning kind of nakedness. (I thought of public exposures, emergencies of bust zipper and collapsed elastic. The needles and pins industry in Morristown must have been enormous, great *patch* fortunes might have been made there—fabulous thread mines in the Morristown hills. Indeed, the town did seem to have more shoe-repair shops and tailors than one would see in a city its size, and now that I think of it, it seems to me that something in the hearts of these people caused them to carry about all the scissors and thimbles and spot sewing equipment I saw.) It seemed to me that all the afflicted people of the world were stuffed into Morristown. It had all it could handle, a cornered market of gimps, a secular Lourdes, but not, withal, ungay. We were a community of arrested diseases, patient patients, developers of fortitude and resignation—all the loser virtues, all the good-sport resources.

"It was something to sit in those Morristown drugstores and see the doting purchases of the healthy, magazines for the relatives they were soon to abandon, cosmetics to make them presentable, pens, stationery, portable radios —all the sick man's sick-room detritus. It may have been a sign of my lassitude at this time that sitting in those drugstores as the cash register rang up the sales I thought no more about it than that it ultimately takes very little to live, that the desert isle and the beachcomber are worthy fictions. I owned a radio myself, of course, and listened to the Morristown stations. I wonder why I never realized while I was there that they were the same as radio stations anywhere. Probably the station managers thought the shut-ins wanted the world on normal terms. But nobody does.

"I lived in the home with Miriam, in the staff quarters, which were really no different from the facilities elsewhere in the home. There were rubber treads in the bottom of our bathtub, and a vertical hand rail screwed into the tile. There were conveniences all about the room, closets deep enough to store wheelchairs and whirlpool baths, a customized feel to the special heights of the furniture, defenses against arthritic stoop and arthritic stretch. We slept in a double bed with hospital sides—I'm just a prisoner of love. There were no locks on any of the doors, not even the door to the toilet. And the coils of our hotplate were a bright, cautionary fire red even when the electric was off. I have not been entirely comfortable in any room I've lived in since. Once one knows the hazards . . .

"That my physical appearance did not certify me an invalid was no special problem. Many of the people there seemed as healthy as myself. In fact there was an entire population of the unscarred: men and women whose lameness was in the blood, ruddy six-foot fellows as hollowed out as chocolate Easter bunnies, their stony-muscled arms piled high with blood pressure, their wrists with racing, warbled pulse. We were—I speak now not only for the community but for myself as well ('as well,' ha ha)—*weaklings,* our strengthlessness imposing an obligation on others, so that it exerted its force too, as everything alive does.

"Miriam, who knew my real condition, labored to make my assumed one come true. She made tight hospital corners on the very sheets we made love on and kept a bedpan for me within easy reach of the bed, and there was always a full glass of ice water on the nightstand. She sometimes gave me bed baths, first outlining one side of my body with towels and pushing the towels against it tightly like one beginning a sand construction, then pulling my pajama bottoms down—'Can you raise your hips a moment?'—the length of the bed, producing them from beneath the sheet at the foot like a minor trick of magic. 'Turn on your side, please,' she'd say. 'Can you turn on your side?' Then, arranging the sheet so that just

73

my back and the upper part of my buttocks were exposed
—I felt prepared, lovingly set up, set off, appetizing as
vegetable-ringed meat on a plank—she would begin to
rub my back with the warm, soaped cloth. She spoke as
she worked, peaceful, passive monologues, her voice more
distant than her hands which turned and rubbed and
stroked, telling me not the jokes now—she had run out of
jokes, though she was always careful to tell me the new
ones her patients told her—but about her life before she
met me.

" 'I have to help people,' Miriam said. 'I thought I'd be
a schoolteacher. In Iowa you don't have to be a college
graduate. You can get a temporary certificate so long as
you're enrolled in college and earn at least six credits a
year. A lot of teachers never graduate. They just sign up
for summer school year after year, but I've known some
who manage to save enough so they can take off every
third year or so and maybe get their degrees in eight or
nine years. Of course, those who get positions in Ames or
Iowa City have an advantage; they can teach and go to
the university at the same time. Those are the plum jobs,
though. They're very rare.'

" 'Mnn.'

" 'When I graduated high school I *did* teach for a year.
Fourth grade. I liked it very well. It was very interesting
and I enjoyed being around the children, but you know—
when it comes right down to it that's not really helping
people, teaching school. I mean, kids aren't in trouble,
not even if they're poor, not even if they don't always get
enough to eat. I mean, they're *kids,* you know? Kids can
play. I guess really the only kind of trouble people can get
into is to be sick.

" 'I mean, their bodies can be in trouble. That's really
all that can happen to a person. I've always been strong.
I'm very thankful for that. I love being strong. I mean, if
we were to wrestle I'd probably win. I wouldn't try to
hurt you but I'd win. Here.' She handed me the wash-
cloth. 'Do your private property.' She giggled. 'That's
what we call it. Or "family jewels." Isn't that silly?
Sometimes we say that to the men.'

74

" 'You do my private property, Miriam.'

" 'Don't be wicked, Marshall.'

" 'Miriam, you do my family jewels.'

" 'Now I've already spoken to you, young man.'

" 'Do my cock, Miriam. You do my prick. Please, Miriam, do my wang wang.'

" '*Marshall!*'

" 'You said you liked to help people.'

" 'People in trouble. You're not in trouble.'

"I turned on my back. 'There's trouble and there's trouble.'

" 'No,' Miriam said firmly. 'Whenever I wash you down there you just come all over the sheets and there's nothing left for me.' She looked down at me and laughed. 'Look at you. You're just like one of the old men around here with their big old things.'

" 'Do the old men get hard?' I was interested; I hadn't known this.

" 'Of course they do. It's a reflex, silly. There are some men around here who get an erection when I feed them.'

" 'Who? Who does?'

" 'Never mind. That's a nurse's confidence.'

" 'Who does? Who gets an erection when you feed him?'

" 'Never mind. You'll never get me to violate my professional ethics.'

" 'What about enemas? Do they ever get one when you give them an enema?'

" 'Enemas too,' Miriam said.

" 'Jesus.'

" 'Turn around. I'll do you back there.'

"Gently she reamed me. When Miriam had finished one of these baths you could eat off me. Then we made love. Me and Nurse. Calmly, not like on the bus, but languidly and with long graceful glidings like paddling canoes in dreams. Afterward I lay back with my hands behind my head, and soon it was me talking. I told her about being on the radio.

" 'Mnn,' Miriam said, for neither of us were much at discussion. There was give and take but it was of a

75

certain kind, like the rules of service in a ping-pong game. I'd serve five times, then Miriam would. It's the way people who will grow closer speak while they still don't know each other very well.

"Miriam talked only when she was doing something—I suspect it was a habit she picked up from her rounds, a compulsion to fill up the silence imposed on patients whose blood pressures or temperatures are being taken. There was something curiously polite, not to say efficient, about this habit, as though language were one more service she rendered. For my part I seemed to speak only when spent, as after lovemaking.

"Miriam was making us some bouillon on the hotplate. She was naked despite the fact that there was no lock on our door; this, together with the domestic tour she made about the room—fetching the kettle and bouillon cubes, going to the bathroom sink for water—seemed very erotic to me, like the establishing of the story line in a stag film.

" 'My father was an unhealthy man,' Miriam said. 'I mean, he was without health. His heart was bad—he'd had three heart attacks, two of them massive—but there were other things: his liver, migraine—more than that even. He'd had operations. But even before he was sick physically, there was something delicate about him mentally. He was very tender-hearted. I mean, he couldn't take bad news. It didn't just make him unhappy as it would others; it affected him physically. That's what his illness *was*—bad news, bad news chipping away at his health. It was a sort of erosion.

" 'We're a large family—from Cedar Rapids originally. We moved across the state to Simms, Iowa, because it was easier to shield Daddy from bad news there. We were away from the family, my father's and mother's brothers and sisters, all of them getting along in years, and all their old friends too, whose illnesses and deaths could be managed better than if we were still with them right there in Cedar Rapids. Now that the news could come through the mail instead of over the telephone, we could plan how best to shield it from Father.

76

" 'But not only physical things affected Daddy. Bad news could come in all sorts of ways—like if my sister or I got a bad grade in a subject, or if business was bad. Father had a little money and was a silent partner in a few small businesses—a grocery store, a barbershop, a drycleaner, that sort of thing—so that except in boom times there was always some bad news coming in from one business or the other. But even political things could upset him, current events from all over the world. My God, how that man had sympathies! Mother tells about the time she had to keep the news of the Lindbergh kidnapping from Father. She just cut it out of the paper —the big front-page headlines and stories and pictures, everything. "Here, what's this?" my father asked her when he saw his paper all cut up. "Oh that," Mother told him, "that's just a recipe I cut out of the paper." *"From the front page?"* Father asked. "Well, the second," Mother said. "The second?" "It's a very newsworthy recipe," Mother said, "it's a big sensation all over the country. It's for a good cheap eggless cake." "Eggs are high?" Father said. "Yes," said Mother, "very expensive." "Oh, that's terrible," Father said, clutching his chest. "But we're saved by the new recipe," Mother tried to reassure him, but Father still held his chest and had grown very pale. "What's wrong?" asked Mother. "I'm not thinking about the cakes," groaned Father, "I'm worried about the omelets."

" 'Well, you can see how it was, how we had to shield him. It wouldn't have been so bad, except that he was an unrelenting questioner. He knew the harm it did him but he couldn't help himself. He was like someone flirting with a bad tooth, teasing and maneuvering it until it hurts.

" 'We had a little dog, the cutest little thing. Well, it was my dog but everyone in the family loved it. We were always petting it and making up to it, even Father. Maybe we loved Roger *too* much because he never really enjoyed being outdoors. Why should he? He had everything he wanted in the house. Well, of course a dog has to go out sometime, if only to make number one or number two, so we would send Roger out once in the morning and once again at night. That was one of the good things—if it was ever too cold or rainy to walk him, why we could send him out by himself without being afraid he'd run away. He'd do his duty and come right back, whining to be let in. But one time when we let him go out he didn't come right back. Mother and my sister Rose and I were concerned but we didn't want to alarm Father so we arranged it that two of us would go to bed and the other would keep a vigil for Roger. Of course we couldn't go outside and yell for him because Father might hear that and then where would we be?

" 'My sister was the one who stayed up, for Roger was *my* dog, remember, and Father might get suspicious if he came down at night and saw me. Also, we weren't sure I could fool Father; I might not be able to hide my concern. Well, he *did* get up and come down that night. He saw the light and came into the kitchen where Rose was drinking from the glass of milk which Mother had cleverly thought to pour out for her so she'd have something to do in case Father came down. "I just can't seem to sleep tonight, Father," Rose told him, "I thought this milk might relax me." "Is something wrong, Rose? Why can't you sleep?" Father asked her. "No, nothing's wrong, Daddy," Rose said. "You know how you get sometimes, you just start thinking about things and you can't seem to fall asleep."

" 'That was exactly the wrong thing to tell Daddy, of course; right away he wanted to know *what* things. Rose made up some stuff about the school elections to tell him. She was in charge of publicity for the candidate put up by her home room and she didn't know where she was going to get the paints and cardboard for the posters. Well, that troubled Father and he had a little angina pain even though both knew the elections were a good two months off, but as Rose pointed out it wasn't the end of the world, and that seemed to calm him some. But then he started to ask where everybody was: were Mother and I in bed, and where was Roger? Well, she had just let him out, Rose said. This satisfied Father for it was a natural thing to do, and so he went back to bed.

" 'Roger still wasn't back in the morning, but fortunately Mother, who rarely was up before Father, this time *was,* and she told him she'd just let Roger out. That started something in our house, I can tell you. From that time on poor Mother and Rose and I had to take turns rising before Father just so's one of us could say we'd just let Roger out. The trouble was, Father usually got up at dawn. We were always tired now because we had to take turns staying up late too. This hurt us in the alertness department. I mean, it was self-defeating, for without sleep we just weren't sharp enough to withstand Father's assaults on us for information. It was wintertime—a cold one in Iowa that year—and suddenly it seemed as if all our relatives and friends were coming down with everything all at once. The three of us were always so tired now that we didn't know what we were saying and would spill the beans to Father accidentally.

" 'It wasn't our fault, but the bad news would just tumble out all over the place and there didn't seem to be anything we could do about it. It was just awful that we couldn't shield him any more, and believe me it took its toll on that dear man. He lost weight and had pain all the time and his parameters—pressure, pulse, eye track—just went from bad to worse. About all we could manage was to keep Roger's disappearance from him, and this at a time when we'd given up hope of the dog's ever returning. For that matter, Father was so generally dispirited and debilitated by now that he rarely ever asked after him. We wondered if it might not be better just to find some way of breaking the news to Father, have done with it altogether, and then maybe manage to get enough control of ourselves to try to deal with the routine day-to day shielding of Father that the situation demanded. But of course we were too far into it now. We couldn't just say we'd lied, and we certainly couldn't tell him one morning that the dog had just gone off. Father had too much sense for that; he'd have seen that Roger had been missing for weeks.

" 'Well, the way it turned out we didn't have to choose any of these alternatives, but frankly I thought it was all over with us when Father himself brought up the subject. "I don't know, Miriam," he said, "I just never *see* Roger any more. The dog is *always* out. He never used to be like that before this damned winter. Oh, these are hard times, Mim. I'm hearing so much bad news lately I'm worried that there might be something wrong with Roger's bladder"—and then he clutched with both hands at the small of his back as though he'd just felt a fierce jolt in his own bladder.

" 'I told Mother and Rose what Father had said and we agreed that we had to do something fast. Well, that very next night Mother went up to Father and said, "You know, Earl, Mim and Rosie have given what you said about Roger yesterday quite a lot of thought, and Mim agreed that maybe it's just too cold for Roger here. We did get him as a pup from that nice man that time we went down to Floria, remember. Anyway, Mim's decided that Roger might be better off if he lived with her Cousin Ernestine down in Birmingham, where the climate's not so harsh. We know how tender-hearted you are, Earl, and we didn't want to burden you unnecessarily with a sad leavetaking, so we've already been down to the depot and shipped Roger off." Well, it caused Father some pain to realize that I'd given up my dog, but after a while, when he saw the thing in perspective, his spirits began to brighten, and the rest of us felt better too because now we could get more sleep. In no time at all we were able to cope and shield Father again from the bad news that seemed to come from everywhere that winter.

" 'It was marvelous to see Father grow lively again. I can't say that he recovered his health, but not having to hear bad news all the time did restore a certain confidence and vigor to the man. And the winter too seemed to be declining in its fierceness, the back of the cold spell had been broken, and though it wasn't actually warm, the terrible snow had begun to melt—though here and there there were still high drifts and all the curbs were piled with the stuff. It wasn't just that we knew how to handle the bad news better now that Roger was off our mind; it was that the bad news itself fell off. One day Father even

80

felt well enough to go out for a walk. It was fun to see him in so fine a fettle—Father was a marvelous man to be with when he was feeling good—and I joined him. He was so cheerful that he didn't seem to be the same man, and once he even bent over to gather up some snow for a snowball. I thought he might hurt himself doing a thing like that but he was up again as spry as any boy and threw the snowball all the way across the street to hit the tree there a lovely bull's-eye. This made him so happy he couldn't contain himself and he just stepped bold as you please into a pile of snow at the curb, but then he got this horrible look on his face, and he dropped down on his hands and knees and began uncovering whatever it was he had felt in the snow. Well, it was Roger's frozen body and when he stepped on it he'd snapped its neck.

" 'I had to carry Father back to the house on my back, and I think he must have been dead by the time we got there. I took his body in through the back door because I knew Mother and Rose would be in the parlor, and out of habit I didn't think they should see this.'

"The funny thing is," Dick Gibson told his audience, "I don't remember *hearing* any of this. I mean, I must have or how would I know it, but I don't recall much of anything that went on in that room the months I was there. Was I silent the whole time she spoke? Was it a monologue? Did I ever drink the bouillon? Did Miriam get into bed with me during her story? Did I fall asleep? What happened?

"I wasn't in love with Miriam. It's more probable, though unlikely, that she was in love with me. She made me comfortable, more comfortable than I'd ever been in my life. Perhaps because she was a nurse. Nurses have lousy reputations because of what they do for men. I mean the bedpans, the enemas and the pubic shaves, I mean the deathbed vigils and hearing folks scream. I could be myself with Miriam, vent my gas, kiss with a bad taste in my mouth, grunt over my bowels in the toilet. So when I ask if I could have fallen asleep it isn't out of fear of not being on my mettle as a lover. I was in a trance, a catalepsy, a swoon, a brown study, a neutral funk. I was languid, gravid, the thousand-pound kit in Miriam's room, sensitized as human soup. And if I heard her at all it was in my ilium I listened—as deep as that—harkened in my coccyx, my pajama strings all ears, and my buttons and the Kleenex under my pillow.

" 'What is wrong with you, Mr. Desebour, may I ask?' Doctor Pasco, the Home's young director wanted to know.

" 'I have the falling sickness, Dr. Pasco,' I told him lazily, dizzily. 'I have the petit mal.' Nor was I lying. I was in the cataleptic's 'aura' state. It must have been something like that.

"Miriam noticed my passivity.

" 'Too many bed baths,' I told her.

" 'We'll cut them out,' she said. 'Are you bored here? Are you tired of me?'

" 'Christ, no. I swear it. If I didn't know you I'd tune you in and listen to you on the radio.'

"It was the truth. That was *exactly* how I listened to Miriam—as if she were some new kind of radio personality. Once I realized this I tried to study her inflections, but she had no inflections. I sank deeper and deeper into my desuetude, the pit of my stomach spreading till I was *all* stomach pit.

"One night she asked me to leave.

" 'Just like that?''

" 'Yes.'

" 'I won't leave. I like it here. I won't leave until I unlock the secret of your voice,' I told her, yawning.

" 'What are you talking about, Marshall? Why are you so difficult?'

" 'Please, Miriam, let's make love. Then fix us bouillon and tell me a story.'

" 'I am not the Story Lady, Marshall. I've told you, I want this ended. You must get out.'

" 'If you make me leave Dr. Pasco will know we're not married. He'll throw you out.'

" 'We could say we're getting a divorce.'

" 'I won't agree to a divorce, Miriam.'

" 'We'll see,' she said.

"I became a laughing stock; Miriam made me a laughing stock. Oh boy, the laughs at my expense, last laughs and best laughs, up one sleeve and down the other. I was their butt, their asshole I was. Miriam's strategy was simple: she cuckolded me. It probably didn't amount to much more than washing the private property of a few of the chronics. From the talk I think there may have been some hanky panky with the man who came when she gave him enemas. (He was a nice enough fellow, unremarkable except for a peculiar inability to pronounce certain *rs* sounds which, in his mouth, came out *tch*.) The place fed on scandal; it was good therapy for those chronics. I could have blown the whistle on her; I could have gone up to them and said 'Look here, I'm no cuckold. Miriam's not my wife,' but then I would have seemed more pathetic than foolish. It's one thing to lose control of your wife, but quite another not to be able to handle your mistress. Besides, I hadn't yet broken the secret code of her voice.

"But it was the strangest thing I have ever endured. For one thing, we still screwed, more than ever probably, for Miriam was determined to make her adultery seem real, and to do that she needed to preserve the illusion of our marriage which could now be maintained only by the further illusion that she was deceiving me. How complicated it all was. For the first time in my life I was involved with someone who actually had motives. I even had motives myself. (How motiveless the world is, when you stop to consider, how unconspiratorial is the ordinary bent of humanity, how straightforward that bent. Drive drives the world, simple inclination is its capstan.)

"Another thing was my standing now with the patients. How they clowned with me, how they made jokes with their joke! For instance, they would pretend that I had this enormous dick. The source of this idea, I suspect, was just the fact that of all the people in the Home—patients and staff—Miriam and I were the only two who cohabited, so that even before Miriam made cuckoldry with the enema man, an aura had built up around us. We stood apart from the rest of those lame ducks and can't-cut-the-mustards, though they didn't see those bedbaths in the double bed with the hospital sides. The conceits they invented were elaborate and insane:

" 'Ah, Mr. Desebour, pull up a couple of chairs, why don't you?'

" 'He's in for rupture,' one man liked to explain to his visitors, 'from carrying great weights.'

" 'Is it a fact, Mr. Desebour, that you had a limb amputated in order to accommodate your incredible cock, and that you now wear a pant leg over that cock and fill up your shoe with its foreskin?'

" 'No, that is not a fact,' I said, and they laughed the harder. Everyone laughed. The man who got hard-ons when Miriam fed him laughed; the Sherpa who had injured his spine in an Everest expedition, and whose employer—a rich Southerner who had taught the Sherpa English—brought the fellow to Morristown to spend the rest of his life in the Home, *he* laughed.

" 'Down home,' the Sherpa said, 'there was this good old boy. Now *he* had a piece on him and that piece, well sir, it was big but it was cuter'n a speckled pup under a red wagon. Folks down home said he could *climb* it. Whoeee, have mercy, have mercy. My daddy told me that old boy went up it like a nigger chased up a tree by a li'l ole ghost. I ain't sayin' a thing 'gainst Marshall's here, I'm just tellin' you all what my daddy reported.'

" 'Down home, down home,' I hissed at him irritably. "You're from Tibet. Why don't you say *up* home?'

"I tell you, it's quite extraordinary to be laughed at— Bob Hope couldn't have touched me in those days—quite extraordinary to know that wherever you go you are something less than the least person there. Not to inspire disfiguring envy or fury or hatred but only merriment is a doom. I had the power to change a mood simply by entering a room. At the sight of me, whatever had been the frictions and cross-currents before, there was now a unity. And it didn't matter what people said to me. I mean this two ways. Many of the patients confided private things about themselves to me, what they regarded as my inhumanity lending me the immunity of clowns—as

84

one fucks one's wife in front of the dog. You don't understand this, do you? There have been cuckolds before. Why, right in your own neighborhood, you think, down your street and up your block, and who laughs, who doesn't go out of his way to be kind to the guy's children, circumspect with him? I don't know, perhaps they smelled something on me that was inhuman *really* or they wouldn't have acted like that.

"They laughed at me openly but never brought Miriam's or the enema man's name into it. As a matter of fact, he was the only one who didn't find me amusing. He even tried to befriend me. The enema man had had two or three divorces himself and knew the rough weathers of love. He told me that this was why he was in the Home, and why he took enemas; his frustration in his marriages had somehow affected his intestines and kept him almost constantly blocked. But he was nice and tried to comfort me. He put his arm about me consolingly. 'Don't depend on women, kid. Forget the broads. They're poison. Put money in your poitch.'

" 'That's easy for you to say.'

" 'Not so easy, not so easy. They took their toll. Agh, none of 'em are any good. They're woitch than a coitch.'

" 'All of them?'

" 'Every last one. They'd be better off dead in a hoitch.' I nodded. 'Kid, good talking to you. I better beat it back to my room, it's time for my enema. Hey, did you see the noitch?' "

"I told him where he would find Miriam. I marveled at my helplessness, astonished to recognize that the conventional parameters of character applied, amazed that a person who had been on the radio; who had traveled and lived alone could not handle himself in a pinch. Why, I should have let them have it for laughing; I should have set Dr. Pasco straight or wrung Miriam's neck. Now I don't know. Now I am surprised I was surprised, for there I was, sidetracked in Morristown and living incognito with a nurse in a rest home, things too strange for your apprentice personality and one-track soul. How could I have known better who had gotten every idea I ever had from what they permitted to be spoken on the air? Why, my greenness was written in the stars. It's a wonder I didn't cry, break out in sweats and pimples, a wonder I didn't sulk in corners or imagine them all at my funeral. I was little more than a teen-ager. How did I not go mad at that first feel on the bus; what kept me from proposing marriage then and there, the first time I felt her hand on my cock?"

But not all of this was for the warmup. Actually, Dick Gibson got no further than the part where he began to describe the sort of place Morristown was. At that point he became conscious of a stirring in the audience, not a restlessness so much as a new interest. He looked behind him—his instinct unerring here, danger always approaching from the rear—where he saw Frances Langford and Colonna and Bob Hope himself. After a while Langford and Colonna went off to their places behind the curtain, but Mr. Hope remained, politely listening at first but increasingly puzzled to know where this was leading, and then at last visibly concerned that all this talk of invalids and cripples could hurt the show. In a moment he signaled for the curtain to be raised, and there was the band in its places and Colonna and Vera Vague and Miss Langford and the rest of the cast in theirs, and Bob Hope came over to Gibson, whispered something in his ear, relieved him of the warmup microphone and did a fast half-dozen snappy minutes of emergency material.

The reaction of the audience was interesting. It sent up a courteous massed *awww* of disappointment when it saw that Dick was not to be allowed to finish his story, but then responded immediately and uproariously to the first of Hope's jokes. But it was Dick Gibson himself who laughed loudest and cheered hardest. As a professional he understood Hope's problem, of course, but there was something else—not sycophancy, not fear that he would lose his job, but his sense that Hope was racing the clock, up against time, the big one. In all the years he had been in radio he had never quite had this sense of time, had never seen it as a dimension in itself, more, a battleground, *the* battleground, and not only the battleground but the enemy as well. It was radio that took time on at its own game, scheduling it, slicing it into fifteen- and thirty- and sixty minute slices, its single master. Forget railroads and buses and planes, forget appointments at the highest levels and the synchronized intricacies of combat and athletics, all you-cut-here, he-fades-there arrangements. Only radio and time were inexorable, and here was a hero who stood up in it, as one stands up in the sea, and splashed about in it, used it, perhaps one day would die in it. Hence he cheered and laughed, little less than literally wild when the director in the control room threw his finger and the red On the Air sign burned bright and Mr. Hope, script in hand, ready behind the stand-up microphone, took his cue.

Afterward Dick Gibson told the rest of his story to Joe Glober and Mel Bell and Jacomo Miller and a few of the people in Skinnay Ennis's band when they all went out to a roadhouse just outside St. Paul. He was a little in his cups—Hope had spoken to him personally, assuring him that his approach was fresh, and that he had never heard anything like it: "Imagine," Hope had said, turning to the man who worked the applause sign, "not to glut an audience with jokes, but merely to depress them so that when the laughs come the people are actually grateful and laugh harder"—and so perhaps his voice was just a bit louder than usual. But louder or not, he was at first addressing just the seven or eight at his table. Only later did he shift over and gradually raise his voice so that he could be heard finally throughout the entire roadhouse, doing his own version of a broadcast from the Copa Lounge, Barry Gray sans microphone and guests—closed-circuit radio, the radio of confrontation, the shout network—and in his cups or not, never forgetting time as he now understood it.

"Listen . . . the old clock on the wall . . . All right, quickly, then.

"There was a picnic. Patients and their guests, staff and their supposititious husbands.

"By now the whole town was talking. The grapevine of

cripples had put out the word on me and Miriam and the enema man. In the drugstore the pharmacist jokingly offered to sell me enema poison.

'I have no enemamies,' I told him, and it was as if I had broken the bank at Monte Carlo, goodsportwise.

"So the day of the picnic finally arrived and all Morristown turned out. The crème de la crème. The blindees, the deafoes and dummies—see no evil, hear no evil, speak no evil. The amputees, the orphans, the folks of ruined blood, as well as your general all-purpose invalids. All of them loved to crash the other guy's picnic. So that Morristown had a season: summer. The deaf would eat the blind man's chicken, and see the colors of the blind man's fruit, and the blind heard the *fsst* of the deaf man's beer. The amputees licked the orphans' candy canes. But our picnic was even more heavily attended than one could have expected, and it may have been our scandal that made the difference.

"I had been blithe for the man at the drugstore, and now I was blithe for Morristown.

" 'Mr. Desebour, I've heard so much about you,' giggled Mr. Latrobe, the blind kennel master of the guide dogs at the institute.

" 'Nice to see you here, sir,' I told him.

" 'Mis-*t*er huff De-se-booor*gh,* huff huff,' growled the deaf Mrs. Garish in that machine-like, exhalated voice of the trained mute, 'I've beeenn huff loo*k*-in*gg* forwar*dt* huff to mee*t*-ing you.'

" 'Good talking to you, ma'm. I've heard so much about you.'

" 'Hi, Mr. Desebour,' said Paul the orphan.

" 'Hello, son.'

"I entered all the contests and potato-raced my heart out, finishing in the money. No mean feat, for a lot of these fellows had been born with only one leg and until you've potato-raced against a congenital one-legged man in a sack you haven't potato raced. I won at chug-a-lug and lagging pennies and swamped them at horseshoes and wheelchair racing, and in the invalid decathlon I was best. Cheating, entered as a patient but using my health, ear-

STATE
SENATOR **LILA SAPINSLEY**

*I hope you like
my record and will
vote for me on November 4.*

METRIC CONVERSION CARD
Approximate Conversions to Metric Measures

Symbol	When You Know	Multiply by	To Find	Symbol
LENGTH				
in	inches	*2.5	centimeters	cm
ft	feet	30	centimeters	cm
yd	yards	0.9	meters	m
mi	miles	1.6	kilometers	km
MASS (weight)				
oz	ounces	28	grams	g
lb	pounds	0.45	kilograms	kg
	short tons (2000 lb)	0.9	tonnes	t
VOLUME				
tsp	teaspoons	5	milliliters	ml
Tbsp	tablespoons	15	milliliters	ml
fl oz	fluid ounces	30	milliliters	ml
c	cups	0.24	liters	l
pt	pints	0.47	liters	l
qt	quarts	0.95	liters	l
gal	gallons	3.8	liters	l
l	liters	0.26	gallons	gal
TEMPERATURE (exact)				
°F	Fahrenheit temperature	5/9 (after subtracting 32)	Celsius temperature	°C

I have found this useful. I hope you will, too.

Lila Sapinsley

**STATE SENATOR
DISTRICT 2**

nest, shooting to kill like a father burning them in to the other guy's kid in the PTA softball. Flinging off my passivity for once, I pushed past the others in the human wheelbarrow, my hands and arms furious as pistons, nearly pulling the poor guy over who held my legs. Concentrating, concentrating, steady as a surgeon I balanced the peas on my knife as the peas of the spastics went flying off in all directions. *There,* I thought, dusting my hands, nonpareil at the picnic, *take that and that and that.*

"Only Miriam knew my real situation—unless, of course, in the throes of passion with the enema man she had disclosed our secret—but the invalids themselves, thinking I was one of them, would have made me their champion then and there. I could have been their Thorpe, I tell you.

"And a strange thing happened. I sensed that they had begun to turn against the enema man, against Miriam. I saw the enema man—I had beaten that constipate in hard-boiled-egg eating—sitting off by himself on a blanket beside the horseshoe pits, a book in his lap, and looking full, stuffed, his face flushed, his skin itself gorged, oppressed by the ruthless satiety of his life. I went over, blithe but burning.

" 'Reading?'

" 'Yeah. Pass the time.'

" 'What have you got there?' I bent down and read the book's title. 'Ah, poetry. A few voitches, is it?'

"I drifted off toward the lake and began to walk round it. Miriam caught up with me. 'Where are you going?'

" 'All that exercise. It's hot.'

" 'Yes. You were very determined.'

" 'Give 'em something to talk about.'

" 'When will you leave?' she asked after a while. 'This is getting crazy.'

" 'When I unlock the secret of your voice. First I have to unlock the secret of your voice.'

" 'You keep saying that. What does it mean?'

" 'How you talk. How peaceful it makes me.'

"We had stopped following the lake and had turned on

to a footpath that led into the woods. It was very cool among the trees but in a few hundred yards we came to a clearing in the center of which was an enormous stone mansion. It was strange to come upon it like that.

" 'What the hell is *that?* Who lives *there?* My God, you don't suppose we've found the leper colony, do you?'

" 'Mrs. Garish,' Miriam said.

" 'What?'

" 'Mrs. Garish lives there. It's the Institute for the Deaf.'

"It was very hot in the sun. 'It looks cool.'

" 'It's open to the public. Do you want to go inside?'

"I shrugged but followed Miriam into the large central hall of the building.

"Miriam told the woman who came out to greet us that we were from the home. 'Oh, that's nice,' she said. 'It's important to understand the other fellow's problem. Look around. Be sure to see the dead room. You'll want to see the dead room.'

" 'The dead room?'

" 'We call it that. We do experiments there. It's 99.98 per cent free of reflected sound. The telephone company built it for us. It's supposed to be the quietest place in the world.'

"Miriam and I walked through the various classrooms and poked desultorily at some of the special equipment. Then, at the end of a long, carpeted hallway, we came to the 'dead room.'

"We pulled open the heavy door and went inside. It was the strangest room I have ever been in. It may have been about twenty-five by thirty-five feet—about the size of a large drawing room—though it was difficult to tell, for no two walls were exactly parallel. The walls and ceiling were broken up in a zigzag pattern and honey-combed with cells of differing shapes and depths like thousands of opened mouths. We walked on a spongy, corklike substance thicker than any carpet.

"The silence was astonishing, a hushed chorus from the mouths of the walls. It was like a darkness. Have you ever been in a room that is totally dark? Late at night,

90

say, and awakened in a strange place, and for a moment you don't know where you are or how they got you there, and you're groping for the door? Well, the things you brush past there in the dark—a chair or a wardrobe— these are like blind spots. But you can *hear* them, hear the blind spots, as if all objects give off this signal, the sonar of material reality felt, sensed in the extinct ear, held in the vestigial eye, prickling across the bone of your forehead like the electric touch of a girl you wish loved you. Well, it was something like that, the silence. Wait, *double* it!

"For the first few moments neither of us spoke or even looked at each other, as people do who spot a marvel. It was all either of us could do to take it all in, all we could do perhaps to get over the inevitable touch of the sad in the presence of all that black mufflement.

"I spoke first. I don't remember what I said, but my voice was small, squeezed, not unloud so much as dis- crete, anechoic, so that sound as such—walking, the noise of our clothes, our breathing—was meaningless, probably unidentifiable, swallowed in the room's million mouths. Only words, however clipped, maintained their existence in this room of aural blind spots and thick silence, only the ideas *behind* words. In that sense the room was intellectual, a place for concepts. Here no teacups could ever tinkle, no spoon rattle in a glass; there could be no chatter, no din, and the report of a gun would be as insignificant as the clink of two glasses touching politely in a toast. There was no hacking or rustle or hiss or whoosh or crackle or crepitation or affricative churn, no tocsin, no knock, no thump at the door or rain on the roof. All that was not language died at its source or was reduced to harmless velvet plips. God might have made the place.

" 'Talk.'

" 'What should I say?'

" 'Speak.'

" 'I don't know what to say.'

" 'Let's hear it,' I commanded.

" 'I don't know what you want me to say. I . . . Be nice

to me. I'm the one they laugh at—*I* am. They know what I do. I'm the one they're laughing at. They think you're a cripple like themselves.'

" 'In the beginning was the Word. Say.'

" '*I don't know what you want!*'

" 'To unlock the secret of your voice. Just that.'

" 'It will end by my being fired. I'll lose my job. All I want is to help people. Why won't you go?' She was crying, though I didn't hear this so much as see it.

"I recalled her stories after we made love. 'Stop. That's enough. Eureka, I've found it. Thank you.'

" 'I wish I never sat next to you on that bus.'

" 'Now I know the secret. I'm leaving.'

" 'The secret,' she said contemptuously.

" 'Certainly,' I said. 'I knew you had one. Now I know what it is.'

" 'What is it?' she asked dully.

" 'You were naked. I'm a sucker for the first person singular.' "

Dick Gibson paused. He leaned back, appearing to rest. "Quick," he said, suddenly leaning forward again. "Let me see your watch." He took up someone's wrist and brought it to his face. "You're left-handed," he said disgustedly, flinging the wrist away. "The numbers are upside down." He grabbed someone else's wrist, bent down over it so that his nose almost touched the man's watch, and studying the dial, he figured to himself furiously. "*Ah,*" he said breathlessly, "*one hour and seventeen minutes. I just made it.*"

He was in Newark that evening, out on a sleeper that night, did not speak to strangers and arrived in Pittsburgh the next morning.

It was strange to be in a big city again—even stranger than to be home—and he realized that except for layovers he had not been in a really large city since he'd left home. It was fitting. Small towns were the historic province of apprenticeship—villages, townships, county seats, flocculent, unincorporated tufts of population—these backwaters were your unheeding witnesses to your new processes and evolving styles. Just the same he felt expansive, auspicion's loved object, young Lochinvar come riding out of the west on a round trip.

As he left Union Station and looked up Mellon Boulevard at downtown Pittsburgh, he was tremendously excited. He perceived with a sovereign clarity, shipping impression like a lovely cargo, and what he saw was to stay with him all his life as the very essence of the city. He admired the black, thick buildings, the dark windows like glass postage or framed deep water. There were high projecting cornices at the top stories like the peaks of caps, and he tried to look in under them to the careful scrollwork, distinctive as the flow of a hairline. Shifting his gaze he watched the smooth, shiny trolley rails that, blocks off, flowed into each other like twin rivers of perspective. At a nearby corner a snagged lace of electric lines floated above the traffic. He sighted along a row of canopies that unfurled above the big display windows of a department store in a parade of identical angles, trawling on the bright and windless morning a still fringe of scallops. He looked up the tall, fluted shaft of an iron light standard. It seemed monumental to him, something to light up outer space. He waited for a traffic light to change and crossed the street, moving with a certain awe toward a bank like a pagan temple, its brass and marble ornament engraved like money.

It pleased him to be in this city of just under a half-million, a large American city of the first class with a major league ball club (in a state with *three* major league teams; no state had more; only New York had as many), three great daily newspapers, and eleven radio stations (all the networks plus KDKA, perhaps the greatest independent in the country). He congratulated himself. Depression or no, soot or no—an industrial pall hung on the buildings like a painted shadow, but it was not unpleasant; it seemed an earnest of the city's value—it was a magnificent place, as finished and fixed for him as a city in Europe. Yet he felt a twinge too, realizing it was merely his home, that he belonged there only in that sense, that despite his years away from it, he was simply its citizen. No great company had called him there, nor had he, prospector-like, shouldered his way through Indian hazard to seek its veins and work its lodes. In this sense he felt it less his than the last traveling salesman's off the train with him that morning. By the time he was settled in a cab he was already down a peg or two, and he no longer knew the city well enough to be satisfied that the driver did not cheat him as he turned up alleys and cut through parks.

His mother was standing on the porch when the taxi pulled up. "Och," she said, recognizing him, "a taxi, is it? Nivver moind that the roof wants fixin' or cupboard's bare. Bother all that, so long as himself here can roid about in the cabs." It was her Maw Green imitation, a doughty Irish washerwoman from the Sunday funnies. He had not thought about it since he'd left home, and was surprised that it could still make him uncomfortable.

"Hello, Mama."

"Saints presarve us," his mother sighed. She moved down the steps toward him. "It's you, it's really you this toime? 'Tisn't a ghost or a trick of the wee folk?"

"It's me, Mama."

She reached out and touched him, then pretended to wipe a tear from her eye. "La, listen to me blather when it's probably hungry y'are from yer journey." She stepped back to appraise him. "Och, and foine it is yer lookin' too, lad. Faith and begorrah," she said, shaking her head sadly, "if only yer father were here to see you."

"Is Papa dead, Mama?"

"No, God love you, boy, but only down t' corner fer a pint. Ah, bejazus, where's me manners?" She took his heavy suitcase from him and would have had him lean on her as they went up the stairs, but he eluded her and walked up them unaided into the house. His mother followed him inside, calling, "Arthur, Arthur lad, ye must guess who's come. It's himself, Arthur, it's young himself himself."

They heard a rough noise, a clumsy banging and clatter from behind one of the closed bedrooms off the hallway.

94

It was exactly the sound of something outsize and heavy being maneuvered into position, a full steamer trunk, perhaps. He looked at his mother, but she would not meet his glance. Her eyes which had burned with a feverish humor when she had done her imitation had now gone dead; her shoulders sagged.

"Mama?" They heard the noise again and his mother turned away from him. He looked around to see his brother Arthur pushing himself down the hallway in a wheelchair.

"Arthur," he said. "My God, kid, what is it?" He rushed to the boy's side.

"I can do it *myself*," his brother hissed. "Hands off," he said sternly. He wheeled himself past his brother and then turned when he was in the center of the living room. He looked at Dick Gibson contemptuously for a moment and then, tilting his head, his eyes so wide it must have pained him, he displayed the utter dependency of love. "Did you make good? Did you, brother?"

"Don't, lad," their mother said quietly.

"No, Mama, I want to know. Did you? Did you find your fortune? Oh, you must have done, you must have. God knows our prayers have been with you—Ma's, anyway. She took money off the table just to buy the damned candles to light for you."

"Shut up, son. Don't blaspheme."

"No, Ma. Tell him. Tell my bigshot brother how you turned the parish into a Broadway with those candles you kept burning for him."

"He came in a cab, Arthur," his mother said shyly.

"Did he? Did he now?" Arthur said contemplatively. He seemed to subside, considering his brother, sizing him up as if looking for a purchase before attempting to scale him. Which of his brother's faces would be the easiest for him, he seemed to wonder. Then, suddenly, he raised both arms, brought his fists down viciously and beat mercilessly at his thighs and legs. "What about *me?*" he screamed. "What about *me?*"

"Arthur," his mother said. "Darling."

"*Shit*," he yelled. "*Shit* on that."

95

Their mother looked helplessly at Dick Gibson.

Dick went to his brother and put a hand on his shoulder. "You say shit to our mama? You're shit yourself." With that he grasped the rubber handles at the back of the wheelchair and overturned it, tumbling his brother.

Arthur bounded up quickly and held out his hand. "Long time no see," he said.

"You had me going at first," Dick said.

Arthur shrugged. "Ah, it's a tic," he said. "Like Mama's imitations."

"Beward of imitations," his mother said, a sybil in a cave.

They were zany, and Dick remembered why his family's characters oppressed him so. It wasn't simply that they worked so hard to show off. Rather it was that their divertissements were a delaying action that held him off. In a while they would drop their roles and behave normally. Their masquerades were reserved for homecomings like this one, or leavetakings, or their first visit to a patient in the hospital, say. It was their way of concealing feeling, thrusting it away from them until all the emotional elements in a situation had disappeared. In this way his family life was as sound, that is to say as even-keeled, as any. It was like living with lawyers, with cops who had seen everything. If he were to die right then and there, they would probably make his body a prop in a game, and the game would continue, the show go on until every last atom of their grief had been absorbed—until, that is, real grief would be ludicrous, coming so past its time. Oh, they were hard. He recalled the story Miriam had told about her father, how she'd had to shield him. Why, *his* family was like that and he hadn't even known it. Why couldn't folks take it? Why did they insist upon the quotidian? What was so bad about bad news? Surely the point of life was the possibility it always held out for the exceptional. The range of the strange, he thought.

Dick asked for his father and was hurt when they brought him up to date in a matter-of-fact, straightforward manner. It meant that they had already absorbed

96

his homecoming and that their long neutrality had begun.

And it had.

Except for his dealings with his father, whose roles were endless and played with a rabid verve, a hammy, polished vehemence. The man had become a missing person. That is, he had somehow done away with the father Dick remembered—once a heavy smoker, he had even given this up—and had taken on a variety of characteristics which had nothing to do with himself. (And nothing to do with the man he'd asked about, whose situation had been subsumed in a painless generality; "Fine," his mother had said when he'd asked. Not even "Foine." Fine, then. But could her placid sketch of the man be another performance? Was neutrality itself a further concealment, a new way of handling the really felt?) His father's behavior shocked him. In the past his dad's performances during those momentary seizures of spirit that were an affliction to all his family—Dick, the exception, was their audience, though his bland submission to their moods, like the drowned man's in a first-aid demonstration, may also have been a sort of performance, as his leaving home may have been, or even his famous apprenticeship—had been strictly amateur, never parodic and thus professional, like Arthur's or his wife's. His father's roles had always been only a sort of graceless variation of his usual condition, as someone with a head cold is said to be "not quite himself" while it lasts.

When Dick Gibson had left home a few years before, Arthur, then a boy just entering high school, had been ferociously exuberant, proud, almost worshipful in Dick's presence, developing the conceit that Dick had enlisted in the navy and was off to see the world, have adventures, fight the country's enemies, get drunk in the world's low bars. He was kid brother to Dick's hero and bounded about the older boy like an excited puppy. Given Arthur's superior height, this was quite patently ludicrous, and Dick was actually physically cowed by the broad, satiric slaps and jabs with which Arthur mocked his brother's shy, serious journey. His mother, on the other hand, called Dick aside and before his eyes transformed herself into the sacrificing mother in a sentimental fable who covertly slips all her life's savings and most trusted talismans into her boy's pockets to tide him on his way. She managed to make him feel like someone off to medical school in Edinburgh, say, fleeing the coal mines in which his father and his father's father before him had worked for years, ruining their healths and blunting their spirits. When he looked in the envelope later he saw that she had given him her recipe for meat loaf. The talisman was no St. Christopher's medal but only a penny some child had laid on the streetcar tracks.

But his father, an inventor who had had something to do with the development of radio and who was essentially a serious man, had merely joked lamely with him, rather embarrassed, Dick thought, and perhaps a little impatient for the train to leave. "Listen, kiddo," he'd told him, "good luck. Stay out of jail." Then he'd made a fist—noticing the fingertips, not tucked into the palm but exposed and almost touching the wrist, Dick was ashamed of his father's forceless fist—and pretended to clip him sportily on the jaw. He'd hit him with the wrong set of knuckles, and Dick had felt the gentle flat of his father's fingernails on his cheek. Now he wondered if this might not have been the subtlest turn of all.

The man never let up. There was something driven and fervid and accusing in his narrow postures. He concentrated the full force of his masquerade on Dick alone, and it was always as if the two of them had never had anything to do with each other before, as if the father, now pontificating, now relaxed and expansive—though always abrupt, like someone speaking out at prayer meeting—was seizing some initiative the son had not even known was at stake, throwing him off balance, casting first stones.

"Today, downtown, I bought my paper from the man at the corner of Carnegie and Allegheny. You've probably seen him though you may never have noticed him. He is a fixture there—the sort of person of whom it's idly said, 'Him? He's probably worth plenty.' He's a cripple, an amputee. His name is Harold, though I don't know how I know this, we've never been introduced, I don't recall anyone ever mentioning his name to me. He has no arms. He merely stands, sentinel-like, behind his stock of newspapers and administers their sale. Customers count out their change from a bowl of coins and bills beside a greasy iron weight that lies across the top paper in the pile.

"Because it was very warm this afternoon, in the nineties, most people had taken off their jackets and walked the streets in their shirtsleeves. Harold had taken off his jacket too, and one could see the long empty sleeves wrapped about his stumps and neatly attached to the body of his shirt with safety pins."

What's all this about cripples, Dick thought. Why cripples? Why always cripples lately?

"Two things struck me. First, that the shirts of such men are almost always blue workshirts. Why is that? Is it simply that Harold, being a member of the working class, would naturally wear denim shirts? Ah, but Joseph, who has a shoe-shine stand on the same corner, wears *white* shirts. Is Joseph affected, is he ambitious? Would you distinguish between Joseph's craftsmanship—he deals in a service—and Harold's mere agency? No. What is that makes blue-shirted Harold an amputee and arms white-shirted Joseph? Isn't it really a roughness of mind that differentiates between them and tears arms from those who could probably use them most?

"But this isn't what concerns me. I mean to speak of the shirt, the shirt itself, of the useless sleeving of the armless, the redundancy in their cloth. Why not sewn short sleeves in which Harold might pocket his stumps? Why does a paralyzed man in a wheelchair wear shoes? What use have so many blind men for glasses? Consider the humiliation of the paralyzed man. Consider what must be such a person's mortification when someone not only has to put his feet into his shoes for him, fitting the dead foot into the dead shoe, but lace them as well,

99

making a lousy parcel of his flesh. And when he is done the man in the chair looks for all the world like anyone equipped for a walk in the park. And the President himself is like that. FDR is. This is how the leader of the most powerful nation on earth begins his day. Regard the doomed, cancer-wizened man whose doctor has given him eight months to live. He wears a tie. Ah."

Is he saying he loves me? Dick Gibson wondered.

"Decorum, decorum's the lesson even when decorum flies in the teeth of reason. Decorum preserves us from the fate of fools even while making us foolish. Would you like to see a section of the paper I bought?"

He isn't, Dick Gibson thought. He's saying something else, but I don't know what.

On other occasions his father might deliver himself of a political speech which Dick felt had been prepared, actually written down in advance and memorized. But the word "Occasion" is wrong. These were not occasions; indeed, a few times when something might actually be expected from his father nothing was forthcoming.

He and his father went to the movies together. It was a love story, and during one of the romantic scenes a man who was sitting in the same row with them suddenly leaped up from his seat and stumbled past Dick and his father and down the aisle toward the stage.

"Look, Dick," his father whispered dreamily, "I hadn't noticed it before but the first seat across the aisle from us has one of those concealed lights at just about calf-level. What are those for anyway? They seem to be staggered in alternate rows on either side of the aisle. Do you suppose they're meant to give a shape somehow to the theater?"

Meanwhile the man had scrambled up onto the stage, where a portion of the film was to be seen projected on his white shirt. Is it Joseph from the shoe-shine stand, Dick wondered. Carole Lombard's hand flashed in an embrace around the back of the man's shirt; because the man stood forward of the screen, the hand seemed *introduced* into the movie house, a projecting presence that would draw him up into the screen, more real than the great undefiled remainder of the image, realer too than the drifting shards of image sprayed like a pale tattoo across the madman's neck and ears and hair and dark pants, as if the pictures reached him on the other side of thick aquarium glass. The man, his head turned in angered, twisted profile toward Carole Lombard's enormous face floating above him, was heard to scream, though what he might be saying was lost, drowned out by the soft but amplified sigh of the kiss's aftermath and the suggestive crackle of the characters' clothing.

His father had nothing to say.

The next day they saw a woman run over just outside their house. His father had nothing to say.

Then, for no reason, or none that Dick could see, his father, unchallenged, would seize upon an issue and explode into opinion. The man would harangue against low tariffs, then against high; now he would condemn Wall Street, now defend free enterprise; now he would blast the Jews, now Hitler, in see-saw postures of a loggerheads passion. In a way it was easier to deal with his father's set-pieces—if only by letting the man run down, or treating what he'd said as a joke (which seemed to delight him), both of them pretending that whatever position he'd taken had been satirically meant, a rebuke—than with his silences, and easier to deal with his silences than with his moods. In these moods, frequently pantomimed, his father, normally a fastidious man, might undertake to go about in his underwear, say, scratching abstractedly at his belly hair or even plucking at his genitals. Or he might suddenly come up to his son while Dick was reading and slap him abruptly on the shoulder. "Come on," he'd say, "I feel mealy, let's go down in twos and threes and toss the ball around." That they had no ball, that it was almost dark anyway, and that if they were to go through with the idea they would first have to find a drugstore that was still open where they could buy a ball, seemed to make no difference to his father. Indeed, the journey on the streetcar to the drugstore was an extension and deepening of his performance, his father nudging him in the ribs with his elbow and winking, or making two parallel, descending waves with his hands to indicate the female shape whenever a pretty girl—or even an ugly one—came on board. Or he might pointedly take a cigarette from a pack he carried for just this purpose and light it in full view of the motorman and the No Smoking signs posted about the car.

What could have been in the man's mind? Was he insane? On the way to a nervous breakdown? Dick Gibson might have thought so had his father not taken pains to be only *selectively* mad—mad, that is, merely in his older son's presence. Dick was reminded of the premise behind entertainments like the *Topper* stories, where the ghosts appeared only to Topper himself. In this way he was pulled into the plot, felt himself, despite his laconic stance, essential to it, a bit player magnetically drawn toward center stage. It was not unflattering that here, perhaps, was a clue to his father's intent.

So he came to associate his father's actions with his recent experience with Miriam, his vain attempt to unlock the secret of her voice. (He'd lied when he'd told her he'd found the secret, though the fact was he'd come to believe it.) That is, he saw them as in some way related to his testing, more grist for his ongoing apprenticeship.

How weary he was of that apprenticeship. How ready to round it off where it stood, declare it finished! He read the trade magazines—*Broadcasting, Variety, Tide*—and saw with an ever more painful anxiety that men as young as himself, a few of them young men he'd worked with, were getting on in their careers. A two-line notice in the "Tradewinds" column of *Broadcasting* about someone he'd worked with in Kansas—"Harlan Baker, formerly with WMNY, Mineola, New York, has accepted a job as junior staff announcer with WEAF, New York City"— was enough to plunge him into the profoundest depression. Baker was a hack with no style and only the most ordinary experience, and here he, who had worked in almost every facet of radio, was jobless and with no leads. Recently he had even begun to bone up on the technical aspect of radio, reading with difficulty the most scientific disquisitions on the subject, studying the diagrams (and in Morristown getting one of the X-ray technicians to explain what he couldn't understand). There were forty million sets in the country, five thousand announcers on more than four hundred and fifty stations, and the FCC was granting more licenses daily. Soon there wouldn't be a town of more than two thousand people that didn't have its own radio station. Though he wanted radio to flourish, he grew jealous as a lover of its success, and uncomfortable the way a lover sometimes inexplicably is in the presence of his beloved.

In the light of his feeling that perhaps his father somehow meant his performances to be a contribution to his apprenticeship, he introduced the subject himself.

"I haven't spoken much of my work in radio."

"No," his father said.

"I've tried . . . you know, to get experience."

"Yes, of course."

"I've had—I don't know—maybe a dozen jobs since I left home."

"A dozen jobs in five years. That's a lot of moving around."

"Yes, it is. But I wanted to do as many different things as I could. I have this idea about apprenticeship. It's how I see myself—as an apprentice."

"It's best to get a good background," his father said, wantonly indifferent.

"The personalities," Dick said, "I don't know if I can explain this, but they're part of our lives, not even a trivial part either because we grow up to their jokes, we tell time by their voices. And what voices! Broadcast. Broad *cast*. Personality like seed, a part of nature, in forests and beside streams, and high up the sides of mountains, higher than the timber line."

"There's good money to be made," his father said. "There's no doubt about it."

"I change jobs and bone up because I want to make myself worthy of my voice."

His father yawned, swept his fingers up under his glasses, rubbed his eyes, and gently rolled the loose skin on the bridge of his nose back and forth. It was another act. The generation gap. A pantomime of stolid misunderstanding. Though he resisted, Dick felt himself drawn deeply into the performance. By his father's gesture—his face had now gone blank and he was vaguely chewing, sucking his cheeks and exploring the flaws in his teeth with his tongue like a nightwatchman aiming his flashlight at doors—the two of them had become partners in some nightshift enterprise, men in a boiler room, say, among complicated machinery, in a mutual vacuum of the night and labor, a half-hour till one of them has to check the dials again. He could get no further with his dad, and was embarrassed that he had exposed himself as much as he had.

In the next weeks he thought about his apprenticeship a great deal, and wondered if this might not be just the effect his father intended. The more he thought about it, the more convinced he was. His dad's routines had been meant to embarrass him because the man sensed that this sneaking shame was Dick Gibson's weak spot—*Dick Gibson,* that name that had come to him out of the air, the best inspiration of his life, consolidating in its three crisp syllables his chosen style, his identity, a saga, a mythic body of American dash, and that he had used just once, keeping it secret since, unwilling even after five years to give it up, saving it, as one preserves the handsomest pieces in his wardrobe and meanwhile goes shabby and ordinary, a miserliness not of money but of strategy, a military notion of reserves or a coach's of bench, an Aladdin idea of one wish left in the lamp—and wanted to purge him of it. He had never been completely unembarrassed while speaking on the radio; this was a fact (his mike fright was something else). He had always felt just a little silly announcing, introducing, selling, describing, interviewing, giving the time and telling the weather, doing local color, acting and reciting bed-time stories, holding up his spokesman's end of the conversation—which in radio was the only end there was. For the truth of the matter was that radio was silence as well as sound; the unrelenting premise was that the announcer's voice occurred in silence, in the heart of an attentive vacuum disposed to hear it. Whereas he knew this was untrue. Didn't his own mind wander, wasn't it inattentive? *Nothing* was worthy of violating such silence; nothing yet in the history of the world had been worthy of it. That's why he was embarrassed. So what his father was doing was meant to demonstrate how easily self-consciousness could be shed. Some such lesson must have been intended. So, he thought sadly, the apprenticeship isn't finished. This thing remained: he had to become immodest, to learn to move dispassionately into the silence. His experience thus far was nothing; it would be a long time before he would be as good as he was meant to be. That was that.

He made plans to leave Pittsburgh, to take up the burden of his apprenticeship a second time.

The day he left home and bid his family goodbye he had expected a scene. But there was none; they did not offer to come to the station with him, and his mother used her mad, broad dialect only once. "A mither's kiss," she said automatically when she kissed him.

Arthur shook his hand and winced in pretended pain. "Yipes, champ, you don't have to break a guy's fingers, do you?"

His father was even more silent than when Dick had left home the first time, but he seemed on the verge of tears. Dick stuck out his hand but his father ignored it and embraced him. His beard felt strange against Dick's, trailing sensation like a scent, as if he'd been rubbed with something dusty and valuable, scraped by flesh in a ceremony. Dick submitted to the embrace and thought it remarkable that his father's eyes were red.

In the next years you might have heard Dick Gibson's voice a hundred times without knowing it, certainly—so much had it willfully become a part of the generalized sound of American life—without thinking to ask whose it was, no more than you would stop to wonder at the direction of the wind from the sound it makes in the street. He went about the country restlessly, always lonely

105

now and ignorant of time, his beautiful but anonymous voice the juggler's humble affair before some imposing altar, a town crier of the twentieth century.

"Leeman Brothers directs the attention of shoppers to its White Sale now in progress in the Linens section on the fourth floor. For a limited time we will be offering genuine first-quality percale sheets for single, twin and full beds at discounts of up to 40 percent. We are also featuring a wide selection of slightly damaged printed cambrics at 75 percent off. Please take the elevators at the State Street entrance."

"Attention! Attention please! There has been a change posted in the results of the fifth race. Please hold on to your pari-mutuel tickets. *Jimson Weed* has been disqualified for crowding on the turn. Repeat: *Jimson Weed* has been disqualified for crowding. The Maryland Racing Commission has declared the official results. *It's Your America* is the winner, *Martin's Muddle* has placed and *Crybaby* has finished in the money to show."

"Will everyone please stand clear of the firetrucks? Will you stand clear of the firetrucks, please? These men can't work. Someone's going to get hurt."

"Welcome to the General Motors Pavilion of the New York World's Fair, 'The World of Tomorrow.' The General Motors Company wishes to apologize for any inconvenience you may have experienced during your wait on the line. Please sit far back in your comfortable chairs so that you may the better hear through your personalized headsets. The Company wishes to remind any of you who may be wearing sunglasses to please remove them now so that you may the better see our exhibit."

"Kibbidge batting for Medwick."

" 'The Congressional Limited' leaving on track fifteen for Newark, Trenton, North Philadelphia, 30th Street

Philadelphia, Wilmington, Baltimore and Washington. Passengers holding chair Pullman reservations will please go to the south end of the platform. All aboard. All aboard please."

"Will the owner of the green, 1940 Pontiac bearing Texas license plates G479-135 please report to the attendant at gate number twelve?"

"On your left is the historic old Cotton mansion built in 1847 by Emmanuel Cotton, to plans drawn up by the distinguished American architect Lattimer Michael Hough. The expression 'King Cotton' is not, as many suppose, a phrase describing the pre-eminent position of cotton in the Southern economy, but a nickname directly referring to Emmanuel Cotton's life-long obsession that he was the pretender to the Hanoverian throne. The pillars you see are the only standing examples of Virginia marble—not a marble at all, actually, but a processed quartz made to resemble the less expensive stone."

"There will be a half-hour wait for seating, a half-hour wait for seating at all prices."

"A lost child, about four or five years old, wearing a brown snowsuit, brown mittens and answering to the name of Richard, is waiting to be picked up at the ranger station just below the ski lift."

"Front. Front, please."

"Is there a doctor in the house?"
"How do you do, ladies and gentlemen, this is Dick 'Pepsodent' Gibson. I'm very happy to be here in Minneapolis tonight. Bob Hope will be with you in a few minutes, but first. . . ."

One day in Chicago's Loop he was coming out of the Oriental Theater on Randolph Street when suddenly the heavens opened and he was caught in what could have been a cloudburst. One moment the skies were clear; the next the rain was pounding the street in the heaviest downpour he had ever seen. He was only fifty feet or so from the shelter of the marquee when it began to rain, but even if he had attempted to run back to it he would have been completely soaked. So he ducked into the stairwell entrance to an underground cafeteria called Eiler's. He had coffee and a sandwich, but even after he had finished the rain had still not let up. If anything, it was raining even more heavily than before; the water was coming down the stairway and under the doors and had already formed a considerable pool, which the busboys were trying to clear away with pails and mops. Many people—mostly middle-aged women, afternoon shoppers—had come in from the street and were gathered at the bottom of the stairs.

The basement cafeteria in which they were all standing was low-ceilinged and crowded with rounded arches. Obviously it was meant to support the great weight of the building above them. Dick Gibson thought of the London blitz, the underground shelters there, where, according to what he'd heard, people whose homes had been blasted sometimes stayed for weeks at a time. As he often did when he was caught in something like an emergency situation, he began to look about for a girl, someone with whom he might talk, or, in some end-of-the-world abandon, kiss, hold, fuck. But there were very few likely prospects. Two pretty girls of perhaps twenty sat not far away, but these he discounted because there were two men clearly more handsome than himself with whom in all probability they would pair off when the time came. This left only a small, sweetfaced, pleasant-looking young woman. The more he looked at her the more feasible the idea of loving her became. Soon he found her plumpness sexually exciting and even the submissive gentleness of her expression, daring. He began to imagine her willing passion, and to project the wonderful things she might do for him. Before long he began to consider himself lucky to have her rather than the two girls whose beauty had probably made them selfish and cold. As he was thinking

108

of his girl and imagining what it would be like to have such heaviness at his disposal, perhaps even gratefully blowing him, she looked up and saw him staring. Maybe she had felt his concentration; at any event she smiled widely as if she recognized him, or as if they were already lovers. Dick blushed and looked away at once, fixing his features in a stern, indifferent mask. Though he knew she was still watching him, he did not dare look up.

In a while the rain stopped and they were free to go. The girl passed in front of him and Dick could see the bewilderment on her face as he failed to acknowledge her stare. He realized that it was the same expression he himself had worn when his father had bewildered him.

My God, he thought suddenly, all it was was love. All it was was love and shyness. Oh Jesus, he thought, oh shit, I do not know what my life is.

The next day he called off the apprenticeship.

3

Which was impossible. He was already too far into it. It would have taken a major revision of his character, a rehabilitation, real eye openers. We are what we are. Dick Gibson went back into radio; the quest continues.

By now he had enough experience in radio to handle anything. He was an accomplished announcer, a newsman, an MC, an actor. He could do special events, remotes, panel discussions. He had a keen ear for which songs and which *recordings* of which songs would be the hits, and was even a competent sports announcer. Though he had not yet broadcast a game from a stadium, he had done several off the Western Union ticker tape, sitting in a studio hundreds of miles from the action and translating the thin code of the relay, fleshing it out from the long ribbony scorecard. More than anything else this made him feel truly a radio man, not just the voice of radio but radio itself, the very fact of amplification, the human voice lifted miles, beamed from the high ground, a nexus of the opportune: See seven states! And everything after the fact so foreknown, the game itself sometimes already in the past while he still described it; often the afternoon papers were on the streets with the final box score while he described for his listeners the seventh-inning stretch or reported a struggle in the box seats over the recovery of a foul ball—his foreknowledge hindsight, a coy tool of suspense: "DiMaggio swings. That ball is going, going— oh, it's foul by inches."

He was able to perform even the simpler feats of engineering, and had a good working knowledge of sound effects. (Strangely, he would sometimes reveal these, giving up his privileged information not so much with a gossip's delight as a betrayer's, enjoying his sense of ruining illusion, fixing forever in the minds of those who heard him that fire was only handled cellophane, rain stirred pebbles on a piece of paper, thunder a tin sheet shaken—so that even afterward that was what they heard, cellophane, pebbles, tin sheets, the metaphors undone, turned, the things they stood for become the things that stood for them.) He was good at all of it.

He no longer experimented nor changed jobs, and though he still had not used the name Dick Gibson, it was not because he was saving it, but merely because he had eschewed the idea of his apprenticeship and with it the idea of his destiny too.

But he must have had a destiny. He had traveled much in the past and was registered with at least fifteen draft boards across the country. One month in the winter of 1943 he received notice from five of them that he had been called up.

It was like being arrested.

He did his basic training at a camp in western Massachusetts. There he experienced the total collapse of civilization. To Dick the army made sense only if one considered the ultimate objectives of the war, but he waited in vain for his superiors to remind him of the Fascists or to outline the goals which he himself had so passionately endorsed in his own pleas to his listeners to buy bonds and save paper and conserve water.

He had brought his portable radio with him and it became his habit, now that he was in it himself, to listen to all the war news, taking particular comfort from Edward R. Murrow's bravely resonant "This is London."

One evening he had just settled back on his bunk to listen when Private Rohnspeece picked up the radio from the window sill.

"Hey, what do you think you're doing?"

"I'm breaking your faggot radio," Private Rohnspeece said, and threw it out the window.

"What's wrong with you?" He grabbed Rohnspeece's sleeve, but his comrade-in-arms pulled a switchblade knife out of his pocket and an enormous blade clicked brightly into position. Then the man calmly cut a piece out of Dick Gibson's hand. Dick screamed and a sergeant came running into the barracks.

"Who the hell's making that goddamn noise?" the sergeant demanded. Dick sucked blood, swallowing it back as fast as it came out of his wound, thinking in this way to preserve his life's precious juices. (At that instant it somehow seemed related to the war effort, like turning off lights and saving tinfoil.) Between mouthfuls he continued to scream, and again the sergeant, apparently myopic, demanded to know who was making the noise.

Rohnspeece pointed to Dick Gibson. "He is," Rohnspeece said.

"He cut me," Dick said.

The sergeant looked without enthusiasm at Dick's hand. It was as if he had been auditioning bloody hands all day and this was just one more in a pretty thin lot. "You'll bleed worse than that once Jerry sticks his bayonet in your gut," he said, but Gibson was scarcely relieved that someone in authority had at last mentioned Hitler's forces.

Afterward he went outside to see if he could salvage his radio, but it was gone. He did not see it again for two days, when it suddenly turned up on top of Private Fedge's locker.

"Where did you get that radio, Fedge?" Gibson asked.

"I found it."

"It's mine."

"You saying I stole it, cocksucker?" Fedge reached for the M-I he had just finished cleaning.

"That's not loaded."

"The fuck it ain't," Fedge said.

"Are you going to listen to Charley McCarthy tonight?" Dick asked without hope.

"What's Charley McCarthy?"

"Fedge, you asshole, Charley McCarthy's the orphan. He lives with Mr. Bergen," Private Laverne said.

"Eat my dick, Laverne."

"Whip it out and I will," Laverne said.

Fedge whipped it out and Laverne ate Fedge's dick. While Fedge's eyes were still closed Dick Gibson seized the opportunity to lift his radio off the top of Fedge's locker and take it back to his bunk. Something had happened to it when Rohnspeece had thrown it out the window, and to hear it at all, Dick had to stick his right foot in his locker and let the radio rest on his neck, steadying it with his hand. He felt this made him look rather like the woman of Samaria toting her water jug back from the well, but he hoped no one would notice. There was a good chance no one would since a crowd had gathered to watch Private Laverne eat Private Fedge's privates.

But Corporal Tuleremia came up to him.

"Who are you supposed to be?"

"Shh," Dick Gibson said. "They just introduced W. C. Fields. He's the guest star."

Tuleremia smashed Dick Gibson in the stomach. "I'll show you stars, you pansy."

Dick decided he would have to listen in the dayroom from then on. There, with the radio page from the Sunday paper spread out before him, he carefully logged an entire week's programs, checking them off with a pencil and starring those he was particularly interested in. On Monday he was listening to *Lux Presents Hollywood*, with Ginger Rogers as Kitty Foyle, when Blitz came into the dayroom. Blitz turned off the lights, walked over to the big console radio, fiddled with the dial and tuned in a yodeler. Then they listened to polkas for an hour in the dark.

Dick turned amiably to Blitz. "Why don't we share?" he suggested.

"We can share your balls," Blitz said neutrally.

We're going to win this war, Dick Gibson thought. We're going to whip the Axis powers, the cunning Japs and vicious Nazis, and then we're going to conquer the world.

He had never known such men existed. For all the imagination that had enabled him to flesh out full-fledged accounts of ballgames from the flimsy data that came in over the wire, he could not have imagined men like Laspooney and Null. These two would wait until the men were seated on the boothless toilets and then come into the john, running amok, goosing and grab-assing.

"Hey, Null," Laspooney would shout.

"What is it, Laspooney?" Null called back.

"Don't you just love these horseshoe toilet seats? A man can just shove his hand down the opening and grab," he'd say, shoving his hand down the opening and grabbing.

"Yeah, Laspooney," Null answered, "there's no place to hide."

Dick thought it odd that the army would take homosexuals, but as it turned out they weren't homosexuals; indeed, off post, they beat *up* homosexuals. They just thought that grabbing people's cocks was a good joke, almost as good as farting. Laspooney could fart a strong unbroken string for twelve minutes. They were real stinkers too. The men just fanned the air in front of their noses and laughed. Only Private Rohnspeece did not fan the air. "I don't know what's wrong with you guys," he'd say, "I *like* the way it smells."

Late one night when Dick went into the crapper to polish his brass, Null was seated on the toilet. Though he was in the act of squeezing out a turd, Null grinned and waved. "Hey," he called out. "Listen to this. Look. Look here." He pointed toward the opening in the toilet seat,

114

grunted and there was a splash. "Well, don't you get it?" Null asked.

Gibson shook his head.

Null grinned and squeezed out a big one. "Now do you get it?"

"Get what?" Dick asked.

Null did it again. "There. That. Don't you get it?"

"I don't get it."

"Null voids, you jerk," Null said, exploding in laughter.

Dick Gibson looked at him.

Still smiling, Null got up off the pot. It was outside the range of possibility that he might flush the toilet, but he didn't even wipe himself. He came over and wrapped his arm about Dick's shoulder. "You know what's wrong with you, soldier?" Null said. "You don't get no fun out of life. Tomorrow me, you and Laspooney'll go out for a night on the town. We'll do things up brown."

Dick gagged. "Will we have to beat up queers and roll drunks?" he asked weakly.

"Nah. Live and let live."

Dick was terrified, but he went with them. Null kept his promise and they didn't beat up any queers or roll any drunks. They found a willing high school girl named Sheila and took her to a motor lodge and gang-banged her, Dick holding back when it was his turn and he was alone with the girl. "It's nothing against you personally, Sheila, but I'm married and anyway I have too much respect for you." He did not tell her that it was the smell of Null's underwear, which seemed to be everywhere in the room, that inhibited him. "Could you kind of moan a little for their benefit, Sheila? They think I'm a grind and don't get much fun out of life."

"Then *you* moan," Sheila said.

When Laspooney and Null returned, it was late and time to get back to the base. Sheila could sleep there and pay for the room, they said. Sheila said she didn't have quite enough money to cover it and asked if they could let her have four dollars.

"What are you, Sheila, some goddamned hoo-er?" Laspooney said.

"Yeah, Sheila, is this one of your fucking slut hoo-er shakedowns?" Null wanted to know.

"Come on, you guys," Laspooney said, and began to slap her around. Null joined in and together they beat her up pretty bad.

When they had finished Dick Gibson looked down at her helplessly. Sickened, his features had somehow formed a sort of grin.

"What the fuck are *you* grinning about, Soldier?" Null said.

Dick Gibson looked at him. "Don't you get it?" he said.

"Get what?"

Dick pointed to the girl lying unconscious at their feet. "Don't you get it? She's bleeding."

"Oh yeah," Null said, laughing, and slapped Dick Gibson on the back.

Radio had badly prepared him for his new life. He had never suspected the enormous chasm between the world of radio with the sane, middle-class ways of its supposed audience and the genuine article. Only the officers—to the shame of his democratic instincts—were at all recognizable to him. Whom had he been speaking to over the air? he wondered. Was anybody listening? Was he the last innocent man? He was sure that he was not innocent, just less brutal, perhaps, less reckless, more hygienic than the next man. Who broadcasts to the brutes? he wondered ardently. Who has the ear of the swine?

He asked permission to speak with his commanding officer.

Captain Rogers, a railroad man in civilian life, pressed his tented fingertips in the classic position of executive consultation when Dick said he wanted to explain the reason behind his request for transfer out of the artillery and into special services. He might better serve the army in a slot for which he was better qualified, he said.

The captain noted that Gibson had done well in artillery work and shouldn't sell himself short.

Dick allowed that that was true, and went on to use other phrases and arguments which he would no longer have dared to use with someone other than an officer. He reminded the captain that Joe Louis was in special services. Had the army made a mistake? Someone like Joe, with his superb physique and physical endurance, would make a splendid infantry man, but wasn't the army and the country better served by using him to raise the men's morale with his boxing exhibitions?

"You've got a point there," the captain said, "but what of the terrific boost to morale if Louis *were* an infantryman? Wouldn't that be just the thing to show the men what democracy is all about? Wouldn't it? I mean, when you take a world champ and treat him just like everybody else, well, something like that might be just the ticket for demonstrating the sort of country we are."

Dick Gibson considered. "Yes, Captain, that's true in Louis's case. But I'm *al*ready just like everybody else."

They were in the office of the man who had been the golf pro for the Berkshire resort which the army had taken over for a training camp. The room still had the wide glass display cases that had once housed its former inhabitant's trophies, and this, together with the rug— Dick, used to the heavy, absorptive carpeting of radio studios, always felt more sure-footed on rugs than on bare floors, or even on the ground itself—lent a pleasant donnish quality to the room. It was conducive to horseshit, Dick sensed.

Well, that was all very well, the captain said at last, but how could he recommend Dick for special services when he knew nothing about Dick's talent?

Thereupon followed Dick's strangest audition. Without a microphone or script and with only the captain for an audience he did what amounted to an evening's mixed programming. He introduced records, paused five seconds, and pleasantly recapitulated the name of the song and the singer. He made up news. He did an inning and a half of a ballgame and then, guessing from the captain's expression that he was no sports fan, rained it out and went back to the studio for a talk on first aid. He

117

re-created this and he re-created that, all the time watching the captain's face for cues to his tastes. For a few minutes he did a creditable job of reproducing an emergency at the transmitter, requesting the audience to please stand by, and had the pleasure of seeing the captain smile, a reaction he was at a loss to account for until he remembered that the man had been a railroader and must have experienced similar breakdowns in his line of work. Thereafter he hit the railroad angle pretty hard, doing all he could remember of the opening of *Grand Central Station,* a half-hour drama, and Tommy Bartlett's *Welcome Travelers,* an interview show with people who had just gotten off the Twentieth Century Limited.

Even in auditions he had been by himself, separated from the sponsor or the station manager by at least the plate glass of the control booth, and there was something so strange to him in this confrontation that soon he forgot why he had come. Each show he re-created now became an end in itself, something to be gotten through, and he had a heavy, hopeless sense of a truck mired in mud, of branches and rocks shoved beneath tires for a traction that would never be attained. He had forgotten that his aim was to capture the consciousness of the brutes, and here he was being polite, elegant and glib. At ten o'clock, an hour and a half after walking into the captain's office, exhausted, he signed off, appalled to realize that what he had been doing was a frightening reenactment of his career.

Shaken, Captain Rogers looked at him for two minutes before finally speaking. "You're a regular show," he said at last. "Request for transfer approved!" He slammed the blotter on his desk three times, left, center and right, with the fatty side of his fist in a mime of someone stamping documents submitted in triplicate.

But it was no different on Armed Forces Radio. Dick's show was broadcast on Sunday afternoons—that traditionally gray and sober time on American radio, after church and before the family-comedy programs of the early and mid-evening—and was called *The Patriot's*

118

Songbook. Though it went out on shortwave wherever American forces were stationed and to virtually every theater of combat, Dick was not pleased with it; he found the rigidity of the format and the endorsed quality of the sentiment burdensome. (Ironically, his audience had never been larger. The program was taken not just by the military but by dozens of independent stations across the country.) He had no illusions that he was reaching the brutes, for the program, thirty minutes of service and popular war songs, was something of a joke even at the London studio from which it emanated. The staff, most of them professionals like himself in civilian life, referred to it as "The Flag Wavers' Songbook," "Uncle Sam's Lullaby Hour," or even worse. The single thing he had to show for it, and this at the beginning, was his promotion to sergeant, an honor that simply reflected Armed Forces Radio's fashion of having several of its programs hosted by noncommissioned officers.

To Dick it seemed absurd to play recordings of rah-rah songs to men who had actually been in combat. He had heard too many vicious parodies of these songs; they were sung in comradely funk in every London pub, so he could imagine the words the men on the actual firing line might put to them. He made efforts to broadcast some of the milder of these parodies—though there were no recordings of them that he knew of—but every request was refused. Indeed, how could it be otherwise when even the innocuous remarks with which he introduced each record ("This next song, 'Semper Paratus,' is the beloved anthem of the generally unsung seadogs in the mighty United States Coast Guard. The Coast Guard is one of our nation's most trusted services. In peacetime it has the responsibility of enforcing maritime laws, saving lives and property at sea, operating as an aid to navigation generally, and preventing smuggling. In war it is a valued adjunct of the navy itself. A 'Patriot's Songbook' salute to the *Coast Guard!*") had first to be checked and approved by his superiors?

Despite, then, his knowledge that Rohnspeece and Fedge and Laspooney and Null and Blitz and the others—if, in fact, they were still alive—had probably heard him, AFR being the only English-speaking radio they could pick up in most of the places where they could be, Dick had no hope that he had changed their opinion of him. He had the brute's ear, but the brute was probably laughing. The brute may even have been pissing into the speaker cone or firing bullets at it or whipping someone's ass with the aerial. He was a celebrity for the first time in his life—*Stars and Stripes* had interviewed him—but it had never seemed less important. In his interview with *Stars and Stripes* the one remark he had really wanted them to print—"Lord Haw Haw and Tokyo Rose are much more effective. As a radio man I envy them both"—had been omitted, and he had sounded as bland as ever he had on the radio.

The show was recorded on Tuesday nights in Broadcasting House, the BBC facility in London. Busy during the day, a few of its studios had been set aside for the use of the Americans late at night. One Tuesday, shortly after the appearance of his interview in *Stars and Stripes,* Dick was making an electrical transcription of *Songbook* when he saw the flashing red light that indicated an air-raid warning. He had been through other air raids in London, though one had never occurred when he was broadcasting. Seeing the light, he gathered together the pages of his script, switched off his microphone and rose to go to the shelter. He was almost out of the studio when his engineer and director, a first lieutenant named Collins, called to him over the loudspeaker from the control room.

"Sit still, Sergeant," the lieutenant said. "There's no telling when they'll sound the all clear. I'm tired. The damn BBC won't give us the goddamn building at a decent hour. We're soundproofed, so I don't think we'll pick up the noise of the bombers in here. Hell, we can't even hear the blasted sirens. Why don't we just go ahead and finish the broadcast?"

Sergeant Gibson looked nervously toward the signal light, which had now gone into a new pattern—a series of four short flashes followed by three long, indicating that the bombers were over the city. Except for the lights they would have had no hint that the bombers were overhead; in their windowless studio they might not have heard even a direct hit, and would have known that they were dying only when the flames had begun to lick at them.

"Damn it, Sarge, sit back down," the lieutenant ordered. "We'll be okay. Watch the On the Air sign. When the sign comes on you cue in again after 'Wing and a Prayer.' "

Dick returned sullenly to the microphone and the lieutenant put the song on the turntable. The signal lights and the insane bravery of the music made Dick more nervous than ever. He wondered if men had ever gone into battle burdened by such themes. It was impossible, and he had a certain knowledge of the impossibility and inanity of comfort, suddenly realizing what must be the enormous irritation to the dying of all brave counsel and all fair words. Such must forever have tampered patience and ruined death.

When the record finished the On the Air sign beamed on. In the brief moment before he began talking Dick strained to hear the bombers. He thought he could detect a buzz or hum, but it might have been only the electric engines in the studio. The lieutenant rapped on the glass with his graduation ring and pointed furiously to the sign. Shaken, Dick lost his place, then found it again. "Fellas, that was 'Coming in on a Wing and a Prayer,' as sung by the Mello-Tones." He heard the alarm in his voice and longed to be in the bomb shelter, where he could hear the bombs when they exploded and feel the slight fleshly shift in the sand bags. He looked toward the booth but the lieutenant had leaned down to pick up the next recording and he could not see him. For all he knew he may have been the only person left in the building. His hand rattled the pages of his script and he lost his place again. " 'Coming in on a Wing and a Prayer,' " he repeated, stalling. Again he found his place and introduced the next song. It was "When the Lights Go on Again All Over the World," and as he listened to the lyrics ("Jimmy will go

121

to sleep in his own little room again") he became furious. If he'd had a pistol he might have taken aim and shot the lieutenant right then. Why, he thought, surprised and not displeased, that's how the brutes think, the ones who treasure their grudge and then, on patrol, calmly shoot their lieutenant in the back. Was *he* a brute? Good! So be it!

He felt himself swell with power, a savage sarge. *"Bullshit!"* he roared into his open microphone over the lyrics of the song. *"Bullshit!"*

The lieutenant's face appeared white and enormous behind the control room window. He seemed not angry, nor even astonished; he looked as bland and mild as a ship's captain just relieved of command by his men. Dick saw his mouth move and his lips form words, but no sound came out; he had forgotten to depress the speaker button in the control room. Dick felt a triumphant flush of heroism, Horatio at the bridge, the Dutchman at the dike, the man in the radio room sending out his S.O.S.'s as the others lowered the lifeboats and leaped into them, all men covering all other men's retreats—the guerrilla achievement. "Ah boys," he cried, exultant, "we're the ones who pay. It's us who bleed, buddies."

The lieutenant's eyes widened. He was livid now, his face contorted with the bitter, contrary exercises of grief and grudge. Gibson knew he had to hurry. Ignoring the officer, he grasped the microphone still more tightly and drew it closer to him, as if the only way Collins could stop him would be to pull the equipment out of his hands. "We're meat, we're meat," he cried passionately. (He saw his listeners come alive, one soldier beckoning the other to approach the radio, crawling out of foxholes in the jungle, gathering together around the Lister bag. He saw snipers leaning down from the trees to which they were tied. Thinking of the bombers that were even now zeroing in on Broadcasting House, fixing its roof between the crosshairs of their bombsights, he began to chatter ferociously, not calling as he might have to a panicky audience falling all over itself to escape a burning theater,

122

"Calm down, calm down," but a sub-articulate commiseration that cut through the traps of language, dispensed with hope and went abruptly into mourning. "Ah," he said. "Oh my. Gee. Hmn. Yuh. Ah. Oh. Tch tch. Whew. Hmph. Boy.")

Behind the glass in the control booth the lieutenant was leaning so far forward that his nose was blunted by the glass. "Tag," Dick said. "We're it. Boom boom."

"You're crazy if you think I'm going to permit any of this stuff to get by," Lieutenant Collins's voice boomed out over the speaker. "What do you think you're doing? Who do you think you are? Not a syllable of this will ever be broadcast! I'm stopping the transcription!"

"They're moving in," Dick Gibson said, "I don't know how much longer I can hold out. I'm by myself. The bombs are falling."

"Hah!" the lieutenant cried. "I've shut you off. You're just talking to the walls."

"I don't know if you can still hear me, boys. I may just be talking to the walls, but I'm sticking to my post. Let's have some music, what say?"

"I won't put it on for you!"

"Over hill, over dale,
Hell, they even read our mail,
As those caissons go rolling along.
In and out, hear them shout,
I can't wait till I get out.
As those caissons go rolling along."

"Well, *ex*-sergeant, are you proud of yourself? *Are you, ex*-sergeant?"

"There'll be bullshit over
The white cliffs of Dover,
Tomorrow, just you wait and see."

"On second thought I *am* going to record this. It will make very interesting listening at your court martial."

"Anger's a way, my boys,
Anger's a way,
Why should we take their noise,
Why don't we run away—ay—ay—ay?"

"That's evidence. Right there. *That's* evidence."

"This is the Army, Mr. Jones,
They'll shoot some bullets in your bones,
You had your breakfast in bed before,
But you dum la de dum in a war."

"You'll get yours, Mister."

"Oh-hh say can you see
How the powers that be
Keep us down, in the groun'
With the lie that we're free?"

He pushed his microphone away and leaned back. He
was exhausted. The lights had ceased to flash. The air
raid was over. Dozens had died, hundreds were wounded,
but the rest of them were safe till next time.

"You didn't sign off," the lieutenant's voice croaked
over the loudspeaker.

"Right," Dick Gibson said. He pulled the table mike
toward him again and held it in his lap. "Fellow animals," he said, "grr whinney whinney oink oink roar. See
you at the crap table, catch you guys 'n' gals in the bars,
keep a candle in the whore's window, meet you in the
alley. Dick Gibson"—he hadn't meant to use the name,
but it slipped out—"signing off."

MP's came. Before they arrived Dick had to be
guarded by the lieutenant. They had nothing to say to
each other, and he was embarrassed that the man had no
gun; it would have been simpler for them both if he had.
As it was it may have appeared to Collins—Dick was the
larger of the two—that Dick was doing him a favor by
not resisting. More probably, he may have thought that
Dick was *seeking* favors. That was what brutes did; time

and again, in difficulty, he'd seen them go boyish, go soft, presuming upon their deprivation to toady—brutes turned housepets. Dick couldn't be sure that he had not intended this last possibility. Perhaps he meant to underscore a new strain in his character. Certainly when the MP's came they didn't seem to see anything strange in arresting him, or in leading him out of the building under armed guard. He was pleased in one way, not so pleased in another. He wasn't sure he knew what to do next. In a sense he looked forward to his conviction, to some actual ruling on his status, a documentation of sorts of his character. Then he could be genuinely what they said he was. (To divide men into officers and enlisted men was a superb idea; he didn't know how he had lived without it.) He was even impatient for the time when he would be turned queer by the absence of women (or the presence of men), impatient to learn their desultory violence and terrifying indifference. He yearned for the debasement of his taste and fastidy—it was a way of being free. Already he was astonished by his freedom, the liberties he took with his guards, for example—"Give us a smoke, chief"—affronts, gaucheries that bordered on risk, swagger the other side of his scruple, swinging from cringe to contempt as though character were nothing more than hinged mood. It was strange and exhilarating to live by the rule of whim.

At the guard house—the British government had set aside a portion of the Inns of Court for use by the Americans as a detention center, and he had the fearful suspicion that the prisoners had been left in London to be bombed—he acted like a guilty man (that is, he behaved as if having committed one crime he could commit another), thus frightening many of the other prisoners, AWOL's, the deserters for love, the careless missers of trains and buses, the cowards. Another prisoner remembered that he had been interviewed in *Stars and Stripes* and this seemed to induce awe, as if there could be no offense like the offense of the respectable. The prisoner, himself an accused murderer, pressed Dick to discover why he was there. It was when Dick admitted that he'd "told them what to do with it" that the man became deferential, words and will to him the ultimate violence. Dick decided that though the man had killed he was not one of the brutes at all.

He stayed in the guard house for a week. After he had cleaned up his room each morning there was not much to do and he listened to the BBC. It was satisfying to him chiefly because of its clear classifying of its audience—even more meticulous and useful than the distinction between officers and enlisted men. During the week he also had three interviews with the captain who was assigned to be his defense counsel, a man who was a dentist in civilian life. Dick thought him too earnest, but in fairness he had to admit that he thought all dentists earnest. Only a very earnest man would be able to stand the sight and feel of an open mouth. (It was probably their excess earnestness that kept them out of medical school.) He was certain the dentist would not be able to get him off—certain also that only the dentist's earnest objectivity kept him from expressing then and there his opinion of Dick's actions.

He learned that his trial was set for the end of the following week. When he was taken from the guard house four days before that date and conducted in a closed car—there was no one to guard him—to a castle in the English countryside, he was terrified. Angrily he asked his driver—a man of lower rank than Dick who, despite the protests of his lieutenant and engineer and director, was still a sergeant until proven guilty—why the dentist was not with him. "Is it a trick? My whole case rests on that guy's arguments. If they've yanked my mouthpiece I'm sunk."

"Gee, Sarge, I don't know a thing about it," the driver said.

Dick saw that the driver was not himself a brute (and where *were* they all, incidentally?) but just another poor innocent as Dick himself once had been. He watched the man's cautious negotiation of the left side of the highway, an effort that obviously still strained him.

"So you don't know a thing about it?"

"That's right, Sarge."

Dick leaned forward, almost pressing his lips against the driver's neck. "Cut that Sarge shit, Mac," he said levelly, "or you and me are gonna tangle assholes." They rode on for a while in silence; then Dick became offensive again. "Fucking left side of the road," he said brutally. "This whole fucking country is eaten up with faggotry and fuckery because the cocksuckers drive on the left side of the road. La la la. Why don't you drive over on the right, you simple bastard? Let these assfarts know the Yanks are coming." He leaned forward abruptly and jerked the driver's arm so that the car swerved to the right. "Ha ha, the Yanks are coming!" Dick screamed. The driver recovered control of the car and Dick sat back, pretending to chuckle at his joke for the rest of the ride. Every once in a while he would glance at the terrorized driver. I must get used to meanness if I am to live in the world, he thought. Otherwise I won't last, I'll never make it.

At the castle he was met not by MP's but by three men in suits, big anonymous-looking men with the blunt faces of U.S. marshals or secret servicemen. Their very business suits suggested magicians' costumes, bulging with what he took to be concealed pockets and trick linings, even their hatbands reversible perhaps, in emergency becoming signal strips seen miles. Two of the men frisked him objectively, touching him heavily about his body, yet with a rapidity that made it all seem routine. They might have been checking him out to see if he was transporting fruit across a state line.

Afterward they led him through the first floor of the castle, which had been renovated and was honeycombed with offices. The women who worked in these cubicles probably knew more about the war and what was going on, Dick thought, than even old Ed Murrow back in London. Two of his escorts left him at a small elevator and he rode up with the third. He was surprised to see the man push the button for the nineteenth floor; he was quite certain that there could not be nineteen floors in the castle. Probably he was in some terrific nerve center and in reconstructing the building they had put in secret floors between floors and beneath ground level, like the extra pockets in the secret servicemen's suits. They stepped out into a richly carpeted hallway that looked more like the corridor of a first-class hotel than it did of either a castle or the offices below (above?). The man led him toward a large door at the end of the hallway, where he made Dick stop and lean against the wall to be frisked a second time. This took longer than the first frisking and was not nearly so objective.

"Okay," the man said finally, "you're clean as a whistle." Then he winked. "Incidentally, if you don't mind my saying so, soldier, you're mighty well hung."

"You must be *some* security risk," Dick said.

The man shrugged and knocked on the door. A voice that sounded vaguely familiar told them to come in. The secret service man opened the door and saluted. Dick gasped and saluted along with him; he was looking right into the eyes of a famous general. Like Dick's guard, the general was dressed in civilian clothes and wore nothing to assert his identity save his famous face and a cluster of four small stars formed by diamonds and pinned to the breast pocket of his suit.

The secret serviceman was dismissed and the famous general narrowly studied Dick's salute. "Pretty loyal all of a sudden, hey, young fella?" he said. Dick remained braced and continued to hold his salute. "By golly, you're a regular West Point cadet. Off the record, lad, are you sure you're the same fella that tells my people they're just meat?"

Dick continued his salute, his chin so tightly drawn in toward his neck that the tendons began to quiver. "I can't hear you, son," the famous general said.

"Yes, sir," Dick said. "I'm he, sir."

"Ha. He admits it," the famous general said, turning around. For the first time Dick noticed that several high-ranking officers from various services were also in the room. He was despondent with panic. What did the chiefs of staff—if that's who they were—have to do with his

128

case? Was he to be made an example? Suppose they charged him with treason? They could shoot him.

The famous general chuckled. "Child, that was sure some swell dodge your signing off that way. I've certainly got to hand it to you. . . At ease there, soldier . . . Yes sir, pulling all that traitor crap and then saying you were Dick Gibson instead of your real name. Of course, that wouldn't win you an acquittal, but it's lucky for you just the same that you thought of it. Isn't it, boys?"

Several of the officers grunted.

"You know, my boy, your program is my favorite. Did you know that, youngster?"

"Is it, sir?"

"Hell, I'll say so. Positively. That's a fact. My favorite. Those songs. Stirring, absolutely stirring."

"I'm very pleased you think so, sir."

"Oh, I think you do a *terrific* job. If I have any objection at all I guess it's that you don't play enough golden oldies."

"Golden oldies," Dick said.

"Well, those were some pretty good songs they had back there in the first war," the general said. "Not to take anything away from the stuff they're doing now, of course," he added quickly.

"He doesn't play any cavalry tunes," a colonel in the tank corps objected glumly.

"Do any of you fellows know 'She's the Mistress of the Quartermaster'?" another asked.

"How's that one go, Bob?" a two-star general asked.

"You're a lucky kiddy, son," the famous general said, breaking in.

"I am, sir?"

"You're mighty well told you are. Why, it's only because I like your program so much that your case came to my attention at all. You know, it's funny; I don't really care all that much for music. My lady can never get me to go to a concert with her. I'm not even all that fond of a military band. I guess that as much as anything else it was *you* I was listening to. There was something about your voice. It reminded me of an experience I had, oh, back a few years now. Anyway, when there was a substitution for you on *Patriot's Songbook* last Sunday I had to find out why. That's how I heard about what you'd done. Well, naturally once I found out I just had to hear that record Lieutenant Collins had made. I can tell you one thing—you made me mad as hell. Why, I was all for hauling your ass up before a firing squad or something. Then, when you signed off saying you were Dick Gibson, why it suddenly came to me why I'd always been so fascinated by you."

"I don't understand, sir," Dick Gibson said.

"Why, I guess you don't. Well, of course you don't. But I'll get to it, son, I'll get to it." The general put his arm about Dick's shoulder and led him toward a chair. "Do you recall a few years back working for a station in Nebraska?"

"KROP," Dick Gibson said, "the Voice of Wheat."

"Yes, that's it, that's the one. Well, sir, my first wife's people live out in Atkinson, Nebraska, and when I was running the Fifth Army headquarters in Chicago, I sometimes had occasion to take old Route 33 to go see them. Well, I use the radio a lot when I drive. I kind of depend upon it; it helps me to stay awake. You see, I don't like to stay in motor lodges or hotels—most of them aren't very clean, you know; 's matter of fact, the only place I like to stop is some army camp where they train inductees; I *know* that sort of place will be clean enough for any traveler to lay down his head—so usually I drive through. That's where you come in. I was near the Iowa-Nebraska border, I remember, and suddenly I picked up this program, with this fella talking. Well, sir, as I already told these gentlemen, there was ice on that highway, and it was getting dark and I was tired—but I mean tired—and I'd already dozed off for a fraction of a second and only the sudden swerve of the car jolted me awake again. That's when I picked up this program. Well, it wasn't like anything I'd ever heard before. Something about the voice . . . but not just the voice, what the voice was saying . . . I was fascinated. It woke me up. I didn't want to miss a word. That was *you* speaking, lad. I remembered the name soon as I heard it again on Lieutenant Collins's record—*Dick Gibson*. I don't even recall now what you said back then. All I know is that whatever it was, it helped. I followed your voice all the way to Atkinson."

"There was something wrong with the equipment," Dick Gibson said.

"No sir. It came in perfect. *Perfect*. Best reception I ever had. Funny thing about that too, because I'd borrowed the car, and up to the time I picked you up the radio had been giving me trouble. But you came in perfect, no static or anything. It was as if you were right there in that car with me."

Dick remembered how good he'd been, how he had thought even at the time that he was in a state of grace. His chest heaved, and he felt tears coming. Whatever the general might tell him now, he knew that it was over; his apprenticeship was truly finished, the last of all bases in the myth had been rounded, his was a special life, even a great life—a life, that is, touched and changed by cliché, by corn and archetype and the oldest principles of drama. In ignorance and absentminded goodness of heart he had taken a burr from the general's paw. And the general had turned out to be *the* general and would now repay him. This was no place for it, but he began openly to cry, simultaneously congratulating and commiserating with himself. Good work, Dick Gibson, he thought. Poor Dick Gibson, he thought. You paid your dues and put in your time and did what you had to. You struggled and fought and contended and strove, and many's the time your back was against the wall, but you never let up, you never said die, even when the night was darkest and it seemed the dawn would hold back forever. You showed them. You, Dick Gibson, you showed the dirty motherfucking fartshits and prickasses. You showed them good. Poor Dick Gibson.

The officers, embarrassed by his weeping, looked away. Only the famous general watched him. He's letting me cry, Dick Gibson thought. He's letting me get it all out. Poor Dick Gibson, he blubbered silently.

The general waited a few moments, then stepped forward. There was a war on. "Feeling better?" he asked gently.

"Yes sir," Dick said, his nose filling.

"Calmed down?"

"Sir, I am," he managed forcefully.

"Talk business?"

"Business as usual," Dick said, and took out a handkerchief and emptied his sinuses.

"That's the spirit," the general said when Dick, his nose clear once more and his eyes dry again, looked at him brightly.

"What's up, sir?" Dick asked.

"We've been playing the transcription," the general said. "Remarkable. You were hysterical. Fear brings things out in you." Dick blushed. "No, you don't understand. We want you to do the same for us."

"We want to hear the war," one of the other officers said.

"Yes," the general said, "this place—" He indicated their surroundings with his arm. For all the fullness of his emotion, Dick understood exactly what the general's gesture meant. It took in the false floors and new walls, the elevator and desks and typewriters and secret pockets of the secret service. But more than anything else Dick understood his gesture as an indictment of the *chairs*.

For all the precision of his understanding of the moods in the room, it was a long time before he could concentrate on what they were actually trying to tell him, however. Only a certain sharpness and impatience in the general's tone impelled him to put it all together.

He was to be sent to the most terrible war zones of all, and from these incendiary landscapes he was to send back reports, transmitting them the thousands of miles to headquarters over special equipment. They were interested not in military information as such, but in the *feel* of the campaigns. He was, in short, to do the color on World War II. Lieutenant Collins was to be sent along with him as his engineer. Except for the incident during the air raid, they worked well together.

Dick asked if the enemy wouldn't be able to pick up his broadcasts.

"Negative," a naval commander from research and development said. "We've perfected this transmitter and receiver that work on a band below three kilocycles. Your standard broadcast band begins at 550."

He was given to understand that the assignment would be dangerous. He expected to be told this. They would understand if he turned it down and chose instead to be court-martialed. He expected to be told this. His infraction wasn't *actually* treasonous. The Judge Advocate representative told him that his punishment wouldn't amount to more than an eleven-year sentence and a reduction in rank. He expected this. *They* wouldn't force him. This wasn't unexpected. No man would look askance if he didn't "volunteer," and of course there was some good-natured laughter at the use of the word "volunteer." Did he understand, then, what was required and that they weren't trying to push him into a corner? He expected to be asked.

"Affirmative."

Did they understand, then, that knowing the risks he was still willing to go through with it?

He anticipated that one too. "Affirmative, *sir.*"

Indeed, after the general's speech, he expected *everything,* all of it. He understood that the exceptional life—the one he had been vouchsafed to live—was magnificent yes, but familiar too, unconventional but riddled with conventions of a different, higher order. The full force of it descended on him; he could almost plot it. There would be—success. And lurking in the success, danger, suffering different from that he'd already endured, which was merely niggling loneliness and his apprentice's uncertainty. Now the loneliness—God, the women he'd have—would exist inside power. Poor Dick Gibson, he thought; poor little rich boy. Now there would be tantrum and flaw, which he would try to guard against, learning to take advice from trusted advisers. And at the apogee there would probably be betrayal and slowish death. (Unless his end came suddenly, stylishly, a la mode—in a private plane he flew himself, perhaps.) But for now he was safe, snug as a bug in their lousy war zones (though he was a little nervous for Lieutenant Collins).

So, he thought, pledging himself, I am ready for things to happen to me. Let the cliches come. I open myself to the great platitudes.

The generals indicated he could leave. They would be in touch with him soon.

He paused at the door and looked at the famous general.

"What is it, son?"

"You saved me too," he told him. "I don't mean the court-martial. I thought I belonged with the brutes. But I feel pride. A brute doesn't feel pride." He saluted, and the general returned it, and Dick left.

"Ah," said the famous general when Dick had closed the door behind him, "but he's the only one who does."

4

**FROM THE ARCHIVES: TRANSCRIPTS OF DICK GIB-
SON'S BROADCAST OF**
Fabulous Battles of World War II: Mauritius.

"Dick Gibson talking low on the low band.

"We're on Mauritius. Formerly Ile de France. Indian
Ocean, east of Madagascar. Breasting the twentieth parallel like a runner breaking the tape. Sister isles, all vol-
canic—Réunion (a French possession), Rodrigues and
the St. Brandon group. Who's St. Brandon, patron of
what? Sounds English to me. How did he get those spic
brothers. Réunion and Rodrigues for sister isles? What
miscegenous, nigger-in-the-woodpile history went on here,
anyway? Who, wanting something for nothing, looking for
what trade routes, asking the way east from the way west
like those other old junkmen of science, the alchemists,
found this place? Who charted it on maps, informing the
old cartographers so they could erase their ancient lame
finesse, *Hic sunt leones?* It is the world, real as Paris.

"The light is terrible, and I have no smoked glasses,
though Collins, an officer, does. There's not much here.

Lieutenant Collins agrees. Wait. I have my map. Hmn. Well. Hmn. Oh. Mnh hmn. Say, let's try that. Here's how I read it. I see from the Miller Cylindrical Projection that we are the last island cluster of democracy in the Tropic of Cancer, a short hop from the Tropic of Capricorn border. We are the Gateway to the Antarctic, a key cog in the bitter battle to control the glaciers. Am I getting warm?

"When I was a boy I imagined war as a cataclysm, an extended chaos. I puzzled where soldiers slept, when they ate. After a while I came to believe that wars had no silences save those of ambush. War seemed to be some eternal fire, sourceless and undying like a nasty miracle. Just a hint of the undisrupted was more exotic than the fiercest massacre. What, the mail goes through? The lottery isn't stopped? The restaurants are full? Imagine. Now I perceive something of the thinness of cataclysm and know that more bombs fall in the sea than on the city, but a piece of my terror hangs on. In neutral Lisbon, where uniformed Germans and uniformed Americans walk side by side and buy papers at the same newsstands and ask the same questions of the hotel porter, and wait behind each other at the gas pumps, and no one draws his gun and there is less skulduggery than in Cleveland, my flesh crawled and I had bad dreams. Collins flew in first class and I in economy on our commercial flight here, and sitting beside me was a Japanese soldier who helped me recline my seat because the button was stuck. Neutrality is the miracle. I do not understand how forces can swirl and swarm and elude each other.

"Unless Collins has secret orders—he swears he hasn't: our proximity has made *us* neutral; already he swears to me—I don't understand what's happening here, or why we came. There's nothing to report. There's a garrison of British soldiers, here since before the war. These men, never rotated or reinforced, seem residents of the place, as much its citizens as the Chinese, Dutch, Indians, French and Africans who live here. Occasionally there are reports that the Japanese have put troops ashore on one of the nearby islands, and then there is a flurry of military activity as the men go out on patrol. There's some evidence that there *are* Japanese around, a few but at no greater than patrol strength, and as they make no move to threaten the garrison at Port Lewis, the island's principal city, the British don't try to engage them.

"It's pretty much a planter culture here—no industry and a rattan feel to life. I guess at its essences. Mauritius would use its barks and leaves and boles. Commerce blooms from its rangy stalks and thorny brush. There are goods in its grasses. I smell high-grade hemps and queer cocoas. I sniff deck tars, caulking syrup and narcotics in the island's fibers—hashish and bhang and cannabis. And there is something brackish and briny in the tangled mat of the growth, as though the vegetation were merely the dried top of the sea.

"As per our orders, Collins and I protect the equipment. One of us is at the transmitter at all times. Off duty I either drink with the British or roam about the place, sometimes, climbing the grassy slopes of the volcanoes that acne the landscape. I've exhausted Port Lewis, seen its single museum—a curious place which in addition to its limited collection of paintings, mostly by the planters themselves, holds the largest collection in the world of the skeletons and reconstructed bodies of the extinct dodo bird which, for some curious reason, once thrived on Mauritius and Réunion isles.

"Is this the sort of thing you want?"

"A tip of the Dick Gibson cap to the High Command. You knew what you were doing, all right. Increased activities among the Japanese. A few small landing parties spotted by some of the planters. They disappear quickly into the jungle. No real alarm at the British garrison yet, as there is no evidence that they are bringing any heavy equipment with them."

"Still more landings reported. They seem to be concentrated on Réunion, though one or two have been seen on the beaches of Mauritius itself. Yesterday a cache of armament, though of a strange sort. Primitive. Perhaps

137

for jungle warfare. The British colonel here says the stuff looks almost like traps. One interesting sidelight: some of the Japanese accompanying the soldiers are dressed in civilian clothes."

"A Japanese task force has been spotted steaming toward Mauritius, about two days off. Vichy France has sent troops to Réunion. The garrison here has been placed on alert. All Asians are under strict scrutiny. The buildup on both sides is terrific now."

"By now there seem to be as many Japanese as British about; though both forces have thus far managed to stay out of each other's way."

"The Royal Air Force is here."

"It's a collision course, all right, though no major engagements yet. One of the Japanese civilians attached to the Jap army was captured and interrogated. He turns out to be a scientist—an ornithologist."

"The report has come back. It's official. HIC SUNT DODOS!"

"The dodo is an extinct species of ungainly, flightless bird of the genus Raphus or Didus. Its incubation ground and later its world was the island of Mauritius. It was closely related in habit and aspect to a smaller bird, the solitaire, also extinct but once indigenous to the island of Réunion. It has long been held by ornithologists that the dodo—both the dodo proper and the solitaire henceforward will be subsumed under the pseudo-generic term 'dodo'—was related to the pigeon, but this is only an hypothesis since the bird has not been available for study since 1680, the year that the last known dodo died. Although the dodo was sent to European museums, no complete specimen exists, and today only the foot and leg of one specimen are preserved at Oxford. The representations one sees, even in the Mauritius Museum of Art itself, are merely restorations, little more than cunning dolls constructed on skeletal frames. Nevertheless, the skeletons, the scattered bones of which are to be found abundantly even today in the Mauritian fens and swamps, have been painstakingly reassembled by Mauritian dodo artisans—the best in the world—and give an accurate picture of what the bird was like.

"He was large, slightly bigger than the American turkey whom he in no mean way resembles. In silhouette the dodo is not unlike a great scrunched question mark. For detail we may refer to the paintings from life that have been made of the bird, many of the best of which are still here in the Mauritius Museum of Art and Dodo Reconstruction. Most of the artists seem to be in agreement that the animal possessed an enormous blackish bill which, together with the huge horny hook in which it terminates, constituted the shepherd's crook of the question mark. Its cheeks, partially bare, seem oddly weatherbeaten and muscular, like the toothless cheeks of old men who have worked out in the open all their lives. Black except for some whitish plumage on his breast and tail and some yellowish white the tint of old piano keys on his tail, the dodo was somewhat formal in appearance, if a trifle stupid looking. This formal aspect is attributable also to his wing, forshortened as a birth defect, which in repose flops out and down from his body like an unstarched pocket handkerchief.

"Dodos are said to have inhabited the Mauritian forests—this is the style of information, of certain kinds of fact; I find it relaxing—and to have laid a single large white egg which they mounted high in a setting of piled grass. Hogs, brought in by the settlers, fed on the dodo eggs and on the dodo young, and in one or two generations the birds were extinct.

"By now you have the reports, the action paced off in the war room, set pin for pin like surveyor's stakes in alignment, the lines drawn in a terrible cat's cradle of possibility. This, what *I* do, is something else.

"The buildup was flawless. Men came from the sea, from the air. They peeled off the landing craft and ran up the beach like barbarians. Paratroopers bloomed in the sky like flowers and grew into the ground. The trade routes are really open. I celebrate the Department of Deployment, reinforcements, fresh troops. (There's something virginal in the sound: showered, shaved, their fight untapped, blossoming in their pink skins. 'Fresh troops'; it sounds pasteurized.) And cooks to feed them and clerks to count them. And the Japs the same, as good as you in producing populations out of thin air.

"But you know. And who am I, Dick Gibson, to be telling you all this? You know what I think, High Commanders, Chiefs of Staff? This broadcast of mine is a little like prayer. Well, not prayer exactly, but still, there's a soupçon of reverence and a touch of review. That's what you want to hear, right? Am I getting warm? That's why the low band was invented, High Commanders on High.

"I'll tell you what happened. History is good experience for me, the itinerant radio man.

"Collins is the officer and must command me to rise. Yesterday he came to my room to wake me but I was already up. I'd awakened before dawn. I'd heard some noises and couldn't fall back to sleep. At first I thought the engagement had begun, but when I went to the window there were just some trucks and black shapes moving in the street. I assumed they were more reinforcements for the garrison. Then it occurred to me that they might be Japanese, but when I called down a British voice yelled up at me, so I went back to bed.

"Then something that has always been undeveloped in me—I mean my sense of place—suddenly surged up and overwhelmed me. Why, here I am, I thought, on Mauritius, one of three or four places on the globe which merely to have seen qualifies a man as a traveler, I mean a wanderer, one of those whose fate it is to be troubled by laundry, mail months old, irregular bowel movements, a certain ignorance about time and a taste gone crotchety through nostalgia for things eaten long before. How did I get this way? I wondered. It can be no accident when one finds himself sizing smooth pebbles on the cold coasts of

Tierra del Fuego. To see a desert is to scorn a city, and to lick a finger that has once been in the Weddell Sea is to eschew the ordinary salts forever. What had earned *me* distance? In America I had crisscrossed the country, leaping in and out of landscape, stitching my wild, erratic journey. The mile is a measure of madness too, and a map is hot pursuit. (This is still the war news.) Gradually the room grew light and I could perceive the objects in it—the four-bladed fan that hung from the ceiling like a great spider, the cane furniture like petrified vegetable, the huge wardrobe, big as a piano crate, the white mystery of the mosquito netting. They were the solid evidences of my own strangeness. Why am *I* far afield?

"I rang for my tea and porkchop—think of that, a porkchop for breakfast—and the little half-naked native brought it up on a tray. Still standing beside my bed he kneaded the warm half-baked dough they use here as rolls and pinched the last counter-clockwise swirls into it. How does he live? He is fourteen and already married and a father. My 15 percent service charge which must be divided with the chambermaids and hall porters and laundry people and maintenance men cannot keep them all. This hotel has been practically empty since the war began. What strange arrangement goes on here?

"As I was finishing my breakfast Collins came for me and we drove straight to the garrison. It was deserted. The troops I'd seen were not reinforcements. They'd been pulling *out*.

" 'Where could they have gone?' Collins said.

"I stood with all my weight on one hip, the deferential stance of one waiting for someone else to make a decision for him.

" 'Something may be up,' Collins said. 'We ought to find out where they've gone. There's probably someone around.'

"We found a man in the infirmary who told us the garrison had gone off to make contact with the Japanese at the southeastern edge of the island, about a half-day's trip over rough terrain.

141

" 'Looks like the real thing,' Collins said. He did not seem very happy. 'What the hell is this about anyway, Dick? How'd a couple of old radio men like us get involved in all this?'

"In a way he was thinking the same thoughts I had earlier, but I only shrugged.

" 'You believe all that shit about the dodo bird?' I didn't answer. 'Bird extinct two hundred and fifty years suddenly shows up. Damned island extinct for about the same length of time, and all of a sudden it's a major theater of operations. It must have something to do with that bird. That's what the talk is, but no one knows. What do *you* make of it?'

" 'I don't know, Lieutenant.'

" 'You said they've got some stuffed dodos at the museum.'

" 'Representations, cunning dolls.'

" 'Let's take a look at them, see what all the fuss is about.'

"We went to the museum. Collins treated. I knew the collection pretty well by now and I started to take him through. He wasn't really paying much attention; be barely glanced at the glass cases. 'We could still be in London, you know that? You had to go haywire.'

" 'No excuse, sir.'

" 'No, hell, water under the bridge. Boy, it sure spooked me when I learned you were so highly connected. What did you have on that general, anyway?'

" 'I once took a burr out of his paw.'

" 'Yeah. Ha ha. You know something? I don't think this war can last much longer. You going back into radio when it's over?'

" 'Yes sir.'

" 'Not me.'

" 'No sir?'

" 'Television.

" 'Oh.'

" 'That's where the money will be. Radio's had it.'

" 'I'll stick to radio.'

142

" 'Will you?'

" 'Yes sir.'

" 'Well, it's all a matter of what you're comfortable doing, I guess.'

" 'It's been pretty good to me,' I said.

"Soldiers had been talking this way for hundreds of years in the respites before big battles. I don't think Collins saw me, but I began to cry. A chill went through me. Something about our voices, the sound of our dropped-guard friendship, told me that something terrible was going to happen. As he spoke hopefully and confidently about the future, I expected to see Collins die, to be hit by a grenade, his head torn off. Before long, I thought, he'll be dead at my feet, his neck broken. I wanted to tell him to hush, but of course I couldn't.

"Then something odd *did* happen. We were in the picture gallery. All about us were the dark oils of the early settlers—pictures of dodo hunts, the excited Dutchmen ruddy and breathless from the chase, the dodo cornered, maddened perhaps by its ordeal; other paintings, still lifes of Mauritian feasts, tables, spread with the island's fruits, halved cuchacha melons white as moonlight, tangled wreaths of the fruit vines that trellis the cones of the volcanoes, the dodo birds prepared for cooking, split, the guts, like long, partially inflated balloons, tossed into a slopbucket, their long necks limp, the beaks open in death and their bare, old men's cheeks flecked with blood. I had thought we were alone, but suddenly I heard a low bark of heartbreak. We both turned. It was the captured Japanese civilian, sitting on one of those benches that they put in the middle of picture galleries. There was a strange rapt expression on his face, and he was weeping. Probably he didn't see us.

" 'How did he get loose?' the lieutenant whispered. I shook my head. Collins drew his service revolver—since that time in Broadcasting House when he'd placed me under arrest he always wore one—and pointed it at the man. 'Hands up,' he commanded. The scientist appeared not to have heard and Collins walked closer. 'I said hands up.' Still the fellow did not acknowledge us. 'Hands up and stop crying.' At last the Japanese turned to Collins. He seemed very tired. He raised his arms wearily.

" 'What are you doing here?' Collins demanded. The Japanese just stared at him. He looked like someone in touch with something really important who was suddenly forced to deal with the ordinary. I was glad I wasn't the lieutenant and didn't have to ask the questions. 'Come on, fellow. You don't have to speak our language to get our meaning,' Collins said. He waved the pistol at him. He shook it in his face. 'Move out smartly . . . I said *move!*' the man merely looked away from Collins again and stared across the room at a large painting of a dodo bird. He rubbed his eyes. 'And you can cut out that sniffling,' Collins said firmly. 'We're not barbarians. We're American soldiers and you're a prisoner of war, subject to rights granted you under the Geneva conventions. You're our first prisoner and we aren't exactly sure of what those rights include. We'll have to look them up, but anyway we're not going to hurt you. You have to come along with us, though.'

" 'I am not afraid,' the Japanese said calmly. 'And I will go with you. But first, can you please give me one moment alone in here? As you can see, this is the last gallery. Obviously I have no means of escape.'

"I must confess something. I was very excited at the prospect of taking a prisoner. 'Don't do it, Lieutenant—it's a trick,' I said.

"The man looked at me contemptuously. 'Please, Lieutenant,' the Japanese said, 'you can see that there is no escape.' He patted his pockets and opened his palms. 'I am unarmed.'

" 'How come you talk such good English?' I asked threateningly. He seemed disappointed in me. I didn't blame him; I felt my sergeant's stripes sear themselves into my arm.

" 'I am a scientist,' he explained coolly, looking at the lieutenant. 'English is the official language of ornithology.'

" 'Hmph.'

144

" 'Please, Lieutenant, I will go with you now. My meditations'—he looked at me—'are over.'

"He rose, his eyes, downcast, his body just visibly stiffening as we went by each of the paintings. In the gallery showing the environments of the dodo birds he would not look up, and once, when his hand accidentally brushed against one of the glass cases, he jumped back as if flung. 'Pretty odd behavior for a so-called *scientist*, wouldn't you say, Lieutenant?' I whispered in Collins's ear, regretting my style even as I spoke. My stripes lashed me, driving me to feats of clown and squire.

"Once outside the museum the Japanese seemed more comfortable. We took him back to the garrison and let ourselves into the guardhouse.

" 'How did you escape?' the lieutenant asked our prisoner.

" 'I didn't. I was abandoned. They forgot about me.'

" 'What were you doing at the museum?'

" 'I'm an ornithologist.'

" 'You're the one who discovered the dodo.'

" 'No. I identified him.'

"I was still smarting from all the things I'd said up to now. 'Listen, Lieutenant,' I whispered, 'I think there's more going on here than we appreciate yet. Give me a few minutes alone with him.'

" 'Why? What good would that do?'

" 'I think I know some ways of getting him to talk.'

" 'He's a prisoner of war, Sergeant.'

" 'Yes sir, but our buddies are out there. I think this gook knows more than he lets on.' The scientist rolled his eyes.

" 'Many hundreds of years ago—' he said.

" '*Talk,*' I hissed.

" 'Many hundreds of years ago, during the dynasty of the Emperor Shobuta—' the man said.

" 'That's it,' I said lamely, 'keep talking.'

" ' . . . there suddenly appeared in Japan, on the island of Shikoku—your Indian word "Chicago" derives from this—a single specimen of the genus Raphidae Didus, what you call *dodos*. How it got there is unknown, for Japan—this was in the thirteenth century, three centuries before the discovery of Mauritius—was an insular nation which had no dealings with the rest of the world. The bird was flightless. Ceramics from the era show that its wing development was even less than the Mauritian representations. Naturally, the bird was a curiosity. The curator of the Shikoku Zoo—we are not barbarians either, Lieutenant; Shikoku had a zoo long before one was ever dreamed of in Europe—did not know how to classify it and was inclined to put it with the animals rather than in the aviary.

" 'Now at this time Japan was plagued by warlords. One in particular, Zamue, a Shikokuan, was a threat to the emperor himself, a man of mild manners and ways whose paths were peace. Zamue, in contrast, was a fierce samurai who, in the course of events, had left a trail of bloody victories from the island of Yezo in the north of Kyushu in the south.

" 'Now it came to pass—you have this idiom in your country?—it came to pass that a court counselor, one Ryusho Mali, recognized the need to instill courage in our emperor, and when he heard about the strange wingless bird that had alighted in Shikoku he sent for it in order to examine it for its qualities as an omen. He had expected something like a peacock, perhaps, or a cassowary—both rare in Japan but not unheard of—or even a parrot, but when he saw the specimen he was extremely disappointed. How could so foolish-looking a bird bode well for the state? Nevertheless, setting aside his prejudices, he proceeded to examine it closely. Perhaps it enjoyed some of the properties of the parrot and could be made to mimic human speech. Ryusho Mali recalled how a predecessor of his had once done something notable for his country through an ordinary crow, and so he closeted himself with the bird and examined it. He tried to train it to say "courage," thinking that perhaps the hard *k* sound might be natural to it, but, alas, he quickly discovered that the bird had no voice at all. It was mute as a turtle. He

146

wondered if something cheering might not be done with the feathers, but there was little inspiration to be had from the lusterless black and dingy yellow with which the bird was covered. In the end, Ryusho Mali put the bird away from him, commanding that it be sent back to the zoo in Shikoku to be stared at by the multitudes for the pointless novelty it was.

" 'The Emperor Shobuta—whose very name means compassion—was himself an animal fancier, no hunter but a lover of beasts. Perhaps he saw that they had qualities which he himself lacked. It is often the way. We have an expression: "The grass is always greener on the other side of the fence." At any rate, it is well known that fish and birds are the most fascinating animals to man for that the one can live in the sea and the other in the air. Be that as it may, it was Shobuta who had decreed that there be a 200—for the two hundred distinct animal types; the z in the word "zoo" is a corruption of the 2—and every day he would visit there, consoling himself with the mysteries of creation.

" 'No sooner was the bird returned to its pen in the 200—as I've said, the curator did not know how to classify it and had ordered that it should be put in with the hogs—'

" 'But hogs—' I said.

" 'Yes,' the ornithologist said. 'Exactly. No sooner was the bird returned to the 200 than the emperor, who had been away at his summer palace when the bird was first discovered, saw the dodo and was furious—as much as it was possible within the terms of his sweet nature for him to *be* furious—that it had been classified with the animals. He had recognized it immediately for what it was. Oh, I don't mean he knew that it was Raphidae Didus, but he saw that it was a bird. He was, as I say, furious. His exact words were: "What iniquity is this? To break off the wings of a bird"—for that is what he thought had happened—"merely to indulge the crowd's appetite for the grotesque! I will not have this! A nation which stoops to the barbarity of a Zamue the samurai does not *deserve* to be sustained. What, are not wings marvelous enough? We have an expression in Japan: "to gild the lily." It is to situations like this that such an expression applies."

" 'It was the first time anyone had ever seen the emperor so angry, and though it was explained to him that no one had tampered with the bird, he would not believe it. He ordered the bird released and brought it back with him to the palace. There he anointed the nub of its wings with precious balms and unguents. I said before that man admires and loves those qualities which he does not himself possess, but he loves also to recognize in other species those which he *does*. Both things are true. Perhaps the emperor's heart responded to something like his own winglessness in the bird's; at any rate, it is known that he cherished the bird as he had cherished nothing before it, and that he kept it with him always.

" 'Now something must be said of the warrior Zamue. Remarkable as it may seem for one so successful, he had no followers. He permitted himself none. The fact is, he was not so much warlord, or even samurai, as he was assassin. He was a man of a thousand disguises and wreaked his havoc through the art of murder, which he had perfected. He had murdered men by drowning them and murdered them with poisons. He'd done murders with knives and murders with clubs. He murdered them awake and he murdered them asleep, and he murdered the sick as well as the well. He had great strength and murdered them by lifting heavy objects and then letting them fall on the tops of their heads. He shoved men off cliffs and lured them from the sea to the rocks with false signal lights. He murdered by loosing beasts and by cruel degrees of torture. He pushed them against walls and squeezed them to death. He murdered with gunpowder and murdered with strangling, by forcing sand up their noses and holding their mouths. He murdered them by repeatedly kicking them hard.

" 'Zamue preempted whole kingdoms by killing the leaders, and had worked his wicked way up the chain of proprietorship till all that stood between himself and the

148

sandal—we say instead of crown in Japan—was the life of Shobuta the Tender. Him he had saved for last, just as one reserves the sweetest morsel of a feast.

" 'Shobuta knew Zamue was coming. He doubled his guards, tripled them, but in his heart he had no faith that he could escape the assassin's depredations. Zamue, as has been said, was a master of disguise. The chances were excellent—better than excellent—that one of his own men was Zamue, and so he reasoned that by increasing their number he had correspondingly increased the chances of Zamue's being among them. He reduced the guard by a third, by a half, by three-quarters. In the end he relieved all but his most trusted attendant and made him his entire guard. I know what you're thinking.

" 'Zamue was a fate—in our country we have a saying. "What will be will be"—and all that the emperor could do in these last days was care for the bird, minister to his new pet's winglessness. "I will be your wings," Shobuta whispered to it. "Surely you are not so high as once you soared," he would tell it—he carried the dodo everywhere—and then add, thinking perhaps of his own circumstances, "We all come down." In this wise the emperor continued for months. Each night as he laid his head on his pillow he could not but wonder if he should ever see the morning.

" 'It is well known that birds tuck their heads under their wings when they sleep, but what of wingless birds? Shobuta took the poor dodo to his bed with him. "I told you I would be your wings," he reminded it softly, and raised his elbow. With an uncanny instinct, the bird nuzzled up to Shobuta's armpit, and the emperor put his arm gently down over the dodo's head. In this wise they remained all night.

" 'As the great feast days approached, Shobuta thought that Zamue would soon make his move. In our country, as in most, there is the old saying: "Strike before the feast days if you would have victory." Each day now he peered outside the door of the imperial apartments and glared accusingly into the face of his most trusted lieutenant.

Should not the suspicion that has occurred to you occur also to the greatest scholar of his time? Every afternoon at exactly the same time Shobuta the Tender would step out just as the circle of his tour brought the man before the doors to the imperial apartments and, at the precise moment when the eyes of the "trusted lieutenant" met his own, he would whisper softly, "When, 'Lieutenant?' How?" In my country we have the expression "battle of nerves." That's what this was. The man never answered, of course, for this is against the basic rule of guard duty.

" 'Why didn't the emperor—?'

" 'Discharge the lieutenant? Zamue was a master of disguise, Sergeant, a master. With his great strength and fabulous muscle control he could alter not only his size but even the actual features of his face. If only he had used his powers for good . . .

" The feast days came and the feast days went and still Zamue had not put in his appearance. "So," the emperor thought, "he did not abide by the venerable saying. How clever the fellow is! How clever *and* how wicked!" Yet troubled as he was . . . Oh. I forgot to mention something. The emperor had little feeling for his personal safety, but very delicate negotiations were going on in Japan at this time, negotiations which the emperor himself had initiated and that required his leadership if they were to succeed. Also, he was disturbed by what would happen to the dodo when he was no longer there to care for it . . . As I started to say, troubled as Shobuta was, he never let on to the dodo bird that he was concerned with anything more serious than the dodo's winglessness. No. With the dodo he was always careful to seem gay. He took up singing and sang for the voiceless bird with apparently unflagging spirits. If the dodo appeared to tire of a particular song Shobuta the Tender immediately removed it from his repertoire and learned two new ones for the one he had discarded. He noted which songs appeared to give the dodo especial pleasure and had the court musicians compose new ones along the lines of these. Only during that brief moment during the day when he went outside to confront his lieutenant did his anxiety surface—and this, thank God, was a moment the bird was not permitted to share.

" 'Things continued in this wise till the next feast days, and *still* nothing happened. Then, one day, after completing a new song that the dodo had never heard before, Shobuta walked down the hallway at the other end of which stood the huge double-thick ivory entrance doors to the imperial apartments, first, of course, setting down the bird and giving his customary admonition that it remain there until he returned.

" 'The emperor went down the long hallway, his tender anger building as he thought of the duplicities and treasons of him who had so long kept him waiting for what he still thought of as his fatality. But then the knowledge that he had recently completed the delicate negotiations softened his heart toward his malefactor. Indeed, by the time he arrived at the enormous doors it was all this tender, gentle man could do to fix his features in a scowl. Though he was now quite empty of hostility, he felt he owed it to his enemy to present a scowling face—since he knew, you see, that the cruelty of a Zamue thrived on such gestures and the tender Shobuta did not have it in him to disappoint even Zamue.

" 'What was his surprise, then, when he opened the door and saw his "trusted lieutenant" laying dead at his feet, his neck broken and his chest struck quite through with a sword! His first words were typically Shobutian. "Hurrah!" he exclaimed. "The bird was spared seeing this!" Then he began to grieve that his "lieutenant" had come to such a dreadful end. He kneeled by the man's prostrate body, his eyes misting over with tears. Only then did he see that he was not alone. He found himself staring at a pair of the largest feet he had ever seen. Horned they were, and scaly. He looked at the grayish shins, hard as broadswords, and up the cutting edge of the thighs, and all the way up the rest of the long, thick body until he was staring directly into the face of—the assassin Zamue!

" ' "But—" the emperor said.

151

" ' "It is I. I come undisguised."

" 'It was the *real* face of Zamue, the powerful muscles relaxed for once, collapsed in the fierce pile that was his natural aspect. It could be no one else. *Aiiiee,* the emperor thought, he means to kill me with his ugliness. I must not look.

" 'Zamue reached down, pulled the emperor to his feet, and was just about to kill him by biting his jugular in two when suddenly he released him and began to laugh uncontrollably.

" ' "Ho haw hoo hoo haw ho ha!" laughed the assassin, pointing to something behind the emperor's back. Shobuta had forgotten to close the door behind him, and when he turned he saw that what Zamue had been laughing at was the wingless, ungainly dodo waddling down the corridor toward them. Shobuta—he did not want the bird to see what Zamue was about to do to him—immediately made to close the doors, but Zamue restrained him. "No, let him come," he roared. "I have never seen anything so ridiculous. Look. He has no wings. A bird with no ho haw hoo hoo wings!"

" 'The bird continued to approach them, his waddle more graceless than ever. In his haste to be reunited with his friend he appeared to stumble, to fall, to pitch, to buckle, to drop to one knee. Zamue thought he had never seen anything so comical as this fat bird, bigger than a turkey, with its glazed, bulging eyes that made it seem so stupid. "Ho haw haw hoo. Just look at that booby, will you? If you want to know, I think it's drunk."

" 'But when the bird had reached our emperor and was nuzzling against his knees, Zamue recovered himself. He drew the sword from the lieutenant's chest and raised it high above his head. "Say your farewells to your clumsy friend, Shobuta, for now I am going to split you two in two!" Zamue shouted. So saying, he raised himself up on the powerful balls of his enormous feet and made to chop with his sword on the emperor's crown—we say crown and not sandal when we are referring to the head—when suddenly the bird appeared to float up into the air. The wingless bird had *risen!*

152

" 'Zamue's eyes widened in horror. *"Yeeeeeghch!"* he screamed, and still stretching for leverage with the sword above his head, his fright and his imbalance and the weight of his weapon toppled him backward. Moving quickly and almost without thinking, Shobuta recovered the sword and plunged it into the assassin's heart. The giant writhed and thrashed. His throes were terrible, but it was all up with him; in minutes he was dead. Interestingly enough—so evil are some men—he had actually lied to Shobuta when he said he had come undisguised, for his features changed still another time, and as death relaxed them his muscles flowed like currents to create a final tidal wave of horror beneath his skin. Only now was he undisguised.

" 'In the excitement Shobuta had lost track of the bird. Now he looked around and found it some yards away, squatting in a corner. It seemed clumsy and stupid as ever. It had flown but one moment—in the instant of its dear friend's need—and now it was as it had been before.'

" 'That's quite a story,' Collins said after a while.

" 'It isn't finished,' the Japanese said.

" 'Keep talking,' I said.

" 'The news of Zamue's end spread throughout the empire, and all at once, in the vacuum created by the death of the assassin, many vicious men began to struggle for power. This was a terrible disappointment for Shobuta and for all those others in the empire whose paths were peace. But—the Japanese have an expression: "First one thing, then another—" terrible as it must have been for him, Shobuta knew that he could no longer sit idly by while the empire was being torn to shreds by contending forces. He was a changed man. From Shobuta the Tender he became Shobuta the Jealous; wherever there was insurrection, there too was Shobuta. He met each challenge forthrightly and with all the force at his command. And this force was now considerable. Reports of the bird's miraculous flight had traveled the length and breadth of the empire, and bit by bit its strange powers were transferred to the emperor. Shobuta had become irresistible, *rosichicho*—invincible. His enemies, and there were many, fell back before him as grain before the wind. Before long almost every pocket of resistance had either been defeated or else dissolved of its own accord. Only one man, the shogun Korogachi, the most powerful of all Shobuta's enemies, held out. A wily warrior, he pretended to encourage a belief among the people in the emperor's new powers. In this way he thought to let the emperor do his work for him, and to inherit a docile Japan once he and the emperor—you say "locked assholes"?

" 'Only when there were no more seditionists save himself did Korogachi declare that he disbelieved the emperor's story about the wingless bird. He let it be known that he thought the bird was a hoax, a desperate fabrication of the emperor's counselors—for example, he presented proof that the bird had been with the cunning Ryusho Mali long before the emperor had ever laid eyes on it—and that when he and Shobuta met on the field of combat, man-to-man, no crippled—ha ha—bird would have any bearing on the outcome. He intimated that the real miracle was the so-called "character change" of the emperor, and declared that he had no more faith in Shobuta the Jealous than he'd had in Shobuta the Tender. "If you want my honest opinion," Korogachi was wont to say, "that mother should be known as Shobuta the Show-boat!"

" 'When Shobuta the Jealous heard what the shogun had been saying about him, he was so furious that he insisted on setting out at once for their confrontation, and he ordered that the bird be brought from the temple where it had been kept for safekeeping and religious observance ever since the day of its fabulous flight. "We shall just take the wondrous bird with us this time, since Mister Korogachi proclaims not to believe in its powers! Perhaps it will show again what it can do. Who knows but what it may fly in his face and peck out Mister Korogachi's eyes?"

" 'In this wise, feeling himself invincible, and now singing marital airs to the bird where once he had sung lullabies and poems and love songs, Shobuta set off with his army, the bird waddling along beside him.

" 'I shall not dwell much longer on this history. Shobuta's forces were met by an enormous army. The holocaust raged for three days and three nights. The noise of battle was fantastic; the clank of armor intermingled with the screams of the dying and the bangs and booms of the gunpowder, which had only recently been invented. The racket was simply terrific.

" 'As you know, in nature there is a law of compensation. When a leg is injured or lost, an arm grows stronger. He who had not the sense of sight is frequently preternaturally blessed with the sense of touch or smell. In the bird world it is the same. For some reason, winglessness may be compensated for by a particular acuity of hearing. Historians speculate that Shobuta the Tender had a lovely voice, one particularly well suited to accommodate the soft nuances of gentle love songs. We scientists think it may have been particularly amenable to the sensitive hearing of the miraculous bird. The martial, fervent stridencies of patriotic petition were something else, as were the harsh noises of that awful battle. They were more than the sensitive auditory threshold of the bird could accommodate. It went mad. There is no other word for it. It dashed its poor head to pieces on the shield of a just-fallen soldier. Perhaps, in its confusion, it had identified the shield with the noise of the battle and sought to stop the sound by breaking its ears upon it. Or perhaps both the historians and the scientists are wrong. Perhaps we have all along paid too much attention to its winglessness and not enough to its voicelessness. Perhaps voicelessness is a choice—the choice of silence. Perhaps winglessness is one. Perhaps there are birds who reject the air and choose the earth. Perhaps even extinction is a choice of sorts.

" 'When Shobuta the Tender saw what had happened, his poor heart cracked. Suddenly he remembered those gentle days when he had been closeted with the bird in his apartments. Laying down his sword, he took the bird up in his arms. "Come," he whispered, his voice broken, "once more I shall be your wings," and he began to croon the bird's favorite song. No longer conscious of where he was, he drifted through the field of death among the fallen bodies of his foes and followers. It was such a touching sight that Korogachi, seeing it, began himself to weep. Blinded by his tears, and following now only the sound of the emperor's voice, he did not notice one of the emperor's warriors creeping up behind him. It was Earaki, a deaf samurai who, since he had not heard the sound of battle, could not now hear that it had ceased. Seizing the opportunity of what he saw only as the momentary lapse of the leader of the enemy, he struck from behind and felled the shogun Korogachi for his emperor. Once again the bird had saved Japan.'

"It was a while before either Collins or I could speak.

" 'You're here for the bird,' I said.

" 'We are losing the war. Only a miracle—' His voice trailed off.

"I nodded. His story had unsergeanted me, dissolved the chevrons from my arms. Silence *is* golden, I thought, and kept quiet, as grateful to the Japanese as I had been to the general. I looked from one to the other. Collins's eyes shone. 'He knows where it *is*,' he said suddenly.

" 'Sir?' I said. I knew enough to be fearful.

" *'He knows where it is.* Don't you *see?* They've already got it. Or maybe they haven't, but they're close. Anyway, it's still on the island. That's why he told us—so we can get word to the troops not to shoot. Can you think what it would mean if we could capture that bird?' The Japanese smiled. 'You see?' Collins said, pointing at our prisoner and talking fast. 'He wants us to try. They *haven't* got it. They haven't got it because he's the expert; he knows its ways and its lairs. The bastard is challenging us to try. He's teasing us to try. That's what he was doing in the museum—studying it. Then he was going after it, but that's when we showed up. Right? Am I right, you?"

" 'All correct,' the scientist said. He was still smiling.

" 'All correct.' Collins laughed. 'You *bet* all correct. He couldn't tell the British because there were too many of them, but there are only two of us. So he wants us to try. We bring him along so he can find it for us, then the Japs grab it back. That's it—that's what it's all about.'

156

" 'But that would only make sense if there were a million Japs around to guarantee that he could get it back,' I said.

" 'All correct, Sergeant,' Collins said.

" 'Well, then,' I said, 'it's a trap.'

" 'A beauty, Collins said. He turned to the Japanese. 'We have a jeep. How long till we get to the area?'

" 'About nine hours,' the scientist said. 'I'm judging by the time it took the patrol to bring me here after I was captured.'

"Collins had risen and was moving toward the door, the Japanese right behind him. 'But there'll be all those *Japs!*' I said.

"Collins turned to me. 'They can't shoot for fear they'll madden the bird. We'll stay out of their way. You'll see. Even if they get the dodo first they can't shoot because of the noise. He won't let them. That's our chance.'

"Collins got on the jeep radio and told the story to the British. He asked them to hold their fire, to give us twenty-four hours to try to find the dodo. He wanted Sansoni—that was the scientist's name—to give him the position where we'd be so he could tell the British. The Jap refused. When Collins drew his gun the man just grinned. 'It's better, Lieutenant, that they *don't* know,' he said. 'They'd be drawn to the area. Something could go wrong.' Collins nodded, and put the gun back. I had been cast adrift among brave men. It is always the case with squires.

"Though I'm not a good driver, Collins made me drive the jeep and Sansoni gave directions. To avoid the British we stayed off the main roads, and after a while we even avoided the secondary roads and were cutting across plantations and through fields. We left Port Lewis in the afternoon, and it was already dark, about ten-thirty or eleven o'clock, before we saw our first Japanese. They were under orders not to shoot, of course, but they signaled us to stop. Collins drew his gun again and pointed it at Sansoni's head. The soldiers recognized the scientist, and when he spoke to them calmly in Japanese they giggled. 'I've explained the situation to them,' he told us. 'They'll inform the others on the walkie-talkie—that is an interesting English orientalization, "walkie-talkie," don't you think—that we're coming. We won't be interfered with.'

" 'Excellent,' Collins said.

" 'Bully,' I said. 'Why were they giggling?'

" 'Oh well,' Sansoni said patiently, 'they expect that you two stand to lose our little contest.'

"It was fantastic. Every few minutes now we passed great clusters of Japanese troops. When our headlights picked them up they would simply turn and smile and wave us on. Soon we were in a forest, squeezing the jeep between the trees. Here and there we could see soldiers crawling along on their hands and knees. Collins was very excited. 'It's true,' he said hoarsely, 'they *haven't* found it yet.' By now it was almost impossible to drive. The crawling soldiers took up so much of the space between the trees that there was no longer any clearance.

"I honked the horn to make them move. *'Don't do that again,'* Sansoni said fiercely. 'We're almost there. Do you want to madden it? Lieutenant, please do something about this man of yours.'

" 'He's right, Sergeant. Calm down.'

" 'Further,' Sansoni said, 'just a little further.' We drove another half-mile or so. 'Now,' Sansoni said.

" 'Lieutenant?'

" 'Do what he says, Sergeant. Stop here.'

"The three of us got out. We had passed all the Japanese soldiers and were alone in the forest. We walked through the woods for a while, and finally came to a bowl-shaped clearing, perhaps two hundred feet across. Though it was very dark—there was no moon—and I'd never seen the place before, there was something familiar about it. Then I realized that it was the landscape of many of the pictures in the museum. Collins was having the same thoughts. 'The glass case,' he said. 'The environment they built for the reconstructed dodo. That was like this place.'

" 'Shh,' Sansoni said. 'Now it is necessary that we do not talk.'

"The grass was strange, leathery, and there was a fierce smell to the ground. It was an odor neither ripe nor rotten, life nor death. It was as if we smelled the molecules themselves, things outside time and form. I turned to see if there were any Japanese behind us, and when I looked back again I had lost the Jap. I moved toward the lieutenant to tell him, but he shushed me before I could speak and pointed to Sansoni. He was down on his hands and knees in the dark. Collins and I both halted. Then Sansoni suddenly began to croon strange songs in a high soft voice. I knew they were Shobuta's thirteenth-century carols.

" 'Lieutenant,' I whispered.

" 'What is it?' The lieutenant was whispering also.

" 'He's seen the dodo.'

" 'We know that.'

" 'He's an ornithologist.'

" 'We know that.'

" 'Even if he only saw it through field glasses—'

" 'What?'

" ' . . . he'd have made . . . *observations*.'

" 'Yes. What of it?'

" 'He knows its lairs, its habits.'

" 'Yes, we know that.'

" 'He can do its signals.' I shuddered.

" 'Will you be quiet?'

" 'He'll find it.'

"The lieutenant shook me off, moved toward Sansoni, and as I watched, went down on his hands and knees. In the dark I lost them both. I was not alone, though; the Japanese had caught up with us and I could hear their creaking movement all around me. I sank down on *my* hands and knees. There we were, Americans and Japanese, crawling around in that queer grass, soundless as Indians. We could have been cats and birds observing some petty detail of a mechanical neutrality, a breach in nature like a child's 'time-out' in a murderous game.

"A match flared suddenly in the darkness, its light rolling across the face of the Japanese who had been on the plane with me, the one who'd helped me with my seat.

He grinned and blew out the match. Someone laughed. It sounded like Sansoni.

" 'Lieutenant?' Perhaps they've already killed him, I thought. I stopped crawling and waited till I could no longer hear the soldiers. I leaned against a tree, but the bark was thorny and I moved back into the leathery grass. I rooted about in it and suddenly came on something soft. I laid my head down and closed my eyes, and something warm and feathery brushed my face. I didn't have to see it to know it was the dodo bird; I'd invaded its nest. I felt the bird's body stiffen and move backward. No, stay, I thought, I'm no hog. Then I grabbed its legs and pulled it to me for a hostage.

"In the dark, directionless, I traveled with the bird for hours. Several times we passed Japanese, but the bird was hidden under my shirt, next to my skin. As I crawled by the soldiers I made the exploratory pats of one searching for something under a bed. Over the old rough ground we went, a trade route of the extinct. I thought of dinosaurs and mammoths and the saber-toothed tiger, and here was I, Dick Gibson, with that other loser, the dodo. *Back,* I thought, cursing it, *back to history, you.* And felt its shape against my skin, its useless, resisting wing that whipped at me percussive as a terrorized heart. It scratched me, it pissed on me, and shit on me. I gagged, and my vomit covered the bird's stench and saved me from the Japanese. When the sun comes up, I'll be killed, I thought.

"Then I heard Sansoni's voice. He was perhaps a hundred yards off, but I could hear him talking to Collins—or to me, perhaps, if Collins was already dead. 'It's useless in the dark,' he was saying. 'Most likely it's asleep. We'll have to wait and look for its nest in the morning. I'll tell them.' He spoke briefly in Japanese, and I heard the men laugh. For all I knew, he had told them to kill us. I froze where I was, and forgetting that the bird was mute, I reached inside my shirt and grabbed its beak. This only made it thrash the more. I think it bit me. Quietly as I could I removed the bird and set it down on the ground. 'Go,' I whispered to it, and shoved it away. I

160

heard the soldiers taking off their packs, and after a while their heavy breathing as they slept.

"The bird wouldn't leave me—don't ask me why—so I sat with it in my lap and waited till morning, and all that night I could think of no plan.

"Just after dawn I heard the soldiers getting up and Sansoni organizing them, telling them what to look for. There was a heavy mist and I couldn't see them very well. I examined my chest where the bird had bit me and thought of the dodo's extinct germs working in my blood.

"Finally I stood up. The bird was in my arms. 'The search is over,' I shouted. 'I have it. It's mine.'

"A Japanese came out of the fog and smiled and called out to the others. I could hear the word go round the forest. They were about two hundred feet from me when Collins pushed through the vanguard. Though I had thought him dead, I was not surprised to see him. I was very detached about everything.

" 'You found it?' he yelled.

"I held it up.

" 'They'll take it. Run. Goon—get going.'

" 'They can't shoot. You said so yourself.'

" '*Run!*'

"The Japanese were still coming toward me. They were only twenty-five yards away now.

" '*They're going to take the bird!*' Collins screamed.

"They were fifty feet off.

" 'Kill it,' he yelled.

" 'What?'

" '*Kill* the damn thing. They mustn't have it. *Kill it!*"

" 'What good will that do?'

" 'That's an order, Sergeant.' Collins was pointing his pistol at me. 'Kill it or I'll kill you.'

" 'It bit me,' I said lazily.

" '*Kill* it.' The Japanese had stopped where they were. They were looking first at Collins, then at me. 'Kill it, Goddamn you. *Kill it!*'

" 'I have no gun.' The loudness of my voice surprised me.

"Sansoni began to plead with me. 'If you let it live we'll

161

treat you as a prisoner. My word. Geneva conventions. My word on that, Sergeant.'

" '*Kill it*,' Collins screamed. 'Kill it, or I *promise* I'll shoot you.' He reached into his pocket, pulled out something black and threw it toward me. He was very excited. 'Here,' he shouted. 'Pick up the knife. Wring its neck. Cut its throat.'

" 'Please, my dear Sergeant,' Sansoni said. 'We'll let you off. We'll allow you both to return to the garrison. All we want is the dodo.'

" 'I'm going to count to three, Sergeant,' Collins yelled. 'I'll shoot you. I swear it.'

"The knife had landed at my feet. 'One . . .' Collins shouted. '*Two* . . .'

"I bent down and picked up the knife. I turned it in my hand and examined it. I opened it.

" '*Good*,' Collins said. 'They mustn't get their hands on it. Remember what we're fighting for.'

" 'It's only a bird. Everybody. Hey, it's only a bird.'

" '*Kill it!*'

"I slit its throat. I heard them gasp. It was as if I'd pressed the blade to their own throats.

" 'Ah,' Collins sighed.

"I looked down. Its blood was all over me. The Japanese were weeping. Holding the bird against my breast, I started walking toward them. 'It's only a bird,' I said. 'Don't you see? It's just a bird.'

"Then the bird was in the air! They fell away from me. Collins was shrieking, they all were. The bird was in the air and the soldiers screamed. Some tried not to look at me, but they couldn't turn away their heads. The bird came down against my breast and then rose again—higher this time. And then, falling again, it rose a third time. The Japanese were keening with grief and ecstasy. I moved toward them and they hid from me.

" 'It's the miracle!" Collins screamed. 'Oh, my God, it's the miracle! I didn't want them to have it. I didn't want them to have their symbol. I never thought . . . Oh, Jesus, it's the miracle.'

"Now the bird fell. I reached out my arms and it

162

settled against my breast for the last time. I carried it to its nest and placed it inside the spongy ring. When I turned I saw that the Japanese had lined up on two sides, making a sort of aisle in the forest. I walked through them. Collins fell in beside me, crying. The soldiers threw down their weapons and I could hear them murmuring. *Rosichicho,* they were saying. Invincible—I was invincible. When we were a few hundred yards past, I heard a sudden burst of machine-gun fire. It was the garrison. They charged into the forest and killed them all—every last Japanese. They've been clearing them out on the other islands too; the battle's been raging for two days now. Casualties are enormous, on the British side as well. I, of course, am *rosichicho.*

"Oh, by now I think I've pieced together what's happened here. Why Collins and I were assigned to Mauritius. It was the equipment, wasn't it? It was a test of the equipment. Am I getting warm? You wanted to check its range, and you picked a place where not much was happening in the event these broadcasts were intercepted. They were *meant* to be meaningless. It was our presence on the plane from Lisbon that attracted the enemy. They sent men to check up on us. That's when they discovered the dodo and sent for the ornithologist. Then they sent out more men because they figured we knew about the bird too. Then we built up our forces to match theirs. But it was all *meant* to be meaningless. But that's very hard, you know? Meaning is everywhere, even in Mauritius.

"Collins is dead. Everyone is. 'Dead as a dodo.' We have that expression. I, of course, am *rosichicho.*

"Only don't bet on it. I tossed the bird. I flung him up myself. With my wrists. It's all in the wrists."

Part II

Hartford Daily Intelligencer
Tuesday, March 3, 1959

WGR	WSQ	WMH	WHCN	WLLD
630	770	900	1320	1600

12:00 Midnight

WGR   Witching Hours (Music & News)
WHCN   The Dick Gibson Show (Talk)
WLLD   The World Tmrw

Dick's guests that night were Dr. Jack Patterson, Associate Professor of English at Hartford Community College; Bernard Perk, a pharmacist, probably the ablest proponent of fluoridation in all New England; Pepper Steep of the Pepper Steep Charm School; and rounding out the panel, Mel Son, the Amherst disc jockey whose experiences with the powerful Democratic machine when he'd tried to run for state office had once earned him Special Guest status. They'd all been on the show before but only Mel had ever been the Special Guest, it being a principle with Dick to choose his panels from the community—panelists were, after all, something like jurors and, as such, surrogates for the audience—but to import his Special Guests from outside.

Tonight his Special Guest was the psychologist Edmond Behr-Bleibtreau. Behr-Bleibtreau did the flying saucer bit from the mass-hysteria angle but was also known for his advocacy of the psychic phenomena people, as well as for some of the new things. As Dick understood it from the little of Behr-Bleibtreau's book that he had read, the man's major emphasis was the old business of mind over matter, though Behr-Bleibtreau called mind "will." Dick had heard that he was a very forceful man, as formidable as any guest on late-night radio. It was also said that he sometimes used his knowledge of psychology in unusual, if unspecified, ways. Despite the expense, Dick considered himself lucky to get him. Special Guests were not paid, but some of them, though they probably collected again from the organizations they represented or from their publishers, insisted on "expenses." Behr-Bleibtreau had presented the station with a bill for his first-class air fare from Los Angeles, and even though the man had been with Long John Nebel on WOR in New York the previous night, WHCN had agreed to pay it. They were also picking up the tab for his Holiday Inn suite. Everything would come out of Dick's tiny budget for the show. For a month or so there'd probably be nothing left over for the loners, those characters who'd written no books and represented no organizations and who really needed to be helped out with expenses. When he'd told Behr-Bleibtreau this, the man had patted his arm to reassure him. "In that case," he said, "I shall have to give you a good show. Something very special."

Several others, guests of the guests, were in the studio. They had begun to gather about a half-hour before air time. Jack Patterson had left his wife, Rose, at home to listen to him on the radio and had a girl friend with him, one of his students probably, an Annette something. One reason he came on the program was that it gave him someplace to go when he was deceiving Rose. Bernard Perk had brought his son and daughter-in-law, in from Chicago on a visit. Pepper Steep came with her sister and Mel Son had brought Victor Ash, the man who had defeated him in the primary. After the election they had become good friends. Even Edmond Behr-Bleibtreau had brought guests, a man and a middle-aged woman in an enormously long fur coat which looked as if it might have been made up for someone a full foot taller than herself. Neither of Behr-Bleibtreau's guests had been introduced to Dick. They were all seated in a single row of theater seats along the wall opposite the control booth.

"Do you think anyone else will drop in?" Dick asked his panel. "I have to know so Jerry can phone in the order for our sandwiches."

Behr-Bleibtreau held up his hand. "I expect someone." He hesitated. "He may come and he may not."

Dick opened his microphone and told his engineer to order for fifteen people. Then he explained the ground rules to his guests and obtained mike levels from each of them. "Bernie Perk," he said, "you don't speak that softly. Let's hear your reaction to Jack Patterson here when Jack says that fluoridation not only doesn't prevent tooth decay but causes cancer of the jaw." Bernie Perk gave an exaggerated groan and the panel laughed, even Behr-Bleibtreau. "The most important thing," Dick said, "is that you don't all speak at once. I'll recognize you either by looking at you directly or by calling your name. These mikes compensate for the different power levels of your voices, so everything comes at the listener at equal strength. If you speak when someone else is talking, it just sounds like babble. Nothing's more frustrating for the listener."

The panel knew all this, but he went through it for his guests' guests, owing them insights. He was only sorry that the show was so much what it seemed. Those who came to the house of magic were entitled to secrets. Besides, he loved the people who saw him work. The capsule-like character of the studio, the heavy drapes hung down over solid, windowless walls, and the long voyage to dawn created in him a special sense of intimacy, as though what they were about to do together was just a little dangerous. Even more than the people who watched him work he loved the people he worked with. They were comrades. For him it was as if all place—*all* place—was ridiculous, a comedown, all studios makeshift, the material world itself existing only as obstacle, curiously unamiable, so that, remembered later, the night they worked together became some turned corner of the life. (A sense, up all night, of emergency, national crises kicked around the anchor desk.) There had been a thousand such comrades in the fourteen years since the war, the seven years he had been doing late-night talk shows. And all place *was* ridiculous, wayside, all towns tank, for him anyway. Though his voice had been heard everywhere by now, he had never been network (unless you counted the small, queer regional networks: the Billy Lee Network in Texas and the Southwest, Heartlands Broadcasting, the Mid-Atlantic Company, Gulfcoast Broadcasting System, the Northwest's Big Sky Company), never coast-to-coast.

"We'll be here five hours," he said. "It's a long time till five o'clock." He turned to Behr-Bleibtreau. "The world looks strange when you've been in a studio all night and go outside. If we all last, I'll take you to breakfast." Now he turned to his guests' guests. "As I say, it's a long time till five o'clock. If any of you *absolutely* has to sack out there's a cot in my office, and another in Jerry's. Some nights I wish *I* could go lie down." This wasn't true; there had never been a show which he hadn't wished would go on longer. Babble or not, for him the greatest moments

170

had been when, losing their tempers or caught up in their ideas, they all spoke at once; in that instant he would feel himself physically touched by their speech, centripetally held by their crosstalk. Nor was he ever nervous, save in some impersonal sense, as now, anxious for the chemistry to be correct, like someone hoping that the fish are biting. If it all went well, if Behr-Bleibtreau found the panel to his taste—not provincial, sufficiently challenging to bother with—something could happen. A truth, or something better than a truth. "I'm here merely to moderate," he said. "I myself am not controversial." He was, to use Madam Modred's term, "a control."

And wasn't *that* a night? WVW, Lockhaven, Pennsylvania. The night of the seance. The medium was the Reverend Abner Ruckensack. Shakespeare had come, the Bard of Avon. A lugubrious Shakespeare, plain-talking, curiously shy. He called Dick Mr. Gibson. It was down in the log. (He still couldn't bear to think of his logs, tapes of all his programs. Fourteen years, seven of them doing these late-night talk shows, almost five thousand tapes. His spoken history of some of the world. The expense enormous, to say nothing of the time that went into indexing them. All but a hundred or so burned to a crisp in the fire. Dick Gibson's burned logs.) He could still remember one part. It must have been about three in the morning. All of them tired, impatient, the Reverend Ruckensack producing dud after dud—farmers he'd known, children he'd baptized, a sinner, an enemy—and the panel sending them back, shade after shade, like failed auditioners, until *he* came, the Bard himself, the Divine Will:

DICK: You don't sound like Shakespeare.
SHAKESPEARE: I'm him, all right, Mr. Gibson.
DICK: You are, eh?
SHAKESPEARE: We're *white* men here, Mr. Gibson.
DICK: Well, if you're Shakespeare, how come you don't speak in blank verse? I always associated Shakespeare with blank verse.
SHAKESPEARE: We're *white* men here, Mr. Gibson.

171

That blank verse was just for the niggers. So's they wouldn't understand.

He still remembered it, and here and there other passages, but without the logs one day it would all be gone, as all conversation was always going, the word disintegrate, busted, and the air come in like a draft. Or all that remained would be the conclusions, with none of the wonderful linkings and marvelous asides. The wisdom forgotten and the madness gone, and only the silence for punctuation.

He could not depend upon his listeners; he had no notion of them. They were as faceless to him as he to them. (They didn't even have a voice.) His panels, his Special Guests were more real. As for his listeners, he guessed they were insomniacs, cabbies, enlisted men signed out on leave at midnight driving home on turnpikes, countermen in restaurants by highways, people in tollbooths. Or he saw them in bed—they lived in the dark—lumps under covers, profiles on pillows, their skulls beside the clock radio (the clock radio had done more to change programming than even TV) while the dialogue floated above their heads like balloon talk aloft in comic strips. Half asleep, they would not follow it too closely.

No, he knew little about his listeners. They were not even mysterious; they were there, but distant as the Sioux. He knew more about the passionate extremists who used his microphones in the groundless hope of stirring those sleepers, and winning over the keepers of the booths—the wild visionaries, opponents of fluoride, palmists, astrologers, the far right and far left and far center, the dianeticians, scientologists, beatniks, homosexuals from the Mattachine Society, the handwriting analysts, addicts, nudists, psychic phenomenologists, all those who believed in the Loch Ness Monster, the Abominable Snowman and the Communist Conspiracy; men beyond the beyond, black separatists who would take over Idaho and thrive by cornering the potato, pretenders to a half-dozen

172

thrones, Krebiozonists, people from MENSA, health-food people, eaters of weed and soups of bark, cholesterolists, poly-unsaturationalists, treasure hunters, a woman who believed she held a valid Spanish land grant to all of downtown San Francisco, the Cassandras warning of poison in the white bread and cola and barbecued potato chip, conservationists jittery about the disappearing forests and the diminishing water table (and one man who claimed that the tides were a strain on the moon), would-be reformers of a dozen industries and institutions and a woman so fastidious about the separation of church and state that she would take the vote away from nuns and clergymen, capital punishers, atheists, people who wanted the abortion laws changed and a man who thought *all* surgery was a sin and ought to carry the same sentence as any other assault with a knife, housewives spooked by lax Food and Drug regulations, Maoists, Esperantoists, American Nazis, neo-Jaegerists, Reichians, juvenile delinquents, crionics buffs, anti-vivisectionists, witches, wizards, chief rabbis of no less than three of the twelve lost tribes of Israel, and a fellow who claimed he died the same year Columbus discovered America.

DICK: Do you mean to sit there and tell me you've actually been to Saturn on a flying saucer? Come *on*, now, Mr. Beckendienst.

HERMAN BECKENDIENST: I have too. I have. The Martians chose me. They come down to my field while I was plowin' and taken me aboard. Then, whoosh, up we went to Saturn. I'd say it taken 'bout half an hour. We didn't land. I ain't claimin' we ever *landed*. Not on Saturn proper we didn't. But we set down on one of the rings. The blue one. Yes sir.

DICK: Well, why? Why did they choose *you*, Mr. Beckendienst?

HERMAN BECKENDIENST: Well, I don't *know* why.

DICK: Didn't you ask them?

HERMAN BECKENDIENST: No sir. They don't have our language.

DICK: Then how do you know they were from Mars?
HERMAN BECKENDIENST: Well, I seen their license
   plates.

And when Dick leaned over and hugged the farmer, the
man had been more startled by Dick's embrace than by
the approach of the Martian saucer itself. He could have
hugged all of them—all the zealots and crusaders and
saints to obsession, as well as the reasonable ones, the
juristic Bernie Perks. Ah, God, would there were an
auditorium to hold them all, to always be there with
them, to keep them forever talking.

He received the signal from his engineer. "A minute to
air time, people," he said. They all stopped chatting and
looked at him. A couple of the panelists coughed. Behr-
Bleibtreau smiled. Dick rubbed the skin along his throat,
and watched for Jerry—there was something vaguely athletic about the gesture, his engineer's arm up like an
official's with a gun above runners—to throw his finger at
him. "Thirty seconds," he said on his own. "All right, be
ready."

In his head he knew the exact instant that Jerry would
signal, and was already talking before the finger came
down the full arc of his engineer's arm.

DICK: Good midnight. I'm Dick Gibson. Till dawn us
   do part. Forgive the glibness, please. I've been in radio practically since it was invented, but I've never
   been comfortable about introductions. There's just
   no appropriate style. UNH UNH UNH, DON'T
   TOUCH THAT DIAL! You see? I don't know you,
   you don't know me. We're strangers. One of us has
   to make a beginning. Why don't I just give you the
   lineup? My colleagues and comrades tonight are
   Professor Jack Patterson, Pepper Steep of the Pepper Steep Charm School, Bernard Perk of the corner
   drugstore, and Mel Son of Amherst.
JACK: Mel, son of Amherst. (laughter)
MEL: Jack patter, son. (laughter)

174

DICK: Come on, you guys. I haven't introduced our Special Guest. Who is—

BERNIE: Boy, with jokes like that I'd give up.

DICK: . . . the noted psychologist, Edmond Behr-Bleibtreau. Dr. Behr-Bleibtreau is an author who has written extensively on the problem of Will—not as a philosopher but as someone pragmatically concerned with the problems of people.

JACK: That'd be like Will's will.

DICK: If my panel *will* restrain itself long enough for me to get through this introduction, we can find out about it from the guest himself. Oh, Dr. Behr-Bleibtreau, one of the things we do on this show is to invite the audience to send in telegrams to the station. We accept about half a dozen collect wires a night, so I have to ask those people who won't be paying for them to keep their messages within a ten-word limit. Later on we'll discuss their comments on the air.

Dick gave his listeners his cable code; then, displeased with his voice—he thought it too high-pitched tonight—and to calm down his panel, he talked some more about the program's format. He watched Behr-Bleibtreau for signs of irritation, but the man merely smiled and seemed to follow everything that was said with great attention. Sometimes a guest tried to make an alliance with Dick against the panel, but Behr-Bleibtreau seemed perfectly at ease, more so even than the people in the theater seats.

Still distrustful of the panel's mood, Dick made some further summary statements about Behr-Bleibtreau's work, for though it was true that he had not read Behr-Bleibtreau's books he had the public person's superficial grounding in all things; he could have gone on for fifteen minutes or so giving his creditable layman's presentation of the psychologist's position. He knew, however, that he was boring his listeners. (The thing about me, he thought even while still speaking, is that I have no humor. And that's because I like being where I am and doing what I

175

do. Why, then, am I so unhappy?) He knew he had to bring his speech to an end, but he saw Jack Patterson's lips pursing for a joke. (They were skittish tonight: he didn't know why.) Anything was better than this, however, and he addressed himself directly to Behr-Bleibtreau, making it seem at the last moment as if his remarks had all been part of a dialogue.

DICK: ... by which I take it you mean the mind. Every day in every way I get better and better. That sort of thing.

BEHR-BLEIBTREAU: Yes. But not so piecemeal. I would take the element of time out of it. We are too patient.

JACK PATTERSON: I'm surprised to hear you say that, Dr. Behr-Bleibtreau. As patient as you were during Dick's program notes. As positively benign as the guest of honor at a banquet.

BEHR-BLEIBTREAU: I'm not in favor of rudeness, Mr. Patterson.

JACK PATTERSON: I think I must call you on that, Dr. Behr-Bleibtreau. I don't wish to be stuffy, but I'm as much Ph.D. as you are, and if I'm going to address *you* as Doctor, I think I deserve the same courtesy.

BEHR-BLEIBTREAU: And shall our druggist friend here insist on being called Doc?

BERNIE PERK: Hey, wait a minute, I'm out of this.

JACK PATTERSON: That was meant for me, Bernie.

PEPPER STEEP: Oh good. Two Doctors and a Doc.

MEL SON: And a Dick.

Dick broke in to introduce a commercial. As Jerry put on the loop in the control booth Dick asked, "What's wrong with you people? Come on, Jack, stop being so damned snotty. You've been horsing around since the program went on the air. Be professional, for God's sake." He looked apologetically at Behr-Bleibtreau. (Guests had walked out. It was not unheard of.) "We're going on again now, and I'm going to try to draw you out,

Edmond, about some of your ideas. All right, everybody. Here we go."

DICK: I'd like to get down to something a bit more specific, sir.

BEHR-BLEIBTREAU: Yes.

DICK: What troubles me is the role of determinism in all this. You don't seem to leave any room for it.

BEHR-BLEIBTREAU: I prefer to use the word "determination." It's—

JACK PATTERSON: Oh, *please.*

DICK: Jack, let the man finish his sentence, will you? I don't know how this hostility built up, but I want to tell you I think you're sabotaging the program.

JACK PATTERSON: Do you want me to leave?

DICK: No, of course not. I just want you to calm down a little—that goes for all of. you—and give Dr. Behr-Bleibtreau a chance to explain himself.

JACK PATTERSON: Because all you have to do is say the word and I'll get the hell out of here.

BERNIE PERK: Come on, Jack. Dick isn't saying anything like that.

MEL SON: Of course not.

PEPPER STEEP: And they say women are temperamental.

JACK PATTERSON: *Don't give me any of that cant, you.*

PEPPER STEEP: Well, I beg your pardon, I'm sure.

JACK PATTERSON: Big charm school operator. Charming.

BERNIE PERK: Please, everybody.

JACK PATTERSON: Because *that's* how the hostility built up. Cant. Cant and crud. I think this is Jack Patterson's farewell appearance on these shows. Either you get the goofs who think all the world has to do is sit around listening to how they were carved out of wood by elves in the forest, or quick-buck artists like the Dr. Behr-Bleibtreau here who make their pile out of positive thinking or some other such claptrap. Nothing *real* happens. You've got the extremists on the one hand and the self-taught, gift-from-the-sea people on the other. I'm thirty-eight years old. I'm a

177

Ph.D. from Harvard. *Harvard!* And all I am is an Associate Professor at Hartford Community College. Oh, God.

DICK: Ladies and gentlemen—a commercial.

He got up and walked around the long table to where Jack Patterson was sitting, his forehead pressing against the microphone in front of him. "Jack, are you okay? Are you? Are you feeling all right?"

"I think the man's having a nervous breakdown," Pepper Steep said.

"Give him room."

"Is he all right? Should we call his wife?"

"Annette, was Jack unwell this evening?"

"Why are you all picking on him?"

"Oh boy, two of a kind."

Only Behr-Bleibtreau's people remained seated. The others had all come up to the table.

"I'll have to ask the guests in the audience to take their seats."

Sitting modestly in his place, Behr-Bleibtreau stared placidly at Jack's slumped figure.

"We're on again. We're on the air."

"What's going to happen about Jack?"

"Shh."

"Well, we can't just do nothing. Isn't it dangerous for him to be touching a live microphone like that?"

"Shh," Mel Son said, "be quiet."

DICK: Uh—Dr. Behr-Bleibtreau?

BEHR-BLEIBTREAU: Yes?

DICK: I was wondering . . .

BEHR-BLEIBTREAU: . . . if I could develop the point I was making about determination?

DICK: Yes.

BEHR-BLEIBTREAU: I think our friend Patterson here could do that even more effectively than I.

BERNIE PERK: Perhaps *I* might. I've been rather deeply involved with the fluoridation campaign here in New England. The average person doesn't realize it, but there's an awful lot of money spent by the anti-fluoridation people on this. Those of us who favor a program of caries prevention, and who have nothing like the funds of those who oppose it, sometimes wonder—

JACK PATTERSON: It's okay, Bernie. I can handle this.

MEL SON: Perhaps Dr. Behr-Bleibtreau—

JACK PATTERSON: No, Mel, really, I'm fine. I apologize to our audience and our guest as well as to the rest of you for flying off the handle like that. Why don't we put it down to a bad kipper? I only hope I haven't embarrassed Annette.

PEPPER STEEP: Uh oh.

DICK: I think we ought to—

BEHR-BLEIBTREAU: I would be interested in exploring what Dr. Patterson meant before when he spoke disparagingly about autodidacts.

JACK PATTERSON: Well, I'm afraid I have to stand by that, Dr. Behr-Bleibtreau. It takes all kinds, and we get all kinds.

BERNIE PERK: That's true.

PEPPER STEEP: Tell him about the memory expert.

JACK PATTERSON: I'll tell him about Laverne Luftig. Do you remember Laverne Luftig, Bernie? Were you on that show?

BERNIE PERK: No, I don't think so.

JACK PATTERSON: You do, Dick.

DICK: The child star.

JACK PATTERSON: That's the one.

BERNIE PERK: I couldn't have been on that night or I'd remember.

MEL SON: That's right, I played her record a few times.

BEHR-BLEIBTREAU: Go on, Jack.

JACK PATTERSON: Well, as Dick says, she was a child star— not an actress, a *singer*. And not a star, I guess, just someone who cut a few records. The thing about this little girl, though, was that she wrote her own material.

BERNIE PERK: Does she sing under another name?

179

JACK PATTERSON: No.

BERNIE PERK: I don't think I ever heard her.

JACK PATTERSON: Well, you mightn't have done. She was just starting out in the business, and to tell you the truth I don't really know what's happened to her.

MEL SON: "The Orphan's Song."

JACK PATTERSON: Yes. That's how she came to be on Dick's program.

DICK: I got a call from New Jersey, and was told that Laverne was going to be in Hartford. They played the record for me right on the phone, and when I learned the kid was only ten and a half years old I said she could come on the program.

JACK PATTERSON: Then Dick had some trouble or something—

DICK: There'd been a fire in my apartment.

JACK PATTERSON: —and couldn't meet her the day she came in. He asked if I'd go down to the train and pick her up. This was on a Thursday and I didn't have any classes. Anyway, I agreed to go down to the terminal. I'd been on the show often enough by then so I could fill her in on anything she needed to know, or what she might expect from the panel.

DICK: This program is unrehearsed, so I don't usually do that, but this was a little girl. I wasn't even sure she could stay up all night.

JACK PATTERSON: Have you been to the Hartford railroad station, Professor Behr-Bleibtreau?

BEHR-BLEIBTREAU: No, Jackie.

JACK PATTERSON: It's very difficult to find a place to park down there. There's a lot of reconstruction going on, everything's all broken up. I asked one of my students— Miss Tabisco; you know her, Annette—if she'd come down with me and sit in the car while I went into the station. If a cop asked her to move she could drive around the block till we came out.

BEHR-BLEIBTREAU: Someone in this studio is carrying a gun.

JACK PATTERSON: I don't know what I was expecting, possibly a Shirley Temple type—you know, all dimples and ante-bellum curls. Anyway, when the train from New York arrived I didn't see the little girl anywhere. I stood right on the platform when the passengers came out of the train, but I suppose I must have missed her. I had just decided to have her paged when this very strange-looking little girl came up and asked if I were Mr. Gibson.

I say she was strange-looking, but I don't really mean *that* exactly. It was summer, so of course she wore no coat. One could see that she was . . . well, that she was a child. Still, her face, all beauty and bone and intelligence, was all that it would ever be. The face of a woman, you see, with less baby fat on it than Annette's. Most kids in show business—particularly if their acts are adult, if they're singers, say, or they play the drums—dress like children, and the reason they look so awful is that their clothes are costumes. I mean, they're not dressed like children so much as dressed *up* as children. Or they go the other way. You've seen the kid tap dancers with their top hats and canes. This little girl was different, though. I don't recall what she was wearing, but there wasn't any . . . well, there wasn't any *starch* in it. I didn't see petticoats. When she went up the stairs I didn't see underwear.

I suppose another reason I may not have noticed her, was that instinctively I had been looking for her mother, some stage-aunt or stage grown-up, but she'd come alone.

"No, honey," I told her, "Mr. Gibson couldn't come, and he sent me to look after you. I'm Professor Patterson." I asked if she'd brought luggage, and she told me that all she had was the overnight bag she was carrying. When I reached out to take it she said she could manage.

We went to the car. Which was gone. I figured a cop had made Miss Tabisco drive it around the block, and I stood in the street so she'd be sure to see me when she came past. We waited about seven minutes, and I found myself explaining about the parking arrangements—as one would to an adult, you see. I apologized for the snag, but though she didn't say anything and was very polite, I sensed she was annoyed. Finally Miss Tabisco arrived on foot to tell us that the car had been towed away. She'd tried to explain I'd only be in the station a few minutes. "Trains are late," the tow man said; the space was needed for the mail trucks. She said she'd drive around the block, but the fellow told her he'd already been called out by the cops. It's a racket. She could see he meant business, that if she stayed with the car she'd just be towed off in it. The man gave her a card where the car could be picked up.

"Well, this *is* a damn nuisance," I said. "I'm sorry, sweetheart," I told the girl.

BEHR-BLEIBTREAU: Which girl? Miss Tabisco? Laverne?

JACK PATTERSON: Oh, I'm sorry. *Laverne*. Miss Tabisco gave me the card and I saw that the garage was all the way across town. When I mentioned this, Laverne looked at her watch. "Listen," she said, "I feel pretty grubby after that train ride. I think I'll just get into a cab and go to my hotel."

"Well, I can't just let you go off by yourself like this," I said.

"Look, really," she said, "don't bother. You'd better go and reclaim your car. They charge for storage after the first hour. I'll manage. Perhaps I'll see you afterward. I see the taxi stand."

"At least let us drop you," I said. "I need a cab myself."

"Very well," she said.

I wanted to go into the hotel with her but she assured me it wasn't necessary. "Goodbye, Miss Tabisco, Professor."

"So long honey," Miss Tabisco said.

DICK: I hadn't heard any of this.

JACK PATTERSON: It took longer than I thought to get

my car, and Miss Tabisco had an exam that afternoon and had to leave. Incidentally, they *do* charge
for storage. Well, anyway, it was almost five o'clock
before I got the car business straightened out, and
after the kind of day I'd had I was really tired. The
idea of going home and eating and having to come
back downtown for the program . . . Well, suddenly I
thought of Laverne Luftig registered in her room in
her hotel and I was envious. I mean, it had all gone
so smoothly for her and so badly for me. *I* was the
one who'd been inconvenienced; it was as if *I* was
the stranger in town.

I can't explain this part very well, but the fact that
I knew someone who was registered in a hotel downtown made me very nervous, very edgy. Do you
understand?

PEPPER STEEP: Sure I understand. This is disgusting.

JACK PATTERSON: No, you don't. I'm talking about
hotels. You sign the register, but you're anonymous.
This isn't very clear, but nothing is ever *yours* so
much as the room you rent. God, the assumptions a
hotel makes about you! All the *towels* they give you.
I mean, you'd have to take eight baths a day to use
them up. The clean sheets and the Gideon Bible and
the whisky mode. The Western Union blanks! As if
all one had to do all day was fire off telegrams to
people. *Oh, the civilization!* Everyone there—do
you realize this?—everyone there will be dining *out*
that night! And the bed like a lesson in function—

BERNIE PERK: (*softly*) Jack—

JACK PATTERSON: No, Bernie, it isn't what you think.
I *registered* in the hotel. I asked the desk clerk
where Laverne Luftig was, and I took a room on the
floor beneath hers. Later I called her up. "Hello,
honey," I said. "It's Uncle Jack, sweetheart. How
are you?"

"You got me out of the shower," she said. "I
thought you were Ben Meadows."

BEHR-BLEIBTREAU: Ben Meadows?"

183

MEL SON: He's a d.j. here in Hartford. The kid was probably after him to play her record.

JACK PATTERSON: I just called to find out if you're all settled, Laverne. I'm sorry about the car."

"It wasn't your fault. Did you have much trouble?"

"No."

"How's Miss Tabisco?"

"She had an exam. She had to leave." I had just come from the shower myself and was lying in my shorts on top of the bedspread. The air blowing through the air conditioning had a lemony scent. Laverne's voice on the telephone was lower than Annette's. "We never did get a chance to speak about the show tonight," I told her. "I thought we ought to do that."

"Where are you now?"

"Well, I'm still downtown."

"Can you come to my room for a drink? Are you near the hotel?"

"Close by."

MEL SON: Hard on.

JACK PATTERSON: Use their underground garage," she said.

"I will, Laverne."

"Give me thirty minutes," she said, and hung up.

I hate waiting. I have the impatience of a better man. The hour before an appointment is a torment for me. I have no skill for slowing down the shave or drawing out the combing of my hair. At the Modern Language Association conventions the same. I go down to the lobby for newspapers I don't have the patience to read, or into bars and finish my drink as soon as it's brought. I never learned to nurse a drink or brood over the salted peanuts. I gulp my food and burn my cigarettes as in a high wind. I get no value from these ceremonies.

After I dressed I *still* had twenty minutes. I sat for two and went up early. Laverne came to the door in towels.

"There's scotch on the desk," she said, and disappeared back into the bathroom. "Pour yourself a drink. I'm sorry, but there isn't any ice."

When she came out, in exactly the thirty minutes she had asked for, she was wearing a sort of shift, very stylish. Her hands were in her hair, fixing it, and there were hairpins in her mouth. "Meadows called just after you did," she said. "He said he didn't have the record, so I sent one over by messenger in a cab. What time is it?"

"Just past seven."

"He'll play it in the segment after the 7:30 news. We'll listen to it here."

DICK: This story, Jack, is it—?

JACK PATTERSON: Oh, yes. Don't worry. It's okay.

I told Laverne pretty much what she might expect on the show that night, and we ordered dinner from room service. She just wanted to go down to the coffee shop and grab a bite; it was for me. *I* wanted to eat off the cart with the big wheels and the white-on-white linen thick as blanket and spoon my fruit from the glass dish in the packed ice. *I* wanted napkin under my chin and the high luxury of sitting in socks and drinking scotch out of a water tumbler.

Laverne put the radio on, turned down low so we could talk while waiting for Meadows to play her song.

BEHR-BLEIBTREAU: What did you talk about, Jackie-bunch?

JACK PATTERSON: Well, nothing, Doctor. We just talked.

BEHR-BLEIBTREAU: Just talked.

JACK PATTERSON: Well, I guess I told her about my job, Professor Behr-Bleibtreau.

BEHR-BLEIBTREAU: You were boasting?

JACK PATTERSON: Well, no, I wouldn't say I was boasting.

BEHR-BLEIBTREAU: Was it the way you talk to Annette, to Miss Tabisco?

JACK PATTERSON: Yes, I guess. In a way. Yes.

185

BEHR-BLEIBTREAU: You were boasting to a ten-year-old girl?

JACK PATTERSON: Yes, sir.

BEHR-BLEIBTREAU: Bragging about Harvard?

JACK PATTERSON: Yes, sir.

BEHR-BLEIBTREAU: Go on.

JACK PATTERSON: Suddenly she hushed me. "Shh," she said, "the news is finished. He'll play it after this commercial." She was very excited, on the edge of her chair, leaning forward, one hand above the table and making rapid motions as if bouncing a ball—you know, the way policemen hold back one line of traffic while signaling the other line to go through—and talking softly to the radio. "Come on, Meadows. Say something nice. Put it on the charts here in Hartford. Get in how I'm only ten years old."

But Meadows only gave the title and her name.

"The fool's never *heard* it," she said. "He's listening to it for the first time."

Her voice was good, stronger even than her speaking voice.

"You sing very beautifully, Laverne."

"Be quiet. I want to hear this passage. The trumpet cuts into the words. I knew I should have made him use the mute."

We listened to see if Meadows would make any comment after the song was finished, but all he did was give the title again.

Laverne turned off the radio. "The d.j.'s aren't playing it in the East," she said. "I think we're in trouble."

"It's a fine tune, Laverne. Did you do the words *and* the music?"

"What? Oh. Yeah."

"Which do you write first, dear, the lyric or the melody?"

"The lyric, the melody. It doesn't make any difference."

"You certainly are an ambitious little girl. I don't think I ever met anyone like you."

"What's wrong with ambition?"

"Nothing, dear.

"Do they give concerts at your school, Professor? Do they ever bring in singers from the outside?"

"Well, they do, Laverne, but I'm afraid I have no influence with the Concert Committee."

"What did you think of the song?"

"I enjoyed it very much."

"Do you think it will be a hit?"

"A scholar doesn't really have much knowledge about these things. Is that very important, Laverne?"

"Well, they don't give out gold records for duds, kiddo."

"Is that what you want out of life, Laverne? A gold record?"

BEHR-BLEIBTREAU: You talked about life with a ten-year-old? *Life?*

JACK PATTERSON: Yes, sir.

BEHR-BLEIBTREAU: Go on.

JACK PATTERSON: "Of course I want a gold record," Laverne said. "That's one of the things I want. Most of the others will have to wait. They don't write leading roles for ten-year-old girls. What can a person like myself expect on Broadway? One of the brats in *Sound of* Music? '*Do* a deer, a female deer, *re* a gleam of golden sun.' "

"Why are you in such a hurry, Laverne?"

" 'Cause I'm dying of cancer, kiddo. I've got twenty-seven minutes to live."

"Laverne!"

"Pour yourself another scotch, Professor."

"Well, thank you very much, Laverne, I think I will. I just wish there were some ice."

"Take it out of my root beer."

"Well, that's very sweet of you, Laverne, but if I do your root beer will be warm."

"Yeah, well, there's a broken heart for every light on Broadway."

"I think I'm getting a little tipsy, Laverne dear."

"The schmuck didn't even tell them I'm ten years old."

"Do you have any brothers and sisters?"

"He didn't even announce the *label* I'm with."

"What grade are you in?"

"The Hartford market is one of the biggest in New England. I think I'm a dead duck. What are *you* giggling about?"

"This is the way I talk to the baby sitter."

"You're married, are you?"

"Yes."

"Who's Miss Tabisco, your chauffeur?"

"Miss Tabisco is one of my pupils. She's one of the scholars here at HCC."

Laverne shrugged. "Listen, I've got to make some phone calls," she said. "Just hand me that little address book, would you, the one on the desk." I gave her her book. It was opened to her page on Hartford. In it she had written down the names and phone numbers of about two dozen people here—the editors of the high-school and junior-high-school newspapers, chairmen of dance committees, even the entertainment editors on the *Courant* and the *Intelligencer*. I lay back on her bed and listened to her on the phone. "Hi," she'd say, "this is Laverne Luftig, the ten-year-old singer. I sent you a letter about two weeks ago, and I'm calling to remind you about my press conference tomorrow morning. Don't forget now, I'm looking forward to meeting you personally and presenting you with an autographed copy of my new recording." Then when she finished with the list, she called the manager of the hotel to double-check the arrangements for the hospitality suite for the press conference. She was wonderful.

"What do your parents think about your career?" I asked her. Then it suddenly occurred to me that her song might be autobiographical. "Oh, I'm sorry," I said, "are your parents living, Laverne?"

"Yeah," she said, "but my manager died. Listen, it was sweet of you to pick me up and fill me in about tonight, but don't you think you ought to be getting back? I mean, won't Miss Tabisco and your wife be wondering what's happened to you?"

"Shall I tell you a little secret, Laverne?"

"What's that?"

"I've checked into the hotel. My room is just below yours."

It was time for station identification and a commercial. During the break Bernie Perk told Jack Patterson that he thought he'd better not go on with his story, but Jack didn't seem even to hear him. He had stopped obediently for the commercial break and now seemed as remote as when he had slumped in his chair earlier. Then, two seconds before being given their cue, Behr-Bleibtreau said again that someone in the studio was carrying a gun.

DICK: What was that? What did you just say?

JACK PATTERSON: "Look, Professor—" Laverne said.

"Don't send me away, Laverne. I just want to look at you. Make some more calls. I like to watch your face when you're on the phone."

DICK: Professor Behr-Bleibtreau, what was that you said?

BEHR-BLEIBTREAU: A ten-year-old girl? A ten-year-old girl's face?

Is that what you're telling us?

JACK PATTERSON: Yes, sir.

BEHR BLEIBTREAU: Go on.

JACK PATTERSON: "Yeah, well, it's time for my nap."

"Don't give me that, Laverne."

"I'm ten years old, for God's sake."

"Juliet was thirteen."

'I may be hip but I'm just a kid."

"Dante fell in love with Beatrice when she was only eleven."

"Just because I'm in show business, don't think I'm loose."

"Lord Byron loved Haidée when she was barely twelve."

189

"I'm *ten*."

"You're ten and a *half*."

"You're mussing my hair."

"Helen of Troy was nine. So was Héloïse when Abelard fell for her. Psyche was six, Laverne. And what about Little Red Riding Hood? When you come right down to it, how old could Eve have been—a day, two days?"

"My dress, you're mussing me. My dress is all the way up."

PEPPER STEEP: This is incredible. You—you—

JACK PATTERSON: All I did was *kiss* her, I *tell* you. It was her face. This wasn't adultery. I swear, Annette. I *swear*. Miss Tabisco. It was her *face*. I mean, she wasn't even well developed. Where was the sex? She had no bust, no hips. I never even *looked* at her legs. All I did was kiss her. The bones and intelligence and beauty. My tongue like a red ribbon in her mouth.

PEPPER STEEP: *Disgusting!*

MEL SON: Where were your hands?

JACK PATTERSON: In her hair, in her ears. Vaulting her teeth. In her syrups and salivas.

BERNIE PERK: Oh, Jack.

PEPPER STEEP: What did she say after all this?

JACK PATTERSON: That I couldn't come to her press conference.

PEPPER STEEP: Now I've heard everything.

MEL SON: I think so.

BERNIE PERK: Jack, you shouldn't have told that story on yourself. Why did you tell such a story?

DICK: I would have stopped him, but he said it would be all right.

PEPPER STEEP: The man's a slime.

BERNIE PERK: What's the matter with you, Pepper? It was a joke.

Ladies and gentlemen, I know Professor Patterson since he first moved into the Hartford area, and believe me he is not the type of person he describes in this story.

PEPPER STEEP: I wish he'd told Professor Behr-Bleib-treau about the memory expert.

BERNIE PERK: Is he all right? Why's he smiling like that?

MEL SON: What's *she* doing?

BERNIE PERK: That's right, Annette. There, that should make him feel better. His color's coming back. Good. I think he'll be okay.

DICK: You can sit there beside him, Annette.

BEHR-BLEIBTREAU: The memory expert?

PEPPER STEEP: Maybe Jack wasn't on that panel. Were you, Jack? Was he, Dick?

DICK: I don't know, I don't recall . . . Jack—do you want Annette to take you home?

BERNIE PERK: *Mrs. Patterson, it was all a joke. Your husband is a very good man. I have been with him when he has fought the anti-fluoridation people to a standstill with the force of his powerful logic. I don't know why he would tell such a joke on himself. There is absolutely nothing to worry about. He's resting quietly.*

PEPPER STEEP: Were *you* on the panel with the memory expert, Mel?

MEL SON: I don't—ha ha—I don't remember.

BEHR-BLEIBTREAU: It's loaded.

PEPPER STEEP: He was on the show because of me. I mean, Dick was just doing him a favor. He needed the exposure at the time.

You have to understand something about my school, Professor. We're not a modeling agency— that is, not exactly. In your large cities where a real advertising industry exists—New York, of course, Chicago, L.A., a few others—there are schools which specialize in training girls to be models. A lot of these places are just phoney, you understand, but some of them are quite good. I myself am a graduate of one of the better agency schools in San Francisco and had a pretty good career as a model in New York during the war.

Anyway, when age, ahem, withered and custom

191

staled my infinite variety, when I entered my thirties, that is—I'm thirty-eight now—

MEL SON: A *perfect* thirty-eight—

PEPPER STEEP: Thank you, love—and saw that the demand for Miss Steep's services was falling off rather too dramatically, I reverted to type, for I'm *not* a perfect thirty-eight, and I do not, whatever my charms of face and figure, exude riches, which is what's called for today—I mean that 5th Avenue look that speaks of a four-year-old boy in the Central Park sunshine with his nanny, I mean that Biarritz aura. It is nature's way. At any rate at thirty-one and a half I reverted to type, which in my case is Big Boned Northern California Rain Forest, and I knew that if I were to keep body and soul together I would have to leave New York. Well! What could a thirty-one-and-a-half-year-old gal do who all her working life had done nothing but watch the birdy? The birdy had flown. To start up a modeling agency or a modeling school in New York or any of those other places I mentioned and hope to make a go of it was simply out of the question. To be myself on the staff of such a school was inside the question but out of the answer. I'd earned too much big money in New York to take that kind of cut. But I had saved some of this money, and I thought I might start up an agency school in some smaller city. She's an honest wench, however. She knew the market, knew the teensy-weensy demand for the graduates of such schools in such places. She would not have been giving full dollar value. The solution was the Charm School. A charm school in a town like Hartford has *some* tie-in with advertising. The big stores will use its girls for their Christmas brochures and ads. The developer may put one of its blondes up on water skis for the Hidden Lake Estates billboard. (Forgive me my style as you did Dick's. Probably as I go on I will work myself out of it. It's just the way those of us who have been around, and are not perhaps too intelligent, talk.) But mostly the function of the

192

Charm School is to teach charm, i.e. (*very rapidly*), "(1) a power of pleasing or attracting, as through personality or beauty; (2) a trait or feature imparting this power; (3) attractiveness—"

BEHR-BLEIBTREAU: "(4) a trinket to be worn on a chain bracelet, etc; (5) something worn for its supposed magical effect; amulet; (6) any action supposed to have magical power; (7) the chanting or recitation of a magic verse or formula."

PEPPER STEEP: Yes. "—*vt* (8) to delight or please greatly by beauty, attractiveness, etc.; enchant."

BEHR-BLEIBTREAU: *"(9) to act upon someone or something with or as with a compelling or magical force!"*

PEPPER STEEP: Yes. I don't do that.

BEHR-BLEIBTREAU: Go on, please.

PEPPER STEEP: We aren't a college, or even a finishing school. We're not accredited. Our girls aren't wealthy, they don't come out or go back into what is called polite society. You might be amused if you saw some of the things we do, there are books in our school, for instance, but we balance them on our heads. You'd be amused, but you'd need some charm yourself if you laughed. We render a service, you see. To the clumsy we do, the shy, the unconfident, to the ungraceful and ungainly and maladroit, to the bunglers and clutzes, the tongue-tied of body and spirit. Oh, we get them—all the wallflowers and fatties, all the unpopular, cripples to acne and dandruff. And I'm not just talking about teen-agers. There are housewives too. I mean the timid, I mean the terrified. There are women—a lot of them mothers—whose husbands have never seen them naked, who undress in closets and bathe only when they're alone in the house—with the bathroom door locked and the radio off. They don't go to doctors and they can't purchase sanitary napkins in a drugstore, or bring themselves to buy a roll of toilet paper. I know one too shy to try on a dress in the curtained booth at the back of the department store, and another who won't stand in front of a three-way mirror. Oh, the terror in Hartford! You just don't know.

We have a winding staircase in my studio. Especially constructed; it cost me two thousand dollars. They come down the staircase with a book on their head. Making their entrances. At the level of the eighth stair they must begin to speak. "How do you do, Mrs. Powers? I'm *so* pleased you could come. Uncle Jim will be down in a moment. He asked me to take your coat and to see if there's anything you'd like." And they have to finish just as their foot touches the last tread. "Oh! Mr. Strong. I didn't know you'd been admitted. Clotilda didn't tell me. Would you like a cucumber sandwich in the library?" "Bless me, it's Roger Thunder. How *are* you, Roger? Back from Persia already? How did you leave the Shah?" Don't laugh—it's true. The girls invent the speeches. And the names—I don't make those up. They always use names like Powers and Strong and Thunder. They're afraid, you see, and invest all other humans—even those of the mind: there's no one at the bottom of the staircase—with strengths and fiercenesses.

"Hello, Mr. Lamb. Leave your umbrella outside, please. You're dripping water on the rug." Only the advanced ones say things like that.

MEL SON: What about this memory expert?

BEHR-BLEIBTREAU: She's coming to that.

PEPPER STEEP: I'm coming to that.

We have toy telephones. They talk to tradesmen, to people who've invited them to parties. Or they call up the most distinguished people in Hartford and invite *them* to parties. They speak to the accounts department of stores to straighten out incorrect billings. Or I give assignments. I tell a woman that her lover is on the line but that her husband is standing in the room. Or that she must speak to the doctor in the middle of the night. "Yes, Doctor. Thank God your answering service was able to reach you. My breasts feel funny. My nipples have turned the color of rootbeer. I've a pimple suppurating in my behind. My vagina is steaming."

We teach them diets and care of the skin, grooming of the hair they learn, what cosmetics to use, the juice of which fruits for complexion. Clothes and color scheme and scents and polite conversation and how to bend to pick up a fallen glove and get in and out of cars.

And we offer instruction in courage and indifference. I take them with me to restaurants and have them return their steak or their soup while I sit by silently. Or we'll go to waiting rooms in lawyers' offices and when no one is looking they'll take a tin of condoms from their purse and ask aloud, "Excuse me, who dropped this?" We—

MEL SON: Dick, she's got to be one of your sponsors. This is the longest plug I've ever heard.

BEHR-BLEIBTREAU: Be quiet.

MEL SON: I . . . I . . .

BEHR-BLEIBTREAU: Go on, Miss Steep. I want to hear about the memory expert now.

PEPPER STEEP: The memory expert. Yes. Arnold. He wrote me a letter. He wanted to enroll in the Charm School. I had been thinking for some time of admitting boys. They do in the dancing classes. Isn't all the terror sexual, anyway? I agreed to see him and we set up an appointment for the following week. He came on a bus from Springfield. As soon as I saw him I knew it couldn't work. I had expected a young man, a teen-ager, but he was older than me, in his early forties.

"Won't the charm schools in Springfield have you?" I asked. "There's Miss Doris's, and a branch of Lovely Young Thing."

"I never looked into them."

"Let's be frank with each other, shall we, Mr. —what is it?—Menchman?"

"Ma'am?"

"Are you straight? Or are you looking for some kind of . . . well—*thrill?*"

195

"Oh, no, ma'am."

"Well, then?"

"I saw your presentation on television."

Sometimes I'm asked to bring over some of the younger girls to one of the local stations. They act out social situations, do tea parties, that sort of thing. You remember this, Mel; you were on one of those shows.

MEL SON: I—I—

PEPPER STEEP: "You saw my presentation on television. Yes?"

"They were so poised. They were just children, but they were so *poised.*"

"Well, that's very nice. Thank you, but I don't—"

"Mignonne Gumbs, 13, Sheila Smith, 12, Pamela Fairfife, 14—I never saw composure like that in such young children. When Pamela Fairfife spilled tea on Mignonne Gumbs—that wasn't planned, was it?"

"No. The tea was too hot. She couldn't hold the handle."

"I thought not. It looked too real. The way Mignonne Gumbs reassured her—telling her that the fabric was stain-resistant, and that she needn't worry about having scalded her because the tea had landed on old scar tissue. She made up that part about the scar tissue, didn't she?"

"Yes."

"Ah."

"Miss Gumbs had a lot of confidence by the time she graduated."

"I could *see* that."

"Those three particular students—that program was more than a year ago. How do you remember their names?"

"Oh, well, I remember."

"I see," I told him. "I really don't think there'd be much for you in our school. You don't want to learn to pour tea or come down steps."

"From behind curtains."

"I beg your pardon?"

"From behind curtains ... onto a stage. Down into the audience. I—um ... in front of people."

"I'm sorry," I said, "I don't understand."

"I'm clumsy, Miss Steep. Your secretary, Miss Ganchi, let me into your office before you arrived or you would have seen. I tripped. I can't even walk into a room. It's as hard for me to cross a threshold as it might be for someone else to step from one car to another in a moving train. I don't know how to stand, what to do with my hands—anything. People laugh."

"I'm sorry. Your presence would be disruptive in our classes. You'd embarrass the girls."

"They were wonderful."

"Yes, well—"

"If it's a question of money ..."

"It's not."

"I need the training."

"I'm sorry."

"I'm—I'm a memory expert. I'm in show business. Or rather, I would be if I weren't so clumsy. Listen, my act is the greatest in the world. I know that sounds very bold, but it's true. I ... I'm a freak, you see."

"Please, Mr. Menchman."

"No, it's so. I am. I mean, there's no trick to what I do. I *do* it. It's not even *talent*. I have an eidetic imagination."

"An eidetic—?"

"It's called that. There are only about a hundred of us in the whole world. Maybe three—I'm one— are true eidetics."

"I don't follow you."

"It's very simple. You've heard of a photographic mind?"

"Yes, of course."

"There is such a thing. Nobody understands how it works, really, but it's visual. Somehow, whatever I look at registers on the retina and on the mind simultaneously. In other people the mind receives the impression a zillionth of a fraction of a moment late, but with eidetic there's no lag. At least that's what the theory is now. Anyway, when an eidetic tries to recall something he sees this picture. All he has to do is look at it. He can even close his eyes—as a matter of fact, he *has* to close his eyes or it would be like a double exposure—and the picture is right there on the eyelids."

"Fascinating."

"Oh, I'm a freak is all."

"Do you remember things forever?"

"No. The pictures fade after a time. Just as a photographic proof will. They even turn that same murky purple. But it lasts for a couple of years at least. Even then I don't forget everything; I just remember the way normal people do."

"Well, I must say . . . Still, I don't see how I'm the person to help you."

"Oh, you *are,* Miss Steep. I'll never forget how grand those children were. Sheila Smith lived next door to me before her family moved to Hartford. She was the sloppiest little girl I'd ever seen. There wasn't a time when her nose wasn't running. When I saw her on television . . . she's so *changed.* Change *me,* Miss Steep. Teach me my body. I know I could be great—my *act*—but my body . . . People laugh. They don't even pay attention to the feats I do; they think I'm a comic. You have to be in control of your body to be in the show business."

"All I could teach you is to move like a woman. They'd still laugh."

"No. You'd teach me grace."

"It's impossible, Mr. Menchman. The girls would be too embarrassed."

"Then take me as a special student. I have money. Charge what you want . . . Maybe you don't believe me. Is that it? *This is what is behind me in this room:* To the right of the door as one enters—eidetics see from right to left, thus giving substance to the speculation that the idiosyncrasy is passed on through a semitic gene; my grandfather on my father's side was Jewish—are three blue bookshelves about five feet wide and held on the wall by twelve brackets, four brackets to a shelf, with three screws in each bracket. One bracket, the second from the right on the highest shelf, has Phillips head screws. On the top shelf are seventeen books, on the middle twelve, on the bottom fourteen. If you pick a shelf I will give you the titles, authors, publishers and colors of the spines or book jackets."

"This isn't necessary."

"You think it's a trick. I work with no assistant. Your trickster has an assistant."

"I don't think it's a trick. It simply isn't necessary."

"It *is* necessary. I want you to know what I can do. Before you turn me down, you must see."

"Please, Mr. Menchman. I believe you ... Very well, what's the fourth book from the left on the bottom shelf?"

"*Titles and Forms of Address. A Guide to Their Correct Use.* Armiger. A. and C. Black. Buff ... Am I correct, madam?"

"Oh, I suppose so. I can't see from here. Anyway, that isn't the point."

"The fifth book—""*Really,* Mr. Menchman—"

"The *fifth* book is *Manners and Conduct* by the Deans of Girls in Chicago High Schools. Allyn and Bacon. Mauve. The sixth—"

"You could have memorized all that before I came in. Turn around in your chair. Go on. Swivel about and face the bookshelf, please."

"Are you—?"

"Just do it ... Watch out!"

"What happened? What was that?"

"You knocked over an ashtray. Never mind, it didn't break. Now keep your back to me."

"Is this a test?"

"There are file cabinets behind my chair—"

"Two stacks, each containing four drawers. Am I correct, madam?"

"On the front of each drawer there's a small frame with a manila card in it. What do the cards say?"

"A-Do. Dr-Hes. Hest-Q. R-Shipman. Shir-V. W-X-Y-Z. Two drawers have no cards. Do I have it right, madam?"

Well, I won't go on about it. There are hundreds of things in even the emptiest of rooms. Looking only once, only casually, Arnold saw and registered them all. Every detail made its impression on him. At first only mildly interested but gradually fascinated, I led him about the Charm School—it was after hours by now—took him into rooms, turned on the lights and let him look briefly. Then he gave me back all of it. All of it. The thousand things, the million details. And it was just as if I were blind and he was giving me sight. Naming everything, hearing my inventory called off—the precise placement of the furniture, bare spots in the rugs, the patterns in the drapes, the number of holes in the speakers of the toy telephones—I had it all for the first time. I hadn't know how much there *was* before.

By the time we'd finished our tour I had decided to help him. I could see he'd been telling the truth, both as to his gifts and his drawbacks. He was immensely clumsy—a stumbler, a toe stubber, a lumbering blunderer—and immensely excited. His excitement fed his clumsiness. Those pathetic flourishes, his corny "Am I correct, madam?" learned from some old fraud in a tent show. But his *mind!* His mind was a gallery of the world, of everything he had ever seen. Stuffed to bursting it was with all the odd-lots of memory, a warehouse of surfaces. No wonder he couldn't move! So I agreed to work with him, though for the sake of the girls it had to be after hours.

We used my studio, and after great effort I got him first to the point where he could stand in place without falling, then to where he didn't knock telephones from desk tops when he sat down, and at last to move across a room without tripping. I didn't dare try him on the stairway, of course, but after two or three weeks, he became relatively adroit in the simple conquest of ordinary human space. We still had no idea how he would behave on a stage— the equipment in my studio was limited—so neither of us really knew whether he was making any practical progress. We devised a curtain, however—that is *I* did; Arnold was a long way off from doing any work with his hands—the area in front of it became Arnold's "stage."

Arnold would stand behind the makeshift curtain and I would introduce him, adopting what I took to be the styles of the various MC's he might encounter. Thus a late night television show: "This next guest is one who'll give pause to any of us who've ever had to take out our Social Security card to look at before writing down the number. He's a memory expert who calls himself an eidetic—a man with a photographic mind. Let's bring him out and have him take some pictures. Ladies and gentlemen—Arnold Menchman." Or: "Mr. Sy Tobin and the management of the Sands Hotel present . . . *'The Great Arnold'!*"

Sometimes Arnold would just be standing there, as in a tableau, when I drew the curtain. Other times he would run out from between the curtains in that snappy locomotive jog entertainers do, their heads down, their hands balled into fists at the level of their chests, the orchestra playing "Fine and Dandy."

After a while we saw the limitations of our makeshift stage. Though Arnold could have gone on right then if there had been an audience. He knew every square inch of that room, at home as a blind man in his square yards of familiar darkness. We had to try him in other environments, for place—mere place— was our problem. Arnold wasn't stupid. Unlike other "mentalists" he enjoyed what he knew; the things he saw when he closed his eyes were full of wonder for him. And he was selective: he didn't get any pleasure out of such stunts as memorizing whole Sears and Roebuck catalogs.

DICK: Does he listen to the radio?

PEPPER STEEP: What? Wait. Or pages from telephone directories, or timetables. Though he knew these too. Knew the Yellow Pages, knew the City and Town Indexes on the back of the Shell Oil Company roadmaps for every state. But encyclopedias, tracts on gardening, rock formations—these were his forte. The positions—listen—he knew the positions of the stars! But it is one thing to know a principle, another to apply it. For instance, Arnold *knew* dexterity— whole books of the dance he knew; he could have given you by heart the choreography of a hundred ballets—but he wasn't dexterous. So place was our problem, the threat of place.

Then I thought of the local television station. After all, this was how Arnold first knew about me, wasn't it? As I told you, I'd done some things for them with my girls. Whenever there was a telethon I volunteered my students to handle the phones. For favors rendered I presumed to ask the station manager to let Arnold and me—after hours, of course: everything we did that year (*giggling*) was after hours, everything we did required keys—use his station.

In the empty studio I would introduce Arnold. I wanted him to learn to step over the cables, you see, to get used to moving across a cluttered floor. Slowly Arnold learned to thread his way between cameras and light stands, to step over coaxial lines thick as roots. Then I would rearrange these, Arnold not looking, so that when he came from behind the Japanese screen where I made him wait before I announced him, it was into a new arena that he stepped each time. At first it was as if he was walking in a minefield. He was that cautious, picking

202

his way, high stepping as a man in heavy weather.

We made it into a game. If he brushed against anything he lost a point. "No, Arnold," I'd call. "You're still too tense. Try to relax. If you do collide with something, personify it. Keep it from falling. Brace its shoulders, smile at it." With practice he became more natural, but it was slow work. When he could finally get through an evening at the TV studio without a serious blunder it was time to start all over somewhere else.

Next we used the auditorium of a high school—the father of one of my girls was the principal—and Arnold came down from the stage into the audience and moved gingerly through a row of seats to wherever I happened to be sitting. This was particularly good practice, because half these acts are audience participation. Then one night I shouted up to him to pretend that there were no steps leading down from the stage and to negotiate the four-and-a-half-foot space to the auditorium floor in some other way. It was awful—as if our weeks of practice had never happened. You'd think I had asked him to jump from an airplane. He got down on his hands and knees and backed tentatively toward the apron of the stage. He looked ridiculous. He pushed a foot out behind him and groped with it for the edge. When he found it, he stuck out the other foot and waved *it* about, as if seeking some purchase in the air itself. Another time he lay prostrate on the stage, belly down, arms straight out in front of him and hands joined, exactly like someone doing a belly flop. He couldn't move. I finally had to take his legs and actually pull him down from the stage. I felt like a fireman taking a housepet out of a tree. When he was on the ground again he slumped down on the piano bench, his head in his hands.

"I never crawled," he said finally.

"What's that, Arnold?"

"I never crawled. My mother tells me I never crawled. Proper crawling is very important."

"Of course you crawled. All babies crawl."

"No. 'Odd as it may seem to parents for whom the clumsy crawling maneuvers of a toddler are "cute" and often comic, the act of crawling is a *sine qua non* of proper locomotor development. Studies have shown a close relationship between later athletic development and efficient crawling.' " Arnold quoted letter-perfect from one of his many sources.

"Then let's *teach* you to crawl," I said.

"I'd feel funny," he said. "You'd laugh. No, it's no good. I'm too clumsy. I'm just wasting your time, Miss Steep."

"You *aren't* wasting my time."

"No," he said, "it's no use."

"Are you going to give up now, Arnold? After we've made so much progress? Am I *wrong* about you? Are you a coward? Is that it? Maybe you haven't got the guts to be in show business. Maybe your guts are as undeveloped as your grace. Because believe me, Arnold, there are going to be places where the stages aren't equipped with stairs and it's a bigger jump than a lousy four and a half feet."

"I can't."

"These are bad times, Arnold. Everywhere our foreign relations are deteriorating. The Middle East, the Far East, Europe. Our neighbors north and south. Wars are coming, Arnold. The USO is going to be bigger than ever. Do you think the theaters in a theater-of-operations are going to have stairways? You're going to have to make up your mind, Mr. Menchman."

"You'll laugh."

"Did I laugh when you fell out of chairs?"

"No."

"Or when you tripped over your shadow that time in the studio?"

"No."

"Well then?"

"Teach me to *crawl*," he said.

So I did.

We crawled together across the stage all night. We played follow the leader on our hands and knees. *It was exactly what was missing in Arnold's locomotor development!* Before we left that night Arnold had learned not only to crawl but to negotiate that jump. He could have leaped from any stage in the world. It was our single most productive session.

Now Arnold could move almost as well as your average man on the street, and in the next two weeks he made even greater progress. Inside a month we were able to make a stage of everything, anything. We drove into deserted parking lots at supermarkets and Arnold burst out of the window of my automobile nimble as Houdini. He climbed the hood and jumped up onto the roof of the car like Gene Kelly. He scrambled up the pedestal of a statue in the park and, holding onto the horse's leg, swayed far out over its base, cocky as a ballet sailor in a dance. He was beautiful, suddenly lithe as a cat burglar. I couldn't have taught him another thing about movement . . . It was at about this time, incidentally, that Dick had him on the show.

"I guess we won't be seeing each other much from now on," I told him one night when we got back to my studio.

"You're a marvelous teacher."

"You're an apt pupil."

"I'm very confident about my appearance. I owe you a lot."

"You worked hard."

"I still really haven't got much of an act, though."

"Oh, well," I said "your act. Your act is your mind."

"I guess so . . . But a person's act has to be structured. There has to be a patter. You know. Style is important, delivery is."

"You'll work it out."

"I don't know. I don't know so much about these things."

"I don't either."

"Oh, you do. Miss Steep?"

"Yes?"

"If I gave you more money, could you . . . do you think—?"

"What?"

"Could you be my audience for a bit? Just for as long as it takes me to work out my routines?"

"I couldn't take money for watching you perform, Arnold."

"I'd be taking up your time."

"I'd love to watch you, but not for money. I've become very interested in your career," I said.

So that's what I did. We still used the makeshift curtain, but the way he moved now it could have been the handsomest setting in show business. He invented his routines right before my eyes. All I did was teach him a few flourishes. Not very good ones, I'm afraid—just that kind of handling themselves that professionals do. You know what I mean—a hand clasping the forehead in concentration, or two fingers buttering the right eyebrow, chin cuppings, scowls to make what he did look difficult. Later we discarded even these. He didn't need them; he was too good. His memory should seem to be what it was: a function as naturally available to him as touch. What was wanted was ease, the juggler's divided attentions, his camouflaged concentration, to be centerless, detached, incorruptible.

BEHR-BLEIBTREAU: Just so, Pepper.

PEPPER STEEP: I had never seen anything so fine. He must have known this, though he still needed assurances.

"Will I be good, do you think?"

"Perfect."

"Do you really think so?"

"I have every confidence." We laughed together at the word.

"Still," he said, "I'm a naturally clumsy man, Miss Steep. My smoothness is only a veneer. Just tonight, getting off the bus to come here, I tripped and almost fell."

"An accident."

"Yes, but suppose I do something like that when I'm onstage?"

"Onstage, Arnold, you'll be magnificent. You move like a dancer."

"On *our* stages. Bare floors, familiar terrain, tamed place."

"Anywhere. Everywhere."

"Do you really think so?"

"Arnold, I'd like to see one last performance."

"Oh?"

"A final dress rehearsal."

"But it's not here I'm worried about. This"—he gestured about him—"this is like singing in the bathtub."

"I don't mean here."

"You don't?"

"The staircase."

"The *winding* staircase?"

"Yes."

"The whole act?"

"Yes."

"Tomorrow?"

"Tonight. Now."

"But I—"

"Come."

We went to the high room where the staircase wound its wide barber's spiral to within six feet of the ceiling. Standing at the bottom and shading his eyes, Arnold leaned his head back and looked up to the top step. "Go on," I said. He glanced at me for a moment and began to move up the stairs, at first holding on to the rail, then letting it go. "Ladies and

207

gentlemen," I announced, "it's with great pleasure and pride that we now present one of the most amazing performers in the world. The man you are about to see isn't an actor, for an actor, properly speaking, is one whose dramas are inflexible and fixed. There is nothing inflexible and fixed about the drama you will now witness. Nor do I now introduce a man who is a mere adept in some unvarying physical routine which, though impossible for average muscles and ordinary limbs, is simply the product of repetitive exercise. Like the actor, however, and like the acrobat as well, he is about to face an extraordinary challenge—a challenge which each of us sitting here tonight faces daily. Ah, but we *fail*. This man won't. It is a challenge of getting and a challenge of having, of keeping and possessing—of reach and embrace itself. For he pits himself not as the stand-in actor against the poet's contrived pressures, nor as the proven tumbler against a previously conquered gravity, but as the one man in the world against—simply—*everything!* To have it all at once, easier than Atlas, bearing all the awful tonnage of impression—the juggler of the living world . . ."

Yes, Dick Gibson thought, yes. Yes.

PEPPER STEEP: "Ladies and gentlemen, I give you . . . *the one and only Arnold Menchman!*"

Arnold stood on the top step, less than an inch between the ceiling and his head. He seemed colossal. He poised there for a moment. His hands—*his hands were in his pockets!* He looked directly at me. Then he closed his eyes, removed a hand from his jacket pocket and put it across his eyelids in a gesture I thought we had agreed to abandon.

"There are thirty-seven steps in this staircase," he said softly, "one hundred and eleven balusters. The stairs are covered by an Oriental-type carpeting about four feet wide. Seven basic colors predominate. In the descending order of their quantitative representation they are: red, dark blue, light blue, rose, white, grayish green and black.

"Pick a number from one to thirty-seven, from one to one hundred and eleven."

I didn't say anything because I didn't know that he meant me to. In the past he had often repeated something he pretended had been called up from the audience.

"A number from one to thirty-seven, please. From one to one hundred eleven. I'm waiting."

"Fourteen, Arnold."

"Fourteen, good. From one to one hundred and eleven. If you will, madam."

"Eighty-three."

"Eighty-three, excellent. Fourteen would be the fourteenth stair, balusters forty, forty-one and forty-two. Eighty-three would be the eighty-third baluster, or the highest baluster on the twenty-seventh stair. Choose right or choose left, madam."

"Left."

"My left or yours?"

"Your left, Arnold."

"Thank you, madam. By the fortieth baluster—*my* left—you will find a rose-tinted curvilinear intersected at three angles by wormlike tendrils of grayish green, the tendrils given a slight suggestion of depth by being outlined on their right sides in a thin black. By the forty-first baluster—my left—you will have a small white snowflake shape sketched within a just larger but less rigid version of itself done in light blue. The forty-second baluster on my left is a simple run of red interrupted by four narrow, thrusting fingers of dark blue. You will have to check this information for yourself, madam, for you will of course have noticed that my eyes are shut!"

"That's marvelous, Arnold. You've memorized the Oriental rug!"

"Am I *correct,* madam?"

"Bravo, Arnold. Bravo. The ninetieth baluster. My right."

"A light blue bell."

"The fifty-second. *Your* right."

"A breast. White. A rose nipple." He opened his eyes. *"Oh, Pepper,"* he said. He ducked his head shyly for a moment and then looked at me. Then he came down the stairs, his body sinking out of sight each time the stairway turned and reappearing as it opened out, his gaze still locked in mine. At the eighth step he spoke. "Oh, Pepper," he said again, reaching his hands out to me. "I'm so pleased." At the bottom step he took my hands and held them.

"You were grand, Arnold," I said. I had to look away.

"What is it?"

"Nothing. You were superb, immense."

"No, please. What?"

"You, Pepper? Oh, no."

I tried to smile. "Well, you don't need me any more—you know that, don't you? Your performance just now. Even the way you came down those stairs, you could have been Fred Astaire. You just graduated from the Charm School."

"Pepper, don't talk like this."

"No, really. Fred Astaire himself. You don't need me any more."

"I wanted to be good for you."

"Well, you were. Very good."

"Pepper?"

"What is it, Arnold?"

"Will you be my . . . manager?"

"I don't know anything about managing anybody, Arnold."

"Well, I don't either. I need to be managed."

I didn't argue. I was honored that he'd ask me, and it must be pretty clear by now that we were in love.

BERNIE PERK: This is the darndest program.

PEPPER STEEP: You have to understand something. I had been a model. A model—a glamour girl. You've seen our outlandish postures in the ads, our arro-

210

gance of shoulders and our hips off plumb. You've seen us standing on the public monuments and barefoot in cathedrals and lying in our spread gold hair on beds. Have *you* been so cool in jungles or had such bearing among the bearers? You've seen our faces, the mouths we make, like people photographed speaking French. Our eyes those of queens and courtesans. What persuades has never been your innocence or virginity. Contempt and scorn, disdain and contumely, and experience in the hatbag with the cosmetics and conditioners. But in bed less than waitresses, less than office girls or schoolteachers, so virgins of a sort still, drivers of harder bargains than those others. And anyway there are just not that many bigshots to go around.

So, I had been a glamour girl. I forgot to tell you—at one point I was a Goldwyn Girl. Do you know what it cost to feed and liquor me in those days? Four hundred dollars a week, and often more. I'm talking about *glamour,* I'm talking about being waved in ahead of the people in nightclubs behind those velvet ropes like a plush corral, about the high cost of living at Trocadero and Bill Miller's Riviera and 21. Nothing's a quarter at the Latin Quarter.

So, I'll be frank, I had had men. Do you know something? Most of the men one sleeps with are called Jimmy, or Coco, or Johnny, or Chuck: glamour boys with yellow hair, big spenders on a first name basis not just with the maître d', but with the kid in the parking lot as well. The tall and the fit—good crawlers, every mother's son of them. To the victors belong the spoiled. But never an Arnold, not one, not once. Even at the end, at the time of his triumph on my staircase, Arnold might have played in nightclubs but couldn't have gotten a good table in one. He was doomed to wait for his car in parking lots, to be seated behind the pillars in theaters, to read in barber shops while men without appointments took the chair ahead of him. And it wasn't as if Arnold didn't mind. He minded. Often, perhaps, there was murder in his heart, but what could he do? If you're not born with prerogative you never have it. What could he do? Recite by heart the *New York Times,* or call off, down to the last item in column four, a thousand menus from a thousand Chinese restaurants?

We won't talk of what I felt now, but of what I meant to Arnold. Imagine what it must have been like for him to have me, a Goldwyn Girl! Never mind that he was served last again, or that I was already a decade past my prime. He loved and desired me more than any man had ever loved and desired me even when I was still really something.

BERNIE PERK: I never knew she was a Goldwyn Girl. I remember those girls from the musicals. They were terrific.

PEPPER STEEP: So . . . *two* things had happened. We were in love, and Arnold was ready to go into show business. I still had one or two contacts in New York and we agreed that I should go down and see what could be done about getting Arnold work. Of course we both knew that once he started getting some dates we wouldn't be seeing each other as much as before. I couldn't leave the Charm School, and naturally Arnold would have to go where his bookings took him.

I allowed myself a week to get him some engagements. I was very lucky. Inside of four days I had him booked in three spots—one of them a two-week run in an important lounge in Las Vegas. When I came back and told Arnold of our good fortune I expected him to be overjoyed, but instead he seemed worried, and I noticed that he avoided looking at me.

"That's just butterflies, Arnold. All performers have them. You'll be fine . . . You do understand why I won't be able to go with you?"

"I guess so," he said.

"Well, then. I think we'd better get started. We've

212

got a lot of rehearsing to do. Your first date is just three weeks off."

"Would you mind, Pepper, if I worked the routines out on my own in Springfield?"

"No, Arnold, of course not."

"If you're not going to be there with me, maybe it's a good idea to get used to performing by myself."

"Certainly, Arnold. If that's what you want." I sounded wounded, I suppose, but frankly I saw his point, and besides, I'd been neglecting the Charm School since I started working with Arnold.

His first booking was a club date at a convention in Atlantic City. At the last minute I decided to take time off and go down with him, but when I told him he said I'd just make him more nervous than he already was. He had to do it on his own, he said. I made him promise to call me just as soon as he got offstage, and I sent him a good-luck telegram at the hotel where he was to appear.

I knew he was supposed to go on at about ten o'clock, and so when I still hadn't heard from him at midnight I called him.

"How did it go, sweetheert? Were you marvelous?"

"It was all right." He didn't sound as if it really was. He's probably tired, I thought. I asked him for details, but he didn't seem to want to talk about it. Indeed, I could almost see him frowning into the phone—a funny little squint which I had seen often in the past few weeks, the sign of his tension, I'd felt.

When he returned to Springfield the next day, again it was I who called him.

"What's wrong, Arnold?"

"Nothing. Nothing is, Pepper."

"Well, it doesn't sound that way. It's almost as if you're avoiding me."

"I love you, Pepper."

"Well, I said, "glad to hear it. You had me

213

worried there. I thought that now you've made it into the big time—"

"I haven't made it into the big time, Pepper."

"You will, darling. Do you know what I thought?"

"What?"

"That maybe . . . maybe you'd fallen onstage."

"No," he said, "I moved very well."

What I really thought was what I'd started to tell Arnold: that he was just another bastard who uses people. Why, he hadn't even paid me, I remembered. We'd fallen in love before that became a point. But it was so absurd to think of Arnold in this light that I was ashamed of myself. I reminded him that his next performance was in two weeks. We saw each other in the interval almost as much as we had when we were still working together, though Arnold still insisted on working on his act alone. And though he was just as sweet as he had ever been, sometimes when he didn't think I was looking I would catch him frowning. Was it possible that having achieved his goal it was no longer attractive to him? I didn't ask, but I decided to wait until after his next engagement before making any additional dates for him.

There was no question about my seeing him work that booking. It was for a week at the Fox Theater in St. Louis, one of the last motion picture houses in America where they still had a variety show between features. This time I waited three days for him to call. Finally he did.

"How is it, Arnold? Are the audiences responsive?"

"They're very kind."

"How do they like the part where you have the houselights turned up and you memorize the first fifteen rows of the audience? Did they go wild for that?"

"I don't do that part."

"Arnold, it's the most exciting thing in the act."

214

"I don't do that part."

When he came back from St. Louis he was as gloomy as ever. Now he always wore that odd squinting frown of his, even when he knew I was watching. It was very strange because he had never looked so good. Evidently he had bought a whole new wardrobe in St. Louis—everything in the latest fashion, the best taste. A couple of his suits looked as if they'd been custom-made. Nor had he ever been so ardent, so clever a lover. But he continued to rehearse alone, and each day he seemed more despondent. By the time he went to Vegas anyone could see that he was miserable.

I had to know what was going on, so without telling Arnold I flew out to Las Vegas on a different plane and dropped into the lounge where he was performing. I took a table in the back, as far from the small stage as possible. When he was introduced and the spotlight hit him, I gasped. He took my breath away—I had never seen him during an actual performance before—so beautiful was he. He seemed magnificent in the new tuxedo he had bought for the engagement. I was reassured at once, but then, when he began his act, it was all I could do to keep from fleeing from the room. He was *terrible*! He moved splendidly, better than I had ever seen him, but when it came time to give them what he had memorized he seemed confused. He stammered and hesitated, he faltered, he stuttered and sputtered. One didn't know if his memory or his speech had given out. He did only a few of the routines we had worked out together, and these badly. For the rest he substituted halting recitations of poems he had memorized in his childhood, violating the first principle of such acts—audience participation. And with his constant frown he seemed almost angry at the audience. It was awful. It was *dull*. It was so bad that the audience took a sort of pity on him and were more patient and attentive than they might have been with an act two or three times better than

215

his. When he was finished they generously applauded.

I hadn't wanted him to know I was there; he would have guessed that I'd come to spy and not to surprise him. But he looked so miserable when he was through that I had to go to his dressing room.

He didn't seem surprised to see me. "Did you see it, Pepper?"

"Oh, Arnold, I'm *so* sorry."

"I didn't want you to know," he said. "I'm so ashamed."

"That's silly," I said. "So you've got a little stage fright. We can lick that. Remember how frightened you were when you were clumsy? We worked on that and today you're one of the most graceful men in show business."

"But I don't *have* stage fright. I was cool as a cucumber up there."

"But, Arnold, the way you stammered, your confusion—"

"It wasn't stage fright. It's my damn eyes."

Arnold told me that ever since he had become graceful his vision had begun to deteriorate. For two months, he said, he had been becoming increasingly far-sighted; each day what he could see moved a little farther off. Since he had an eidetic imagination and could remember only what he saw, and most of what he saw was a blur, his photographic memory had inevitably been affected—even the beloved poems from his childhood. When he closed his eyes the print was indistinct. That's why he squinted; he was trying to make things out.

"But surely you've been to an eye doctor," I said.

"Yes. It's severe astigmatism."

"Well, then, he can prescribe glasses."

"He made a pair up for me. They're *thick*, Pepper. They're awful."

"Well, so what about it?"

"If I wore them, anybody could tell I'm far-sighted. Since you taught me to move so well I just

216

couldn't; they'd detract from my appearance. I'd only be clumsy Arnold again. I even tried contact lenses, but they hurt my eyes and made them water. Onstage I looked like I was crying."

So he was vain. That was what had been underneath the clumsiness we'd rubbed off. I'd taught him to move and now he couldn't stand not to be graceful, glassless Arnold.

I'll say this much: he didn't give up. He was determined to stay in show business. That must have been part of his vanity too, even in the beginning. I mean, maybe the idea of show business didn't even have anything to do with his talent. Maybe his memory was just a lucky excuse he could use to justify being on a stage. By now, he was terribly far-sighted but he decided to make a strength of his weakness, and he conceived a plan to move his act outdoors. He went into the desert around Las Vegas and started to memorize larger and larger objects further and further off. He began with cactuses a hundred yards away and ended with a mountain range twenty miles in the distance. Arnold had become a living map!

BERNIE PERK: Incredible!

PEPPER STEEP: It was impractical, of course. He couldn't get a good crowd to come with him into the desert, and even if he had only someone as far-sighted as himself could have appreciated his accomplishments. We gave it every chance. While in the West we went to Arizona, and Arnold committed to memory the entire south rim of the Grand Canyon, and every bend and twist of the Colorado River for two hundred miles. The Forest Ranger was very impressed and offered him a job. He might have taken it, but the Park Service wouldn't let him wear his tuxedo.

It was all absurd, of course, but Arnold was as determined to work up his new act as he had been to learn how to move well. It was all he could think of. He had an idea that he needed to be in a dependable

217

climate, one where it was always clear, and so he chose Palm Springs. He asked me to come with him, but I told him I couldn't. It broke my heart to have to leave him, but I had my career in Hartford—and frankly, I couldn't see abandoning it in order to chase a will-o'-the-wisp. I tried to talk him into coming back with me, but he was obsessed with his act. I tried to persuade him to sacrifice a little of his appearance, but he was convinced he could still have both.

I saw Arnold only once more. About a year after Las Vegas he sent me a wire saying that he was returning to Hartford and asking me to meet his plane. For old time's sake I did.

When he appeared in the doorway of the big jet he looked like a movie star. He was wearing one of those cream trenchcoats and a smart little cap. Though it was winter and already past nine o'clock in the evening, he had on huge green sunglasses and carried a chic airline suitcase of olive green leather—one of those things with enormous bulging zippered pockets. Somehow I knew that his sunglasses were not prescription lenses.

We went back to my studio.

"I've given up the idea for the act, Pepper," he said.

"Oh?"

"It was silly. I've enormous land masses in my head, but it could never come to anything as an act."

"It was too ambitious, Arnold."

"Yeah. When I was still in California I took a plane up to Seattle. I've got the shoreline of practically the entire West Coast memorized—except for cloud cover and fog banks."

"I see."

"There's no way to use it."

"You still won't wear glasses?"

"No."

"What happened to the things you used to know? What happened to the carpet on my staircase?"

"Gone. All gone, kid. I can't see it. The light that failed."

"Oh, Arnold."

"What the hell? Let's not be so gloomy. How d'ya like my shirt? I had about a dozen of them made up in Springs. In pastels, stripes. No breast pocket, did you notice? That's one of the latest wrinkles."

"Oh, Arnold."

"The shoes are reindeer suede. Handmade, of course. The heels are meerschaum."

"What's the lettering on my card index file?"

He closed his eyes and opened them again. "Can't make it out, Pep."

"Oh, Arnold."

"That's all over. I've given up the act. I've come back, sweetie. We're together again."

"No, Arnold. We're not. I met your plane, but it's over between us. You'd better leave now. My friend is terribly jealous."

"Oh, Pepper."

"Please go, Arnold. I'd prefer there were no scene."

At the door Arnold turned once and shrugged. He tipped his funny little hat forward on his head and shoved his hands deep into the pockets of his raincoat. He was the elegant lonely man, like Frank Sinatra on an album cover.

There wasn't anyone else, of course . . . There *isn't* anyone else. And all Arnold had meant to do in the doorway was make me love him. He thought I would love him if he was handsome and graceful, but I'd loved him for what was in his mind, for what he could remember. He was a peacock now, the world as much a blur to him as it is to the rest of us.

I'm sorry. Forgive me. I'm sorry I'm crying. I don't mean to cry. Please. I'm sorry.

BERNIE PERK: Oh, Pepper.

DICK GIBSON: Ladies and gentlemen, we pause now for station identification.

Among the guests in the studio all hell broke loose during the station break. They talked excitedly to one another, and called back and forth along the row of theater seats like picnickers across their tables. Through they had nothing to say themselves, Behr-Bleibtreau's people turned back and forth trying to follow the conversation of the others. Indeed, there was a sort of lunatic joy in the room, a sense of free-for-all that was not so much an exercise of liberty as of respite—as if someone had temporarily released them from vows. School was out in Studio A, and Dick had an impression of its also being out throughout the two or three New England states that could pick up the show. He saw people raiding refrigerators, gulping beers, grabbing tangerines, slashing margarine on slices of bread, ravenously tearing chicken wings, jellied handfuls of leftover stews.

Pepper Steep had joined Jack Patterson in exhausted detachment; though he said nothing, Mel Son looked animatedly from one to the other. Behr-Bleibtreau also seemed exhausted.

Of the members of his panel, only Bernie Perk seemed keyed up. He jabbered away a mile a minute, so that Dick couldn't really follow all that he was saying. The druggest wanted to know what had happened to everyone. "What's got into Pepper?" he asked. "What's got into Jack?"

Dick couldn't tell him. He had no notion of what had gotten into his comrades. All he knew was that he was impatient for the commercial to be finished and for the show to go back on the air. He couldn't wait to hear what would happen next, though having some dim sense of the masquelike qualities of the evening, and realizing that thus far his guests had "performed" in the order that they had been introduced, he had a hunch that it would involve Bernie.

It did.

BERNIE PERK: May I say something?
DICK GIBSON: Sure thing.
BERNIE PERK: Okay, then. What's going on here?

What's got into everyone? What's got into Pepper? What's got into Jack? I came here tonight to talk about psychology with an expert in the field. But all anyone's done so far is grab the limelight for himself. Everyone is too excited. Once a person gets started talking about himself all sorts of things come out that aren't anybody's business. I understand enough about human nature to know that much. Everybody has his secret. Who hasn't? We're all human beings. Who isn't a human being? Listen, I'm a mild person. I'm not very interesting, maybe, and I don't blow my own horn, but even someone like myself, good old Bernie Perk, corner druggist, "Doc" to one and "Pop" to another, could put on a regular horror show if he wanted to. *But it isn't people's business*.

Look, my son and his charming wife are guests in the studio tonight. Pepper Steep's sister is here. How do you think it must be for them when an intimate relative sticks his foot in his mouth? If you love people you've got to have consideration.

DICK GIBSON: Bernie, don't be so upset. Take it easy.

BERNIE PERK: Dick, I *am* upset about this. No. I mean it. What's it supposed to be, "Can You Top This?"

DICK GIBSON: Come on, Bernie—

BERNIE PERK: Because the temptation is always the one they yielded to. To give up one's secrets. La. La la. The soul's espionage, its secret papers. *Know me*. No, thank you. I'm pretty worked up. Call on Mel.

DICK GIBSON: Take it easy.

BERNIE PERK: Call on Mel.

DICK GIBSON: Mel? (*no answer*)

BERNIE PERK: Mel passes. (*He giggles.*) Well, that's too bad, for thereby hangs a tale, I bet. The truth is everybody likes to see his friends with their hair down. Well, okay, I'll tell the audience something maybe they don't know. We don't see each other off the air. The illusion is we're mates. You want us to be, but we're not.

JACK PATTERSON: Here goes Bernie.

221

BERNIE PERK: (*fiercely*) You *had* your turn: You were *first*. Don't hog everything. You had your turn. Just because you couldn't do any better than that canned ardor, don't try to ruin it for everyone else.

The truth of the matter is, I had to laugh. The man's a schoolteacher. Big deal. He sees up coeds' skirts. Big deal. He has them in for conferences, he goes over their papers with them, he bends over the composition and her hair touches his cheek. Enormous! Call the police, passion's circuits are blown. I know all that, I *know* all that. But if you want to see life in the raw, be a pharmacist, buy a drugstore. You wouldn't *believe* what goes on. It's a meat market. No wonder they register us. Hickory Dickory "Doc." Let me fill you in on the prescription. Yow. Wow.

You know what a drugstore is? A temple to the senses. Come down those crowded aisles. Cosmetics first stop. Powders, puffs, a verb-wheel of polished nails on a cardboard, lipstick ballistics, creams and tighteners, suntan lotions, eyeshadow, dyes for hair—love potions, paints, the ladies' paintbox!

Come, come with Pop. The Valentine candy, the greeting cards, the paperbook racks and magazine stands. The confessions and movie magazines dated two months beyond the real month because time, like love, is yet to be. Sit at the fountain. See the confections—banana splits and ice cream sundaes like statues of the sweet, as if sweetness itself, the sugary molecules of love resided in them. The names—like words for lyrics. Delicious the syrups, the salty storm of nuts and tidal waves of spermy cream. Sing yum! Sing yum yum!

All the shampoos, all the lotions and hair conditioners proteined as egg and meat. Files and emery boards, the heartsick gypsy's tools. Sun lamps, sleep masks, rollers, bath oils and dipilatories, massaging lotions. Things for acne, panty hose—the model on the package like a yogi whore. Brushes, rinses, bath oils and shower caps like the fruits that grow on beaches.

To say nothing of the Venus Folding Feminine Syringe, of Kotex in boxes you could set a table for four on. Liquid douches—you can hear the sea. Rubber goods, the queer mysterious elastics, supporters, rupture's ribbons and organ's bows. Now we're into it, hard by diarrhea's plugs and constipation's triggers. There's the druggist, behind the high counter, his bust visible like someone on a postage stamp, immaculate in his priest's white collar. See the symbols—the mortar and pestle and flasks of colored liquid. Once I sipped from the red, the woman's potion. I had expected tasteless vegetable dye, but it was sweet, viscous, thick as oil. There are aphrodisiacs in those flasks to float your heart.

And there *I* am, by the refrigerated drugs, the druggist's small safe, the pharmacopoeia, the ledger with names and dates and numbers. A man of the corner and crossroads, scientist manqué, reader of Greek and Latin, trained to count, to pull a jot from a tittle, lift a tittle from a whit, a man of equilibriums, of grains and half-grains, secret energies locked in the apothecary's ounce.

Fresh from college I took a job—this was the depression—in another man's store. MacDonald's. Old MacDonald had a pharmacy, eeyi eeyi o! An old joke but the first I ever made. "I'll fill the prescriptions," MacDonald told me. "You're a whipper-snapper. You'll wait on trade and make the ice cream sodas. If that isn't satisfactory, go elsewhere. If I'm to be sued for malpractice I'll be the malpracticer, thank you very much." It was not satisfactory, but what could I do? It was the depression. How many young men trained for a profession had to settle in those days for something else? And do you know what I found out? (What's got into Bernie?) I found out *everything!*

The first week I stood behind the counter, smiling in my white lab jacket, and a lady came in. A plain woman, middle-aged, her hair gone gray and her figure failing. "Doctor, I need something for my hemorrhoids," she said. "They are like to kill me when I sit. It burns so when I make number two that I've been eating clay to constipate myself."

I gave her Preparation H. Two days later she came back to the store and bought a birthday card for her son. Somehow the knowledge that I alone of all the people in the store knew something about that woman's behind was stirring to me. I was married, the woman was plain; she didn't attract me. I was drawn by her hemorrhoids, in on the secret of her sore behind. Each day in that novice year there were similar experiences. I had never been so happy in my life. Old MacDonald puttering away in the back of the store, I up front—what a team we made.

A young woman came in. Sacrificing her turn she gestured to me to wait on the other customers first. When the store was empty she came up to me.

"I have enuresis," she said.

I gave her some pills.

"Listen," she said, "may I use your toilet?"

I let her come behind the counter. She minced along slowly, her legs in a desperate clamp. I opened the door of the small toilet.

"There's no toilet paper," I said. "I'll have to bring you some."

"Thank you," she said.

I stood outside the door for a moment. I heard the splash. A powerful, incredible discharge. You'd think she'd had an enema. But it was all urine; the woman's bladder was converting every spare bit of moisture into uremic acid. She could have pissed mud puddles, oceans, the drops in clouds, the condensation on the outside of beer bottles. It was beyond chemistry, it was alchemy. Golden. Lovely.

I got the paper for her.

"I have the toilet tissue, miss." Though she opened the door just enough for me to hand the roll in to her, I saw bare knees, a tangle of panties.

Her name was Miss Wallace, and when she came into the store for her pills—need is beyond embarrassment: only *I* was embarrassed—I grew hard with lust. I made no overtures, you understand; I was always clinical, always professional, always offhand.

"Listen," I told her one day. "I suppose you have rubber sheets."

"No good," she said.

"You'll ruin your mattress."

"It's already ruined. When I tried a rubber sheet, the water collected in the depression under my behind. I lay in it all night and caught cold."

The thought of that pee-induced cold maddened me. Ah God, the bizarre body awry, messes caught in underwear—love tokens, unhealth a function of love.

There were so many I can't remember them all.

I knew I had to leave Old MacDonald. I was held down, you see. Who knew what secrets might not be unlocked if I could get my hands on the *prescriptions* those ladies brought in! When my father died and left me four thousand dollars, I used it to open the store I have now. I signed notes right and left to get my stock and fixtures together. My wife thought it was madness to gamble this way in the depth of the depression, but I was pining with love. There were so many . . . Let's see. *These have been a few of the women in my life:*

Rose Barbara Hacklander, Miss Hartford of 1947, 38—24—36, a matter of public record. What is *not* a matter of public record is that she had gingivitis, a terrible case, almost debilitating, and came near to losing the title because of her reluctance to smile. She wanted to shield her puffy gums, you understand. Only I, Bernie Perk, her druggist, knew. On the night before the finals she came to me in tears. She showed me—in the back of the store—lifting a lip, reluctant as a country girl in the Broadway producer's office raising the hem of her skirt, shy, and yet bold too, wanting to please even with the shame of her beauty. I looked inside her mouth. The gums were filled, tumid with blood and pus, enormous, preternatural, the gums of the fat lady in the circus, obscuring her teeth, in their sheathing effect seeming actually to sharpen them, two rings of blade in her mouth. And there, in the back of her mouth at the back of the store, pulling a cheek, squeezing it as one gathers in a trigger—cankers, cysts like snowflakes.

"Oh, Doc," she cried, "what will I do? It's worse tonight. The salve don't help. It's nerves—I know it's nerves."

"Wait, I can't see in this light. Put your head here. Say 'Ah.' "

"Ah," she said.

"Ah," I said. "Ah!"

"What's to be done? Is there anything you can give me?"

"Advice."

"Advice?"

"Give them the Giaconda smile. Mona Lisa let them have."

And she did. I saw the photograph in the newspaper the morning after the finals. Rose Barbara crowned (I the Queenmaker), holding her flowers, the girls in her court a nimbus behind her, openly smiling, their trim gums flashing. Only Miss Hartford of 1947's lips were locked, her secret in the dimpled parentheticals of her sealed smile. I still have the photograph in my wallet.

Do you know what it means to be always in love? Never to be out of it? Each day loving's gnaw renewed, like hunger or the need for sleep? Worse, the love unfocused, never quite reduced to this one girl or that one woman, but always I, the King of Love, taking to imagination's beds whole harems? I was grateful, I tell you, to the occasional Rose Barbara Hacklander for the refractive edge she lent to lust. There were so many. Too many to think about.

My mind was like the waiting room of a brothel. Let them leave my imagination, I prayed, the ones with acne, bad breath, body odor, dandruff, all those whose flyed ointment and niggered woodpile were the commonplace of my ardor.

Grateful also to Miss Sheila Jean Locusmundi who had corns like Chiclets, grateful to the corns themselves, those hard outcroppings of Sheila Jean's synovial bursa. I see her now, blonde, high-heeled, her long, handsome legs bronzed in a second skin of nylon.

I give her foot plasters. She hands them back. "Won't do," she says.

"Won't do? Won't do? But these are our largest. These are the largest there are."

"Pop," she whispers, "I've got a cop's corns."

A cop's corns. A cornucopia. I shake my head in wonder. I want to see them, Sheila Jean. I invite her behind the counter, to the back of the store. If I see them I might be able to help her, a doc like me. Once out of view of the other customers Sheila Jean succumbs: she limps. *I* feel the pinch. That's right, I think, don't let *them* see. In my office she sits down in front of my rolltop desk and takes off her shoes. I watch her face. Ease comes in like the high tide. Tears of painless gratitude appear in her eyes. All day she waits for this moment. She wiggles her toes. I see bunions bulge in her stockings. It's hard for me to maintain my professional distance. "Take off your stockings, Miss Locusmundi," I manage. She turns away in my swivel chair and I hear the soft, electric hiss of the nylon. She swings around, and redundantly points.

"I see," I murmur. "Yes, those are really something." They are. They are knuckles, ankles. They are boulders, mountain ranges.

"May I?" I ask.

She gives me her foot reluctantly. "Oh, God, don't touch them, Pop."

"There, there, Miss Locusmundi, I won't hurt

227

you." I hold her narrow instep, my palm a stirrup. I toss it casually from one hand to the other, getting the heft.

"Ticklish," Sheila Jean says. She giggles.

I peer down closely at the humpy callosities, their dark cores. There is a sour odor. This, I think, is what Miss Hartford's gingivitis tastes like. I nod judiciously; I take their measure. I'm stalling because I can't stand up yet. When finally I can, I sculpt plasters for her. I daub them with Derma-Soft and apply them. When she walks out she is, to all eyes but mine, just another pretty face.

Grateful too—I thank her here—to Mary Odata, a little Japanese girl whose ears filled with wax. I bless her glands, those sweet secretions, her lovely auditory canal. Filled with wax, did I say? She was a candle mine. I saved the detritus from the weekly flushings I administered.

Her father took her to live in Michigan, but before she left she wrote me a note to thank me for all I had done. "Respected R. Ph. Perk," she wrote, "my father have selectioned to take me to his brother whom has a truck farm in the state of Michigan, but before I am going this is to grateful acknowledgment your thousand kindnesses to my humble ears. In my heart I know will I never to find in Michigan an R. Ph. as tender for my ears as you, sir. Mine is a shameful affliction, but you never amusemented them, and for this as for your other benefits to me I thank. Your friend, M. Odata."

When I closed the store that night I went into my office and molded a small candle from the cerumen I had collected from her over the months, ran a wick through it, turned off the lights, and reread Mary's letter by the glow of her wax until it sputtered and went out. Call me a sentimental old fool, but that's what I did.

Not to mention Mrs. Louise Lumen, perpetual wetnurse, whose lacteal glands were an embarrassment to her three or even four years beyond her delivery, or flatulent Cora Moss, a sweet young thing with a sour stomach in the draft of whose farts one could catch cold. There were so many. There was Mrs. Wynona Jost whose unwanted hair no depilatory would ever control. Her back, she gave me to understand, was like an ape's. Super-folliculed Mrs. Jost! And psoriatic Edna Hand. And all the ladies with prescriptions. I knew everybody's secret, the secret of every body. And yet it was never the worm in the apple I loved but only a further and final nakedness, almost the bacteria itself, the cocci and bacilli and spirilla, the shameful source of *their* ailment and my privilege. I was deferential to this principle only: that there exists a nudity beyond *mere* nudity, a covertness which I shielded as any lover husbands his sweet love's mysteries. I did not kiss and tell; I did not kiss at all. Charged with these women's cabala I kept my jealous counsel. I saved them, you see. Honored and honed a sort of virginity in them by my silence. Doc and Pop. And knight too in my druggist's gorget. I could have gone on like this forever, content with my privileged condition, satisfied to administer my drugs and patent medicines and honor all confidences, grateful, as I've said, for the impersonal personality of the way I loved, calling them Miss, calling them Missus, protecting them from myself as well as from others, not even masturbating, only looking on from a distance, my desire speculative as an issue of stock.

But something human happens.

One day . . . Where's my *son* going? Why's he leaving? Edward? Connie, *don't* go. Youth should have a perspective on its parents . . . Well, they've gone. I must have shamed them. Isn't that the way with the young? They think the older generation is stodgy and then they've no patience with confession. Oh well, let them go. Where was I?

BEHR-BLEIBTREAU: "One day—"

BERNIE PERK: Yes, that's right. One day a woman came into my drugstore I'd never seen before. She

229

was pretty, in her early or middle twenties perhaps, but very small. Not just short—though she was, extremely short; she couldn't have been much more than five feet—but *small*. Dainty, you know? Maybe she wore a size six dress. I don't know sizes. She could probably buy her clothes in the same department school girls do. What do they call that? Junior Miss? Anyway, she was very delicate. Tinier than Mary Odata. A nice face, sweet, a little old-fashioned perhaps, the sort of face you see in an old sepia photograph of your grandmother's sister that died. A *very* pretty little woman.

I saw her looking around, going up and down the aisles. Every once in a while she would stoop down to peer in a low shelf. I have these big round mirrors in the corners to spy on shoplifters. I watched her in the mirrors. If I lost her in one mirror I picked her up again in another. A little doll going up and down the aisles in the convex glass.

I knew what was up. A woman knows where things are. It's an instinct. Have you ever seen them in a supermarket? They understand how it's organized. It has nothing to do with the fact that they shop more than men. A man goes into a grocery, he has to ask where the bread is. Not a woman: she knows where it's *supposed* to be. Well, this woman is obviously confused. She's looking for something which she knows is always in one place, whatever store she goes into. So I *knew* what was up: she was looking for the sanitary napkins.

Most places they keep them on the open shelves to spare the ladies embarrassment. I don't spare anyone anything. I keep them behind the counter with me. I want to know what's going on with their periods. They have to ask.

Finally she came over to me. "I don't see the Kotex," she says.

"This is the Kotex department," I say, and reach under the counter for a box. "Will there be anything else? We have a terrific buy on Midol this week. Or

230

some girls prefer the formula in this. I've been getting good reports; they tell me it's very effective against cramps." I hand her a tin of Monthleaze. "How are you fixed for breath sweetener?" I push a tube of Sour-Off across the counter to her.

She ignores my suggestions but picks up the box of Kotex and looks at it. "This is Junior," she says.

"I'm sorry," I say. I give her Regular.

"Don't you have Super?"

"I thought this was for you," I tell her, and give her the size she asks for.

A month later she came in again. "Super Kotex," she said. I give her the box and don't see her again for another month. This time when she comes in I hand her the Super and start to ring up the sale.

"I'd better take the tampon kind too," she says. She examines the box I give her. "Is there anything larger than this?"

"This is the biggest," I say, swallowing hard.

"All right."

"Tell me," I say, "are these for you?"

She blushes and doesn't answer.

I hadn't dared to think about it, though it had crossed my mind. Now I could think of nothing else. I forgot about the others. This girl inflamed me. Bernie burns. It was astonishing—a girl so small. My life centered on *her* center, on the prodigious size of her female parts.

BEHR-BLEIBTREAU: Say "cunt."

DICK GIBSON: Wait a minute—

BEHR-BLEIBTREAU: It's all right to say "cunt."

BERNIE PERK: . . . *Cunt.* The size of her cunt. The disproportion was astonishing to me. Kotex *and* Tampax. For all I knew, she used the Kotex *inside.* I *did* know it. I conceived of her smallness now as the result of her largeness. It was as if her largeness *there* sapped size from the rest of her body, or that by some incredible compensation her petiteness lent dimension elsewhere. I don't know. It was all I could think of. Bernie burns.

I had to know about her, at least find out who she was, whether she was married. I tried to recall if I had seen a wedding band, but who could think of fingers, who could think of hands? Bernie burns. Perk percolates.

That night I counted ahead twenty-eight days to figure when I might expect her again. The date fell on September 9, 1956.

She didn't come—not then, not the next month.

Then, one afternoon, I saw her in the street. It was just after Thanksgiving, four or five days before her next period. I raised my hat. "Did you have a pleasant holiday?" I asked. My face was familiar to her but she couldn't place me. I counted on this.

"So so." The little darling didn't want to embarrass me.

"I thought you might be going away for Thanksgiving," I said.

She looked puzzled but still wanted to be polite. "My roommate went home but I stayed on in Hartford," she said. "Actually she invited me to go with her but my boss wouldn't give me Friday off."

Ah, I thought, she has a roommate, she's a working girl. Good.

"I'm very sorry," I said, "but I find myself in a very embarrassing position. I don't seem to be able to remember your name."

"Oh," she said, and laughed. "I can't remember yours either. I know we've seen each other."

"I'm Bernie Perk."

"Yes. Of course. I'm Bea Dellaspero. I still don't—"

"I don't either. You see what happens? Here we are, two old friends and neither of us can—*Wait* a minute. I think I've got it. I've seen you in my store. I'm the druggist—Perk's Drugs on Mutual."

"Oh." She must have remembered our last conversation for she became very quiet. We were standing outside a coffee shop, and when I invited her to

232

have a cup with me she said she had to be going and hurried off.

Her number was in the phone book, and I called right from the coffee shop. If only her roommate's in, I thought, crossing my fingers for luck.

"Where's Bea? Is Bea there?"

"No."

"Christ," I said. "What's her number at work? I've got to get her."

I called the number the roommate gave me; it was a big insurance company. I told them I was doing a credit check on Bea Dellaspero and they connected me to personnel. Personnel was nice as pie. Bea was twenty-four years old, a typist in the claims department and a good credit risk.

It was something, but I couldn't live on it. I had to get her to return to the store.

I conceived the idea of running a sale especially for Bea. My printer set up a sample handbill. Across the bottom I had him put in half a dozen simple coupons, with blank spaces where she could write in the names of the products she wanted to exchange them for. She could choose from a list of twenty items, on which I gave about a 90 percent discount. I sent the flier in an envelope to Bea's address.

Normally I'm closed on Sunday, but that was the day I set aside for Bea's sale. I opened up at ten o'clock, and I didn't have to wait more than an hour. When she came in holding the pink flier we were alone in the store.

"How are you?" I asked.

"Fine, thank you." She was still uneasy about me. "I got your advertisement."

"I see it in your hand."

"Oh. Yes."

She went around the store picking up the items she wanted and brought them to the counter. When she gave me her coupons, I saw that she'd chosen products relating to a woman's periods or to feminine hygiene. She'd had to: I'd rigged the list with men's shaving equipment, pipe accessories, athletic supporters—things like that.

"What size would these be, madam?"

"Super."

"Beg pardon, I didn't hear you."

"Super."

Super *duper*, I thought. I put the big boxes on the counter and added two bottles of douche from the shelf behind me. It won't be enough, I thought. She had a pussy big as all outdoors. Imperial gallons wouldn't be enough. "Let me know how you like the douche," I said, "I've been getting some excellent reports."

God, I was crazy. You know how it is when you're smitten. Smitten? I was in love. Married twenty-three years and all of a sudden I was in love for the first time in my life. Whole bales of cotton I would have placed between her legs. Ah love, set me tasks! Send me for all the corks in Mediterranea, all styptic stymies would I fetch!

In love, did I say? *In* love? That's wrong. *In* love I had been since Old MacDonald's. *In* love is nothing, simple citizenship. Now I was *of* love, no mere citizen but a very governor of the place, a tenant become landlord. And who *falls* in love? Love's an ascent, a rising—touch my hard-on—a soaring. Consider my body, all bald spots haired by imagination, my fats rendered and features firmed, tooth decay for God's sake turned back to candy in my mouth. Heyday! Heyday! And all my feelings collateral to a teen-age boy's!

So I had been in love and now was of it. Bernie burns, the pharmacist on fire. I did not so much forget the others as repudiate them; they were just more wives. Get this straight: love is adulterous, hard on the character. I cuckold those cuties, the Misses Odata and Locusmundi. Horns for Miss Hartford! Miss Moss is dross. Be my love, Bea my love!

I bagged Bea's purchases, punched the register a few times to make it look good, and charged her fifty-seven cents for the ten dollars' worth of stuff she'd bought.

"So cheap?"

"It's my special get-acquainted offer," I said. "Also I knocked off a few dollars because you mentioned the secret word."

"I did? What was it?"

"I can't tell you. It's a secret."

"You know, it's really a terrific sale," she said. "I'm surprised more people aren't here to take advantage of it."

"They're coming by when church gets out."

"I see."

As she took the two bags in her thin arms and turned to go, it occurred to me that she might never come back to the store. I raced around the counter. I had no idea what I would do; all love's stratagems and games whistled in my head.

"I'll help you," I said, taking one of her bags.

"I can manage."

"No, I couldn't think of it. A little thing like you? Let me have the other one as well."

She refused to give it up. "I'm very capable," she said. We were on the sidewalk. "You better go back. Your store's open. Anyone could just walk off with all your stock."

"They're in church. Even the thieves. I'll take you to your car."

"I don't have a car. I'm going to catch the bus at the corner."

"I'll wait with you."

"It's not necessary."

"It isn't safe."

"They're all in church."

"Just the thieves, not the rapers."

"But it's the dead of winter. You don't even have a coat. You'll catch cold."

"Not cold."

235

"What?"

"Not cold. Bernie burns."

"Excuse me?"

"Not cold. The pharmacist on fire."

"I'm sorry?"

"Don't worry about me," I said. "I'm hale." I jumped up and down with the bag in my arms. "See?" I said. "See how hale? I'm strong. I huff and I puff." I hit myself in the chest with my fist. "Me? Me sick? There are things on my shelves to cure anything."

Bea was becoming alamed. I checked myself, and we stood quietly in the cold together waiting for the bus.

Finally I had to speak or burst. " 'There's naught so sweet as love's young dream,' " I said.

"What was that?"

"Its a saying. It's one of my favorite sayings."

"Oh."

" 'Who ever loved that loved not at first sight?' "

"I beg your pardon?"

"It's another saying."

"Do you see the bus coming?"

" 'Love makes the world go round.' "

"I've heard that one."

" 'Love is smoke raised with the fume of sighs.' " The fume of *size*: super. " 'Take away love and earth is tomb.' 'Love indeed is anything, yet is nothing.' "

"I think I hear it coming. Are you *sure* you can't see it."

" 'Love is blind.' " I said gloomily. She *had* heard it: it lumbered toward us irresistibly. Soon it would be there and I would never see her again. She was very nervous and went into the street and began to signal while the bus was still three blocks off. I watched her performance disconsolately. " 'And yet I love her til I die,' " I murmured softly.

When the driver came abreast, Bea darted up the steps and I handed her bag to her. "Will I see you again?" I said.

"What's that?"

"Will I see you again? Promise when you've used up what you've bought you'll come back."

"Well, it's so *far*," she said. The driver closed the door.

"I deliver!" I shouted after her and waved and blew kisses off my fingertips.

DICK GIBSON: Remarkable!

BERNIE PERK: So's love, so are lovers. Now I saw them.

DICK GIBSON: Saw whom?

BERNIE PERK: Why, lovers. For if love is bad for the character it's good for it too. Now that I was of love, I was also of lovers. I looked around and saw that the whole world was in love. When a man came in to pick up penicillin for his wife—that was a love errand. I tried to cheer him. "She'll be okay," I told him. "The pills will work. She'll come round. Her fever will break. Her sore throat will get better." "Why are you telling me this?" he'd ask. "I like you," I'd say. " 'All the world loves a lover.' "

For the first time I saw what my drugstore was all about. It was love's way station. In free moments I would read the verses on my greeting cards, and my eyes would brim with tears. Or I would pore over the true confessions in my magazine racks. "Aye aye, oy oy," I'd mutter, "too true this true confession." I blessed the lipstick: "Kiss, kiss," I droned over the little torpedoes. "Free the man in frogs an bogs. Telltales be gone, stay off shirt collars and pocket handkerchiefs." All love was sacred. I pored over my customers' photographs after they were developed. I held a magnifying glass over them—the ones of sweethearts holding hands in the national parks or on the steps of historic buildings, the posed wives on the beach, fathers waving goodbye, small in the distance, as they go up the steps into airplanes. People take the same pictures, did you know that? We are all brothers.

Love was everywhere, commoner than loneliness. I had never realized before what a terrific business I did in rubbers. And it isn't even spring; no one's on a blanket in the woods, or in a rowboat's bottom, or on a hayride. I'm talking about the dead of winter, a high of twenty, a low of three. And you can count on the fingers of one hand the high-school kid's pipedream purchase. My customers meant business. There were irons in these lovers' fires. And connoisseurs they were, I tell you, prophylactic more tactic than safeguard, their condoms counters and confections. How sheer's this thing, they'd want to know, or handle them, testing this one's elasticity, that one's friction. Or inquire after refinements, special merchandise, meticulous as fishermen browsing flies. Let's see. They wanted: French Ticklers, Spanish Daggers, Swedish Surprises, The Chinese Net, The Texas Truss and Gypsy Outrage. They wanted petroleum jellies smooth as syrups.

And I, Pop, all love's avuncular spirit, all smiles, rooting for them, smoothing their way where I could, apparently selfless—they must have thought me some good-sport widower who renewed his memories in their splashy passion—giving the aging Cupid's fond green light. How could they suspect that I learned from them, growing my convictions in their experience? Afterward, casually, I would debrief them. Reviewing the troops: Are Trojans better than Spartans? Cavaliers as good as Commandos? Is your Centurion up to your Cossack? What of the Mercenary? The Guerrilla? How does the Minuteman stand up against the State Trooper? In the end, it was too much for me to have to look on while every male in Hartford above the age of seventeen came in to buy my condoms.

Bea never came back—I had frightened her off with my wild talk at the bus stop—yet my love was keener than ever. I still kept up my gynecological charts on her, and celebrated twenty-eighth days like sad festivals. I dreamed of her huge vaginal landscape, her loins in terrible cramp. Bernie burns.

I formed a plan. The first step was to get rid of her roommate. I made my first call to Bea that night.

Don't worry. It's not what you think. I didn't disguise my voice or breathe heavily and say nothing, nor any of your dirty-old-man tricks. I'm no phone creep. When Bea answered I told her who it was straight off.

"Miss Dellaspero? Bernie Perk. I don't see you in the drugstore anymore. You took advantage of my bargains but you don't come in."

Embarrassed, she made a few vague excuses which I pretended cleared matters up. "Well that's okay, then," I said. "I just thought you weren't satisfied with the merchandise or something. You can't put a guy in jail for worrying about his business."

In a week I called again. "Bea? Bernie."

This time she was pretty sore. "Listen," she said. "I never heard of a respectable merchant badgering people to trade with him. I was a little flustered when you called last week, but I have the right to trade wherever I want."

"Sure you do, Bea. Forget about that. That was a business call. This is social."

"Social?"

"That's right. I called to ask how you are. After our last conversation I thought I'd be seeing you. Then when you didn't come in I got a little worried. I thought you might be sick or something."

"I'm not sick."

"I'm relieved to hear it. That takes a load off my mind."

"I don't see why my health should be of any concern to you."

"Bea, I'm a *pharmacist*. Is it against the law for a pharmacist to inquire after the health of one of his customers?"

"Look, I'm not your customer."

"Your privilege, Bea. It's no crime for a man to

239

try to drum up a little trade. Well, as long as you're all right. That's the important thing. If we haven't got our health, what have we got?"

A few days later I called again. "Bernie here. Listen, Bea, I've been thinking. What do you say to dinner tonight? I know a terrific steakhouse in West Hartford. Afterward we could take in a late movie."

"What? Are you crazy?"

"Crazy? I don't get your meaning. Why do you say something like that?"

"Why do I say that? Why do you call me up all the time?"

"Well, I'm calling to invite you to dinner. Where does it say a man can't invite a young lady to have dinner with him?"

"I don't *know* you."

"Well, *sure* you know me, but even if you didn't, since when is it illegal for a person to try to make another person's acquaintance?"

"Don't call any more."

"I'm sorry you feel that way, Bea."

"Don't call me Bea."

"That's your name, isn't it? You don't drag a person into court for saying your name. Even your first name."

"I don't know what your trouble is, Mr. Perk—"

"Bernie. Call me Bernie. Bernie's my first name."

"I don't know what your trouble is, Mr. Perk, but you're annoying me. You'd better stop calling me."

She hung up.

I telephoned the next night. "My trouble, Bea, is that I think I'm falling in love with you."

"I don't want to hear this. Please get off the line."

"Bea, dear, you don't lock a fellow up for falling in love."

"You're insane. You must be at least twenty-five years older than I am."

"There *is* a difference in our ages, yes. But they don't arrest people for their birthdays."

240

She hung up.

My plan was going according to plan. "Bea?"

"I thought I convinced you to stop calling me."

"Bea, don't hang up. Listen, don't hang up. If you hang up I'll just have to call you again. Listen to what I have to say."

"What is it?"

"One of the reasons you're hostile is that you don't know anything about me. That's not my fault. I don't take any responsibility for that. I thought you'd come into the store and gradually we'd learn about each other, but you didn't want it that way. Well, when a person's in love he doesn't stand on ceremonies. I'm going to tell you a few things about myself."

"That can't make any difference."

" 'That can't make any difference.' Listen to her. Of course it can make a difference, Bea. What do you think love between two people is? It's *knowing* a person, understanding him. At least give me a chance to explain a few things. It's not a federal offense for a fellow to try to clear the air. All right?"

"I'll give you a minute."

"Gee, I'd better talk fast."

"You'd better."

"I want to be honest with you. You weren't far off when you said I was twenty-five years older than you are. As a matter of fact, I'm even older than you think. I've got a married son twenty-six years old."

"You're married?"

"Sure I'm married. Since when is it a crime to be married? My wife's name is Barbara. She has the same initial you do. But when I say I'm married I mean that *technically* I'm married. Babs is two years older than I am. O woman ages, Bea darling. All the zip has gone out of her figure. Menopause does that to a girl. I'll tell you the truth: I can't stand to look at her. I used to be so in love that if I saw her sitting on the toilet I'd get excited. I couldn't even wait for

241

her to wipe herself. Now I see her in her corsets and I wish I were blind. Her hair has turned gray—down *there*. Do you know what that does to a guy?"

"I'm hanging up."

"I'm telling the truth. *Where's it written it's police business when someone tells the truth?*"

I sent over a carton of Kotex and a carton of Tampax, and called her the following week. "Did you get the napkins?"

"I didn't order those. I don't want them."

"Order? Who said anything about order? You can't arrest a man for sending his sweetheart a present. It wouldn't stand up in court."

And again the next night.

"It's you, is it? I'm moving," she said. "I'm moving and I'm getting an unlisted number. I hope you're satisfied. I've lost my roommate on account of you. You've made her as nervous as me with these calls. So go ahead and say whatever you want—it's your last chance."

"Come out with me tonight."

"Don't be ridiculous."

"I love you."

"You're insane."

"Listen, go to bed with me. Please. I want to make love to you. Or let me come over and see you naked. I want to know just how big you really are down there."

"You're sick, do you know that? You need help."

"Then help me. Fuck me."

"I actually feel sorry for you. I really do."

"What are you talking about? I'm not hiding in any bushes. You know who I am. You know all about me. I'm Bernie Perk. My place of business is listed in the Yellow Pages. You could look me up. It isn't a crime to proposition a woman. You can't put a man behind bars for trying."

"You disgust me."

"Call the police."

242

"You disgust me."

"Press charges. They'll throw them out."

Her threat about an unlisted number didn't bother me; a simple call to the telephone company the following afternoon straightened *that* out. I gave them my name and told them that Bea had brought in a prescription to be filled. After she'd picked it up I discovered that I had misread it and given her a dangerous overdose. I told them that if I were unable to get in touch with her before she took the first capsule she might die. And they'd better give me her new address as well so that I could get an ambulance to her if she'd already taken the capsule and was unable to answer the phone. Love *always* finds a way!

I gave her time to settle herself in her new apartment and get some of her confidence back. Then, a week later—I couldn't wait longer: it was getting pretty close to her period—I took the package I had prepared and drove to Bea's new address. Her name on the letter box had been newly stenciled on a shiny black strip of cellulose, the last name only, the little darling—you know how single girls in big cities try to protect themselves by disguising their sex with initials or last names: the poor dears don't realize that it's a dead giveaway—along with her apartment number. I walked up the two flights and knocked on the door.

"Yes?"

"Mr. Giddons from Tiger's." The building was managed by Tiger's Real Estate and there's actually a Mr. Giddons who works there.

"What do you want?"

"We have a report there's some structural damage in 3-E. I want to check the walls in your apartment."

She opened the door, the trusting little cupcake. "It's you."

" 'All's fair in love and war.' "

243

"What do you want?"

"I'm berserk," I said, "amok with love. If you scream I'll kill you."

I moved into the room and closed the door behind me. What can I say? In the twentieth century there is no disgrace. It happened, so I'll tell you.

I pushed her roughly and turned my back to her while I pulled on the rubber. As I rolled it on I shouted threats to keep her in line. "One false move and I'll kill you. I've got a knife. Don't go for the unlisted phone or I'll slit you from ear to ear. I'll cut your pupick out. Stay away from the window. No tricks. I love you. Bernie burns, the pharmacist on fire. Don't double-cross me. If I miss you with the knife I'll shoot your head with my bullets." At last it was on. Still with my back to her I ordered her to stand still. "Don't make a move. If you make a move I'll strangle you with my bare hands. Don't make a move or you die. I'm wearing a State Trooper. They're the best. I'm smearing K-Y Petroleum Jelly on me. Everything the best, nothing but the best. All right," I said, "almost through. I just have to take this box of Kleenex out of my package and the aerosol douche. I'm unfolding the Venus Folding Feminine Syringe. There: these are for you. *Now.*" I turned to her.

"My God!" I said.

She had taken off her dress and brassiere and had pulled down her panties.

"Oh God," I gasped. "It's so *big!*"

"I didn't want you to rip my clothes," she said softly.

"But your legs, your legs are so thin!"

"Pipestems."

"And your poor frail arms."

"Pipecleaners."

"But my God, Bea. Down *there!* Down there you're magnificent!"

I saw the vastnesses, the tropical rain forest that was her pubes, the swollen mons like a freshly made

244

Indian tumulus, labia majora like a great inverted gorge, the lush pudendum.

"Fantastic!"

"I've the vulva of a giantess," she said sadly.

I reached out and hid my hands up to the wrists in her pubic hair. As soon as I touched her I felt myself coming. "Oh, Jesus. Oh, Jesus. I love you—oo—oo—oo!" It was over. The sperm made a warm, independent weight in the bottom of my State Trooper. It swung against me like a third ball. "Oh God," I sighed. "Oh dear. Oh my. Let me just catch my breath. Whew. Holy Cow! Great Scott!

"Okay," I said in a few moments, "now you listen to me. I'm at your mercy. How can you throw a man in the hoosegow when you know as much about him as you do? I didn't jump out at you from an alley or drag you into a car. Look—" I turned my pockets inside out—"I'm not armed. There's no knife. I don't carry a gun. These hands are trained. They fill prescriptions. Do you think they could strangle? Granted I threatened you, but I was afraid you'd scream. Look at it this way. I was protecting *you*. You're just starting out in the neighborhood. It's a first-class building. Would you want a scandal? And didn't I take every precaution? Look at the douche. Everything the best that money can buy. And what did it come to in the end? I never even got close to you. To tell you the truth I thought it might happen just this way. It's not like rape. I love you. How can you ruin a man who loves you? I'm no stranger. You know me. You know my wife's name. I told you about my son. I'm a grandfather. Take a look at these pictures of my grandchildren. Did I ever show you these? This one's Susan. Four years old and a little imp. Boy, does she keep her parents hopping! And this is Greg. Greg's the thoughtful one. He'll be the scholar. Are you going to put a grandfather in jail? You got me excited. Perk perks, the pharmacist in flames. I love you, but I'll never bother you again. I had to, just this once. Give me a chance. It would

245

break my wife's heart to find out about me. Okay, they'd try to hush it up and maybe the grandkids would never hear about it, but what about my son? That's another story.

"I'll tell you something else. *You're the last.* A man's first woman is special, and so's his last. He never gets over either of them. And how much time do you think I have left? You saw how I was. I can't control it. I've had it as a man. I'm through. Give me a break, Bea. Don't call the police. I love you. I'm your friend. Though I'll let you in on a secret. I'd still be your friend in jail. All I really wanted was to see it. I *still* see it. I'm looking now. No, I'll be honest: *staring.* I'm staring because I've never seen anything like it, and I want to remember it forever. Not that I'll ever forget. I *never* will. Never."

I was weeping. Bea had started to dress.

"There are jokes," I said when I'd regained control, "about men on motorcycles disappearing inside women, or getting lost. There's this one about a rabbi married to a woman who's supposed to be really fabulous. One day the cleaning lady comes into the bedroom where the rabbi's wife is taking a nap. She's lying on the bedspread, all naked except where she's covered her genitals with the rabbi's skullcap, and the maid says, 'Oh, my God, I knew it would happen one day. The rabbi fell in.' I used to laugh at stories like that, but I never will again. You're *so* beautiful."

"I didn't scream," she said, "because it was my fate."

"What?"

"People find out about me. In high school, in gym, the girls would see me in the shower, and they'd tell their boyfriends. Then the boys would humiliate me. Worse things were done than what you've done. We had to leave town. In the new high school I got a note from the doctor so that I could be excused from gym, but they still found out. Maybe someone from my old town knew someone in the

246

new town, maybe the doctor himself said something—I don't know. Boys would take me out and ... want to see. When I graduated I moved away and started all over in a different state. There was a boy ... I liked him. One day we made love—and *he* told. It was terrible. I can't even wear a bathing suit. You know? Then I came to Hartford. And you found out. I didn't scream because it was my fate. At least you say you love me—"

"Adore you," I said.

She said something I couldn't quite hear.

"What was that?"

"I said it's my burden. Only it carries me. It's as if I were always on horseback," she cried, and rushed toward me and embraced me, and I held her like that for two hours, and when I was ready we made love.

During the commercial break Dick discovered that apparently his guests had lost their voices.

After his confession the druggist had slumped in his chair, his hands in his lap, his mouth slack-jawed. His eyes were glazed, stunned by the violation of his character. Dick murmured his name and shook him gently, then turned to the others. "Do you think he's okay?" he asked. But Jack Patterson and Pepper and Mel were as somnolent as the pharmacist. The cat had their tongues. Behr-Bleibtreau was smiling. "Listen," Dick told his panel, "you can't poop out on me. We've got almost two hours to go." Pepper Steep's eyes were closed. Jack Patterson was catatonic. Bernie was off in some private world. "You've got to be able to talk," he said. "It's bad radio." He turned to Mel Son. "Come on, Mel, you're the professional. Give us some help here. When we go back on the air, get with it." Mel scowled; he winced and blinked. He *seems* alive, Dick thought, but helpless, like someone gagged by robbers.

Meanwhile the commercial tapes were being played over the loudspeaker in the studio. At this time of night there were only the public service spots: enlistment pitches for the Naval Air Reserve, appeals for Radio Free Europe, "Only You Can Prevent Forest Fires," "Watch Out for the Other Guy." Dick loved the ragged shrillness of these messages, their martial musical backgrounds, the sense they gave of a low budget and a moribund style: the sound man's cellophane fires, more cozy than ominous, the long scream of a car horn gone awry that was, in these pieces, an inevitable signal of an accident proclaiming itself, a fanfare of the accomplished fact. He loved the starched treble of the announcer's anti-Communist voice, and enjoyed—the discount for broadcasting public-service messages was enormous at this time of the morning—the sense the commercials created that his show was self-sustaining, a public service itself, that the equipment operated for *him,* existed to carry *his* voice out over the mysterious air incredible distances, into receivers (those strange extensions of his mouth), a sign in the night that there was no death.

Ordinarily he had to shush his guests who, suddenly relaxed, chattered nervously during these commercial breaks, annoying to him as if they drowned out the strains of some favorite song. Now he began to panic as the commercials came toward their end. Hurriedly he opened the key on his mike and spoke to his engineer. "Put up another commercial. Give me some time here." He looked at Behr-Bleibtreau. If his panelists wouldn't talk he'd be alone with him. He was getting scared.

Then Vendler came in with the sandwiches.

"Vendler," Dick said, "where've you been? We're all starving."

From time to time Dick had attempted to put Vendler on the air, but the man wasn't interested. The popular late-night television shows all had their Max Asners and Mrs. Millers and pet bartenders, even their favorite barbers and regular cab drivers: fans who never missed a night, who out of some inexplicable urgency were always in the studio audience and were never surprised when they were called on. But Dick had never been able to draw this man out. Probably he did not even listen to the show. He was content merely to wait around until Dick mentioned his delicatessen and then would pick up the empty lazy susan from the previous night and depart.

This time Vendler wouldn't get away so easy. Dick pulled a chair up for Vendler and sat him down in it. Grabbing Bernie's microphone, he put it in front of the man, gave him one of his own sandwiches and took one himself. Quickly he removed it from the wax paper envelope and took a great bite, pantomiming monumental chewing, holding it up in front of him and waving it about like a man eating on the run. Though he hadn't said a word, it was as though he was speaking to them with his mouth full. He spun the lazy susan as if it were a roulette wheel and pointed to it with his sandwich hand inviting everyone in the studio to partake. No one made a move except for Jerry, his engineer, who came out of the control booth, grabbed some sandwiches and coffee and rushed back into the booth.

They were on the air.

DICK GIBSON: [In a split second balancing these factors: he was no longer alone with Behr-Bleibtreu. Vendler was with him. A laconic man but a presence from the outside, one of the best he could have right now. Yes. Vendler from Vendler's 24-Hour Kosher-Style Delicatessen, with the smell of lox on his fingers, a suggestion of the briny deeps of pickle jars, his hands red from frankfurter dyes, dark bits of pastrami herb on his white shirt, a vaguely kosher-style lint. A man refulgent with the fluorescent light from his massive delicatessen cases, a solid fellow, full as salami casing, smooth as the formica tabletops he rubbed with damp rags. A generous man with cardboard placards for the Sisterhood Lecture Series using up the precious space in his windows, with slotted collection cans all along the top of his white cases, for Leukemia, Heart Fund, obscure agencies in Israel. A man with a bread-slicing machine, with the butt ends of corned beefs and bloody, delicious ropes about roasts, with sliced lox spread out on oily paper like cards in a card trick. Such a bright, glowing guy! And he wouldn't be tainted by what had gone on that night! Yes! It was Vendler he would use against Behr-Bleibtreau.

But his habit was to leave right after his name was mentioned. So here was Dick's problem: Should he guarantee the man's staying on by never mentioning his name, or should he risk it and even throw in the plug? Vendler was in the chair, the mike in front of him. He had never been this close to being on the air before; he might even like it. If Dick was skillful enough, he might even forget they were talking on the radio after the first five minutes. Subjects, subjects, he needed subjects.

Subjects? He had a ready-made one: It was a family joke among those who listened to the program regularly that Dick's engineer had a voracious appetite. Indeed, it was Jerry—whom the audience never heard—who was the center of the feast. His appetite was the only legend attached to the show, its single myth. (Why was that?) He got fan mail, requests for pictures, recipes, actual cakes, diets, pennies to weigh himself. Dick sometimes read Jerry's mail over the air or repeated certain comments he had made about the food. The audience pictured the engineer chewing his way through the night as he turned his various dials. It was as good for the program as Jack Benny's feud with Fred Allen, Phil Harris's drinking, Don Wilson's weight, Crosby's sport shirts, Jessel's girls. It neither added to nor detracted from the legend that his engineer's appetite was real, that the man *was* a pig and, further, a *cheap* pig who ate this much every night only because it was free. So there was his subject: Vendler meets Jerry, the King of Breakfast confronts the Emperor of Freeloaders.

All this in that split second between the red illumination of the On the Air sign and Dick's opening his mouth to speak. And then this: *Because my character is my mind. Bernie's is his obsession, Pepper's her generosity, Jack's his meanness, Jerry's his*

250

freeloader's appetite. God knows what Behr-Bleib-treau's is, maybe his mystery, but mine's my mind, what I think and nothing else. And this: He was a character as other people were amoral.]

Vendler is with us, ladies and gentlemen.

[Surprised because he felt no resistance when he reached out to hold the man in place. Then, realizing that it was because he had not yet mentioned the delicatessen, that the one required the other, that he'd clicked only one tumbler in the lock, he gives the plug to get the resistance over with at once.]

. Of Vendler's 24-Hour Kosher-Style Delicatessen.

[And there *was* a shiver, thinner even than the faint, indecisive shift of the body that signals some-one's intention to rise from a table after a meal has been eaten. So Vendler had a character too, or at least habits. But he was still fixed by Dick's stiff, outstretched arm.]

Just exactly what *is* kosher style, Arthur? Some of our listeners might not know.

ARTHUR VENDLER: Chopped liver. Lox—that's smoked salmon. Kosher pertains to the dietary laws.

DICK GIBSON: [Not bad, actually, for a man who didn't know this was going to happen to him. His voice a little loud, though; probably raised because he's uncertain about the equipment—look at the way he bends down and brings his mouth right up to the microphone. I have no character; I am what I think. And what I say on the radio. What I think and what I say. My *voice*.]

ARTHUR VENDLER: Very few people keep kosher any more. You have to be a fanatic. Even most rabbis don't keep kosher except on the high holidays. It's a style. Kosher style is a style. It's not actually kosher, just the kind of things people like to eat. I don't know if I can explain it. Rye bread, herring, smoked white fish. If you've ever been to the mountains, they serve it in the mountains. I guess the best way I can put it is New York style. What you get in your New York delicatessens.

251

DICK GIBSON: Well, it's delicious. Look at Jerry, will you? That's called Jerry-Style 24-Hour Eating. How would you like a guy like that for a steady customer?

[*How's Behr-Bleibtreau taking all this?*]

Wouldn't *he* run up a tab? Maybe he doesn't swallow, what do you think?

['Tain't funny, McGee. Get into this, Vendler, please. Help me out.]

He eats for a whole town.

[Behr-Bleibtreau is frowning. He shifts in his chair and looks toward the control booth. What is this? What's he doing? He points his finger at Jerry. Jerry puts down his sandwich. He puts down the cream soda. My God, *he spits out what's in his mouth!* He pushes the food away from him. There goes *that* subject.]

How's business, Vendler?

ARTHUR VENDLER: Business is good. I can't complain.

DICK GIBSON: You can't complain, eh?

ARTHUR VENDLER: No.

DICK GIBSON: No, eh?

ARTHUR VENDLER: No.

DICK GIBSON: Well, that's good that business is good.

ARTHUR VENDLER: Yes.

DICK GIBSON: [Getting mad at him: there is no reason for grown men to clam up before a microphone. He imagines Vendler in his delicatessen, kibitzing the customers, his mouth going a mile a minute as he slices meat at the machine, the authority of the merchant on him. What was there to fear from a microphone? He spent too much time reassuring his guests, talking them down from where they were treed in their shyness. Damn their timidity, their deference. Then, when they finally did speak out— just look at Jack and Pepper and Bernie—they went around with a hangover from their words.]

Yes, eh?

ARTHUR VENDLER: (*nervously*) Sure.

DICK GIBSON: You know what I'm thinking?

ARTHUR VENDLER: What's that?

DICK GIBSON: [Terrific—a regular Mr. Show Business, this Vendler.]

It must cost you twenty-five to thirty dollars a week to make up these trays for us. That's four weeks a month, twelve months a year. You'd be better off taking a regular spot on the show, buying time and letting us do a commercial for you. You'd be surprised how low the rates are this time of night.

[Mad at Jerry too, now.]

Of course Jerry might quit if you didn't bring the sandwiches around, but maybe not. He seems to have lost his appetite anyway. Think it over. Of course you might be doing something on the tax angle. I didn't think of that aspect of it.

ARTHUR VENDLER: Listen, I don't—

DICK GIBSON: Sure. What do *I* know about it?

ARTHUR VENDLER: I've got to be getting back.

DICK GIBSON: Haban Nagila, kid.

ARTHUR VENDLER: Where's my lazy susan?

DICK GIBSON: Lying down.

[Vendler leaves the studio. Dick Gibson thinks, I am cutting my losses, and stares at Mel Son—*this is air-time, this is while they are on the air, no one is saying anything, their silence is being sent out over the ether*—and scowls Behr-Bleibtreauly. He has some hope. Mel's uneasy. His eyes dart angrily. His behavior isn't the withdrawal of the others, but seems, rather, an effort to keep control of himself. Perhaps Mel is Jewish; maybe he resents the way Dick has treated Vendler. But the man won't talk. Dick gives him every opportunity. Well, Mel, tell, he thinks. But it's hopeless. Perhaps three minutes have gone by since they came back on the air. And then he thinks—the guests in the studio. He announces their names, making up one for those he has forgotten or never knew. Then he makes up other names and gives their place of business. Then he thinks: the telegrams.]

We should be getting some telegrams about now.

[He looks at Jerry.]

No? Nothing in yet? Well, the lines are open. If anyone has a question for Professor Behr-Bleibtreau, send us a telegram at WHCN, Hartford, Connecticut. I'll accept collect wires. Please keep your messages under ten words. Ask the Professor. Or, if you have questions for one of the panel members—*Mr. Son, for example*—we'll entertain those as well. Or perhaps you don't have a question at all. Maybe you just want to make a comment. Make it at our expense.

[Interrogatives. Declaratives. Let's see, that leaves exclamatives.]

Just tell the operator you want to send a collect wire to me, Dick Gibson—that's D-i-c-k G-i-b-s-o-n—care of WHCN—W-H-C-N—Hartford—H-a-r-t-f-o-r-d—Connecticut—C-o-n-n-e-c-t-i-c-u-t. Or, if you'd rather abbreviate it, C-o-n-n. Talk it over with the Western Union operator; see what she says.

[Okay, that's another minute. Only a hundred and five to go. Now what?]

But he *knew* now what. Behr-Bleibtreau, that's what. Behr-Bleibtreau knew too. The man still smiled, but Dick sensed that the smile had shifted, amusement no longer but something preceding damage. Perhaps he sensed Dick's dread and was annoyed that it had not been enough to silence him. (Though in a way he had been silenced; he could think of no more ways to kill time.) Looking at his panel, Dick was suddenly consumed with sympathy for them. The professor had their tongues, and now he was after his. He thought of signing off early, declaring the evening at an end, paying the lost revenues from the remaining commercials out of his own pocket. But then the professor would have his tongue too. Dick, who had no character, wanted to beat him.

The mistake the others had made was that they had gone too far. He would keep it down. He would ask Behr-Bleibtreau how he liked Hartford, to compare it with other places he had been. Behr-Bleibtreau was waiting to see what he would do. Just keep cool, Dick warned himself, small talk, everything low key and easy, no more drama. Just relax and say—

DICK GIBSON: (*almost shouting*) *All right, Professor, what the hell's all this crap about a loaded gun?*

BEHR-BLEIBTREAU: Please pass the sandwiches.

DICK GIBSON: The sandwiches? I'm talking about loaded guns.

BEHR-BLEIBTREAU: I'm talking about sandwiches. Is there turkey? Is there dark meat?

DICK GIBSON: [Grabbing his microphone suddenly. If they saw him his radio audience might think he was an ace reporter, urgent, shirt-sleeved, like someone on the radio in the movies with a scoop.]

Ladies and gentlemen, you don't know what's been going on here tonight! My panelists are unable to speak! This man has something to do with it. It's a trick. Perhaps they're hypnotized. I don't know how he does it, he doesn't touch them, he swings no pendulum, but *something's* happened, *something's* up! He's after me too. (*to Behr-Bleibtreau*) Is that it?

BEHR-BLEIBTREAU: I don't see the bottle opener. Would you swing the lazy susan around this way, please? Perhaps it's on your side of the tray. Oh, never mind. Here it is.

DICK GIBSON: Don't listen to him. He doesn't have a bottle opener. He's not looking for one. There isn't even any soda in his hand. I don't know what his game is, but he's giving you a false picture.

BEHR-BLEIBTREAU: No more turkey? I'll take the corned beef. I'm asking for indigestion, I think, but it looks marvelous.

DICK GIBSON: Don't believe him. He's *not* asking for indigestion. He's not *eating!*

BEHR-BLEIBTREAU: The bread's stale. Where's the mustard? Would you pass me that plastic knife?

DICK GIBSON: 'The bread's *fresh!* There's *already* mustard on the sandwiches!

BEHR-BLEIBTREAU: It's rather warm in the studio. May I take off my jacket?

DICK GIBSON: He's wearing a sweater.

BEHR-BLEIBTREAU: Whoops, sorry. That was clumsy of me. I seem to have smeared some ketchup on my glasses while I was getting out of my jacket. Could you hand me one of those paper napkins?

DICK GIBSON: He's still in his sweater. He doesn't wear glasses. The napkins are right in front of him.

JACK PATTERSON: Here you are, Doctor.

BEHR-BLEIBTREAU: Thank you, Professor Patterson.

DICK GIBSON: Patterson never opened his mouth. Behr-Bleibtreau's a ventriloquist! What's going on here? Why are you lying to my listeners?

BEHR-BLEIBTREAU: But it's *you* who are lying, Mr. Gibson. I must confess I don't understand what you hope to accomplish.

DICK GIBSON: What do you want?

BEHR-BLEIBTREAU: I want a napkin. I want the mustard. I want the plastic knife.

DICK GIBSON: What color are the walls in this studio?

BEHR-BLEIBTREAU: The walls? Pale yellow, aren't they?

DICK GIBSON: They're *white!* What color's my tie?

BEHR-BLEIBTREAU: Well, it's all colors. There's red and there's green. It's a pattern. It's all colors.

DICK GIBSON: It's *blue,* it's *solid* blue! What are you doing? I'll ask the people in the studio. What color is this tie I'm wearing?

BEHR-BLEIBTREAU: All right, there's no point in that. Leave it alone. All right, I'll confess. I've been having some fun with you.

BEHR-BLEIBTREAU: Very clever imitation of my voice, Mr. Gibson. You ought to do this sort of thing professionally—in nightclubs.

DICK GIBSON: Thank you very much, Doctor.

DICK GIBSON: You mean *you* ought to. Ladies and gentlemen, I didn't imitate him. He imitated *me*.

BEHR-BLEIBTREAU: *Look out!*

DICK GIBSON: He also imitated me saying "Ladies and gentlemen, I didn't imitate *him*. He imitated *me*." I haven't said anything since I asked the studio audience about the color of my tie.

DICK GIBSON: He said that too.

BEHR-BLEIBTREAU: *Look out! He's got a gun!*

DICK GIBSON: Oh, ho! *That* was a mistake, Dr. Behr-Bleibtreau. I think I'll just sit this one out. *I* don't see any gun. If he has one—whoever *he* may be—he should be making some demands along about now. He should be saying "Hands up! Give me your money and nobody'll get hurt," or "Don't anyone move, I'm taking the woman with me." People with guns can be very articulate about what they want.

BEHR-BLEIBTREAU: *What if they're suicidal?*

DICK GIBSON: What are you talking about? What do you mean?

BEHR-BLEIBTREAU: What if they intend to kill themselves? What if the gun is still concealed and they intend to shoot themselves?

DICK GIBSON: Look, come on. Who's supposed to have this gun? If someone *really* has a gun—

BEHR-BLEIBTREAU: Tell him (*silence*) Go ahead, tell him. I release your tongue. You may speak. (*silence*)

DICK GIBSON: There. You see? I don't deny, of course, that Mr. Behr-Bleibtreau could come up with an appropriate voice, but I wonder how convincing his bang bang would be.

BEHR-BLEIBTREAU: *Tell him!*

DICK GIBSON: Tell me.

BEHR-BLEIBTREAU: Ncy *chλmyc* Tell him.

MEL SON: What do I have to lose? It's almost all up with me anyway. Gibson's tie is brown and yellow stripes. The walls are green.

DICK GIBSON: Mel? Is that you, Mel? Is he doing your voice?

257

DICK GIBSON: (*whispering*) (I didn't ask that.)

MEL SON: It's me.

BEHR-BLEIBTREAU: Show him the gun, why don't you? [Mel Son takes a revolver out of his pocket.]

DICK GIBSON: What is this? Mel, what's happening?

BEHR-BLEIBTREAU: Does he have a gun?

DICK GIBSON: Yes.

BEHR-BLEIBTREAU: Did you say yes or was that me imitating your voice?

DICK GIBSON: I said yes.

BEHR-BLEIBTREAU: Speak up. Will Dick Gibson deny that Mel Son has a weapon in his hand? Supposing for a moment that the audience has been hearing two Dick Gibsons, a real one and an imposter— which is not the case—that would still leave the real Dick Gibson to deny the existence of the gun. *Does* he deny it?

DICK GIBSON: I already said he has a gun. I already said so.

BEHR-BLEIBTREAU: There are no disclaimers? It's not too late.

DICK GIBSON: The gun's real. The real Dick Gibson says the real gun is real.

BEHR-BLEIBTREAU: Very well, then.

BEHR-BLEIBTREAU: You really are a superb mimic, Mr. Gibson.

BEHR-BLEIBTREAU: Stop that.

DICK GIBSON: Is that loaded?

BEHR-BLEIBTREAU: Show him.

[Mel Son holds the gun out and Dick Gibson peers into the chambers of the revolver. The leaden tips of the bullets resemble dull stones in a bracelet.]

DICK GIBSON: (*softly*) You want to put that back, Mel. What would you need a thing like that for?

MEL SON: I'm hunting. I'm a hunter.

DICK GIBSON: (*to Behr-Bleibtreau*) Why don't you talk to him? Can you talk to him?

BEHR-BLEIBTREAU: Me? Shall I hypnotize him?

DICK GIBSON: Why would a man bring a gun into a radio station? He's supposed to be a professional.

That's got to be against FCC regulations. I just hope this program isn't being monitored. There'd be one hell of an investigation.

[There is a click.]

BEHR-BLEIBTREAU: He's cocked it.

DICK GIBSON: Listen, I don't like what's happening here. I think we need the police. *(to the listening audience)* Ladies and gentlemen, this is Dick Gibson, WHCN, Hartford, Connecticut. There's a man in my studio waving a revolver around. If the police are listening, would you get over here, please? Maybe one of you listeners ought to phone them and tell them what's happening.

BEHR-BLEIBTREAU: Do you think that was wise? He could kill half a dozen people before the police even got close to him. He means to die, anyway.

DICK GIBSON: We don't know that.

MEL SON: We *know* it.

DICK GIBSON: *(to the listening audience)* Forget what I said. Don't phone the police. *(to Behr-Bleibtreau)* If the police heard me they'll be coming. They'd have to; it's their duty. There's no way to stop them.

BEHR-BLEIBTREAU: They didn't hear you.

DICK GIBSON: They didn't? *(suspiciously)* They didn't, eh? *(whispering now)* (Ladies and gentlemen, this is Dick Gibson, WHCN, Hartford, Connecticut, the *Qui Transtulit Sustinet* State. A fantastic thing is going on at this station. I'm sitting in Studio 2A, where several people have gathered for an informal midnight-to-dawn talk program called *The Dick Gibson Show*. The guests, Jack Patterson, Bernard Perk, Pepper Steep and our Special Guest, Psychologist Edmond Behr-Bleibtreau, together with Jerry the engineer and yours truly, Dick Gibson, the show's host who is wearing a solid blue tie, are being held virtually at bay in the white-walled studio along with several of *their* guests by Mel Son, an Amherst,

Massachusetts, disc jockey and former unsuccessful candidate for the Massachusetts State Assembly. I don't know how long I'll be permitted to speak into these microphones, ladies and gentlemen, but as long as I'm able I'll try to give you a picture of what's happening here. There are, of course, several eyewitnesses to these events, and I'd put them on the air to let them describe in their own words all that's occurred, but unfortunately, all their voices seem to have been stolen, with the exception of my own, Mel Son's, and Dr. Behr-Bleibtreau's. The pussycat's got their tongues. Dr. Jack Patterson of Hartford Community College made a brief remark a little over an hour ago to Bernie Perk, the registered pharmacist, but since then has lapsed back into silence. Listeners to the program heard Patterson's voice again a few moments ago when he reputedly handed Behr-Bleibtreau a napkin to wipe some ketchup off his glasses, but both the remark and the ketchup incident itself have been challenged by your reporter who believes the learned psychologist to be some kind of hypnotist/ventriloquist. At any rate, the three principals seem to be Behr-Bleibtreau, Mel Son and Dick Gibson. Wait, Behr-Bleibtreau is about to speak. Let's listen . . .)

BEHR-BLEIBTREAU: *Ncy chλmc.*

DICK GIBSON: (Did you get that, folks?)

MEL SON: I . . . My . . .

BEHR-BLEIBTREAU: Ync *hcmyć.*

DICK GIBSON: It's really kind of wonderful the way you guys worked all this out between you to take over my program. It's really very funny.

MEL SON: [He brings the barrel of the gun down heavily across the bridge of Dick's nose, drawing blood.]

My name is Mel Son. I've been in a trance, but I've just been released—I get the feeling temporarily—in order to tell my story. I've never been in a trance before. It's queer. It gives you a funny feeling. Everything in the trance but Dick's tie was sort of blue—oo—oo and soft. Your eyes are blue, Dick.

DICK GIBSON: My eyes *are* blue.

MEL SON: Your blood—where I cut you—your blood is blue . . . gee, I just can't get over this trance business. Once I was hypnotized in a nightclub. There were fifteen of us and we all went under, but this was nothing like that. This was like being sick or something. I don't really mean sick—nothing hurts or anything like that—but it's . . . well, *dreamy*, as if you were heavily medicated or just beginning to come down with something. It's like the way you're sensitized sometimes in a barber's chair getting a haircut in winter. The back of your head gets all prickly. It's terrific. I mean, I was really getting excited. And I'll tell you something else. I never felt—this is important—I never felt *humble*. I mean, you'd think if a guy's in a trance his will would be rendered helpless, that he'd be going around Yes, Mastering everything in sight. But it isn't like that at all. As a matter of fact, you feel very *proud* in a trance, almost stuck-up. You have a lot of confidence. It's all very dignified. That's the truth about trances. If you want my honest opinion, I think you're making a mistake to waste your pity on enchanted princes locked up in trees. I can't get over it. It's really fantastic. I tell you, there's more than is dreamt of in your philosophy.

DICK GIBSON: Less.

MEL SON: No, Dick, more—much more.

DICK GIBSON: Why don't you put the gun down, Mel?

MEL SON: Not just yet, Dick. I've got to shoot myself with it. I'm going to put the barrel in my mouth and blow my head off. Brr. What a way to go! That's a phrase that's always gotten to me—you know what I mean? Another one is—you get this on the news wire every once in a while—"So-and-so killed his wife and three children and then turned the rifle on himself." That sounds horrible, but I don't get the logistics of it. A man would have to have incredibly long arms to turn a rifle on himself. "He put a bullet through his brain": that's another one. How discrete that sounds. So definitive. That's the sort of thing *I'm* after. As a matter of fact, that's one of the reasons I chose to do it on the radio. It'd be a different thing altogether if I snuck off in a corner by myself. I've have done it on my own show but I don't reach the market you do.

To tell the truth, I haven't settled how I'll do it yet. I thought I might sit on the pistol. Or stick it in my ear. Or against the part in my hair. Or through my eye. Or inside my shirt, or under my arm. Or against my heart. Or across my Adam's apple. Do you get what I'm aiming at? Ha ha. Ignition, explosion, obliteration, smear. Something really dirty: he died as he lived. Before and After—that's it. Here today, gone tomorrow. And a stain that won't wash out. Something in me green or blue in the woodwork like grain. My nostrils divorced and my eyes disappeared, hair in the wound and skin on the floor. Bone around like shattered glass. Pieces of tooth, and my ingrown toenails out. My sideburns on fire and a hole in my birthmark. My death archeological, my corpse my body's palimpsest. Mel melded. Jigsaw Mel the Son-saw puzzle. Mosaic me. Blood and blood. Mel Sundry. Mel the Sonset. Mel the Melted. Molten Mel the Sonburned. The Sonspot.

DICK GIBSON: [Upset. His wound, where Mel struck him with the revolver, is throbbing. Fantastically, it occurs to him that if Mel kills himself or if Behr-Bleibtreau takes his voice, he will never have done a quiz show.]

Ladies and gentlemen, welcome to ... *Night School!* This is your host on the college of knowledge, quizzer whizzer Dick Gibson. Tonight's contestant is Mel Son the Suicide, Amherst d.j. and d.o.a. Let's try to get some answers—Mel?

MEL SON: Quizzer whizzer?

DICK GIBSON: Yez zir, yez zir. Are you ready for the first question?

MEL SON: I am. For the time being I am. But hurry,

hurry. I'll plug my pulse and blast my blood. I'll shoot my shirt and kill my collar. I'll—

DICK GIBSON: All righty. (*to his mute guests*) No coaching from the audience. The question is . . . Why? Do you have that? Would you like me to repeat the question?

MEL SON: Would you repeat the question?

DICK GIBSON: Surely. *Why?*

MEL SON: Sin.

DICK GIBSON: Sin?

MEL SON: Sin, sir.

DICK GIBSON: Sincerely?

MEL SON: Sine qua nonly.

DICK GIBSON: Could you develop that a little? This is an essay question.

MEL SON: Well . . . *because.* Let's just say that I'm petitioning for an undress of griefiness.

Mel Son's Story:

Mel Son was a normal child, no more curious than any other child his age—and no less. His hands had spent time in his mother's brassieres; he'd fingered Dad's jock and spied on Sis. But necessity wasn't involved. It was just that same neutral obligation that makes an older boy smoke his first cigarette or one ten years younger sit behind the steering wheel of the family car while his mother shops.

Puberty hit him as hard as it does others, but if he was uncomfortable he was no more so than anyone else. It was as normal as the day is long. There were wet dreams—I don't remember them, only the sensations—and some masturbation—I found it difficult; I could never really decide what to think about—and once in a while dates. It was a routine adolescence, steady as she goes.

Then, one night when I was fifteen years old, an old man sat next to me in a movie theater. He put his hand on me and stroked me till I came. It felt good and I let him. Maybe it was because there was a girl with me and my senses were already aroused, or that I knew that there was no chance, absolutely

263

no chance in the world, that this girl would do to me what the old man was doing. Or it may have been something else, something about the old man's surreptitious skill. Sly and smooth he was as a pickpocket ... Whatever, I let him.

Do you see what I'm driving at? Do you know what I'm saying? That I'm queer? No! It was *normal*. That the pressures I felt, the feelings I had—they were *mine,* my own. What did they have to do with girls or women? What did they have to do even with that old man in the theater? Do you see? It was *my* thigh, *my* neck, *my* cock, *my* balls. Not pussy, not tits. It was my young man's own ass I sat on, my skin I lived in, my reflexive flesh. *I never made the leap of sex.*

And how *is* it made? What round peg/round hole argument in sex waiting on puberty like the plain geometry? How *does* it happen? What Noah instinct is it—in me omitted—that drives us two by two to beds like polite company approaching table? By what inevitable degrees does bent become inclination, inclination tendency, tendency penchant, penchant disposition, disposition fate? Is there glue in those brassieres? What lodestar astrology shoves our lives? Where's it written, eh? As if love could only be the *prescribed* friction! Hah! I'll write you a new prescription! Why, love *machines!* Marry the bus that takes you to town, *that* throbbing thing! Embrace wind, kiss the earthquake, hold the sea! Make up to gravity! To all the physics of adversity!

Feelings' other was never for me. Erection was extension, not tropism. I was born sexually intransitive, a sort of mule, but complete too. Or now complete—since that old man complete. *Anyone* would have done: the girl I was with that night, men, whores, boys, wives—anyone. Or anything: my prick lapped by dogs, flys walking the white underside of my arm, tight squeezes, the warm pressure of the bathwater, Foot-Eeze machines, spot-reducing

264

machines, whirlpool baths, a fast trot on a warm day on a good horse over rough ground!

And I was no more grateful to the man than I would be to the fly or the horse! And I wasn't reciprocal; I have never wished to hold or mount or touch or taste another human being. Oh my body's buttons, oh its levers, oh its zones! I want hands on me, in me, breath in my ears, fingernails on my back, a tongue at my toes, cunning massage. And I'll tell you something else: it's too damn much *work* to jerk off. Though after the old man I at last knew what to think of: why *me,* why *myself!* After the old man I couldn't look at my naked reflection in the full-length mirror in the bathroom without getting excited!

So that's about it, quizzer whizzer. I've lived with bad men, men so bad they've never wanted anything from me in return.

[He winks at State Assemblyman Victor Ash.]

DICK GIBSON: You're killing yourself for your sins?

MEL SON: Foo on my sins. Nah, what do they amount to? Lust and sloth. Nah. I'm killing myself because my gloss is going, because I'm heavier, because my hair's falling out, because my teeth are rotten and my breath is bad. Even dirty old men draw the line somewhere. I will not live without pleasure. Where's the solace, eh? I'll put a ball in my balls. That's it! Up my testicles to death. Whoops, confession's over. I'm back in the trance.

DICK GIBSON: This is terrible. Will he do it?

BEHR-BLEIBTREAU: Of course he'll do it.

DICK GIBSON: [There is still the possibility that it is all a joke, but he is caught up in the strange program, the strangest he's ever been on. Not really understanding how they've worked it, but suspecting— where were the telegrams?—that the show might not be going out over the air at all. (The engineer, given great powers, emergency powers, one of those like tugboat captains or bombardiers, say, who rise to

265

command for brief interims, or secret servicemen who under certain conditions tell Presidents what to do, bishops crowning kings while the kingdom floats leaderless and unmoored—ultimate privilege hiding in them, all the more awesome for its ordinary invisibility and its provisional quality—could have cut all of them off the air whenever he chose.) But even if it wasn't actually going over the air—and he still had the feeling that it was—it might be on tape, and even if it wasn't on tape there was still the studio audience to think about, and even if they were all deaf as well as dumb, then there was still Behr-Bleibtreau and Mel and himself. The show *must* go on. And this, he thought, is all I have for principles.]

When? *(softly)* Shouldn't we try to take the gun away from him?

BEHR-BLEIBTREAU: If you struggle with him you could be killed yourself.

DICK GIBSON: Mel? *(no answer)* Mel? *(nobody home)* Mel. *(out to lunch)* Mel, it's Dick. *(closed for the duration)* Mel Son. *(Nobody here by that name; try down the street)* Professor Behr-Bleibtreau. *(This sotto voce: in the style of the outnumbered, the beleaguered, two pals in ambush)* (This is serious, Professor. That gun could go off any minute. Maybe if we could get him to keep talking ... Why don't you release his tongue again?)

BEHR-BLEIBTREAU: (It's too late, but that gives me an idea. There may still be a way.)

DICK GIBSON: (Is it a long shot?)

BEHR-BLEIBTREAU: (Yes.)

DICK GIBSON: (Is it risky?)

BEHR-BLEIBTREAU: (Yes.)

DICK GIBSON: (Is it one chance in a million?)

BEHR-BLEIBTREAU: (More or less.)

DICK GIBSON: (What is it? A man's life's at stake. It may be worth a try.)

BEHR-BLEIBTREAU: His life for your silence!

DICK GIBSON: Hey, what is this?

BEHR-BLEIBTREAU: Your silence for his life. An even trade.

DICK GIBSON: Hey, cut it out. Come on. Hey!

BEHR-BLEIBTREAU: Shh.

DICK GIBSON: *(fiercely)* The show must go on!

BEHR-BLEIBTREAU: It will.

DICK GIBSON: *I must be on it!* The show must go on and I must be on it. I'm the show.

BEHR-BLEIBTREAU: But you've got nothing to show. I'm taking your voice.

DICK GIBSON: No.

BEHR-BLEIBTREAU: Yes. I'm having it. I'm shoving it down your throat. Give it up. Let him live.

DICK GIBSON: What are you talking about? No!

BEHR-BLEIBTREAU: They'll board up your mouth like plate-glass smashed by the thieves. I'm taking your voice, I'm making you still.

DICK GIBSON: No. What do you think this is? *No!*

BEHR-BLEIBTREAU: Some reticence there.

DICK GIBSON: The show—

BEHR-BLEIBTREAU: Hold it down. People are sleeping.

DICK GIBSON: I will not hold it down.

BEHR-BLEIBTREAU: Dummy up, Dicky.

DICK GIBSON: I will not dummy up.

BEHR-BLEIBTREAU: Stow it. Break off.

DICK GIBSON: I will not stow it. I won't break off.

BEHR-BLEIBTREAU: *Unutter! Muzzle!* Give me your word you'll give me your voice.

DICK GIBSON: [He means to speak but can't think of anything to say. Perhaps he can do the alphabet, and go on to numbers. He can't remember the alphabet. What's the first number? That's it: *First* is the first number.]

First!

BEHR-BLEIBTREAU: Be mute, you turtle. You giraffe.

DICK GIBSON: [*faintly*] First . . . and . . . another . . .

BEHR-BLEIBTREAU: I have your voice. I almost have it. I have the others' and I'm getting yours.

HENCEFORTH I CONTROL THE BROAD-

CAST PATTERN OF THIS PROGRAM. I EN-
GINEER THE ENGINEERING. I USURP THE
SIGNAL. I DIRECT IT AND REDIRECT IT. I
WHISPER . . . (and we are blacked out in New En-
gland). (*in a normal voice*) I'm changing the sound
patterns. I raise my voice . . . (*He raises his voice.*)
AND I AM HEARD ACROSS THE MISSISSIPPI.
COME IN KANSAS, COME IN CALIFORNIA.
(*To Dick Gibson*) Now. Give me your voice, give up
the rest of it. The voice is the sound—

DICK GIBSON: *of the soul!* (*determined*) You'll never
get it. Not as long as I wear this solid-blue tie in this
white-walled studio. You ought to wear glasses;
you've buttoned your sweater wrong.

BEHR-BLEIBTREAU: (*ferociously*) The Virgin Mary
sucks!

DICK GIBSON: The opinions expressed on this program
are those of Dr. Behr-Bleibtreau and not necessarily
those of this station or of the sponsors. I repeat, Dr.
Behr-Bleibtreau's opinions are his own and not necessarily those of the Naval Air Reserve or Only You
Can Prevent Forest Fires.

BEHR-BLEIBTREAU: It's useless, Gibson. I'll have your
silence. I'll get your voice.

DICK GIBSON: Want to bet (*to the panel and guests in
the studio*) Let's hear it. Everybody sing. Let's hear
it. *You,* Jack. One word. Say the word. Pepper?
Come on, Pepper, old pep pot. You're the lady.
Ladies go first. A word. A noise. No? Not yet?
Catch your breath, dear; I'll get back to you. Bernie? Say something in Latin, Doc. Recite a prescription. Mel? Give us a sigh, Mel. Give us a lovegroan.
Somebody *cough,* for Christ's sake! What? No one?

BEHR-BLEIBTREAU: They can't help you. I've only been
playing up to now. I've been teasing you. The rest is
real.

Are you ready? *Listen:*

I do the sailors' knot in your vocal cords. I twist
your tongue, I tie it. I give you pause, lump in the
throat, I give you stammer and smoker's cough. I

give you sore throat and ache your tooth. I give you harelip. I chap it. I huff and I puff and the roof of your mouth comes down. I murder your breath. Shush, man. Hush. Mum's the word. Soft spoken, there. Silent night, holy night, all is calm, all is bright. Speak softly and carry a big stick. Still waters run deep. Quiet Please, Hospital Zone.

Now . . . Say "She sells seashells down by the seashore." Say "The Leith police dismisseth us." [Behr Bleibtreau pauses. Gibson is silent. Then:] Because I am perfect, because I am straight, because I am without flaw, because I am correct, because I am pure, because I am unblemished and upright, because I am without stain and without aberration, because I have never looked up a dress on the stairs or handled myself in the shower or stolen from dimestores or forged Mother's name on a note from home; because I have never broken and entered or eaten between meals; because I have never fired a shot in anger or hoarded or said "ain't" or gone on a binge or butt into line or chewed gum in class or overslept or failed to share; because I have never hit-and-run, told fibs, raped, played the radio loud while others were sleeping or stuck out my tongue or been a bad neighbor; because I have never picked my nose or stood or parked where I shouldn't; because I've never cheated at cards, made rude noises, scrawled bad words on walls in toilets or kept books overdue from the library, lied to Customers, drunk while driving, fudged my taxes or broken windows with balls or stones; because I've never murdered or lived in sin; because I have never clipped, high-sticked, fouled the shooter, never talked back to the umpire or jumped the gun; because my backfield's never been in motion and I've never not hung up my things—because of all this and more, I exercise my right to call on demons, spirits and avenging angels!

Solomon collected the demons in a bottle and sealed them with the Seal of Solomon—the six-pointed Star. We'll need that. Wait. I have it.

[Behr-Bleibtreau reaches forward, takes the Hebrew National Salami from the lazy susan, turns the meaty cylinder in his hand and locates the trademark—a Star of David. Placing this face up on the table, he draws an imaginary circle around himself with his finger, then leans forward and touches the Star.]

This! We'll use this! *This* will be the Seal of Solomon!

Calling the demons, thanking the demons, useful demons who teach us things—who put the new math in our heads, and help us with piano, French, the point of jokes.

Calling the demons, Lucifer's demons, Lucifer's troopers, Lucifer's dead; calling the demons, praising the demons, nothing fulsome, nothing false, praising the demons, commending the demons, extolling the demons, giving dem demons all dere due. Giving them medals, honors, Hosannahs, giving them all that they deserve—

Calling the demons, needing the demons, up from the bottle where they are sealed, calling the demons, demanding the demons, up and up from the jar of hell. Come to us. Come now. No false alarms for demons, no crying wolf for demons, no dry runs at demons' expense—

Calling the demons, paging the demons, inviting the demons, summoning them. Calling the demons, Lucifer's demons, Lucifer's sidekicks, Lucifer's men:

In the name of the magician Moses, the magician Jesus and the magician Solomon, I call you forth.

Come incubus, come succubus, come Hell, come djin.

Here demons, here boys, darlin' demons, demons dear.

I call on . . . Sordino. Sordino the Soundless. Sordino the Mute. I call Sordino. Silent Sordino. Come,

Sordino. Come to us now. I offer you your sign. My finger's at my lips.

(to Dick Gibson) Each demon has his own sign, like the hallmark on silver or the brand on a cow. This is Sordino's:

I call Sordino, silent Sordino, pensive Sordino, taciturn one. Ncy *cm hycm cym nc* Yen
Come Sordino, come to us now.

Come sad, secret, silent fellow. Come to us, our melancholy baby.

(A pause. Then:) He's here. Can you feel the pall? That's Sordino's doing. That's Sordino. Pall's his sign too. He's with us in the studio. Can you sense the pall? He's with us, all right. That's him. (They each have something by which they're recognized. This one has bad breath, that one breaks wind. One will appear as a naked child, another will stammer. One has loose teeth—they lie on his tongue or awash in his saliva—and another black and blue marks on his privates. The pall is Sordino's.) Do you remember before the program when I told you I was expecting someone?

My God, what's he doing? *That's* rare. See. Look there—he's *materializing!* In the corner. *Sordino!*

Take over Gibson's voice, Sordino.

DICK GIBSON: There's no one.

BEHR-BLEIBTREAU: That's it, Sordino. You sound just like him. Was it you before too?

DICK GIBSON: There's no one.

BEHR-BLEIBTREAU: Perfect, Sordino. Now. Take it all. Take the rest of it. There was a fire. His tapes were consumed. So it's all gone, all but your mimicry of his sound. Now. Take that too. Pull even that out of his throat. Take it with you down to hell. Wonderful, Sordino. Be careful. He'll struggle. Take his rattle, his groans, get his gasps. Take it all.

271

DICK GIBSON: *(choking)* Don't . . . What—

BEHR-BLEIBTREAU: That's it.

DICK GIBSON: *(coughing now, sputtering)* Please . . .
  You're . . . I can't . . . No . . . I can't . . . breathe . . .
  He's—

BEHR-BLEIBTREAU: Wonderful, Sordino.

DICK GIBSON: *—choking me!*

> [He tries to pull Behr-Bleibtreau's hands off his
> throat, but the man has a stranglehold on him. With
> his teeth he tries to snap at Behr-Bleibtreau's arms,
> but all he manages is to get a piece of Behr-
> Bleibtreau's sweater in his mouth.]

BEHR-BLEIBTREAU: *(giggling, then recovering himself)*
  That's it, Sordino. That's the way.

DICK GIBSON: *(strangling, gasping for breath)* Please
  . . . I'm . . .

> [With both hands he tries to bend back one of
> Behr-Bleibtreau's fingers.]

BEHR-BLEIBTREAU: Ow. Ouch. The pall. Sordino's
  pall. The pull of the pall. You wouldn't think a pall
  could hurt so much. Never mind, Sordino. Let the
  chips fall where they may.

DICK GIBSON: *(hoarsely)* Listen, you can't . . .

> [It is futile to struggle further. All Dick's strength
> is gone; he has never felt such hands. He looks
> wildly at Jerry in the control booth, but the man is
> bent over his dials.]

  (weakly) Help me, Jerry—

BEHR-BLEIBTREAU: Good,   Sordino.   Wonderful.
  You're getting it.

DICK GIBSON: Oh God, *some*body . . .

> [His swivel chair is on casters, and in the struggle
> he has been turned violently about. As he renews his
> efforts to get away, he pushes forcefully against the
> floor with his foot and the chair swings around,
> temporarily upsetting Behr-Bleibtreau's balance.
> One of Behr-Bleibtreau's hands flies from Dick's
> neck. Dick lunges forward and ducks his head; the
> other hand slips away. Out of the chair now, he runs
> around to the other side of the table. Standing be-

hind Mel Son, he sees the gun in his lap. He reaches down for the gun—and misses; instead, he has grabbed Mel's penis beneath the cloth of his trousers. At Dick's touch Mel's cock almost instantly hardens; he grabs Dick's hand with both of his own and tries to keep it on his prick. Dick brings his other hand around and plucks the gun off Mel's lap.]

BEHR-BLEIBTREAU: [Coming around to the side of the table where Dick is standing.]

Watch it, Sordino. Gently. He's got a gun.

DICK GIBSON: [Holding the barrel in his hand, Dick reaches out and hammers at Behr-Bleibtreau's throat with the butt of the revolver. He chops wildly at the man's neck, smashing at his Adam's apple. Behr-Bleibtreau falls across the table and Dick Gibson hits him repeatedly in the throat.]

There. There.

[Behr-Bleibtreau, his breath knocked out of him, holds his throat. Mel Son rises and looks at Dick; he still has his erection. Dick shrugs and aims the pistol at Mel's cock. Mel leaves the studio, and Assemblyman Ash follows him. Behr-Bleibtreau lays writhing on the floor. The woman in the long fur coat and her companion come up and help Behr-Bleibtreau to rise. They leave the studio. Dick looks around and sees that Jack Patterson's coed has already left. He had not seen her go. Neither had Jack; coming out of his stupor, he looks toward where she had been sitting. Dick hears the man fart. Seeing her gone, Jack leaves too. Pepper Steep's sister is sound asleep. Dick Gibson looks at Bernie Perk and sees him wink at Pepper. Pepper smiles and Bernie pats her arm and they go out together. Dick understands; Bernie is in love with the bad breath that Dick has noticed on other occasions when Pepper has been on the program. It is something that happens in her stomach at about three o'clock in the morning. Jerry has put on the last commercial of the evening—a one-minute spot for a dusk-to-dawn drive-in theater north of the city. It is played this late because it is an appeal to lovers, automobile-trapped kissers and huggers, lovers with roommates at home, or parents waiting up—bleary yearners domestic in cars. They cruise the highway. Perhaps they don't have the money for a hotel room, or perhaps they are not yet at that stage. They have nowhere to go. For the first time, Dick understands that it is precisely *his* audience the message directs itself to, and so the spot depresses him. Perhaps Bernie will take Pepper there. He sits back down at his table and waits until the commercial is finished.]

Then he talks till 5 A.M., rambling, filling in, not always aware of what he is saying, or even if the program is still on the air, but using his voice because he still has it, because it's still *his*—uniquely inflected, Gibson-timbreed, a sum of private frequencies and personal resonances, as marked as his thumbs—because the show must go on and he must be on it. As he speaks, it occurs to him that Behr-Bleibtreau could never have taken it, that poor Dick Gibson had nothing to confess; like Behr-Bleibtreau, his own slate is clean, his character unmarked, his history uneventful. But he has had a close call.

"Well, ladies and gentlemen," he says, "there is no astrology, there's no black magic and no white, no ESP, no UFO's. Mars is uninhabited. The dead are dead and buried. Meat won't kill you and Krebiozen won't cure you and we'll all be out of the picture before the forests disappear or the water dries up. Your handwriting doesn't indicate your character and there is no God. All there is—" He looks over at Pepper Steep's sister asleep in her chair and wants to cry. He wishes he had something with which to cover her to keep her warm, something to put over her shoulders. Somehow Jack Patterson's fart still hangs in the air—"are the strange displacements of the ordinary."

Part III

1

From an address at the annual "Annals of Broadcasting" Dinner:

Mr. Irwin Schlueter, Chief of the American Radio Institute's Division of Research and Development, suggested that the technological development which most influenced the character of radio broadcasting in the United States in the decades of the fifties and sixties was television, that it produced an impact on the medium at least as powerful as the impact of the talkies on the silent films of the twenties, but that after television the next most powerful influence, and in the long run an influence which could outstrip even the influence of television, had been a series of "gadgets" developed in the sixties—none of them, from an engineering standpoint, spectacular in themselves, and some of which were merely the application of principles known for years.

It's almost [Mr. Schlueter said] like observing the piecemeal development of the wheel. I say "development" because almost certainly the wheel was never "invented," but was instead a slow, cumulative serendipity.

Tape, of course, has liberated the radio man from his studio and given him a mobility he never had before. Miniaturization has contributed further to this process. The ongoing evolution of the cassette with its terrific convenience has provided additional acceleration of the trend, and "solid-state," or the so-called instant-on, because of the reporter's new ability to begin his on-the-spot broadcast without waiting for tubes to warm up, has had even more far-reaching effects on field radio, and has given the radio man not only mobility but time, and not only time but the potential to make of himself a peripatetic broadcasting station.

But if these gadgets have exercised an influence on the broadcaster, think of the enormous consequences for the listener. Consider instant-on itself. In the thirty-five to forty-three seconds it used to take to "build a sound," the listener's mood—this has been repeatedly demonstrated in psychological testing—becomes one of honed impatience. He wishes, say, to hear a particular program and turns on his radio. There is solid scientific evidence that by the time the radio has warmed up, a small antipathy has developed in the listener, an aggression which has first to be overcome before receptivity can be properly exploited. Thus the broadcaster's burden is a double one: he must sell his listener *before* he sells him. By eliminating "dead time," solid-state obviates this. Indeed, futher studies have shown that by instantly responding to his will, solid-state actually predisposes a listener to accept a program. The average listener is not a scientist, of course, but even if he understands the basic principles of electronics he does not consciously think of them when he turns on his radio. For him there is only the subliminal impression—solid-state increases this—that there is a continuous entertainment or dialogue going on in the world which he may bring in or exclude instantly, as though by magic. This gives him a sense of power. It is no accident that the operating manuals accompanying new radios designate the various knobs and dials under the pseudo-generic label "controls."

Where solid-state has thus far had its greatest effect is in the area of car radio, where, depending upon the time of day, the listenership may sometimes be as high as 84 percent. Try to imagine what conflict there could be in a driver's mind when, on the one hand, he was pushed along through space at a mile a minute while on the other he was stymied by a cold car radio. He might have traveled as much as a mile, or even further, before bringing in the first clear signal of a broadcast. Was he in time or wasn't he? For the listener in the car the time lag meant not impatience or hostility, but confusion—an emotion more difficult of placation than even those others, and more dangerous, too, when you consider that this man was "at the controls" of a murderous, powerful machine. With the highway development program what it is today, and with cars every year given greater and greater horsepower, the discrepancy between speed and its tube-radio opposite could only have become greater, and the burden of the programmers—who have to keep all sorts of audiences in mind—heavier. Undoubtedly, highway safety would suffer. Nor do I make a callous joke when I say that it is not the radio man's first duty to kill off his market. Radio is a business dependent upon revenues from advertising. Advertising is dependent upon sales. Humanitarian considerations aside, when a man dies in a crash you have not lost simply a good customer —and make no mistake; he *is* a good customer; he's driving a car, *advertised on radio,* for which he buys gas, *advertised on radio,* to or from a home which he has bought with a bank loan, *advertised on radio,* and furnished with a thousand things, *all advertised on radio*—but the good customer's family as well. There is inevitably a period of mourning, and mourning—I don't care what religion you're talking about—means one thing and one thing only: *abstinence.* And abstinence, humanitarian considerations aside, is bad for business. Solid-state does away with all this.

Yet it is one of the peculiar paradoxes of our age that while reducing the time lag between broadcast and reception has had an unparalleled effect in shaping broadcasting, there has been, collaterally, a development which goes in an opposite direction altogether, and is, as of this moment, the single most important event in the entire history of radio.

I am speaking, of course, of the so-called tape delay, the small, inexpensive instrument which by utilizing extra gears and blind-alley loopings forces the recording tape though false waystations so that by the time it is played a six-second interval has been created in which the broadcaster can cut or, in more sophisticated models, edit offensive statements before they go out over the air. What this has meant for programming is only now beginning to be realized. Unquestionably, however, its greatest effect has been in the area of the audience-participation principle—specifically the telephone talk show. Without the six-second delay tape, or something very much like it, this kind of programming would be impossible. Most of the American public, of course, is decent and responsible and have no need of instrumentation to monitor them. Nevertheless fail-safe equipment will be a necessary adjunct of the telephone talk landscape as long as we live in a society part of whose vocal instincts, emboldened by the cloak of anonymity, are vicious and disturbed and exhibitionist. It's inconceivable that a sponsor could continue to support a show which did not have the safety valve provided by a system like tape delay. This despite the fact that advertisers have known—known from the beginning—the incredible attractiveness of audience-participation programming.

Indeed, the self-entertainment principle has always played a major role in our industry, in local as well as network programming. At its most oblique level it manifested itself in the presence of the studio audience itself, its laughter, its spontaneous and sometimes not-so-spontaneous applause. One of the old-time host's key phrases, *perhaps the single most classic sentence in radio,* so deep-seated in our culture and consciousness that whenever it is uttered today it takes on the dimensions of a joke, was "Keep those cards and letters coming in." What was this if not a direct appeal to the audience-participation instinct? But there is a whole history of shows which flourished entirely on the strength of their dependence upon the audience, an audience which provided not only a presence at the entertainment, but was in fact the entertainment *itself.* One need only point to the success of the *Major Bowes Amateur Hour,* whose origins date almost to the beginning of radio. I don't think I have to remind anyone here tonight that "The Amateur Hour" is still with us in its adapted TV format, or that CBS's *Ted Mack's Amateur Hour* has had the longest continuous run in television.

But there have been many such programs—everything from "man on the street" shows and quiz programs to good old *Mr. Anthony,* where people with problems could come to seek help. There was *Candid Microphone,* and most of you will remember *Bride and Groom,* where real couples actually got married on the air. Nor should I omit from this list the famous *Don McNeil's Breakfast Club,* which when it recently went off the air at Don's retirement was the longest continuous program in the history of broadcasting, not just in America but in

281

the entire world! There was Arthur Godfrey's *Talent Scouts*, a hit on radio long before it ever went on television, and there was and still is *Art Linkletter's House Party*, the very name of which conveys my theme. Further, the dominance of daytime TV's popular game shows must seek its origins in radio programs like Art's. Many of these programs have been responsible for some of the biggest billings in the industry.

I am not here tonight to stir up nostalgic memories or to enunciate glorious names from the putative Golden Age of Radio, however. Suffice it to say that industry executives and advertisers have always been aware of the rich possibilities of participation programming. The development of magnetic tape—and before that of wire—led naturally to news interviews, press conferences and the like, the whole "voices in the news" syndrome being still another instance of audience participation. With McLuhan and his celebrated "global village" concept we get only the articulation of a principle which the industry has understood instinctively—that the listener needs to become a *communicant*. The elaborate production radio of the thirties and forties— your "Big Broadcasts," et cetera—were never the *natural* function of radio, but arose merely as substitute, pro tem arrangements, groping and expensive, a settling for less by shoveling on more. And isn't it a fact that in the so-called Golden Age of Radio your biggest shows—*Amos 'n' Andy, Fibber McGee and Molly, The Great Gildersleeve, Henry Aldrich, Jack Benny,* and every single soap opera that was ever on the radio—by attempting to portray the ordinary lives of ordinary people with whom listeners could identify, was making an effort to get around the audience-participation principle? Is it too far-fetched to suggest that *Allen's Alley* was the comic prototype of today's telephone talk program?

I think we ought not to proceed—in a deeper

282

sense this is not a digression—without first acknowledging that we in radio owe much to a great engineer with a great idea. Probably, shamefully, most of us do not even know his name—I know *I* didn't —despite the fact that many of us here tonight owe our professional lives to him. I refer, of course, to Brandon Sline, the developer of the tape delay. When I knew I was to address you I cast about in my mind for a suitable topic. When I looked around me at the not inconsiderable achievements of radio in our own age, I naturally came in the course of my deliberations to consider the tape delay, and determined to have on the dais with me the man chiefly responsible for it. It wasn't easy tracking him down; indeed, it took considerable research just to discover his name. Thus our debts go often unpaid because we are simply unaware of them. Working in his own spare time in his home on a means of providing the broadcaster with what he thought of as a margin for error, this man, unaffiliated with any network, a staff engineer—I had almost said an *ordinary* staff engineer—at WSNO, Rutledge, Vermont, invented a simple device which has become a contribution more sweeping and more telling than any since Marconi's. Yes, *since Marconi's*. For with just this device and the ordinary house telephone, he has made every home in America its own potential broadcasting station, and every American his own potential star. I'm going to ask him to stand. Brandon? That's right. That's right. Applaud him you well may. Brandon Sline, ladies and gentlemen. Thank you, Brandon. You know, ladies and gentlemen, as we were all applauding Brandon it occurred to me that he, the tinkerer engineer, though a professional, working on his equipment in his own workshop as he did, encompasses the best principles of amateurism, and that it is fitting indeed that his device gives voice to amateurs.

It isn't for me so much as for psychologists to explain the public's urge to communicate directly.

Be that as it may, the instinct seems to be the deepest one in entertainment; I don't think I need point out to you that "ham" radio existed before commercial radio. At the same time that this urge is basic, however, it is also dangerous. Just as an agency like the FCC must regulate and oversee our industry, so must there be machinery to regulate and oversee the public when it is given *its* voice. It would be instructive, but depressing, I'm afraid, to play for you some of the excisions that have been recorded and preserved from even a single program. You would think we lived in Pandora's box. A friend of mine who works one of these shows has said that if he had a dollar for each time he has had to black out the word "kike" or "nigger" or some even less fragrant obscenity, he wouldn't have to work again for the rest of his life. He claims to have heard more filth than any member of the vice squad in the wickedest streets of New York City. It seems a pity that a minority should have it in its power to distress and frustrate the good listener for even the few seconds of silence that follows an unacceptable remark. Have we developed solid-state and instant-on only to have our radios go dead on us in the middle of what is often the most interesting part of a conversation? Aren't we likely to re-create the same psychological blocks we have been at such great pains to propitiate?

It is for this reason that we are currently working on a tape delay that does all that present tape delays do but then accelerates the tapes so that the next decent conversation may be heard immediately—creating, in effect, if not in fact, an apparently seamless conversation. We're close to a breakthrough on this one. And when it occurs we will truly have pulled time's teeth at last. Indeed, as the entire industry now gears itself to the telephone talk show, the fabuous "two-way radio" concept seems a fullfilment of what radio has always promised—a means of open discourse, of people-to-people priorities. Of course there is always room for improvement. One area that must be explored is the area of sound itself. If two-way radio is to take its rightful place on the American air something must be done to soften the sibilant "tunnel effect" of telephone sound and bring it closer to studio standards. We're working on that too. In the meanwhile, so much has already been accomplished that I think we may say with as much accuracy as pride that only now is the *real* Golden Age of Radio upon us. . . . .

2

The Golden Age is upon me. Heavy. I think it really *is* Pandora's box. "Dick Gibson, WBOX, and all I know is what you tell me." (I live in a box.)

I used the phones as early as '53. Before there was even amplification equipment, let alone tape delay. Repeating laboriously, like a translator at the UN, everything the caller said, and not just words but inflections too, mimicking the voice as well as I was able, and not just the voice but the accent, and not just the words and the inflections and the voice and the accent, but also the passion, the irritation and complaint and sulking triumph, listening so closely and working so hard that my head hurt and when it was my turn to answer I couldn't shake the caller's style and borrowed his vocabulary and traded on his posture so that he thought I was baiting him and grew angry, and then I had to mimic *that* and that made him angrier which raised the ante of my imitation once more until at the end we were shouting at each other and one of us finally had to hang up. And still so involved after the call was finished that when I took the next call the first caller's style sometimes continued to prevail, intruding itself into what I repeated of the new conversation, fading only as I began gradually to catch the new caller's emphasis—a round robin of personality. Dick Gibson, KOPY. Dick Gibson, KAT.

Then, when technology at last caught up with us innovators and pioneers, going to the phones again, at last empowered to be myself. But something else changed, though at first I couldn't identify it. When I understood, it was very odd. I had something in my hands again. In Hartford I'd been empty-handed. The phone was like the scripts I used to hold during my apprenticeship.

It seemed right to be burdened. It seemed appropriate that a man on the radio should be connected and not permitted that merely conceptual and apparent connection—his voice—like a beast in Whipsnade, seemingly loose. Fetters give me. Let there be heavy equipment; attach me by cords, electronic leashes, to my microphonic stakes.

(Alternatively, how would it be if I *could* roam free, speak in deserts as in auditoriums, ad lib while swimming, mumble on mountains, ask strangers for the time of day in the streets and have my sounds picked up in Texas or Timbuktu? Build me of crystal, Lord. I would be Jesus Crystal. *In Excelsis Diode.*)

He was already forty years old when he was asked to resign from the station in Hartford. A playback of the tapes satisfactorily demonstrated to the managers that he had not initiated any of the foul language; he had merely been unable to control it. Probably he would have resigned anyway, for that night had shown him how tired he was of all spurious controversy, as well as of his own unconscious baiting of his guests. Besides, he had fallen in love with Carmella, Pepper Steep's sister.

He took her with him to Pittsburgh in the spring of 1959, two months after he had been asked to resign. It was Carmella herself who decided they could not be married. Strangely, it was on religious grounds that she turned him down. She had asked him what he was.

"Me? I don't know. I'll be what you are."

"I'm nothing."

"Then there's no problem. Neither am I."

"Then there's a problem. I want my life to be regularized. I was born a Gentile. That was the name of our little sect in California when I was a girl—the Gentile Church. It was the only one in America. As the elders died off and people moved away there was no one left to carry on the traditions. The Mosque was abandoned."

"The Mosque?"

"Jesus was a Jew. The Jews were Arabs. Arabs worship in mosques. Pepper and I went back a few years ago. I thought of staying on, but the firehouse isn't there any more."

"The firehouse?"

"The Mosque was in the firehouse. Anyway, I've been nothing since. I could be a Catholic if my husband was one, or a Jew, or anything at all. I want to be *something*."

"Look, I was born a Methodist. You could be a Methodist."

"What do Methodists do? I couldn't be Methodist if it went against my conscience as a Gentile."

"Well, I don't know what they do. I don't remember. Maybe we could take instruction."

"Can they smoke?"

"Yes, of course."

"I've been trying to give up smoking."

"Well, there's nothing in the religion that says they have to smoke . . . *I* know—Baptists aren't supposed to smoke. We could be Baptists."

"Would you promise to be a good Baptist?"

"Certainly."

"I don't believe you. Besides, it all seems so artificial. I'd much prefer just to stay with you and wait until I fall in love with someone who's already something."

And that became their arrangement.

The normal and ordinary and the public were her

passions, not instinctively so much as self-consciously. For example, she loved to prepare long lists of electric kitchen appliances, such hardware being to her what jewels and furs were to other women. Dick often found her doodles on telephone pads where she had drawn, with some skill, electric carving knives, blenders, toasters—all the latest products from GE. She would have made a superb interior decorator of a very special sort. Museums could profitably have come to her to furnish typical rooms of the mid-century middle class in the best of popular taste. She watched what everyone else was watching on television. Her opinions were almost always consistent with the samplings revealed in polls. When they weren't she would steep herself in the arguments of the majority until there wasn't a dime's worth of difference between its position and her own.

It was very odd. He knew that one day she would cheat on him. Not because of money or love or youth or power or sensuality; one day her heart would be captured by someone so respectable, someone so responsible and normal, that he would even have to be told that Carmella had "set her cap for him." (That the fellow would have to be told in the first place was certain, for he would be a passive man, flattered and frightened by her and not believing his luck. It was almost as certain that the news would have to be broken to him in just such phrases, the only style that would not kill him.) So someday her prince would come, and he could be almost anyone—though there were some things he could not be. He could be married but not Catholic, he could be Catholic but not married; Carmella would not begin her new life by being damned out of her old one. She was already thirty-four, which set additional imperatives, not for herself, for in a way she was selfless; for example, she had no ordinary greeds, did not require riches or excitement, and had no urge to prolong her youth as such.

But at thirty-four sociology and raw percentages took over. How many men were still bachelors at thirty-four? (The man could not be as much as five minutes younger than herself. She was unwilling to live under even the least psychological aspersion. Thus, she forbade the unsavory and pined for the prescribed. Even during the short time she stayed with Dick she insisted that the daily paper and the milk be delivered—not because she was lazy, not even because she read the paper or drank the milk, but because these things were tokens of decency.) And of those who were still single at thirty-four and born before April 11—her birthday—how many were homosexuals, mama's boys, playboys whose heterosexual profligacies were the danger signals of a too extravagant need? How many were losers or becoming losers? (Was Dick Gibson—when he resigned from WHCN he once again withdrew the name—a loser? He was already forty and sensed that the great apprenticeship, like some recurrent disease from childhood, would soon be on him again. Was he normal? He had been told by Carmella that he had none of the normal man's accouterments, and he could have told her that he did not even possess a character. Was he even *sexually* normal? He had not lived with a woman since Miriam in Morristown almost twenty-one years before, and although he was not virginal, sexually he had the past of a nineteen-year-old boy.) There were other requirements. Even if she were able to find someone who was sexually acceptable, he would have to be a man who was already established, his goals not already realized, perhaps, but within marching distance. It would not do for him to be a beginner, for once a beginner always a beginner. (That, he thought, was still another strike against himself.) Then, on a lower order of the imperative, Carmella would want him to have friends—old army buddies, perhaps—whom she would not entirely approve of, and one failing friend from childhood, say, regard for whom would be a measure of her husband's loyalty and manliness. It was pretty slim pickings. But though he understood the percentages, he also knew how determined Carmella was and that people always get what they want, that *all* goals are within marching distance.

So the adultery was inevitable and placed an extraordinary burden on Dick Gibson (now, as he had been twenty-one years before with Miriam, Marshall Maine again, having, in his own mind, retired "Dick Gibson" when he lost the Hartford show), because the assumption ordinarily made about two people who live together without being married is that the relationship is invulnerable to outside pressures. For a man the least approachable woman is the woman who already has a lover. She seems inviolate as a newlywed or nun. Carmella's open flirting confused men; they never comprehended their eligibility. (Shy men, decent men, why would they?) As often as not they thought themselves toyed with. The burden of proof was on Carmella. She had to allay their fears, and she allayed them at Marshall's expense, cuckolding him out of wedlock. He dreaded their public appearances together. More than once, even before they left Hartford, he thought of calling the whole thing off.

Yet Carmella's very need of the normal was the most fascinating thing about her. It was pathological. To the degree that she yearned for respectability she lacked it, so that as long as he stayed with her he enjoyed a heady sense of the forbidden. For all her absent-minded doodles of electric frying pans and steam irons, she seemed to him the most abandoned woman he had ever known, wilder than the Creole girls of Mauritius, crazier than the brutish whores he had been with in London during the war. It was her need to convert everything into the routine and domestic, her necessity to pretend even with him that they were just the nice couple next door, that fueled his lust. It was very clear; she was inviting him to play House, a game which she played so ferociously that there was something sinful in their suppertimes, a wickedness in her burned meats and scorched vegetables, something so tantalizing in her bridey pout over a failed cake that he grew hard contemplating the unrisen dough. A vagrant smell of the amiss from the oven was often enough. For him Carmella was a French maid come to life out of pornography. In his imagination her bare behind bloomed just out of sight beneath her pinafores, and he often thought he could see the wide twin grins of her rump. Their arguments—it never went this far; they didn't have argu-

291

ments—would have had to have been settled by sexually seditious spankings. Sometimes she made perky mouths at him, as if she was his daughter as well as his bride, and it was both his torment and a source of his pleasure that she never stopped thinking of the day when she would have a real husband.

They had gone to Pittsburgh for his mother's funeral, but Carmella liked the city and it was she who decided that they would not return to Hartford. Then she wept, understanding that she could make such a decision only because her life was so irregular.

Though Marshall's father was an old man by this time—Carmella told him that they were married—he still enjoyed performing as much as ever. Only a week after he had buried his wife he was playing the role of a dirty old man, and Carmella was an ideal prop for him. Leering, he might pretend to a sudden palsy. Then, his right hand twitching uncontrollably, he would bring it up to the level of Carmella's breasts. In this way he managed to brush them at least a half-dozen times a day, or, in passing, to strum her behind every hour or so. Lest he be misunderstood—his peculiar pride wanted it made perfectly clear that he was lascivious and not physically impaired—he occasionally arranged to get his hand tangled inside Carmella's skirt, where it thrashed about like a fish in a sack making rash plunges and rushes. All Carmella said at these times was "Please, Dad," or "Now Dad, you know that's just perfectly silly." She probably assumed that every family had its eccentric, and that it was perfectly normal for old men, even supposititious fathers-in-law, to turn lewdly on their sons' wives.

With his brother Arthur it was something else again.

Like Marshall, Arthur had never married. In real estate now—they were staying with him until they found an apartment—Arthur lived in a big house in the Squirrel Hill section of Pittsburgh. After his mother's death he had tried to convince his father to come and live with him, but had been unable to budge the old man. Carmella and Marshall were present on one such occasion, Carmella sitting on the sofa between Arthur and the father.

"Be reasonable, Papa. Why do you need the aggravation of a house? List it with me. I'll give it my special attention. We'll put it on the market for twenty thousand, add another thousand realtor's fee, and when I dump it you can keep the extra grand yourself. The buyer doesn't have to know I'm your son. Then you come in with me. There's the solarium, for God's sake. Remember how you and Mama used to enjoy sitting in the solarium when you came out to see me in Squirrel Hill? You don't need this cave?"

"*Cave?* You call where your Mama and me lived our lives and raised our children a *cave?* Are you a cave man? Is your brother a cave man? Am I? Did I ever pull your mama around—may she rest—by the hair? Did I hit her on her head with a club? Music you had. Every Saturday afternoon these walls were alive with the sound of the Metropolitan Opera on the radio. What's the matter, you don't remember Milton Cross? Is music like that heard in a cave? Carmella, tell him."

Carmella, looking from one to the other, was taking it all in.

"That's not the point, Papa. What I'm—"

"It's not the point? It's not? Big shot, what's the point? What's the point, teddy bear? That you got a solarium, that my big-shot son owns the sunshine? You don't own the sunshine. I want sun I go in the yard. My backyard is covered with sunshine like a lawn. You think you get more in your solarium? In fact you get less."

"Papa, why are you so upset?"

"I'm not upset, sonny, I'm not upset. But when you ask me to give over my memories, you ask something which will never happen. Your mama's spirit is in this house. A woman don't live in a home forty-two years so her spirit can be listed with her son for twenty-one thousand dollars." Here his hands flew up like a bird to Carmella's tits, one finger getting caught in the décolletage.

"Mama's dead, Papa. When are you going to face that?"

"Mama's dead not even two weeks, Arthur," Marshall told his brother quietly. "You've got to give Papa time."

He had never called them Mama and Papa in his life. Neither had Arthur.

"Now, Dad, you know that's perfectly silly," Carmella told the old man, pulling his hand out from where it had become caught in her brassiere.

"*Time,*" Papa said fiercely, turning on Marshall. "You could give me a million years. I'll *never* forget her." His palsied old hand floated down to splash about in Carmell's crotch.

Carmella took the hand and held it in both of her own. "Please, Dad," she murmured sweetly.

The two sons were having the time of their lives. Biblically ferocious, they shouted back and forth at each other like Italian sons in melodrama. They glowed with a Fifth Commandment intensity. Meanwhile the old man was now a wild Greek patriarch, now ancient Bulgar, now wily WASP whittler and fisherman, now proud old chief, between the peaks of his wrath declining to mournful Jew, actual tears in his eyes when he spoke brokenly of his dead wife, the late lady who for years had led him a merry chase with her Maw Green stunts. Carmella might have been on the sidelines of some three-sided tennis match as she followed the volleys from father to son to brother to father to brother. For her their vaudeville turns were like a dream come true; the vague religiosity of their syntax was holy to her. There was *gemütlich* in the room like sunshine in the backyard.

"I didn't know Methodist families were this warm and close," she broke in during a lull.

"What, are you kidding?" Arthur said. "Methodist families are the closest families there are. The *closest*. We'd kill for each other. Anything, anything at all. One for all and all for one among Methodist brothers. Right, kid?" He punched his brother's arm.

"Right," Marshall said. "Right, kid."

"You know," Carmella said shyly, "you all make me feel ashamed."

"Ashamed?"

"Of what, dear?" Papa asked. In a sudden seizure, his fingers leaped across her cleavage to her far nipple.

"Of the way I've deceived you."

"Deceived?" Arthur said.

She covered her eyes with her hands. "We're not really married," she said, and peered out at Arthur from behind what would have been her ring finger.

Marshall had been expecting a widower, someone with children in high school. He had looked jealously on the balding and pot-bellied and pin-striped. Love would come from that quarter, he thought. And it *would* be love, hearts erupting in floozy passion, Carmella the Queen of the Cocktail Lounge and Wild West, a Claire Trevor knocking like last opportunity on Mr. Right's storm doors and aluminum siding. He had been wary of just such a juxtaposition; even at Mama's funeral he had steered her clear of all avunculars, his brother's corny cronies, men in liquor, furniture, restaurants and automobiles. He had been rude, accepting their condolences with perfunctory replies as he jerked Carmella next to him as if for support—though the gesture was vicious, like a man with a beast on a stage doing hidden, close-order things with the leash. For the truth was he loved her as much as the man in liquor ever could—perhaps even more since it was still rare and grand for him to be with a woman. It was lovely waking up beside her. On those mornings when she was out of bed first he felt deprived of some special treat he had come to depend on. It was lovely to be in rooms with her or to sit with her in taxicabs, lovely to share space. It was lovely to have her with him in restaurants, to see her head bent over the big menu as in prayer.

Carmella loves Arthur.

In an instant his brother had been transformed. From a life-long kibitzer he had become one of the earnest of the world. Suddenly he seemed to acquire wrists, great rawboned red things that hung from hick cuffs. He had become all that Carmella wanted merely by Carmella's wanting it.

But now Arthur took them for lovers and grew shy. Even his father had to find some other role to play. It was all right to feel up a daughter-in-law but a mistress was a perfect stranger. Carmella's strategy in revealing the true

295

state of their arrangement was superb. What followed was inevitable. Arthur grew more sedate and Carmella more ardent, his humility like a sign to her from an astrologer. Now she had a focus for her needs. She was convinced—and so was Marshall—that Arthur was the one and only. For Marshall it was as if all the torch songs he had played all those years on the radio were suddenly coming true, a delphic Tin Pan Alley. His heart *was* breaking. It was terrible, but not unpleasant.

One day he told Arthur—they were in Arthur's solarium—"She's set her cap for you."

"Aw, come on," Arthur said, "what are you talking about? I'm your brother, for gosh sakes."

"She's got a crush on you, kid."

"Blood is thicker than water."

"You're the apple of her eye, I get a feeling."

"Say, what do you think I am?" Arthur said. "We grew up together. We lived under the same roof. We're flesh and blood."

"My impression is the love bug has bit her. That's the long and the short of it."

And it *was* love. Seeing it in her, Marshall was as embarrassed and awed in its presence as his brother. It was profane, it was passionate. Ah, his heart. Breaking, breaking, broken. He had the blues. He had the blues to his shoes. He moped. He moped and hoped. He saddened and baddened. He felt the terror of exclusion and loved Carmella the more, estrangement dislocating him and making him feel as he had as a child tuning Atlanta, St. Louis, Cleveland or Toronto.

Carmella joined them, and Arthur, decent but flustered and guilt working in him like a decision, went off to fetch tea.

"I suppose you haven't actually slept with him yet," Marshall said miserably. Of course he knew that she hadn't, that she wouldn't dream of going to bed with his brother until he was out of the picture, so that by her propriety the adultery became deeper than the mere technical one of flesh.

She seemed as miserable as he did, her pain—she

wasn't very intelligent, the strategy had been a lucky stroke—conceiving how to get out of her difficulties. "What are you going to do?" he asked her.

"Oh Richard"—he hadn't told her he was no longer Dick Gibson—"what's going to happen? He loves you."

"Blood is thicker than water. I'm the apple of his eye."

"He's so ashamed. Sometimes I think he hates me for what he's doing to you. I could be a good Methodist wife to him—I know I could. Redemption happens, people change. We could have kids. The house is marvelous, but there's a lot that needs to be done. Once we were married we might even be able to talk Dad into staying with us. Children need grandparents. Did Arthur have grandparents?"

"He used mine."

"Oh Rich, forgive me. I didn't mean—"

"Has he made his move?"

"He's too good. He wants your word that it's all right."

He hadn't thought Carmella would stay with him after she blew their cover, but if anything she was with him more than ever now. Their lovemaking grew wilder in the last days. It was as if she understood the criminal source of Arthur's feeling for her and tried to make herself worthy of it.

One night about a week later, she put him to sleep with the most incredible lovemaking of all. He rode Carmella about the room like a horse, slapping at her ass as she, bucking and running, strong as a wrestler in her passion, carried him. Later, he inexplicably woke up. Knowing he wouldn't be able to fall asleep again, he got up without even looking toward Carmella's side of the bed and went up to the big solarium at the top of the house and entered the great diced glass room. He had never been there at night before. Rain fell heavily on the glass ceiling and he kept ducking his head involuntarily. Remaining dry under the steadily ticking rain seemed another facet of the illusion. Great storm-trooper shafts of lightning flashed all about him and he blinked timidly. He walked to one huge

297

vaulting wall of glass and looked out. Though he was higher than the trees and saw nothing moving, he sensed a great wind. The rain simply appeared, visible only as it exploded against the glass. It was if he were flying in it. He thought of radio, of his physics-insulated voice driving across the fierce fall of rain; it seemed astonishing that it ever got through. Now, though he was silent, it was as if his previous immunities still operated, as if his electronically driven voice pulled him along behind it, a kite's tail of flesh. He stood in the sky. He raised his arm and made a magic pass.

"This is Dick Gibson," he whispered, facing the thunder, "of all the networks, coast to coast." The lightning burned along its fuse. "Latest flash from Dick Gibson: Dick Gibson loves Carmella Steep." It exploded and made an electric alphabet soup of the wet, dark sky. "This is not Dick Gibson," Dick Gibson said. "This is God," he called softly across the heavens and raised his right arm and threw a thunderbolt at downtown Pittsburgh. It was just possible that because of all this turbulence his voice *would* get through, that someone might pick him up on the rib of an umbrella or the buckle of his galoshes. And he thought of Carmella as of some mortal woman he had loved, the memory of his recent ride apt, as if he'd had to change her into a horse in order to love her.

Arthur was touching his shoulder.

The radio man wheeled. "I want you to have Carmella," he said. "I want you to teach her the laws of calm and Methodism and to get all that dreck out of her pussy and line it with mortal children before it's too late. I want her to be charming to your clients and rearrange the furniture and mix it up in the Mix-master. I would marry her myself but I am not religious, though I am a god."

"Don't," his brother said. "I'm sorry, I'm—"

"Can you stand in the sky?"

"Please," Arthur said, "I feel lousy about this."

"Don't be silly. You've been very decent. You've—what's that? Who's there?" A pale shape was moving in the darkness. "Carmella?" The lightning flashed again and he saw that she was naked, as was Arthur. So she hadn't waited. It was exactly as if she had broken an appointment with him.

Now his heart *was* broken. It was a Dick Gibson first. He went downstairs and packed. There wasn't much. He played the radio as he put his few belongings together.

He had been off the radio for three months when he left Pittsburgh. For the next few months, into the winter of 1960, he traveled about the country. He had some money—he had saved perhaps $30,000 over the course of his career—and he used planes and rented cars as he had once used trains and buses. Since the apprenticeship was on him again, he went to the places where he had first broken into radio: to Kansas and Maine and eastern Washington, to Roper, Nebraska, where he had worked for the Credenza brothers on KROP, to Arkansas and Montana, to all those unbeaten paths and peripheral places on the American pie where he had been young. There were motels everywhere; it was all beaten paths. He stayed in the motels and listened to the radio, monitoring the stations he had once worked, referring to his log, the by-now thick notebook in which he kept records not only of the programs he had done but the times at which they had been broadcast. He listened out of some deep anniversarial sense, not celebrational but memorial. These time slots were his birthdays and sacred holidays, the ear's landmarks, and what he heard came across to him not as news or music or sports but as the sound of time itself.

A few of the stations for which he had worked had become network affiliates, and in such cases he stayed only long enough to absorb some of their local programming before moving on to the next town. Once or twice he found that a station had long since closed down and he had a nervous, complicated sense of stricken time, the place's mornings and evenings and afternoons without demarcation for him, as if invisible bombs had fallen on abstractions. These occasional disappointments apart, he discovered that most of his old stations were not only still in operation but were almost the same as during his apprenticeship. Even some of the voices he heard were familiar to him, for the voice ages less than anything; it is more constant than a nose or the shape of the mouth that houses it. There were familiar commercials, intact after all these years, slogans he hadn't thought about for a quarter of a century but which lined his memory like nursery rhymes and released in him surges of affection for jewelry stores, all-night restaurants, lumberyards, nurseries and farm-equipment agencies. Yet even when he recognized a familiar voice he never called the station to remind an old colleague of their mutual past. He was content merely to listen, reassured by the familiar, his nostalgia a sort of credentials.

Despite change, much had remained the same—or else progressed sequentially that having known the beginning he might have anticipated what came afterward. Again he was struck by his old sense of the several Americas; he knew that lurking behind the uniformities of federal highway system and the green redundancy of enormous exit signs that made Sedalia seem as important as Chicago, and the blazing fifty-foot logotypes of the motels, and colonial A&P's and Howard Johnsons' like outposts of Eastern empire in west Texas's scrub country, and teller's cage Dairy Queens wantonly labeled as old steamer trunks, and enamelly service stations, and in back of all the franchised restaurants and department stores—there was a Macy's in Kansas City—dance studios, taco stands, drugstores, motion picture theaters and even nightclubs, and to the side of the double arches of the hamburger drive-ins and the huge spinning chicken buckets canted from the perpendicular like an axis through true north, America atmospherically existed. It wasn't the land; he had no mystic's or patriot's or even householder's sense of the land at all. Region somehow persisted inside monolith. The Midwest threw a shadow as exotic as Spain's. He believed in all of it. New Englanders were salty, Southerners proud, Westerners independent, Easterners sophisticated, Appalachians wise and taciturn and knew the old, authentic songs. And beneath all that, beneath all the clichés of region, he believed in further, ultimate disparities between rich and poor and lovely and ugly and quick and dull and strong and weak. And structuring even *these,* adumbrating difference like geologic layer, character, quirk, personality like a coat of arms, and below personality the unspoken, and below the unspoken the unspeakable, so that as he walked down Main Street he might just as well have been in Asia. It didn't matter that the columnists were syndicated or that the rate of exchange was one hundred cents on the dollar; he felt a vague, xenophobic unease. He stared at people as at landmarks or battlegrounds or historic sites; he moved up and down the aisles of Rexall's Drugstores as through someone else's church, and picked at the Colonel's fried chicken like some fastidious visitor to Easter Island pantomiming his way through a feast of guts.

He came away renewed, refreshed, his youth somehow confirmed in the spectacle of his abiding uneasiness. The apprenticeship could continue; he was anxious to go back on the radio.

It was at about this time he began to send out his demonstration records.

But he was restless. He preferred thirteen- or twenty-six-week contracts to anything longer, and developed a reputation in the industry as a drifter. Strangely, this didn't hurt him. Somehow his itinerancy was attractive to station managers; it even lent him a certain glamour. What he was looking for was the ideal format. It formed in his mind slowly. What this was all about, what his apprenticeship meant, was that he wanted to do the perfect radio program. He didn't know what that was, but he began to suspect it would have something to do with the telephone.

In Ames, Iowa, at KIA—he was Bill Barter—he did one of the first telephone swap programs in the United States. Called *Merchandise Mart,* it was really a sort of classified ads column. People called up, described an

301

article on the air they wanted either to trade or sell and left their telephone number. When the caller hung up Bill would describe the article again briefly and give out the telephone number a second time. The program was popular, and Bill, who had never owned much himself, had a genuine curiosity about his callers. He was surprised and even confused by how casually they offered to exchange one plum of possession for another. Their notions of trade indicated whim, sudden decision, mysteriously changed minds, ways of life and thinking that hinted at Hegelian alternatives. Thus upright pianos went for motorboats, motorboats for lawn furniture, lawn furniture for air conditioners. In their descriptions the items were almost always new or used only once or twice or for part of a season, and Bill Barter imagined unspoken tragedy, disqualifying accident, sons fallen overboard and drowned and the outboard cast out. The objects seemed to come with a curse, a heavy resonance of ruin and loss. It never occurred to him that they might not work and needed repairs; his callers did not seem horsetraders seeking an advantage. Indeed, the only times he was suspicious were when something was offered for outright sale.

Other calls—hi-fi for a power mower—suggested windfall, upward mobility, some sudden unmiring intimate as disaster. So that he seemed continually caught in waves of disparate fortune, high and low tides of luck. He had a feeling of horserace, a seesaw sense of change. As the middleman he was untouched, a node through which the currents raced, and this, despite the innocuousness of the program, made him uneasy about it.

Sometimes he could not resist thrusting himself into the deals of his callers. It was frustrating; the middleman was always dropping out of the middle, and he never knew if the traders found each other. It probably seemed playful to the audience, but he was in dead earnest.

A woman called.

"Good morning, Merchandise Mart."

"I want to speak to Bill."

"Bill speaking. Go ahead, please."

"Bill, I've got a nice double plot in Ames Gardens Cemetery. I'll trade it for a washer and dryer or sell it outright at a 20-percent discount. My number is Field 3-8927."

"Aren't you going to die?"

"What's that?"

"Aren't you going to die? Did what you have go away? Are you cured?"

"Listen, I want to speak to Bill."

"I'm Bill. You *are* speaking to him. Are you and your husband splitting up? Are you a spinster? Have you been living with your sister and now she's getting married? I'm Bill."

"Quit horsing around, then, and take my number."

"Field 3-8927. I'm Bill. Are you marrying someone from an old Ames family with its own section in Ames Gardens? I'm not horsing around. Why a washer and dryer? Your voice is young. Maybe you have a lot of children and too many dirty clothes. Are you looking for a larger plot? Have you decided that your babies will be buried with you? I'm not horsing around. Do you have different ideas about death? Don't hang up. I'm not horsing around. I'm Bill. Have you made up your mind to be cremated? Don't ha—"

An old man with a cultured voice called.

"Bill Barter's Merchandise Mart. Go ahead, please, you're on the air."

"Sir, I have an eighteenth-century Chinese Chippendale stand made of aromatic tea wood and in mint condition. The piece has been in my family for two hundred and thirty-seven years."

"Gee, what would you take for something like that?"

"Well, I thought if I could get a real nice Barca-lounger or Simmons Hide-a-Bed—"

People's conceptions and arrangements bewildered and terrified him. A young man wanted to exchange a motorcycle helmet for a crucifix. Gardening tools went for animal traps, sheet music for rifles.

A teen-age boy called up. "I've got nineteen pair of

women's high-heel shoes in sizes 7A through 9 double B. Assorted colors. I've got eleven pair of brown pumps. I'll take yellow belts and percale pillowcases."

Once or twice he offered to buy things from his callers. He simply wanted to get to the bottom of at least one mystery.

A woman called the program. "I've got a sixty-pound bow, Bill, and a complete set of newly re-feathered arrows plus quiver and arm guard."

"That's just what I'm looking for."

"You?"

"How much? What do you want?"

"Have you got puppets? I need puppets."

"I'll give you cash. Buy the puppets."

"I need used puppets."

"Why? *Why,* for God's sake? I'll give you a hundred dollars."

"It isn't the money," the woman whispered. "Only used puppets will do."

The program made him nervous and he left it when his contract ran out.

A few months later he did a straight telephone request show in Fort Collins, Colorado.

" 'The Theme from *The Apartment*' for Roger." It was a man's voice.

" 'Days of Wine and Roses,' " a little girl sobbed. "It goes out for Phil and Doris."

"Is that your mommy and daddy? Do they drink? Is someone with you?"

There were experiments. At KBS in Needles, California, he arranged to call old colleagues who had telephone shows of their own. They kidded each other about former employers and sent out regards over the air from mutual friends. He was trying to create an aura of the thick past, an untrue sense of ebullient history. They should seem to have been boys together—close, loyal, raucous as student princes from operetta.

"Go on, Jeff, give my KBS listeners one of your famous commercials." And as Jeff, across the country, complied, Dick—he was Marty Moon in Needles—drowned out his friend's voice in campfire guffaw.

One night in Ohio he called backstage to the Shubert Theater in New York and talked a stagehand into leaving the phone off the hook. By manipulating sound levels his listeners were able to hear a hollow performance of the second act of *Hello Dolly,* together with comments by the principals as they stood in the wings waiting for their cues.

He tried to impart a sense of the spontaneous and wacky by giving his audience the impression that it had just occurred to him to telephone some world leader. Then he attempted to call De Gaulle or Nehru or Khrushchev. Most of the program was taken up with just the mechanics of placing such a call, with kibitzing the operators here and overseas. He never got through, of course, but once he reached a minor official in the Soviet Union who spoke a little English. Neither knew what to say to the other.

He placed calls to whorehouses. He called a Mafia drop he had heard about, the town drunk, the village idiot. By now he was as obsessed with the telephone as he had once been with radio.

One Monday night (he was off on Mondays) he was drinking in his hotel room in Richmond, Virginia. He'd had a letter that day from Arthur. Carmella was pregnant but was having difficulty. She was older than either of them had thought, probably too old to have an easy pregnancy. She was very sick, and it was a question of whether they would be able to save the baby. The doctor was afraid her water bag would break. She would have to be in bed for five months. Dick started to think about his old mistress and about his brother and about his life. He had drunk enough to be very sad. The radio was on, as it nearly always was whenever he was home—for years he had been unable to live without the sound; it often played all night; it influenced his dreams and was the first thing he heard when he woke up in the morning—tuned to a

305

controversy show, one very much like the one he'd had five years before in Hartford. The guest, a Klansman, had even been on his old show once. He was very outspoken and people called up either to support him or to ask him annihilating questions. Since he had been in the game a long time, he was just as equable with his enemies as with his fans.

Dick hadn't actually been listening to the program, but now he picked up the phone by his bed and absent-mindedly began to dial the station. When he was connected he was put on hold. As he waited his mind was empty, not confused so much as fiercely blank. He had no idea what he was going to say, and when his turn came he began to talk about his life. He told about his childhood and his family, about his apprenticeship and about Miriam, about the war and about Carmella, who he said he loved, and all about Carmella's trouble. The show's host must have recognized his voice and didn't try to interrupt him, letting him go on as long as he wanted. Then he talked about the last five years without Carmella, and he began to cry.

This got to the host; the man tried to reassure him gently that everything was all right.

"No, it isn't. But if you want to know who I am," he said, "I'm Dick Gibson."

3

"Dick Gibson?"

"Yes."

"Dick Gibson?"

"Yes. Turn your radio down. We're on a six-second tape delay."

"What? Oh. Yeah. Just a minute. I'll turn my radio down."

"Please. . . . It's two-fifty on the Sun Coast, a balmy seventy-one degrees outside our WMIA studios on Collins Boulevard."

"Dick Gibson?"

"Yessir."

"I've been trying to reach you two months."

"I'm pleased you finally got through. Go ahead, sir."

"Dick Gibson?"

"Yes. Go ahead, please."

"Your feet stink."

"Oh?"

"I smell them over my radio."

307

"But you turned your radio down."

"I smell them over my telephone."

The crank hung up. Dick took another call.

He'd had the program for a little more than two years and had been Dick Gibson uninterruptedly all that time. He would never *not* be Dick Gibson again; he had even had his name changed legally. Laying to rest the apprenticeship forever, he had at last found his format.

The program was a simple one, a variation of something he and radio had done for years. It was a telephone talk show, but slightly different from the hundreds of other telephone talk shows. *Dick Gibson's Night Letters* was a sort of club really, a kind of verbal pen pals. WMIA, a powerful clear channel, 50,000-watt station, sent out its signal in a northerly and westerly pattern, regularly reaching states throughout the South and Middle Atlantic regions. His listener/callers, chiefly from Florida and Georgia, though almost as often from Tennessee, Kentucky, the Carolinas and Virginia to the north and Alabama, Mississippi, Louisiana, Arkansas and Texas to the west, were loosely organized into clubs called Listening Posts or Mail Bags. There were perhaps 15,000 members who for a fee—which barely covered the cost of printing and handling—received a directory of the membership. (Countless others who were not members listened regularly and called the program.) Meetings were rarely held, but from time to time Dick traveled to one Listening Post or another and met fans. Though he preferred talking to them on the phones, it was something the members wanted.

Anyone could telephone the program, but many of his callers were regulars, people who through some trick or other of dialing or patience were able to get through repeatedly. He recognized many of their voices, but he could even identify those who called in less frequently. Crank calls like the one he had just taken were rare. He barely ever had to cut anyone off the air; the six-second tape delay was a nuisance, and he wouldn't have bothered with it except that the FCC required it. As it was, he used it sparingly; his Southerners were gentle in their speech, however violent they may have been in their private lives.

The show went on from one A.M. until four, and during the course of a program Dick might take anywhere from fifteen to forty telephone calls. He was in no hurry to move things along or to get in as many calls as possible. He had become very patient, learning in the course of the show's run that you got the most out of people when you let them go at their own pace. He would not, for example, have cut off the man who told him his feet stank.

A light was blinking on the Arkansas line.

"Night Letters," Dick Gibson said.

"Gibson Bwana?"

It was an old friend, the caveman from Africa, the last member of the mysterious Kunchachagwa tribe. He had been discovered by anthropologists near the Fwap-dali digs on the great Ennedi Plateau in eastern Chad. The last of his race, Norman—no one could pronounce his real name, an indecipherable gaggle of clucks and chirps—had been found by the scientists as he wandered helpless and distraught outside the opening of his cave. The night before, the very night his people had discovered fire—the story had come out slowly, painfully—they had panicked and been asphyxiated in the ill-ventilated cave when a group of young, zealous hunters, made too daring by the novelty of the flames, began to throw everything they could find onto the pyre. The anthropologists comforted him and taught him English.

"Oh awful," Norman had told Dick on the air one night, "eberyting hot, eberyting in flames. Burn up our mores, artifacts an' collective unconscious. Eberyting go up hot hot. Young bucks burn totems, taboos, cult objects and value system, entire shmeer go up dat ebening. Whole teleology shot to shit."

Norman had spent a happy summer with the anthropologists who debriefed and photographed him. He slept in a tent under mosquito netting. "I don't care what you say," Norman confessed one night, "white fellers *got* to be gods. Dey introducing Norman to mosquito netting. In cabe we don't hab dis convenience." Now, he slept under

309

the stuff on his farm in Arkansas even in winter, using the same netting the anthropologists had given him, though it was much worn and there were holes in it. Dick tried to convince him that it should be repaired, but Norman thought it was white man's magic that made it work.

In the fall, after that first pleasant summer, while Norman's trauma slowly healed, the anthropologists could not decide what to do with Norman when they returned to their various universities.

"It's not fair to the poor fellow to take him back with us to civilization. His ways are not our ways. He'd only be lost in New Haven."

"A chap can be acculturated," Norman had pleaded.

"I don't see what else can be done with him," another of the scientists said. "He's little better than an orphan now. Intelligent though he is, he wouldn't be able to survive alone. He'd be just as miserable by himself here in Chad as he would in the States."

"No, Doctor. We live in two different worlds. It couldn't work."

"Den dis las' one take Norman by de han' an' lead him into de forest. Get funny look in he eyes an' whistle 'Born Free.' But Norman find way back to digs."

The discussion went on until it was time for the anthropologists to leave. "Can we sell him to the circus, perhaps?" one of the scientists finally asked. They consulted Norman and he consented to be sold to the circus.

"Poor Norman, him culturally disoriented," Norman told Dick on one of the first evenings he called. (Norman owned no radio; as far as Dick could tell, he had no notion that he was even on the air. Dick supposed that when the phone was installed in his shack in Arkansas some practical joker had given him Dick's number. Possibly Norman thought it was the only number he could get.) "Him all alienated thoo and thoo. How you like dat Norman for de culture lag?"

"Were you really a caveman?" Dick asked him on another occasion.

"Oh, sah," Norman said passionately, "my people hab

nuttin'. We *so* backward. We neber heard ob cars or planes or tools. We so backward we neber heard ob de wheel or trees. Shee-it, we neber eben heard of *air*."

Norman had not been a success with the circus. His masters were kind—it was from them that he picked up much of the rest of what he knew of English—but the public dismissed him as a fraud. No amount of newspaper clippings or reprints from scientific journals could convince them of his authenticity. They didn't have the patience to read them, and his gentle demeanor and essential passivity destroyed whatever confidence they might have placed in a wilder, club-swinging Neanderthal. "Norman too hip, too cool for dem public cats. Him speak to owners. Dey say hokey Wild Man of Borneo ruin it for legitimate cabeman like Norman, and advise him to go into different business. 'What public *really* go fo',' day say, 'is if Norman sit up on platform above tank and let rubes th'ow baseballs at him.' But Norman don' like dat. Whut de hell? I son of Aluminum Siding Salesman when I back wit' my people in de cabe."

"An Aluminum *Siding* Salesman?"

"Yassuh. Dat's our Kunchachagwa word for 'chief.' Yassuh"—Southerners had taught him all the rest of what he knew of English—"How you call in yo' language'—chief.' Aluminum Siding Salesman way we say dat."

So when Norman refused to become a target for baseballs the circus owners had to let him go. He signed up with a lecture bureau and traveled briefly around the South giving talks, but fearing the same reaction he had received in the circus he took measures to improve his act. He appeared before them naked.

"Folks," he would say, "ya'll see befo' you a tragic essample ob de noble sabage. I looks out ober dis yere audience ob ladies an' gennelmuns in yo' all's fancy finery an' it gibs me de culture shock. Acherly, if No'man not be so perlite he lak to bust him sides laughin' jest to look at yo' all's suits an' coats an' whatnot.

"Shoot! Yo'all eber lib in a cabe? You prob'ly tink sech ting all dark an' slimy. But I tell you sho as ah lib de

311

Stone Age was de bes'. Ain' no air pollution in de Stone Age, ain' no angst, ain' no sech ting as identity crisis. Course we had our shibboleths and societal taboos, dass true. Fo' essample, we worship peanut shells, an' ebery autumn when de leaves fall offen de trees we tink it's gone be de end ob de worl' for sho'. But whut *dat* mean? It all relatib. Eberyting relatib. Norman, him see fire an' him see wheel, him see television an' him see Indiana, an' dere ain' no comparison. When de blood ob Aluminum Siding Salesman run in yo' veins, I guess yo' neber be satisfied wit cibilization. But I say *one* ting fo' yo'all— I sho' laks dat mosquito netting. De proper study ob mankind is man."

Usually he was arrested.

After the lecture tour he took a job in a foundry, and with the money he saved he was able to buy a little piece of bottomland in Arkansas.

"Norman," Norman told Dick one night, "trace de whole entire history ob western cibilization all in his own self. Start out in de Stone Age, in on de birt' ob fire—may dey rest in peace—go into de foundry fo' de Iron Age, an' now he a farmer. Eben do some time in show biz. It jest goes to show dat it's true whut dey say—ontogeny sho' nuff recapitulates phylogeny an' make no mistake! Him all tuckered out do. Tink dis nigger skip de Industrial Rebolution!"

Dick wondered how Norman was feeling tonight. The caveman was a moody caller, and at times recently he had seemed almost deranged with gloom. "Norman, how are you?"

"Norman all messed up, Gibson Bwana. Crop come up. Norman get him 'nudder culture shock."

"What's happened, Norman?"

"I buy farm fum white man, neber tink to ask what he planted. Norman just a jerk, neber make it in de white man's worl'."

"Come on, Norman, that's no way to talk. You're very adaptive."

"You know whut dat son bitch planted?"

"Well, let's see—"

312

'*Peanuts!* Him planted peanuts. I neber *see* so many peanuts. In cabe in Chad we got maybe altogedder five peanuts. My people worship little feller peanut. Now Norman got him more peanuts den de Kunchachagwa Pope. Make him nerbous to tink he got so many. If Mama only alibe to see..." His voice cracked and trailed off.

"Norman—you've got to stop thinking like that. Your mother's dead. She died when the tribe discovered fire."

"Sho, Norman know dat. Still, Mama very religious woman, very ortodox. Her stay in de temple all de day, make holy holy. Wouldn't she be pleased to see her Norman wit all dem peanuts!"

"She'd be very proud."

"Also—har, har—Norman in lub."

"What was that?"

"Norman fall in lub."

"That's wonderful, Norman. Who's the lucky girl?"

"Her—tee hee—her—No. Norman dassn't say. Not 'llowed speak name ob female fo' de marriage ceremony."

"Oh?"

"I speak to she fadder do. Him 'gainst de marriage."

Dick could imagine what the prospect of a caveman in the family might do to a parent. "Well, sometimes these things happen," he said soothingly. "Still, if the girl loves you—"

"Dat's jus' whut Norman tell he sweetheart. She say she want to finish school."

"That isn't unreasonable. If you both still feel this way after she graduates—"

"Can't wait much longer. Norman no chicken. Him be forty yar nex' comet. An' little girl just startin' de kindergarten."

"You've fallen in love with a child in *kindergarten?*"

"Otre temps, otre moeurs."

"Norman, that's ... You can't—"

"Gibson Bwana prejudiced as de udder white man," Norman said sourly.

"Prejudiced? What's prejudice got to do with it? ... What other white man?"

313

"Udder white man—de redneck. She fadder."

"The little girl's *white?*"

"Whut dat matter? After we married we go back to Chad. Whut dipperence color make in a cabe?"

"Norman, you live in Arkansas! Listen to me. I want you to promise—Norman, listen to me. Listen to me, please."

"Norman got to go. Some fellers poundin' at de cabin do'." Gibson could hear it, an alarming rattle and some confused shouting.

"Norman?"

But the line went dead.

A newsbreak and a couple of commercials followed. Dick took the next call at seven minutes after three. It was from an Atlanta man who couldn't sleep and called Dick to share with him the thought that had kept him up all night. He worked as an adjustor for an insurance company and was puzzled by the fact that people always told funny stories at lunch. "Why lunch? Why humor?"

"Well probably you eat with your co-workers, and most of them are men, right?"

"Yes, but you're on the wrong track. These aren't dirty jokes. Mostly they aren't even jokes at all. They're anecdotes, amusing things that happen to them in the business, or about odd people they used to know. Sure, sometimes people are smutty, but that's not what I'm talking about."

"My point is that you're with your colleagues. It's mostly an all-male company."

"That's so, but just as often the secretaries come with us, or some of the girls from the typing pool. It isn't *just* men. Why humor? Why lunch? That's what I'm driving at."

"That's what *I'm* driving at. You're with colleagues. Isn't it natural for people who know each other this way to talk about the oddball things that have happened to them?"

"Sure, but why *lunch?* We see each other socially at other times and it isn't like that. I see Schmidt. Schmidt's probably my best friend. But when we go to parties or out

314

to dinner, Schmidt's a totally different person. We talk about issues, or the news, or maybe our kids. There isn't all that *laughing*."

"I don't understand. Does it bother you to hear a humorous story?"

"I didn't say it bothered me. I never said it bothered me. But don't you see? Everything is funny; it's always *funny*. Everybody in my department is an adjustor, but often we eat with underwriters or salesmen or computer personnel or even with the company physicians. We're a big company, one whole floor is a clinic where people come to be examined for their policies. But it doesn't make any difference if a man is a doctor or a salesman or an adjustor like myself. Whenever he speaks up at lunch it's to tell a funny story or make some wisecrack. That's the way it was with the last company I worked for, and the firm I was with before that when I was in another business. It's universal."

"Well, if you enjoy these stories—"

"Certainly I enjoy them. I laugh as hard as the next guy, but what is it? We're adjustors. We see *awful* stuff. I mean, our nose is in it every day of the week. Probably the only time you ever saw an adjustor was when some guy sideswiped your car while it was parked outside your house. He looked at it and told you to go ahead and get it fixed. But that isn't the half of it—it isn't a tenth of it. Every day I see someone with his neck creamed or his leg torn off at the pocket, or his house up in flames and his kid third-degreed in her bedroom. You see pictures of accidents in the papers, but you don't see these. They don't show you the totals.

"And the underwriters know what's going on too. They know everything there is to know about casualty and percentages, and the docs the same. Either you're realistic in the insurance business or you go under. Do you know that 39 percent of the people who apply for life insurance are uninsurable unless they pay some fantastic premium, and 7 percent are uninsurable no matter *what* the premium is? There isn't a premium large enough they could pay to insure themselves. And they'd pay it too."

"Well, there's your answer, then. You people see so much horror that you've got to have some sort of safety valve or you couldn't take it. That's why you tell each other funny stories."

"*No!* It's the same in any business. It's the same in your business. Don't the announcers all kid around when you go to lunch?"

"Yes, but—"

"Certainly. In *every* business. I used to be in the toy business before I went into insurance. It was the same there."

"Well, then, the pressures," Dick Gibson said, genuinely interested now in the problem. "Or perhaps it's the fact that it's mid-day. The temperature is highest then. You've moved your bowels, you're not tired out yet, you've got all your energy. You've—"

"*No.* What is that? The temperature, your bowels? What is that, astrology? No. Why *humor?* I'm talking about good will—people wrestling to pick up checks or at least to leave the tip and the sky's the limit; the world's their oyster and good mood on them like the birthmark. No. No," the caller said excitedly. "And all the fear that engines us gone, the personality seamless as brushstrokes on a painted wall. And to get as good as you give—the ears open and the heart as well. Lunch's good democracy. The menu a ballot, you're voting your appetite."

"Certainly," Dick Gibson said, "that would put you in a good mood."

"What? Yes ... But maybe a joke is a shyness, an anecdote no assertion and good will a finesse. I think maybe it's strategy, a camouflage, some Asian nuance of delay. Sure. To miss profundity is to lose face."

"I'm glad I could help you."

"Well, you have. I think I'll be able to sleep."

"I'm sorry to lose a listener."

"What? Oh. Yes. Ha ha. Why lunch? Why gags, humor, good will? *Why can't it always be lunchtime?*"

The voice cracked, trailed off, and the connection was broken. Dick took three more calls and signed off for the night.

316

He left the studio and walked to the Fontainebleau where he garaged his car. Mopiani, one of the Negro night men, complimented him. "That was a good program, Dick. I listened on a '68 Cadillac. Used both speakers. Drained the battery."

He got into his car and started up Collins Boulevard to the Deauville. He loved Miami Beach, as he admired and loved all excess. He was at home in inflation, and saw the bizarre luxury hotels along the strip as a unique and lovely manifestation. Air conditioning and paper bathing suits, celebrities, amphibious automobiles, the open bus-trains that pulled tourists up and down the shopping mall on Lincoln Road, marinas, eleven different varieties of bagel, the infinite quinellas of pancake combination in the delicatessens ("Woolfie's" and "Googie's" were his home cooking), glass-bottom boats, weather, Italian knit, suntan lotions and the parking problem. (Mopiani was only one of several personal attendants; indeed, he had never owned a car in his life and had purchased this one merely to have it parked.) He was visible in Miami Beach, a celebrity; he'd never been one before, not in this way. He was an intimate of bartenders, cigarette girls and wandering girl photographers (they still had them here; for all its modern patina, one of the Beach's excesses was the past: thus, the entertainers were often older stars, the Tony Martins and Jimmy Durantes and Joe E. Lewises who were famous from a vintage of fame he had known as a boy). He enjoyed the vaguely North African sense of the place, its spanking whitewash and tiny Oriental-like shops. Though the vegetation was at first unreal to him— as though it too, like the bagel styles and lush semi-kosher mood of the hotel kitchens, might have been imported—he had come to look upon palm trees as the very essence of tree, and to dismiss the familiar oaks and elms and maples of his past as spurious and faintly contrived. He knew beach boys, towel boys, the captains of fishing boats and their one-man crews, girl lifeguards, maître d's, chambermaids, Cuban bookies, cops. And they knew him. To be a celebrity, he decided, was to be part of an intricately hierarchical staff, to know semi-secret passageways, backstairs, greenrooms, to have an inexhaustible supply of first names and exist placidly at last with one's world, to belong to it as to a country club.

He lived in the Deauville Hotel facing the Atlantic in a small celebrity suite which he got at a discount, and his pockets were always filled with Deauville matchbooks—changed regularly as the sheets each morning—a Vandyked cavalier, the hotel's symbol, on the front cover. Though he was trying to give up smoking, for some reason he could not give up the matches, and when he offered a light it was always with a strange flourish that he tossed the matchbook on the table. There were Deauville matchbooks on top of the dash of his car, in his jackets, in his rooms, in the studio, everywhere, his small, semi-official litter. Similarly, he stuffed his pockets with the tiny, wrapped hotel soaps, using them as sachets, so that he always smelled faintly of Dial and Deauville. There were other things, cavalier-topped swizzle sticks—though he was not much of a drinker—and Deauville stationery on which he jotted down memos to himself and which he actually preferred for his business correspondence to the official WMIA letterhead. For some reason these souvenirs had become important to him; he did not know why.

It was a beautiful night. The hotels seemed capable of storing energy, and now mysteriously reflected their whiteness. He drove a new convertible, the top down, like a well-paid private detective in movies, and as he drove, privileged at red lights which he stopped for or ignored according to some delicate discretionary sense of his own, he had a notion of coast, a feel of margin. Behind him lay the long drought of his inland life, his singleness (here raised to bachelordom; there were many bachelors in this place) and apprenticeship, which of late he had begun to grudge, resentful of it as of a detour. He played the radio low as he drove slowly along the attenuated strip of twenty- and twenty-five-story hotels like eccentric figures in geometry with their ramps looping like doorman's braid and their cantilevered balconies that shoved out from the shoulders of the buildings like the epaulets of drum majors—and the buildings themselves, amok parabolas of frosting or the ribbed pockets of gadgets for slicing hard-boiled eggs. Sandcastles! And beyond the great wall of hotels that traced the soft veer of the strand, the sea itself, the fishy Atlantic, a new element. It was this—all that water—that now joined the air, fire and clay of his life, and seemed to make it whole. Here he lived, *here*, behind the deep water, exactly at sea level, where his voice with nothing to stop it might climb miles, a straight, clear trajectory of sound, spraying old Heaviside's umbrella of ionosphere, deep as stars, sharp as night. He loved his luck, but it made him nervous. It might turn out to be merely temporary, like a spell of good weather. (Was that why he loved Florida, because the weather was more constant here and he took it as a sign of other, deeper constants?)

He drove up the ramp outside the main entrance to the Deauville and turned his car over to Geraldine, Nick the night man's girl friend.

"How are you, Geraldine?"

"Not so hotsy, not so totsy. Wisht I was back in 'bama on the farm. Nick and me tuned in the show tonight on a Lincoln Continental while we necked. Turned on the air conditioning and it give me the swollen glands."

He went inside and picked up his key from the night manager.

"Hi Dick."

" 'Lo Rick."

"Seen Nick?"

"Nick's chick."

"That hick?"

"She's sick."

He wasn't sleepy and went past his suite to Carol's room, a few doors down. Carol was one of the entertainers in the lounge.

He rapped their signal. "Carol?"

"What is it? Who's there?"

"Dick, honey. I'm a little   nudgy tonight. Okay if I come in for a few minutes and talk?"

He heard someone ask who the hell was out there at this time of night. "Dick, I can't," Carol said from behind the door. "Not tonight."

She must have let one of the guests pick her up, something that happened only when she was very blue. She was married, but her husband had abandoned her and her two children. Now the kids lived with her folks in Michigan; he guessed she missed them pretty bad. Sometimes she used his shoulder to cry on, though he would have preferred her to call up and tell him about it on the air.

"See you tomorrow, Carol," he said. He leaned closer to the door. "You didn't remember our signal," he whispered.

There was soft music playing behind the door of Sheila's room. Sheila was the dance instructor at the hotel, but occasionally she picked up extra money by dealing for the house in private games around Miami. He rapped their signal and when Sheila opened the door he saw that she was still in her Gwen Verdonish skin-tight clothes— musical-comedy red bell-bottoms that went up and around her body like a scuba diver's rubber suit. She probably had a dozen such outfits. Something about her wiry, dancer's body struck him as vicious, but he liked her very much.

He asked if he could come in. "My God," she said, "you too? Everyone's making a play for the help tonight. I saw Carol bring a tourist up earlier, and what's-his-name, the swim pro, Finder, has some minky old bag from Cleveland with him. I guess that other one, Mrs. Loew, must have checked out today."

"Finder's keepers."

"Finder's keepers. Ha ha. These corridors are snug with sin, I do declare. Must be the moon. Whassamatter, Dicky?"

"I want to learn Rhumba."

"You're too old to learn Rhumba. Whassamatter, Dicky? Got the heebie jeebies?"

He loved show folk. They were just as worldly and understanding in person as on stage.

"Not the heebie jeebies, no. Say," he said, "*I* have an idea. Why don't we make love?"

"Well, come on in," she said. "I do declare."

He sat down on the side of her bed.

"You never tried to put the make on me," she said. "What's up?"

"To find out if you will is why. To see if you're as worldly and understanding as you are on stage."

"Whassamatter, Dicky?"

"Yes or no."

"Well, yes then. Heck, yes."

Taking her hand, he brought her down beside him on the bed and gave her a kiss. Then he tried to undress her, but he had trouble with her skin-tight clothes.

"Hey, what the hell are you doing? Hey! What are you doing?"

"I think I tore it. Send me the bill."

"It's a costume, dummy. It doesn't work like regular clothes. The bell bottoms go up over my head. You take it off like a sweater. Don't you know anything about dancing girls?"

She took the bottoms of the strange pants and rolled them up her long legs as if pulling on stockings, maneuvering her body intricately as they rose astonishingly above her hips where they unsnapped at the crotch like a baby's pajamas. She was naked underneath. Dick gasped and gazed in wonder. "Send me the bill. I *want* to pay it."

They made love and smoked. Dick offered her a light from his matchbook, but was disappointed to see that she had plenty of Deauville matchbooks of her own. Then they drank Sheila's scotch, which he stirred with the cavalier-topped swizzle stick. The FM played "Lara's Theme" from *Dr. Zhivago* and Dick saw through a chink in the drapes that there *was* a full moon. Naked, he got out of bed and opened the curtains. Sliding back the glass doors, he stepped out on the balcony. Below him the illuminated swimming pool glowed like an enormous turquoise; beyond it the narrow, perfect lawn of beach meshed with the dark Atlantic, the uneven, concentric tops of the waves seen from above like the curved rows of an amphitheater.

He sat in a wrought iron and rubber chaise longue and crossed his arms on his chest. Looking back over his shoulder, he saw that Sheila was watching him from the bed. "Come on out," he said. "This is swell."

"Do you know what your ass looks like pressing through those rubber straps? Like a zebra's."

"Come on out," he said. "The sun will be coming up in a little bit. It's going to be terrific."

Reluctantly she got up and put on a dressing gown. She brought Dick's underwear out and sat in a chaise next to his. "Here," she said, "put this on."

"Why? I'm comfortable."

"How old are you, Dicky?"

"Pushing fifty. Why?"

"You're not in the first bloom of youth is all."

"Oh. Aesthetic reasons. Okay." He took the underwear and pulled it on. "Is my body really that bad?"

"Pushing fifty's pushing fifty. But actually, if you want to know, you surprised me tonight."

"Not bad for an old man?"

"Not bad for an old man."

He leaned over and kissed her. "Hey," he said, "how come you were still up?"

"Oh," she said, "like you. I had the blues."

"Not like me," he said. "I'm terrific. Say, look at those palm trees over on the Nautilus's patio. That's really beautiful. I never noticed them before. You can't see them from my angle. They must be Royal Hawaiians or something."

"I guess."

"Gee," Dick said, "the palms, the beach, the sea, the moon and stars and air. It's really terrific, isn't it? Listen to what they're playing on the FM. That's 'Mood Indigo.'"

"I guess."

"That's one of my favorite songs, 'Mood Indigo.'"

"I used to do a kind of ballet thing to 'Stardust.'"

"Did you? I bet it was beautiful."

"It was *corny*."

"Well, sure it was corny. Hell, yes, it was corny. But what could be cornier than this, any of this? Listen," he said, becoming excited, "once, long before I ever pushed fifty, during the war, I had this idea about what my life would be like. It was going to be special, really *something*. I mean *really* something. Do you know what I mean?"

"Do I ever," Sheila said. "I grew up thinking I was going to be another Chita Rivera and have the dancing lead on Broadway. I thought I'd be on *Hollywood Palace* one week and introduced from Ed Sullivan's audience the next."

"But your life *is* special," Dick Gibson said. "It *is*. You're here. Excuse me, but you're here with me. *My* life is exceptional too. I mean, what I thought back then was that it would be touched by cliché. Look, *look*, the sun's coming up! I can hear the seagulls screeching! It's dawn. . . . That it would be as it is in myth. That maybe I might even have to suffer more than ordinary men. Well, I was prepared. If that's what it costs, that's what it costs. Sure. Absolutely. Pay life the two dollars and let's get going! . . . That I would even have enemies. Well, face it, who has enemies? Is there a nemesis in the house? People are too wrapped up in themselves to have it in for the other guy. But anyway, that's what I thought. That was my thinking about it, that I'd have enemies like Dorothy had the Witch of the West . . . Look, *look,* the sun is like a soft red ball. The wind's coming up. You can hear it stir the palms . . . That I'd have this goal, you see, but that I'd be thwarted at every turn. I've always been in radio. I thought maybe my sponsors would give me trouble, or my station manager. Or the network VP's. Or, God yes, I admit it, the *public*. That somehow they'd see to it I couldn't get said what needed to be said. That I'd be kicked and I'd be canned, tied to the railroad tracks, tossed off cliffs, shot at, winged, busted, caught in traps, shipwrecked, man overboard and the river dragged. But that I'd always bounce back, you understand; I'd always bounce back and live in high places where the glory is and the tall corn grows. That my birthdays would be like third-act curtains in a play. I didn't remember any of this until tonight. That's funny, that I'd forget about it when it was all I wanted, all I've been waiting for . . ."

"Whassamatter, Dicky?"

"Nothing. Nothingsamatter. Nothingsamatter. *Nothing!* Listen, they're playing 'I Get Along Without You Very Well.' You want to go steady?"

"Shh," she said, "don't shout so."

"Was I shouting? Was I really shouting? Well, I'm sorry," he said. He looked hard at the sunrise. "I *thought* it would be trite," he said. "I thought it would be trite and magnificent."

"You're a funny guy."

"Ha ha."

"Poor Dick."

"Boo hoo."

"It's late. Why don't we go inside?"

"I'm all right. It's beginning to happen. I was waiting for it to start and it's starting. I should have come to Florida years ago. It's beginning. I can feel it. This is it, I think. I think maybe this is it."

4

"I have a call on the Florida line. Hello. Night Letters."

"Hello? Hello?" A kid's voice.

"Turn your radio down, sonny."

"All right." A pause. Dead air. He had stopped trying to fill up the time it took for a caller to turn his radio down. What did his listeners care what the temperature was in Miami? As for the time, they'd been up all night too. They knew the time—none better.

"Hello?"

"I'm here, sonny. Up kind of late tonight."

"Yes."

"No school tomorrow?"

"There's school."

"Where you calling from, sonny?"

"Jacksonville."

"Want to ask me a riddle?" When kids called they usually had jokes to tell or riddles to ask. A good sport, Dick gave up even when he knew the answer.

"Naw."

"Naw, eh? Well, what's on your mind? What's the temperature up in Jacksonville?"

"I don't know. I'm not outside."

"I'll bet you're not. Where you calling from? Is there a phone in your room?"

"Yes."

"Do your parents know you're using it at this hour? I'll bet when they put that phone in they told you that having your own extension was a privilege and not a right. What do you think they'd say if they knew you were using it to call a radio station at a quarter of two in the morning? You think they'd approve of that?"

"No. But they're dead."

"Oh. . . . Well gee, son, I'm sorry to hear that. That doesn't change the principle, though. It's still kind of late for a youngster to be up. Youngsters need sleep . . . Are they both dead?"

"Yes, sir."

"I'm sorry, son. What did you want to talk about? Do you want to give me your name?"

"Henry Harper."

"What did you want to talk about, Henry?"

"How do I join a Listening Post and get your Night Letter Directory? Is there a certain age you have to be?"

"How old are you, Henry?"

"I'm nine."

"I don't think we have anyone your age in any of our Listening Posts."

"Oh."

"But in all fairness, Henry, I'm sure there isn't anything against it in our bylaws. All you do is send your name and address care of this station and write me a little something about yourself for the Night Letter. You write, don't you?"

"I print."

"To tell the truth, Henry, I think you'd be better off in the Cub Scouts."

"That's best left up to me, I should think."

326

"Just as you say, Henry. Maybe you'd better get some rest now though."

"I can't sleep."

"Oh?"

"I would if I could."

"Do you want to talk about it, Henry? Do you want to talk about your Mommy and Daddy?"

"They're dead. I told you that."

"I see."

"They died in a freak accident."

"What grade are you in, Henry? What's your favorite subject?"

"Third grade. Social Studies. Mother and Father were hobbyists. There's money. This isn't an extension."

"I see."

"Mother and Father were hobbyists. They'd done everything. They'd gone spelunking in Turkey and all along the Golden Crescent in Iran. They once sailed in a dhow from Dar-es-Salaam in the Indian Ocean all the way round Dondra Head to Columbo. There were motorcycles, of course, and skiing and safaris, and once they were the special guests of the Norwegian whale fisheries on an Antarctic whale hunt. Both of them raced cars and were licensed balloonists. They were fun parents," Henry said, sighing.

"The freak accident?" Dick Gibson said gently.

"Yes. They'd become interested in sky diving. It happened right here in Jacksonville on the estate. I was there. I was seven. Father jumped first and then Mother. Only something went wrong. Father's chute opened, but Mother delayed opening hers, and she fell right on top of him at about two thousand feet. She must have killed him instantly, broke his neck. They fell together another few hundred feet or so. Mother tried to open her chute but her lines must have been all fouled with Father's. She got the reserve pack open, but the chute never bellied properly. She was able to hitchhike the rest of the way down on the buoyancy in Father's chute, but she had no control over her drift, and they tumbled down over the trees into the private zoo. Since she was all tangled up in Father's

327

lines, she wasn't able to disentangle herself in time. She spooked the tiger and it killed her. She never had a chance.

"You *saw* this?"

"I didn't see the tiger part," the boy said. He began to cry.

"Don't cry, son. Don't cry, Henry."

"Yes, sir," Henry said. "Sorry."

"Listen, son, why don't you go into your grandparents' room and tell them you're upset?"

"They're dead. They died in a freak accident."

"The tiger?"

"No, sir. They were John Ringling North's guests on the circus train, and they'd gone back to talk to the alligator woman and the midgets and the four-armed boy in the last car when the bridge buckled. Every car made it to the other side but the freaks."

"I see. Your uncle, then. Your aunt."

"They're dead too. Everybody's dead," Henry said.

"Well, who's home, son? Who's home, Henry?"

"Nobody's home. They're all dead."

"Well, somebody's got to be there. Who do you stay with?"

"I live by myself."

"What about the housekeeper?"

"I fired the housekeeper. She wasn't thorough."

"You said you lived on an estate. What about the gardener?"

"The gardener's dead."

"Henry, children often have terrific imaginations. Sometimes they like to tease grown-ups."

"I don't like to tease grown-ups. I don't have a terrific imagination. What do you want me to do, swear that everybody is dead? Okay, I swear it. I swear it on my honor."

"Well, what about the legalities?"

"How do you mean?"

"How can you live by yourself? Legally, that is. Don't the courts have anything to say?"

"Plenty. They have plenty to say. When my parents died I was given over to the custody of my grandfather. But then he and Grandmother died in the freak accident. There were no other relatives. I had an executor and he died, and the man who took over for him, he died too. I guess all the provisions for me just finally ran out. I don't blame anyone. There's a curse on me, I think. My guardians are wiped out. There's a trust fund which I don't get till I'm twenty-one, but there's cash. There's a lot of cash around the house—about three quarters of a million dollars—and I use that to live. I'm all alone here. But I go to school. I never play hooky."

"Henry, a boy needs adult guidance. How can you live in a big house all by yourself? What about your meals?"

"I'm all right. I'm fine. I make my own breakfast and the school has a hot lunch program. At night I eat in restaurants. I take taxis to them, or sometimes if I don't feel like going out I have a cab bring over some chicken from the Colonel."

"Well, that's all very fine, Henry, but I really think you shouldn't be by yourself."

"If I had a little brother . . . They wouldn't let me adopt one, do you think?"

"No, Henry."

"I didn't think so."

"Listen, Henry, I'd like you to make me a promise."

"What?"

"Will you promise?"

"I'll have to hear what it is first. I won't step into anything blindfold."

"I want you to promise that first thing tomorrow you'll get in touch with the authorities and tell them about your arrangements. Will you promise me that, Henry?"

"Certainly not. I can take care of myself. Listen, I pay the bills. I'm never behind on the gas or electricity. The phone's always taken care of. I go for my checkups when I'm supposed to and I leave the cash with the nurse right after the examination. They never have to bill me. If I need a plumber or a roofer I know how to get in touch with one. I use the Yellow Pages. I'm fair with the merchants. Cash on the barrelhead—which is more than a lot of adults can say. I even give to charity."

"Well, who do you play with, Henry?"

"I don't play much. But I go to ballgames whenever I want. Last September I wanted to see the World Series, so I just hopped on a jet and went. I got the tickets from a scalper outside the stadium but they were good seats. Listen, I'm very responsible. I'm no wild kid or anything."

"It's your life, Henry, but I think you're making a mistake."

"Don't get me wrong. It was fine living with my grandparents. They were nice people. When they died I had a good relationship with my executor. He was an old friend of the family and we got along very well. The man who took his place when *he* died, that's another story. Well, he was a perfect stranger. I'm sorry he had the heart attack, of course, but I didn't mourn or anything. I just don't want anyone adopting me for my money. Listen, I'm all *right*."

"Except you can't sleep nights."

"What? What's that? Well, yes, but your program helps a lot. That's why I called. I want to join a Listening Post. I mean, I listen to all these old people who call up and tell you their troubles and they try to put a good face on things but you can tell they're scared and that their hearts are broken. They break *my* heart. They remind me of my first executor. He was terminal, just like that Mrs. Dormer who calls from Sun City. I think it would help if I could write some of those people. I don't mean I'd give them advice—though I could probably give them some pretty good advice. I could tell them that it doesn't matter, that it's important to have courage, that *that's* what matters. But I don't *mean* advice. Anyway, they probably wouldn't take it from a kid. But maybe I could help some of them with money—you know, to get their operations or bring their sons home from San Diego to see them before it's too late. I have all this cash lying around. I don't need much. I'd move into a smaller house like a shot, but I can't put the estate on the market because I can't enter into contracts yet. That's the big hitch about being a kid and living by yourself, you can't enter into contracts. I think I might move into a smaller house anyway and just close down the big one. Anyway, I'd like to join one of the Listening Posts. I probably have more in common with some of these people than you might expect, and—let's face it—it would make *me* feel a whole lot better to be able to help out. So that's why I called. I wanted to thank *you* too. You do very good work."

"You're a good boy, Henry," Dick said, and he hung up after promising to send the materials as soon as he got the boy's application.

Moved by Henry's call, but not quite certain that it wasn't a joke, he felt strangely troubled the rest of the evening. The callers seemed similarly affected; they were subdued and even the number of calls fell off sharply. Dick had to stretch out conversations with people he normally wouldn't have kept on the air more than five minutes.

The Refugee called. He had come to the country before the war but that's how he referred to himself. It was never clear what country he had emigrated from, and he spoke with no trace of an accent. He was a boring sort of refugee. The only clue to his foreign origin was that when he became excited—and being on the radio usually made him excited—he often confused the usages of "how" and "why" and of "good" and "well." He would say that he liked his meat "good done," and once he had made an impassioned speech in support of his local police. "It's wrong, Mr. Gibson, why the public doesn't support its policemen. The way these young punks scream 'police brutality' every time one of them is arrested is positively sickening. We should honor every last cop on the beat, and instead of castigating him we should get down on our knees and tell him 'Good done, thou well and faithful servant.'" Maybe the Refugee was a joker too.

"Why are you tonight, Mr. Gibson?" the Refugee asked.

"Fine, and you?"

"Can't complain. I've got my health and well name. What more could I want?"

"Not a thing."

"That's what I say. The important thing is to be merry, get along with your neighbors and show your wellwill."

Dick wondered if the man was putting him on. Perhaps his callers were all unemployed actors.

"Are you still there, Mr. Gibson?"

"Here I am."

"Good, as I was saying, it's always a well idea to be friendly. It doesn't cost a thing and it's often good worth it."

"Hmn."

"That's my thinking on it, anyway."

"You're probably right."

"Sure I am. It doesn't make sense to grouse and pout when you can wear a smile and be a well friend. I don't know how these pessimists always look on the dark side of things. I ask myself how, but it just doesn't make sense."

"I'm sure you're right."

"Good, I don't want to take up any more of your time. I just wanted to call and tell you why things are going."

"Wellnight," Dick Gibson said.

"Wellbye," the Refugee said.

"Your feet stink."

"Dick boy."

"Mrs. Dormer?"

"Yes, Dick boy. That's right, Dick boy."

"How are you, Mrs. Dormer?"

"Not so fit as a fiddle. I don't suppose it will be too much longer now."

"That's foolish, Mrs. Dormer. You've had these sieges before. You'll get over this one just as you got over the others. Are you taking good care of yourself?"

"I've been in bed for the past week. Frances had to put the call through. I can't hold the phone. Frances is holding it for me right now. I haven't the strength."

"How is Frances, Mrs. Dormer?"

"Frances is fine, Dick boy. I'm afraid I've been a terrible burden to her, but she's a good girl. Do you know she missed Tom's graduation to come out here when she heard?"

"She must be a comfort."

"She certainly is, Dick boy. She is a comfort, but I don't see why she didn't wait until her son graduated to come out. It would just have been a few days. That Dr. Pepper can be a terrible alarmist sometimes."

"Well, he just wanted you to be comfortable, Mrs. Dormer."

"I know that, Dick boy, but I'm thinking of poor Tom. He's got no father and now here's his mother who won't even be at his graduation."

"He'll be fine, Mrs. Dormer."

"Lord, I hope so. That's my prayer, Dick boy."

"You just try to be comfortable and don't worry about anything. That way you'll get better sooner."

"I don't really believe that, Dick boy, do you?"

"Well, certainly I do. Of course I do. You're just a little discouraged now because of Tom."

"She's stopped taking her medicine, Mr. Gibson."

"Who's there? Who is that? Frances?"

"It's Frances, Mr. Gibson. Mother's stopped taking her medicine. She won't take any of her pills. Would you say something to her? Just say something to her, would you, Mr. Gibson?"

"Mrs. Dormer?"

"I'm here, Dick boy."

"This is shocking, Mrs. Dormer. I'm really surprised. Here's Frances, come to be with you all the way from Chicago, missing her son's graduation. All she wants is for you to get better, and here you are acting like a naughty child who won't take her medicine! How do you think that makes Frances feel?"

333

"I've called to say goodbye, Dick boy. I'm weaker every day. I'll slide into a coma soon. You shouldn't try to trick an old woman on her deathbed."

"Now Mrs. Dormer, you mustn't say things like that. You're a religious woman, Mrs. Dormer. Only God can tell when a person's going to . . . what you just said. You believe that, don't you?"

"I called to say goodbye to you and all my friends in the Listening Posts, and to thank all the nice people who took the trouble to send me cards and little notes. I don't think I'll be able to speak to you again, and I want you to listen. It's a great effort for me to speak at all, and you shouldn't make me argue about what is obvious. Now you've got to listen. Will you listen, Dick boy?"

"I wish you wouldn't—"

"Will you?"

"Yes, ma'm. I'm listening."

"Mr. Gibson, she won't even take her pain killers. I'm sorry to blubber like this, but you don't know the agony my mother's in."

"Frances?"

"Gracious, Mr. Gibson, do you know she's actually lying here naked on the bed because the pressure of her night clothes is just too painful on her skin? I never saw my mother naked in my life, Mr. Gibson, and now she won't even cover herself with a handkerchief. She's going to get pneumonia. Besides everything else, she's going to come down with pneumonia. If she'd take her pain killers we could dress her properly and then she wouldn't come down with pneumonia. She won't listen, Mr. Gibson. I'm going to put the phone back to her ear. You make her listen, will you?"

"Frances, Dick boy doesn't want to hear all this. Shame on you for making such a fuss. I've got wonderful friends in the Listening Post organizations who love me and who I love, and a lot of them are just as sick and broken as I am, and you've got no right to upset them like this. I wanted to say goodbye to my good friends, and it looks like no one is going to let me do that."

"Mrs. Dormer?"

"What is it, Dick boy?"

"Look, Mrs. Dormer, you *have* got wonderful friends in the Listening Posts. You *have*. And because they *do* love you they don't like to see you give up like this. They want you to fight back, just as you fought back in the past. Why don't you take your pain pills and whatever else Dr. Pepper thinks you ought to have. Don't let those good friends down. Don't give up. Will you promise that? Will you make that promise to me and to your good friends in the Listening Posts?"

"No, Dick boy. I won't. And who said anything about giving up, Dick boy? It's because I *haven't* given up that I won't take those pills. That boy who was on last week, that Henry Harper, he mentioned my name and said he wanted to give me advice, that old dying people should have courage. Well, I'll show him courage! What does *he* know about it? That's why I won't take those pills. Do you know how it hurts me? I hadn't meant to talk like this, but it seems no one will let me say what I wanted to say, that you all want me to believe everything's all right, not so's you can believe it too, but so's you can believe I believe it and be comforted. I call that selfish. And everything *isn't* all right. Do you know how it hurts? Do you know how bad it is? My voice, just my own voice coming out of my throat is enough pressure to pull the skin off me. Just my *words*. Just the weight of my words in my throat is like being cut with knives. Just that. Just to say 'flower' is a torture to me. Just to whisper it. I'm killing myself, I'm killing myself to speak and now you make me say all this. I want to be *still*. All I want is to be still."

"Hush," Dick said, frightened. "Hush, Mrs. Dormer. Please hush."

"I'm going to say it. Let me, for God's sake, *will you please?* You're killing me, Dick boy."

"Go ahead, Mrs. Dormer. Go ahead, ma'm."

"I want . . . I want . . . to thank you *all*. You've been . . . my family. Now I know, I know it's awful for an old dying woman to call up and oppress folks this way and give them bad dreams. It's awful. It's vulgar, a phone call from the death bed. It's inexcusable and I'm sorry, and now all this other has come out and I've made a mess— but I did have to tell you all goodbye and thank you for the happiness you've given me. And this is the only way I have, don't you see? I had to make peace with my friends and give them my love. I had to. Goodbye, all my good friends, and God bless you. God bless *you,* Dick boy. Goodbye, my dear."

"Goodbye," Dick Gibson said. "Goodbye, Mrs. Dormer. I love you." He waited a moment to see if she would answer, but he heard nothing and finally he hung up and took another call.

There was a call on the Tennessee line.

"Night Letters. Go ahead, please."

"You can wish me a happy birthday."

"Happy birthday. Who is this?"

"Don't you recognize my voice?"

"Help me out. Where in Tennessee are you calling from?"

"Knoxville."

Dick opened the directory and turned to the Knoxville page. The voice was thickish with no hint of a Southern accent. Quickly he ran down the one- and two-word descriptions of voices he had penciled in beside each of the names. Next to one he found the word "whiskey." He had a go. "Harold Flesh?"

"That's right."

"Get any cards from the Mail Baggers?"

"Them Mail Baggers come through when you're laid up in the hospital. When you got a broken leg they come to your room and write their names on your cast."

"Well, Harold, so many of the Mail Baggers have trouble, you see." Recently he had begun to detect a note of piety in his voice. It was not unpleasant. "They're kept pretty busy cheering up our Mail Baggers who really need it. An awful lot of our people have trouble, Harold."

"They're trouble shooters."

"Well, there's a lot of fun in them too, Harold."

"They pitch in for a wreath. They sit with the kids when it's time for the funeral."

"That isn't all there is to it, Harold."

"They knit and they bake. They read to the blind from newspapers."

"I think you've got it wrong, Harold."

"Have I, yeah? They have the names of cleaning women and lend you *Consumer's Report*. They bring back an ice cream when they walk to the corner. Naw, I didn't get no cards from them. I can stand on my feet, nothing's broken. I didn't get no cards."

"Do you know what I think? I think that as soon as you hang up folks are going to call to wish you a happy birthday. I'll bet that's exactly what happens. I'll bet some of them sing their greetings right over the phone. You see if I'm not right."

"Big deal."

"You'll see."

"Big deal."

"I'm certain of it. They'll wish you happy birthday and sing 'For He's a Jolly Good Fellow.' "

"Sure, sure."

"Yeah, yeah, I'll bet. I can imagine."

"Mark my words."

"Big deal. Federal case."

"That's what I think, Harold. The Mailbaggers——"

"We'll see," Harold cut in. Hurriedly he told Dick goodbye.

Then Henry Harper called.

"I've been trying to get Mrs. Dormer in Sun City since that night she spoke to you. Nobody answers the phone. Is she alive? Is she all right?"

"I don't know, Henry. I haven't heard."

"Tell her she's got to take her pills. That was foolish what I said about courage. She has to take her medicine. Mrs. Dormer, do you hear me? Please take your pills. You mustn't have pain. You mustn't have pain on my account."

"My ears were pierced when I was ten years old," a woman told him from Ft. Lauderdale. "It was the central event of my life."

"How come?"

"My mother did it herself. She used a needle—like the gypsies—and for an anesthetic she held ice cubes to my lobes. The ice melted and soaked the collar of my dress. There was a lot of blood. It mixed with the melted water from the ice cubes, and with my tears too, I guess. Ice isn't a good anesthetic. And Father was weeping to see me in pain, but Mother saw that the aperture would close. 'Run,' she said, 'bring something we can slip through the hole.' You're supposed to use an earring, but Mother's own ears had never been pierced and we didn't have any. The colored girl offered hers but Mother wouldn't take them. Father brought nylon fishing line. 'It's fifty-pound strength,' he said, 'it's all I could find.' They tried to push the fishing line through my ears, but it was too thick, of course, and Mother jabbed at my ears some more, pressing with the head of the pin this time, and a little white flesh fell off on my shoulder like the rolled-up paper in a punchboard, and after a while they could just slip the fishing line through. Father had used it before and there was salt from the ocean on the line—"

"This is a terrible story," Dick said.

"Wait. The point isn't pain. Wait. It isn't the mess they made. There's mess at birth. Wait."

"Well, go on."

"You'll see," she said. "Wait. . . . I slept with the fishing line in my ears and the wounds suppurated and they took me to the doctor. The doctor was furious, of course. He removed the fishing line at once, and treated me with salves and antibiotics. 'We'll be lucky,' he said, 'if the ears don't turn gangrenous. You came to me just in time.'

"But evidently we didn't, or the infection hadn't run its course, because the pain was worse than before and every morning there was blood on the pillow. Father wanted to take me back to the doctor, but something had happened to Mother. She'd become fierce. As I say, like a gypsy.

338

'The doctor's a fool,' she said, and brought a newborn kitten and set it beside me on the bed and poured milk on my ears, and the kitten licked the milk, licked the ears, nursing my lobes. It felt strange and fine, and when the kitten wearied of licking at the dry lobes I would daub more milk on them and set the kitten back at my ears.

"In a few days the kitten came by herself and would lick at the lobes even without the milk. Maybe she thought the blood and the pus were part of the milk. Mother was a modern woman. I don't know where she learned about this; maybe she read it, or maybe she just knew. So there we were, this ten-year-old Madonna and kitten, and even after my ears had healed I went around with it on my shoulder, transferring it from one shoulder to the other, its tongue at my ear, as though it were itself an earring.

"Then one day the kitten was gone. It disgusted Father, Mother said. Anyway, it had already done its job, she said. I cried, but Mother said Father had forbidden me the kitten and that was that.

"But it wasn't Father—it wasn't Father at all. It was Mother. Wait. You'll see.

"Two days after the kitten disappeared my mother came and examined my ears. She took each lobe and rolled it between her fingers like dough. 'They're beautiful,' she said. 'They're lovely and strong. I have a surprise.'

"They weren't beautiful. They were hideous and mysterious to me. The holes had collapsed and were clean as scars. Like navels they were, with just that texture of lifeless second growth. Or properly speaking, not holes at all. One was a crease, an adjustment that flesh makes, like the change in a face when a tooth has been pulled. And one *was* a hole—a terrible absence where a feature should be. Or like a child's sex organ, perhaps, unhaired and awful. Awful—they were awful.

"Mother's surprise was earrings, of course. I was ten when this happened. Do you follow me? My character had already been formed. It had been formed on the beaches of Ft. Lauderdale with the characters of my friends, and at motion-picture theaters and at pajama parties on weekends and by the long, extended summer of my Florida life.

"Then Mother showed me the earrings. Two pairs. One the post kind—button earrings, they're called. Tiny coins like gold beauty spots. She put them in my ears and showed me my reflection in a glass. 'Take them out, Mother. Please.'

" 'Are they heavy?' she said. 'Are you sensitive there? Don't worry. We'll butter the posts, or dip them in fat from a chicken I have. They'll be all right.'

" 'Please, Mother. Oh, please take them out.'

"It was what I saw in the mirror. I was someone *foreign,* someone old. Like the gypsy again, or an aunt in a tintype. Like a man who tells fortunes, or someone who died. Like a child on a stage who plays the violin.

"Mother took the earrings out and put in the other pair of earrings. These hung from a wire, a treacherous loop, and when they went in they opened fresh wounds. 'How do you like them?' my mother asked. This pair was silver, a long, thin, antique lattice and a queer wafer which swung from it. 'Do you like them?' she asked. She was so fierce. I knew they cost a lot. I knew more: *I knew she had bought them even before she had pierced my ears!* 'They're very nice,' I said, and when she left I took them out, unwinding the loop from my ear as you might detach a key from a keyring. I slipped into the bathroom and got some of Mother's vaginal jelly and greased the lobes. In the morning I left the house before she could see I wasn't wearing the earrings.

"But now, now I was so conscious of my ears. I thought, I thought boys stared at them—you know? Nasty *naked* things. I went back and put the earrings on just to . . . well, *cover* myself. Again I was transformed into someone foreign, some little strange girl.

"That's when everything began to change.

"All my girlhood, all my life, I had lived in the sun, but now my darkness wasn't tan but something Mediterranean, a darkness in the genes, something gone black in the blood. There was pumice in it, a trace of volcanoes that slope to the sea, carbon on kettles from fires out-doors.

"I couldn't ride a bicycle any more, or rollerskate. And the imagination of narrow disaster whetted: What if I should stumble? What if I should fall? The posts like actual stakes to me, the loopy wire hardware medieval. *And dirty,* dirty germs beyond the reach of sterilization—though I dropped the earrings every night in boiling water—as if the germs might be part of the metal itself, collected in its molecules, a poison of the intimate, the same reciprocal bacterial play as between a head and a hat or hair and a sweatband, toes and socks, a foot, a shoe. Foh! I was fearful not just because of the simple ripthreat to my ears, but because once the sores were reopened, once the crease had become a slash, the flood-gates of disease would open too, death by one's germs, one's own now un-American alien chemistry.

"I took up music, one day simply appearing among my schoolmates with a violin (just as one day my surfboard disappeared: it was simply gone—my fierce mother, I suppose). And do you know that though I had no talent I played even from the beginning with a certain brooding seemliness? And the earrings like actual yokes, gyroscop-ic; I might have been fetching water from the well, bal-ancing buckets up hills. Yes! Something even more Orien-tal than Mediterranean in the way I shuffled through childhood.

"Even in real summer I no longer wore shorts or jeans or went down to the sea in bathing suits. When skirts were short mine were long, when long, short—again that gyroscopic balance I spoke of—and don't forget the ear-rings themselves, those gold and silver alternatives. (Why I could have been an alternative myself, a community reference point like a hyphen on a kitchen wall, Ft. Lauderdale's little historical girl.)

"The boys were afraid of me, and gave off some dark respect, taking my gypsy bearings and seeing me even at thirteen and fourteen as whatever the adolescent equiva-lent of a divorcee might be. Thinking me hot where I was cool, cool where I burned. And although they sometimes asked me out—this was when I was sixteen or seventeen —it was as if there were chaperones behind a curtain, duennas, or invisible brothers, say, a troupe of jealous acrobats, dark ethnic stabbers with Mary's medals on their necks.

"I am never without the earrings now—the collection has become enormous—and only take them off to boil them in water or sink them like teeth in a glass by my bed. I continue to soap my ears with vaginal jellies. And sometimes there are kittens too, still, which I train in the old way to pull at my cream-sweet lobes while I dream in my bed. I am thought reclusive, silent, but my silence is only the open secret of my ears. My hearing has been affected. Ears, I have ears. *The better to hear you with, my dear.*"

Ears, Dick Gibson thought, ears, yes. A chill went through him. The woman continued to talk, but he could barely follow her now; he was thinking of ears. Then she broke through his reverie. "—your fragile orphan, your soprano, or someone recovered from polio but not quite, who walks with a limp, the body's broken English, something nasty there, the kind who groans in orgasm, who shouts dirty words during sex. Oh, my adoptive styles! I crochet but don't drive, I stay in the house during menses, I burn easily, I go to museums, and am never seen without my sheet music."

"Listen," a caller said from Cincinnati, "I'll tell you the truth. I'm a schemer. That's how I happened to catch your show. Certainly. A schemer lies awake nights, what do you think? I'm calling from the kitchen. The wife's in bed. Sometimes when the schemes aren't there, I come down and make myself a sandwich and drink some milk. I try to relax. Listen—it's the first time I've called—I've been meaning to ask. How many of your callers are schemers, do you think? How many are up nights, looking for angles, thinking up ways, dreaming of means?

"You know what they say? 'Build a better mousetrap and the world will beat a path to your door.' But let's don't kid ourselves, how many of us are inventors, how

342

many of us are equipped? On the other hand, I'm not just talking about pipe dreams. A schemer has to look out for those. Because things look possible at night. Hope's there, wishing is. But I'm looking for something sensible that would go, something meaningful that could really take off. As good as metals in the ground, opportunity like a national resource.

"After my wife had the baby I'd see her sterilizing bottles, preparing formulas, and I thought, what if there was a company that delivered that stuff already made up? What a boon *that* would be. I went to the milk people with my idea and they showed me why it wouldn't work. (Though some outfit out west does it now and are making a killing.) Then I had this idea about renting shirts. You'd get them from the laundry and never have to buy any. They'd have your size on record and bring you fresh ones every week, different styles and colors, ties to match. So I went to this laundry company and they proved to me how it wasn't feasible. That's the secret, of course: it has to be feasible. Feasibility's what separates the men from the boys schemer-wise. We're always running up against the brick walls of the real; we live in a medium of reasons as other people live in a medium of air—on the one hand and on the other hand like left and right."

"Why wasn't it feasible?"

"What's that, friend?"

"Why wasn't it feasible for the laundry to rent shirts?"

"Oh. They have those now too. There's a firm that does that now. Not the one that said it wasn't feasible. . . . It's timing. It's timing and force. A schemer has to have those too. He has to know when to plunge."

"I see."

"Desalinization—that's where the money is. Or steam cars, electric, you'd think you'd clean up. But it isn't *feasible,* Detroit says. I dream of getting in on the ground floor of these things. And the Americanization of Europe, of Africa, the far East. Jungle drive-ins and ice cream on the Amazon and suits off the rack on Saville Row. The bottom of the sea—there's a ground floor for you. The whole world is ground floor if you know where to stand.

343

"I'm a schemer. I'm a schemer and dreamer. In the army—Korea was on back then—I figured if you were in the Canine Corps they'd have to keep you stateside that much longer. It stands to reason—you train at the brute's rate. A dog's brain isn't as quick as a man's. Then I wondered if there might not be a difference between leashed dogs and unleashed. That figures too. Well, reason it out. A dog on a leash can be forced to do what you want. It's harder when he's not connected to you. So I put in for unleashed and saw to it that I was assigned the dumbest dog there. I stalled them for months. Then I applied for kennel master. My C.O. told me it wasn't feasible to make me kennel master. You had to be a vet.

"I'm scheming still. Sometimes the ideas come so thick and fast I can't keep up with them—laundromats in motels, movies in airports, house sitters for people away on vacation. You know something? There's never been a Western on the stage. I'm no writer, but something like that would go over big. If you could figure out what to do about the horses and cattle drives it might be feasible. I have these ideas. I swear to you, I no sooner begin the research on one plan when another pops into my mind. I count opportunities like sheep. How many of your listeners are like me? I'd be interested to know."

"We'll try to find out for you."

"Sure."

"Thanks for your call."

"I was doing some reading about wines. There's this one wine—Lafite Rothschild—which sells for eighty to ninety dollars a bottle once it's matured. It takes years to mature properly, *years*. In France, down in cellars, it's carefully turned—they call that 'laying wine.' A man could spend his whole life on the job turning it, and then it might be his son or even his grandson who's finally the one to bring it up. That's why it's so expensive. But once in a while they put it out on the market for the wine buffs before it's ready. That's called 'first growth,' and it can sell for as low as $2.00 a bottle. Well, I had an opportunity to buy out a shipment of this 'first growth' wine. I thought about it carefully. I considered it from every angle. I tried to look at it from the point of view of the big distributors. I weighed the pros and I weighed the cons, and finally I decided to do it. I invested all my savings and bought up about three thousand bottles at $2.38 a bottle. I built this special cellar and spent a lot of money to get it at the right temperature, and now I go down and I turn the bottles—a quarter turn clockwise in winter, a quarter turn counter clockwise in fall. And once a year I bring the bottles up to stand in the shade for a day in the spring when the barometer's low. It's a long shot, don't think I don't know it, a long-term proposition —thirty years, maybe more—but I'm a schemer, no pipe dreamer, I mind the feasibility and to hell with your get-rich-quick."

"Well good luck," Dick Gibson said.

"This year I had a heart attack—not a bad one, very mild really. 'You can live a long time yet,' the doctor told me. 'Just get plenty of rest and try not to worry.'

"Say I *do* get plenty of rest, say I *don't* worry. It isn't feasible."

Toward the end of that evening's program, the anthropology professor called for the first time in months. Dick had never learned his name but always looked forward to one of his calls. The anthropologist was full of fascinating information; he was one of the few callers who apparently had no interest in talking about himself but simply enjoyed sharing some of the conclusions of his research with Dick and his audience. They chatted pleasantly for a time, the anthropologist feeding Dick a lot of interesting facts about the Seminole Indians who lived along the Tamiami Trail just west of Miami. Dick had seen their wretched cardtables along the roadside, makeshift lean-to "stores" hardly more sophisticated than a child's lemonade stand, and had glimpsed their terrible hovels through the broken fences meant to screen them from the sight of tourists.

"They're so poor," Dick said.

"Oh Dick, the Navajos could give them a run for their poverty. Many tribes could. That's not the point. The

Seminoles are the only tribe that makes its camp outside a great metropolitan area. They've always done this. They did it when the land still belonged to the Indians. They lived on the doorstep of the Creek and Chickasaw and Choctaw. Seminole—*Sim-a-nóle,* or *Iste Siminóla*—means 'separatist' or 'runaway' in the Muskogean language."

"I didn't know that," Dick Gibson said.

"They were the first suburbanites, you see . They conceive of their destiny as a Mighty-Have-Fallen warning to other people. In times of slavery they set up their villages outside the slavequarters. They were offering the example of their condition as a gift to the slaves."

"Gee."

"There's a deep instinct at work here. Follow closely. The significance of the suburbs—I'm doing work on this —is that all peoples are in exile. Your two-week summer vacation is an example. (Traffic patterns and roads, by the way, follow morale patterns closely.) It's all related to the Vacant-Throne theory of history. The czar had his summer palace, the President his summer White House. These are Diaspora symbols."

Unfortunately it was time for Dick to sign off. He had to break in on the professor.

"Put me on hold," the anthropologist whispered, "I have something to tell you." Dick regularly received such requests, and sometimes the phones were lit up for as much as an hour after he went off the air. It may have been that people felt that reaching him privately lent a distinction even more profound than speaking to him on the air. Recently he had frequently obliged them, sometimes hearing terrible things in this way—awful things. People who were well spoken on the air often made no sense at all when they spoke to him privately afterwards —or they might suddenly lapse into some of the vilest language he had ever heard.

After signing off he came back to the professor. "What did you want to say?" he asked.

"Tell me," the anthropologist said urgently, "whether a man sits or stands up to wipe himself, and I'll tell you everything else about him. This cuts through cultures,

Dick. It obliterates history and geography. Dick, it's the single distinction between men. It annihilates everything else. Religion, laws, custom—these things are nothing. He stands because his mommy wiped him. Do you see this, Dick? He stands now because he *still* expects some great, warm soft hand to rub his shit away. All else is nothing. Freud never really understood the true significance of the anal-retentive concept. It's his own term, but he missed the boat. Incidentally, I'll bet you dollars to doughnuts Freud himself was a stander."

"I thought this had something to do with the Seminoles."

"Forget the Seminoles. They're nothing but a bunch of poor-mouth bastards. Poor mouth, poor mouth, that's all they know. All that Mighty-Have-Fallen crap. Forget the Seminoles. The Seminoles aren't my real work anyway. Dick, I have so many ideas, I'm exploding with insights. Truth is everywhere, Dick; significance is as available as gravity. Do you know the best place to learn about a people's legal and penal system? Its zoos! Go to its zoos, Dick, and you'll find out more about its laws and prisons in a half-hour than you would in its courts and jails in a year."

"I don't—"

"Did you know there are three fundamental pieces of furniture—the table, the bed, and the chair—and that a people behaves according to the article of furniture dominant in its culture? Did you know that the living-room sofa, or couch, is only a sort of hybrid bed, and that it was introduced by the degenerate Assyrians as a means of formalizing adultery?"

"You're going too fast, I can't take all this—"

"There's more. There's always more. If you miss one truth there'll be another along. It's like streetcars. Wait, wait. The Axis Powers were the only nations involved in World War II which didn't conclude their news broadcasts with weather reports. No question of secrecy was involved; it was simply a matter of the lack of regard for one's fellows. Since the people within the range of a given broadcast knew whether it was raining or the sun was shining, they didn't care what was happening in the rest of the country."

"I don't see—"

"Flags! Red, green, blue, white, black and gold are the predominant colors used throughout the world for its flags because those are the colors—with the exception of red, which is always blood—that symbolize not only the basic forces of nature but the particular natural forces most valued by a culture. Your flag is a dead giveaway."

"What has this—"

"Sandwiches! What's the thickness ratio of the contents of a sandwich relative to its bread? Is lettuce used to add height? This gives us the hypocrisy quotient. Or those little soaps with a hotel's trademark on the wrapper—"

"What? What about those soaps?"

"Or *matchbooks!* Matchbooks *particularly*. Why does a man become attached to the iconography of a particular trademark?"

"Why does he? Is that significant?"

"What's to be made of the fact that *soaps* wane with use, that fire consumes the matchstick, that the height of a pile of *letterhead stationery* goes down in a drawer, that a *swizzle stick* is made to be snapped in two?"

"What? What *is* to be made of it?"

"Oh Dick, Dick. My real work isn't the Seminoles, it isn't zoos, it isn't furniture or artifacts. It's your program. My real work is your program, Dick. Look out, Dick. Be careful. Please be more careful. Watch your step. A scientist is warning you. Don't take calls after the show. Don't put people on hold. Get your rest, try not to worry. Be like the man in Cincinnati."

"Who is this? What's this all about? What are you saying to me?"

The anthropologist giggled and broke off; Dick heard the buzz of the broken connection. He couldn't be sure, of course, but he was almost certain that the man had been disguising his voice. The giggle had been a sort of sudden relaxation. Something about it had seemed familiar.

And then he remembered. A name flashed into his

mind. No, he *couldn't* be mistaken. *Behr-Bleibtreau!* It had to be. The idea was disquieting at first, but later, going back to the Deauville in the car, he was filled with a marvelous sense of relief. An enemy! He had an enemy. An *enemy* had appeared!

5

Angela called. Dick asked after Robert and the baby. They were both asleep, Angela said, but Robert would be getting up soon. If he wanted she could wake him now. Dick told her to let him sleep.

He asked if she'd be working in the fall—she taught third grade in an all-black Tallahassee public school—but Angela was vague about it. It was very difficult, she said, to get someone really reliable to come in, and the baby was on a schedule which it might not be a good idea to upset just now.

Dick asked if Robert, who was on the Attorney General's staff, was involved in that Ft. Myers business. (Recently there had been a ghetto revolt in the Gulf Coast town, and the local authorities had been pressing for the death sentence under Florida's Anti-Sedition Act.) Angela told him they were both so busy now they didn't discuss each other's work much. In fact, she said, she didn't really know what had happened in Ft. Myers because she hadn't been reading the papers. Dick started to explain, but Angela broke in to say that she thought she heard a sound from the baby's room. He held on while she went in to check.

The Sohnshilds were New Yorkers who had come to Florida in a spirit of missionary zeal, Robert believing it was more to the point to guarantee due process in the South than in New York. From the occasional references to him in the newspapers Dick knew that Robert was highly respected and very effective.

Oddly enough Dick Gibson had heard of the couple even before they became Mail Baggers; he had read an article about the Sohnshilds in *Esquire* in the early sixties. Angela, the article said, had graduated from Smith with a Magna in Philosophy and had met Robert when both were graduate students at Harvard. By the time the article appeared each of them had already been through a number of successful careers. Angela had given piano recitals at Carnegie Hall and had appeared as a soloist with the London Symphony at the Royal Festival Hall. Her essays on the New Left, written in the fifties while she was still a graduate student were said to be the best philosophic justification that radical politics had ever had. She had even been—though this had not been publicized because of her associations with the left—a speech writer for the Kennedys. Robert Sohnshild, as illustrious as his wife, had given up a successful private practice and an inherited seat on the New York Stock Exchange to become the first major news analyst on National Educational Television, and, as an adviser to SCLC, had helped develop the principle of the Mississippi Freedom Schools. Somewhere he had also found time to establish the first successful, nationally distributed underground newspaper.

The article in *Esquire* had been entitled "The Silver Spoon Set," and in it four immensely successful young couples had posed, grinning, in full color in their lovely New York, Washington and Boston apartments, with silver spoons dangling from their mouths like cigarettes. In the text Robert was quoted as wanting to extricate himself from the tangled skein of personal success. "Cut your winnings," he had said. "It's a Thoreauvian thing. I

351

refuse to be a great man. There are too many great men already. They explode on the world like bombs. What I want, and Angela agrees, is for men of talent and judgment and imagination—for men of success—to turn their backs on the 'world' and begin to pay some attention to the community."

The Sohnshilds had come to Florida at about the same time Dick started his show, and had called the program as a sort of lark the first week it was on the air. Robert, slighty tipsy and evidently very happy, had taken the phone away from Angela to announce his wife's pregnancy. Though they had been married twelve years, it was to be their first child. Excited by their celebrity, Dick said that the unborn child would be the program's mascot, and he invited the couple to become regular callers. Though they stopped phoning after the baby came, Angela had begun to call the program again about five months before.

Angela returned to the phone.

"It was nothing," she said, "she probably just stirred in her sleep."

The baby was born with irises white as shirt buttons. It was blind.

One of them was always awake when the baby was asleep. They had not been out of the house together since its birth and kept a constant vigil over its crib, convinced that its odd eyes were the signal of a crippled chemistry. When Angela called now she often sounded wild, offering an incredible picture of their grief. One night Dick had had to cut her off the air when she went into the details of her fifty-five hour labor.

"You know," Angela said, "Robert thinks I'm foolish, but I really think her irises are beginning to darken."

"That would be wonderful."

"Oh they'll never be black, of course, but many people have gray eyes and see perfectly well. Robert's eyes are grayish."

"Why don't you get some sleep, Angela?" Dick said gently.

"You know," she said, "when Carol's sleeping and her

eyes are closed, she's *so* beautiful. You can't tell there's a thing wrong with her. She's just like anyone else. Maybe that's why I don't mind staying up half the night. So I can watch her and see how lovely she is with her eyes shut. Is that disloyal? Do you think it's selfish?"

"No, Angela, of course not." Then he asked if she still kept up her piano.

"Oh, yes," Angela said. "Carol loves to hear me play." She paused, and added fiercely, "Her hearing sense is no more acute than *any* child's her age. I consider it a plus that she hasn't begun to compensate. Perhaps she perceives light; perhaps that's why. She's no more tactile than another child. She's hardly ticklish."

The baby would be two years old soon. The quality of their resistance seemed awful to him, worse even than their luck.

"I still have them," Angela said, and laughed bitterly.

"I'm sorry, Angela, what was that?"

"The silver spoons," she said. "I still have them. I feed Carol her cereal from them."

Now whenever he picked up the phone he expected the caller to be Behr-Bleibtreau.

He picked up the phone.

"Hi," a woman said, "this is Ingrid." It was not a good connection. A baby, crying in the background, further impaired his understanding. "I called once before. On the occasion of my divorce. You probably don't remember." Offhand, he didn't.

"How are you, Ingrid?"

"Never better," she said glumly.

"What have you been doing with yourself, Ingrid?"

"Well, I'm a gay divorcee, the merry widow." He hoped she wasn't drinking; he didn't want anything to happen to the baby.

"Hey, you want to hear something wild? I bought this '69 Buick hard-top and it's got this gadget on it, a sort of memory device. It buzzes when you leave the key in the ignition and the door is open or the engine isn't running. It's optional, but I'm queer for inventions—autronic eyes

353

that dim your headlights at the approach of oncoming cars, remote control TV sets, garage doors that open at the sound of a horn, timers that turn things on and off. I've got tortoise-shell prisms. I wear them like glasses and watch TV while I lie on my back and stare at the ceiling. There's a spigot for ice water on the door of my refrigerator. I have a ten-speed blender. I dissolve frozen orange juice in it. Oh, the things I've bought—there are Magic Fingers in my beds, great underwater lights in my swimming pool, water softeners, FM stereos, tape decks, rheostats, garbage compressors—you name it. Last month my electric bill was one hundred and seventy-eight dollars and fourteen cents. And I'll tell you something—my life's no emptier than the next one's. I can take electricity or leave it alone. Things don't corrupt you; they barely distract you.

"I was at this party—my husband was there; we often run into each other; well, we know the same people and they know we still see each other; it's no big deal—and it was getting a little rough and I thought maybe it was time to go. Well, when I left my friend's house I could hear that gadget on my car. I don't know why I hadn't heard it when I'd parked; maybe I had. It was a kind of whining, not a buzz. It was like the sound of an animal in a trap, or like a child when it's sick, or—you'll laugh—like my own whimpering. Only I don't whimper, never. This just sounded like whimpering would if I did. I'm not being dramatic—I was fascinated. When I got in and turned the key the noise stopped. Well, I know this sounds silly, but I thought, My God, maybe I've killed it. I suppose I was a little high. Sometimes I drink too much.

"You know what I did when I thought I'd killed it? I turned off the motor to hear it again. Some people from the party found me there. They thought I was too drunk to drive or something. Well, I couldn't just sit there all night, and these people meant well, but of course I couldn't tell them what I'd been up to, so I pretended that I *was* too drunk, and I let them take me home in their car. When I got there I ducked in and asked the baby-sitter if she could stay for another thirty minutes, and called a cab and went back for my car.

"You know I never stopped hearing it? When I got back it was the same as in my head. Maybe I have a sort of perfect pitch for machines.

"I got in my car. There were still some people at the party and I didn't want them to find me when they left, so I started the engine and of course the sound stopped at once. I remembered that if the door wasn't shut properly the gadget was supposed to whine then too, so I opened my door just enough to disengage the lock, and the sound came back. Whenever I made a left turn and the door swung free the whine rose to a howl. I went out of my way to turn corners to hear it howl, to punish it.

"It was crazy. I couldn't get home. My left turns pushed me in circles, taking me places I'd never been. I realized that if I was to leave the door open I had to stay in good neighborhoods. The only one I could think of was my own, so I kept circling my own block. When I passed my house I could see the baby-sitter looking out the window for me. Maybe she heard the sound. Driving the car must have charged the battery and it seemed to scream, to sing like a siren. Maybe she even recognized the car, but I couldn't stop.

"By now I was low on gas. I found a station that was open all night, and the attendant asked me to turn off the engine while he checked under the hood. I pulled the key out of the ignition and shut the door tight. I still heard it in my head, but it wasn't the same, it wasn't as real; my pitch was imperfect finally. I have all the major credit cards, but I was impatient. I gave him cash and told him to keep the change. When I got back to my neighborhood the sitter's father was looking out my window. She lives next door and he must have come over to take her place. I knew I had to go in. I gave him the money for his daughter, three dollars more than she was supposed to get. He was angry at first that I'd kept her out so late, but then he . . . well, sort of looked at me. I've known the man years; we're friends. It was the hour; the lateness of

355

the hour excited him. A woman coming home alone at four-thirty in the morning was thrilling to him. A woman giving him money out of her purse worked him up. God knows where he thought I'd been or what I'd been doing. He tried to kiss me, touch my breasts. 'Oh, Ingrid,' he said. He forced me down on the couch. 'Please, Jack,' I said. 'Come on, Ingrid, what's the difference? You're one hell of an attractive woman.' I know what he thought. Years we'd known each other, and he'd never made a pass. Not during my lousy marriage, not during my divorce, not once when he saw me going out with men or my ex spent the night at the house. The lateness of the hour, that excited him. Taking money from me for his daughter, the three dollars extra I gave because I'd inconvenienced her and which he thought was hush money.

" 'I've been driving,' I told him. 'Jack, I left the party hours ago. I've been out driving by myself. Let me up, Jack. Jack, let me up.' I think I embarrassed him; I think I hurt his feelings.

"I put the car in the garage, left the key in the ignition and opened the windows. Maybe I heard it in my room, maybe it was only the whining in my head.

"I can't sleep without it. It has to be on. I use up batteries."

Then Ingrid said something which Dick couldn't quite make out. "I think we have a bad connection," he said.

"I said it's not an animal in a trap, not a baby crying."

"Have it disconnected. You don't need it."

"I need it. It's what—" The last word was lost.

"What was that?"

"I said it's what mourns. I need it. It's what says that everything isn't okay. It's my gadget for grief."

"Get rid of it," Dick said.

"Who would keen, who would cry?"

"Look, this connection is very bad. I can hardly hear you. There's some sort of interference."

"That—"

"What did you say?"

"That's it. What you hear. I had a phone put in my car. I'm in a lover's lane I know. The doors are locked and the engine's off and the key's in the ignition. Listen."

She must have put the phone up to the noise, because suddenly it became louder. Or perhaps she had opened the door and was swinging it back and forth on its hinge, for the sound would rise to a howl and then suddenly grow softer.

Dick Gibson listened to the queer yowl of the device, then heard the woman's voice again. She seemed to be crooning a sort of encouragement to it. He strained to make out the words.

"You tell 'em," she was saying. "Tell him when he comes in. You tell him, sweetie, I st-st-stutter."

"Hello."

"Hello, Henry." It was Henry Harper.

"What? Who? Oh, yeah."

"Isn't this Henry Harper?"

"You don't think I'd be fool enough to give my right name, do you? Yes, I'm the boy you know as Henry Harper."

"Henry Harper isn't your name?"

"No it isn't, and it's a darn good thing I never told you what it really is. I had a lucky hunch when I called that first time and decided I'd better not be entirely open with you."

"Well, I don't know how to respond to something like that, Henry. You put me at a terrible disadvantage. You're free to misrepresent yourself as much as you please, and there's nothing I can do about it except cut you off the air. I don't like to do that to any caller, Henry. ... You see? I called you Henry. I must sound pretty foolish if that isn't who you are." Dick was genuinely upset. "I suppose all the rest of it, your being rich and nine years old and all alone in an enormous mansion, that's all misrepresentation too."

"Of course not. It's an evidence of their truth that I couldn't give my name out over the air."

"I see," Dick said coolly.

"I'm afraid you don't at all. Do you know something?

357

There are a whale of a lot of nosy parkers who listen to this program. If you look me up in the supplement to the Directory you'll see I gave a P.O. box number instead of an address. That was another precaution, of course."

"A precaution against what?"

"Why, against interference with my way of life. Look, I'm an immensely wealthy orphan. There's the estate itself and three-quarters of a million dollars cold cash in my piggy banks, and I stand to come into a good deal more than that when I achieve my majority. Don't you know these things represent enormous temptations to wicked and unscrupulous persons? My age makes me extremely vulnerable to vultures, and my status in the eyes of the authorities trebles that vulnerability."

"Has anyone actually tried to take advantage of you?"

"Oh, Dick, please—don't be such a naif. You should see some of the letters in that P.O. box. When I drove to Jacksonville to pick up the first batch—"

"*Drove* to Jacksonville? You said you *lived* in Jacksonville."

"I maintain a post office box there, yes, but just as I was reluctant to give my right name, so was I loath to declare my true place of residence. How many estates of the kind I described do you suppose there are in a city the size of Jacksonville? As I've been at one time or other a guest in them all, I know only too well how easy I would be to trace. Look, everything I told you before is substantively true. I wasn't trying to deceive you personally, and I didn't intend my natural precautions to be taken as a slander on the Mail Baggers themselves. The people in the Listening Posts are good people, but there are others—voyeurs—who listen to this program who have never bothered to list themselves in the Directory. It's these people who aren't my friends."

"You lied once, and you lied twice. You could be lying a third time."

"The Harpers are not liars, Mr. Gibson."

"Hah."

"Nor are we sitting ducks. I've explained why it's necessary to misrepresent myself, why it's necessary for me to hire a car to take me to Jacksonville to pick up my mail. If you read that mail you'd understand. I have money. People want to trick me. They make the most blatant overtures. There are people who will do anything for money, Mr. Gibson, and while I don't care for the money itself, I have no intention of turning over my fortune to gold diggers and picklepusses. Not so long as that fortune can be used to relieve the miseries of my friends—and I consider all the *legitimately* unfortunate my friends. There are operations, medicines, birthday presents for children whose parents can't afford them. There are vacations, holidays, financing alcoholics and addicts at sanitoria. There are so many *good* purposes to which my money can be put."

"You're a good boy, Henry. I've already told you," Dick said bitterly. He felt that perhaps he was being unfair. The kid's reasons—if he was a kid—were excellent, but a program like this was peculiarly susceptible to masquerades. His phones must not be used for disguises.

"Why are you doing this?" Henry pleaded. "I'm a child, an orphan. Do you think I'm Tom Sawyer? That I find being alone romantic, or that the enormous estate I live on is some dreamy little treehouse place where I can escape from the realities of the adult world? I'm a child. A child needs guidance, security, love. It's his *instinct* to have these things. Do you suppose I'm the only little boy ever to overthrow his own instincts? *I sleep with a light on,* Mr. Gibson! *When* I sleep. Why do you suppose me so unnatural as to wish myself naked in the world? Is a little boy naturally a loner? Absurd! No. I place myself in this awful jeopardy because in addition to a child's instinctive need for guidance and security and love, he has an even more powerful instinct for virtue. It's like a tropism with us. We're innocents, sir, every mother's son of us, innocents who would legislate a just world where no one is deprived or disadvantaged, where virtue is rewarded and evil punished, and all needs annulled. I place myself in jeopardy not by choice, not by dint of rebellion, but because only by operating outside the law am I able to operate at all. Only in this way am I able to do my part, pull my own small boy's weight in the world and do something with my little shaver's instinctive sympathies. How long do you think I would be permitted to contribute to my favorite charities or allay with money—yes! I admit it; money, alas, is all that ultimately makes the difference—the sufferings of my fellows? How long would I be able to accomplish these things if I were to turn myself over to an executor or allow myself to be legally adopted? The best-willed bankers and trustees in the world would turn down my requests for funds to make my little gifts. And I'd *respect* them for it. I wouldn't blame them one iota, for anything less would be a betrayal of *their* instincts and duties! The most loving, abnegative adoptive parents would do the same. *That's* why I didn't give my name."

"You lied to me over the air on my program," Dick Gibson said stubbornly.

"I'm a *child,* Mr. Gibson," Henry Harper told him tragically. "I've a child's emotions. Don't expect self-control from me. Don't look to me for emotional continence. I'm little and my passions are everywhere closer to the surface than in an adult. I'm small and may be bullied. It's often difficult for a child to distinguish between pressure and the guidance his childishness requires. I warn you of this, for I know I will not be able to stand up to you. In any contest of wills between us yours is bound to emerge triumphant."

"You lied," Dick Gibson said. "I trusted you and you lied. Over the air. On my program. What's your real name?"

"Very well then," Henry Harper said. He was sobbing now and could barely catch his breath. "Very well then. My real name . . . my name . . . is . . . is Richard Swomley-Wamble. I live in Tampa, Florida."

"How do I know that's your real name?"

"It is."

"How do I know?"

"I tell you it is."

"How do I know it isn't *Edmond Behr-Bleibtreau?*" It was thrilling to him to speak the name aloud. He listened

360

for a reaction, some dead giveaway, but all he heard were the boy's unbroken, now uncontrollable sobs.

"It's what I said it is," Henry Harper said, "and you'll know it by the damage you've just done."

A lady was on the phone. Her voice was familiar, though Dick was sure she had never called the program before. For one thing, she was shy and hesitant. Also her voice, though familiar, seemed altered.

Dick tried to help her out. "Take your time," he said.

"Well, this is embarrassing to me."

"Oh, come on," he kidded, "we only go out to twenty-three states. There couldn't be more than a million and a half people listening to you right now."

"I was going to ask you a personal question."

"Sure."

"I don't exactly know how to put it. I'm not really one of your regular listeners."

"Win a few, lose a few."

"I've only been listening to the program two weeks— since I'm on this case."

"Are you a detective?"

"Oh, goodness no." She laughed.

"That's better. Well, since you're *not* a detective, go ahead—*shoot*."

The woman laughed again. "I'm calling from Ohio," she said.

"How are we coming in up your way?" He was not as cheerful and expansive as he sounded, for Behr-Bleibtreau was on his mind. Ever since he had mentioned the man's name on the air all his heartiness had been intended for Behr-Bleibtreau. He was showing the flag.

"Your station fades sometimes, but mostly it's very clear."

"Glad to hear it. Excuse me, let me just do a station break here. . . . WMIA, Miami Beach, the 50,000-watt voice of the Sun Coast. . . . I'm sorry, go ahead, ma'am."

"Well, I was almost certain I was right, that's why I

called, but hearing you speak on the telephone, now I don't know."

"Don't know what, ma'm?"

"Whether I know you."

"Oh? Well, you know what? I was thinking your voice was familiar too."

"I used to know somebody, oh years back. Gosh, if I'm right I'll be giving away both our ages. He had [a voice something like yours, only your name is different. Marshall Maine?"]

Dick Gibson took her off the air. The six-second tape delay was enough to excise the passage.

["I don't use that name any more,"] he said into the phone while they were still off the air. ["Please don't refer to it."]

"That's right," he said easily when they were back on the air again. "Who might this be?"

"Well, I was Desebour then. Miriam?" He didn't recognize the name. "I was working at the time in Morristown, New Jersey. A nurse? That's why I laughed when you asked if I was a detective when I said I was on a case. Do you remember now? I don't blame you if you forgot, me springing it on you like this. Why, it was only a few nights ago I was able to place *you*."

Then he remembered the time they had lived together in the nursing home. "Well, of course," he said. "How are you . . . Miriam, is it?"

"Miriam Kranz. You knew me as Desebour."

"You're originally from Iowa."

"That's right. Say, you've got a good memory. I'm glad to see you haven't forgotten me."

"No, of course not."

"Old friends are the best friends." Her voice had lost its reluctant edge, and she had become genuinely jolly.

"Kranz, eh?" He was surprised to find that he was slightly jealous.

"I'm a widow. You know, now that I think of it, you *knew* Kranz."

"*I* did?"

"I'm sure he was around during your time. Let's see

[this would have been '38, '39. I left Morristown in '40. You and I knew each other when I first got there. Kranz was there that whole time. He was one of my patients, a little fella. He had to be fed."

"The one who got a hard-on when you gave him his dinner? *Him?*"

"Marshall! That's terrible. We're on the radio."

"No, we're on a tape delay. I've taken this part off. Don't call me Marshall. Is that the one?"

Miriam giggled. "It is," she said. "I married him right there in the nursing home.] He was a very nice man, you know."

Now Dick remembered Miriam's strange effect on him, how her voice telling a story, going at its own pace, random as landscape, had worked its cozy hypnotic sedation on him.

["Whatever happened to the old bastard who came when you gave him enemas?"]

"Gracious sakes, man, I'm an old woman now. Let's not go into all that. Folks must think we're terrible."

["I took that part off. What happened to him?"]

"Well, that was just prostate trouble was what that was. He had a preternatural prostate. You know—tee hee—at the end, I could get that same reaction by taking his temp or just sitting him up in his chair? He knew he was dying, and do you know what he said to me one time? 'Noitch Miriam, I'm a family man. I have grandchildren. I always tithed my church and believed in God. I am as convinced of Heaven as I am of Kansas, and though I know I'm dying I want to tell you that you have made me happier in these past months than I have ever been in my life.' Those were almost his last words, and I'll never forget them."

"What happened to you, Miriam? It's been years since we've seen each other," Dick said fondly.

"Oh," she said, "a lot of water has flowed under the bridge. Kranz . . . Are we on the air now, [Marshall?"]

"Yes. [No, not that part. Call me Dick.]"

"Kranz had many wonderful qualities. If you didn't know him well you might not have recognized them and

363

just have dismissed him as a dirty little beast, but when you got to know him better he was a very fine gentlemen."

Hearing her, it came back to Dick again how her voice had once been able to pull him out of time, float him snug as someone towed by swimmers. Her voice was quiet, historical almost; there was something in its cool timbre that assumed it would never be interrupted. As he listened to her he played absently with the six-second tape delay button. "For one thing, he was terrifically acute. He had a lot of savvy about current events. He knew more than the politicians, believe *me;* he was one of the canniest men I've ever known. He saw there was going to be a world [war] long before the rest of us dreamed of such a thing. 'We're sitting on a powder keg, Miriam,' he used to say. ['The Axis Powers,] those fellas over in [Germany,] Bulgaria, Finland, [Italy,] Rumania, [Japan] and Hungary, are out after everything we hold near and dear, and they're not going to be satisfied till they get it. Why, everybody's going to get into it—[France, England,] Costa Rica, [America,] Ecuador, San Marino, Syria—everybody. Now it's an unfortunate thing, but there's going to be some mighty big money made during all this. It's going to be dog eat [dog, sure as you're a] foot [high.] It's coming, all right. Why, I wouldn't be at all surprised if some country like Japan weren't planning its attack right now. It'll be a sneak attack, I'll bet you. We won't have any warning. They'll probably pick some out-of-the way place like Pearl Harbor and do it on a Sunday morning in December after Thanksgiving and before Christmas when nobody's expecting it.' He had a terrific acumen in the political line."

"It certainly sounds that way."

"You know what he told me once? He said that probably once the war started there'd be a lot of technological advancement. He said you couldn't tell him a smart man like Einstein didn't have a little something extra up his sleeve, like unharnessing the power of the atom or something, and that's what would finally win the war for us. He got all this just from reading between the lines in newspapers. I never saw anything like it. I tell you, he was one of the most logical men I've ever met. I'm sorry you didn't have a chance to know him better. Anyway, he kept insisting that we all ought to be prepared, that there were going to be a lot of personal opportunities for people once the war started. He figured there'd be a black market. He was too old and sick, he said, or he'd be in there with the best of them. And he would have been too. He knew there'd be shortages once it started. He told me to buy up as many pairs of silk stockings as I could, that it didn't make any difference what size they were. And Hershey bars. He was always after me to stockpile Hershey bars. He knew that meat and gasoline were going to be at a premium too, and he had this notion about rent control. The thing to do, he said, was get the most expensive penthouse apartments you could find up along Riverside Drive in New York City. He figured that rents would be controlled in those places for years and that you could sell them at terrific profits. Another thing was theater tickets. They'd be hard to get once war came. He said that if a terrific composer like Richard Rodgers ever teamed up with a wonderful lyricist like Oscar Hammerstein, Jr., and they did a musical together set in some Western state back before the turn of the century, that it would be a wonderful escape for people all caught up in the war effort, and that anybody who invested money in such a show would make a fortune. I didn't pay too much attention to any of this or I'd be a rich woman today.

"But you know, one thing he *did* convince me of was that there was going to be a terrfic demand for R.N.'s. 'You get your degree, Miriam,' he said. 'You get your R.N. license and you'll have it made once war breaks out. Finish up, then enlist in the Army Nurse Corps. Don't wait until December 7, 1941.'

"So that's what I did. I enrolled as a student nurse at Morristown General, and I went into the Army Nurse program as soon as I graduated. Everyone on active duty as of 2400 hours on 6 December '41 was promoted to first lieutenant, and if they agreed, as I did, to sign up for the duration they were jumped to captain. I was a major by V-E Day, stayed in for twenty years and rose to colonel before I retired.

"After we were married Kranz put me through my student year at Morristown General and I made him the beneficiary of my $10,000 G.I. life insurance. He died just before the close of the war. I was with him at the time, on a stateside furlough. He had a hunch his time was up and, not wanting to die in bed, asked me to dress him. I got him into his clothes and tied his tie. When I finished knotting it he just looked down at it kind of thoughtfully for a moment and said, 'You know, Miriam, styles come and styles go. Wide ties like this one aren't going to be considered very fashionable in a while, but then, in about twenty-five years, they're going to be more popular than ever.' Marshall, these were the last words he ever spoke."

Miriam related all this in her lazy style. Listening to her, Dick had a sense of the piecemeal forces of erosion. He never interrupted; even when she slipped and called him Marshall he let it pass. He was tilted back deep in his chair, his feet on the desk next to the microphone.

"I take only private cases now," Miriam was saying. "The money's better, for one thing—though I don't need money, really. There's my army pension, and Kranz, who had this terrific business sense, told me back in Morristown that the big thing in the fifties and sixties was going to be office equipment—copiers, things like that. I made some good investments and I've got a pretty fair-sized nest egg now."

Yes, Dick thought, nest. He remembered their nest. He undid the buttons of his shirt and scratched his belly.

"I take cases mostly because it lets me travel—I'm with an agency that sends nurses all over the country. I meet a lot of interesting people. The sick are wonderful folks, Marshall. If you recall I once told you I have to help people. Thank God that's never burned out in me. Well, they're just so gentle. Sedation does that, of course, helplessness does. It hurts them to move and you have to do everything for them. And if they're old they're that much weaker anyway. Why, some of my patients I just

366

take and tote them around as if they were babies. I was always strong, you'll remember, and I'm a big old gal now. You probably wouldn't recognize me."

He had an erection. The pressure of his clothing was irritating, so he unzipped his fly and his penis sprung out of his pants. His director rapped on the glass of the control booth with a key. Marshall Maine glanced at him and waved lazily.

"Course, maybe I wouldn't recognize you either," she said. "Oh Lord, I was with so many young men in the army. You know, you get tired of young people after a time. Of course if they're really sick they're just as good as anybody else, but most of the time they don't want to take their pills, and they *never* get over being embarrassed. You just can't do for them like you can somebody who's had some experience and seen the world and knows its ways. My patient here in Ohio, now; he's a man about our age. Marshall, a widower with a bad phlebitis. A *very* interesting man. 'Mrs. Kranz,' he'll say, 'with my leg the way it is I just can't handle myself on the bedpan. Would you mind very much if I just let go? You don't have to do the sheets—heck, just throw them away and buy some more over the telephone through the Home Shopper.' He's very generous. I just can't say enough about it. Naturally I have to clean him up afterward; you can't let a person lie in his own dirt. Now you couldn't do that with a young man; a young man would just as soon be constipated forever before he'd let you touch him.

"I want my patients to want my hands on their bodies," Miriam said. "How else can I help them? Men in their fifties—I suppose you're up there now yourself—whose stomachs have gone soft, who don't try to hide their bald spots with fancy hair styles, and if they don't shave for a couple of days, what of it? Who aren't always squeezed up tight to keep their gas in, and are smooth on their chests as babies—those are your interesting men."

He could not picture her as she had been. He remembered her voice, but couldn't recall her face or the shape of her body. He didn't know if she had been tall or heavy or anything about her. Nevertheless, though he had not seen her in thirty years, he had what he was sure was an exact impression of what she had become. He saw her dowager's hump, the features of her face, the nose rounded and gently comical, the crow's feet and wide mouth, the precise color of her hair, the immense rounds of breast, full as roasts, the wide lap beneath her nurse's white uniform with its bas-relief of girdle and garter like landmarks under a light snow. He had removed his shirt and slipped out of his pants and underwear, and was almost as naked as he had been in Morristown when she had bathed him in bed, or as she herself had been when she padded about their small room doing her little chores and telling him stories of her life in Iowa. He closed his eyes for just a moment, content, irritated only by the distortion of her voice on the telephone.

"Well," Miriam said, "it's awfully late. I have to give my little man his pill. Maybe before I leave Ohio I'll call again. I'm proud you made such a success, Marshall."

He thanked her comfortably. He had pulled off one stocking and was rolling the other down his leg. "Ohio?"

"Yes. I told you that."

"Cincinnati?" Behr-Bleibtreau, if that's who the anthropologist had been, had made a pointed reference to the caller from Cincinnati.

"That's right, Marshall. How'd you know that?"

"Your patient—what's your patient's name?"

"Well, that's a matter of professional ethics, Marshall."

"Does he know you listen to this program?"

"Why, yes, of course he does. He's the one who told me about it. We're listening to it together right now."

"Listen," he said, "his name's Behr-Bleibtreau, isn't it?"

"Marshall, I can't tell you a patient's name when I'm on a case, and that's final."

"It *is* Behr-Bleibtreau, isn't it?"

"Final is final. You don't know me when I make up my mind. I can be pretty darn stubborn. Goodnight now, Marshall."

He looked down and saw that he was undressed. One

knee-length sock, bunched over his heel, was all he was wearing.

"Listen—" he said.

"Goodnight now." She hung up. Dick Gibson angrily pulled the sock the rest of the way off his foot.

"Your feet stink."

He was talking to an old fellow. The man had been driving along the rough back road between Aliosto, Georgia, and Clendennon, Alabama, on his way to visit his son-in-law who was foreman of the Pepsi-Cola bottling plant in Anniston, when he spied a tree, uprooted and lying across some power lines near the side of the road. The tree was not a large one, but its weight was great enough to bow the lines, pressing them down to about the level of a man's shoulders.

Before the old man retired he had worked for many years as a drill-press operator in a factory which manufactured and assembled playground equipment. He said that this is what had given him his great love for children. During his last five or six years with the company he had been appointed by his union to be the shop safety officer, and it was his responsibility to be on the lookout for potentially hazardous situations and to figure out means by which accidents could be cut to a minimum. Not only had he supervised the posting of several dozen instructive signs throughout the plant, but he had developed what he called a "check list," a series of precautionary steps which a worker took before ever turning on his machine.

When the old man saw the tree lying in its treacherous sling, he said his first thought was that here was a terrific potential for an accident if he ever saw one. If the lines snapped, live wires would go jumping and bucking all over the place. The lines were close enough to the side of the road to hook a passing car. Even more urgent was the fact that some kid might be lashed by the energies in the broken cables. "There'd been a terrific wind up in Aliosto the night before last," the old man said, "and I figured maybe some tornado had touched down in the woods and

369

just picked up that old tree and set it down on them lines.

"Well, sir, I was at that point in my journey where I didn't know would it be better to turn back to Aliosto or press on to Clendennon. I drive an old Hudson which the feller I got it from turned back the odometer, and it ain't worked proper since. It don't register at all except every ten thousand miles the first two numbers over on the left change, so was no way to tell how far I already come. That's all woods and dirt road between Aliosto and Clendennon. You don't pick up County double 'S' to Anniston till the other side of Clendennon, so one mile don't look no different than another. Speedometer's bust, too, so I couldn't tell how fast I'd been coming, and I don't wear no watch so I didn't know how long neither. Anyway, I decided to continue along to Clendennon. Which it turned out come up a good deal faster than I thought it would.

"There's a general store in Clendennon, and I went inside and asked the feller could I use his pay telephone. I called the phone company business office down to Anniston and told them what I seen. The girl there put me through to the service department, and I told them again.

" 'Well,' says the feller in the service department, 'we didn't get no reports of any interruption in service. Whereabouts this happen?'

" 'On the road between Aliosto and Clendennon.'

" 'No,' he says, 'in which state, Alabama or Georgia?'

" 'Why, there ain't no state line marker on that road,' I told him. 'I didn't see one.'

"So he asks me where I'm calling from and I tell him Clendennon, and he says Clendennon's pretty close to the Georgia line and that if that tree was down on those wires in Georgia no Ala*bama* truck could go out there and fix it.

" 'Well, man,' I said, '*some*body better. Them lines ain't gonna hold up that tree much longer. Some kid could get hurt.' This was summertime. There's fishing all along back in them woods in the lakes. I'd already passed some boys on bicycles. So he says, well, could I do *this*

370

much for him then—could I go back and get the shield numbers on the two poles holding up the wires that tree was flung across, and call him back.

" 'What shields are those?' I asked.

" 'Why, the shields,' he says. 'The little tin plates that are on every telephone and power pole. They're fixed about five and a half foot up the west side of the pole.'

"You know I never noticed them? I'm seventy-one years old and been around telephone poles all my life and I never *did* see that they had any tin plates on them. Well, I thought all this was his business and not mine and I told him so, but he tells me he just ain't got no trucks available at this time. I probably would have dropped the whole thing, but I couldn't stop thinking 'bout them kids that could get hurt. My son-in-law didn't know I was coming, he didn't expect me, and it didn't make no difference what time I finally got there, so I decided I'd go back.

"Well, that's what I did, and a good thing too, because now those lines were no higher than a man's belt, and when I looked up I could see that where they was attached at they was under more strain than ever. They could have bust loose from their connections right while I was standing there. *Well.* I looked for the plates the feller told me about and there they was, on the west side just like he said, and five and a half foot up, too. You ever see one?"

"No."

"Well, they're just like—what do you call it—insignia on a train conductor's hat, and they're tin, and they got these letters and numbers stamped on them, raised up like the figures on a license plate. Some kind of code. I wrote down the numbers and went back to Clendennon and called the fella again and give him the information.

" 'That's Georgia,' he says. 'That's a Georgia pole. You'll have to call them.' "

"What a lot of red tape," Dick Gibson said.

"No, no, that ain't the point. Hang on a minute. You see, just like you, I thought it was all one company, but it isn't. Georgia is Southern Bell, and that part of Alabama

371

where I was is Talladega County Telephone Company."

"Well, you went to a lot of trouble."

"Wait. I called the phone company in Marietta, Georgia. That's where they come out from to service Aliosto where I live, so I called them. This time I didn't tell my story to the girl who answered the phone but asked to be put right through to the service department. I had the numbers of the shields right in front of me, and as soon as the man got on the line I told him, 'Sir, I'm a stranger who while driving along the back road between Aliosto, Georgia, and Clendennon, Alabama, this morning happened to notice a tree pressing down on the lines between poles LF 644 and LF 643. When I first noticed the tree it was lying on the lines at about five and a half foot. When I went back, I would estimate about an hour and a half later, it had sunk to about three feet off the ground. That's about one foot, three inches each hour. That tree is straining desperately at them wires, and I fear for the children in the area if the lines should snap. In fact, they may already have snapped.' You know what he told me?"

"What?"

"That if the lines did snap, all that would happen is that the phone service in the area would be interrupted, and that they couldn't have snapped or I wouldn't be talking to him right now. He said there was no danger from exposed telephone cable, but that I'd better call the electric company because if there were power lines there —see, I thought power lines had something to do with phones, but it turns out they're two different things—and *they* broke down, then there *could* be trouble. I asked him for the number of the electric company, and he said I'd have to get it from Information."

"What a lot of—"

"Wait. I got the number of the electric company from Information and I asked for the service department. I told my story. Do you know what they told me in the service department?"

"What?"

"That I wanted the maintenance department."

"I'll be," Dick said.

"No. Don't you see? What's the service department at the phone company is the maintenance department at the electric company."

"Did you finally get the right department?"

"Sure I did. Once I knew what to ask for, sure I did."

"Did you have any more trouble?"

The old man laughed. "You don't understand," he said. "I can see you just don't understand. I called the maintenance department. See, I thought I knew what was coming. That they'd want to know was there any power lines between them two poles in addition to the telephone cables. That they'd have to tell me what to look for and I'd have to go back again. Well, they asked me if I got the shield numbers and I told them I did and they said let's have them, and I gave them to them and they said well, sir, thank you very much, we'll look into it right away."

"You certainly had yourself a morning," Dick said.

"I said to this fella, 'How do you know whether there's power lines as well as phone cable along in there?'

" 'Why, sure there are,' he said. 'The *F* in the code tells us that.' "

"They took care of it, then?"

"I drove back from visiting my son-in-law the next day. The tree was gone. Not a sign of it. The lines was all taut as good fencing. For my own satisfaction I stopped the car to check the poles. I'd stopped at LF 663, so I counted the poles and finally come down to LF 644 and 643 and everything was clean as a whistle. That's a terrific system. It's better than an address. Course it *is* an address; that's what those shields actually are."

"Well, I'm glad they got it before somebody was hurt," Dick Gibson said.

"Sure," the man said. "This didn't happen yesterday or last week."

"No? From the way you were talking I thought it was a recent experience."

"No. This was three years ago. I'm retired eight years

and this was five years after I retired. It's been three years since this happened."

"I see." He was anxious to take the next call. Perhaps Behr-Bleibtreu was trying to get through.

"There's order," the old man said.

"I'm sorry?"

"There's order. There's procedure. There's records on everything. There's system."

"I suppose there is."

"You bet your life. When I was in Anniston that time I asked my son-in-law to take me through the Pepsi-Cola bottling plant. He showed me how everything worked. I asked a lot of questions. I couldn't take it all in just that one time, so I went back. I had to go back two or three times. I found out all about it. There's system, there's order. I'm in a gas station anywhere in the country and I look at the bottom of the soda bottle and I see where it came from and I know how it got there. I know what happens to that bottle when they take it back. I look for certain tell-tale signs and I know approximately how many more times they'll be able to use it. I know what happens to the glass when they throw it away.

"Then there's cans. I know about them too. It's what I do now. I find out about things. If I don't understand something I get somebody to explain it to me till I do. I don't rest till my curiosity is satisfied. I know how a letter gets from this place to that, just what the zip code does, who handles it. There's organization, there's process, procedure. There's steps—like that check list I made up for the men in my plant. There's a system and intersecting lines and connections. There's meaning. My son-in-law gave me a shirt for Father's Day. I put it on yesterday for the first time. You know what I found in the pocket?"

"What?"

"A slip of paper. 'Inspected by Number 83.' The shirt's a Welford, 65 percent polyester, 35 percent cotton. It's union-made in Chicago. I read the tags on it, the instructions they give you for washing. How can some shirt outfit you never heard of have eighty-three inspectors? And I'm taking eighty-three as an *inside* figure, mind you;

374

probably the numbers go higher. I'm going to find out. I'll find out what that number actually represents. I wrote Eighty-Three today. If I don't get an answer I'll write Eighty-Two. I'll find out. I'll see how it works, how it's all connected. *Everything's* connected. There's order, there's process, there's meaning, there's system. It ain't always clear, but just stick with it and you'll see. Then you'll be amazed you never saw it. It'll be as plain as the nose on your face. If it was a snake it would bite you."

Behr-Bleibtreau didn't call.

Richard Swomley-Wamble called.
"How are you, Henry?" Dick asked distantly.
"You still don't trust me, do you?"
"Oh, well."
"It no longer makes any difference whether you trust me or not," Henry said. There was a catch in his voice.
"Come on, Henry," Dick Gibson said, "you needn't cry just yet. We've barely started our conversation."
"I'm a child. Children cry."
"Very well. Let's drop it. What's been happening, Henry?"
"Richard's my name."
"Richard, then."
"I'm active."
"Your charities?"
"You make it sound ignoble. Please don't pick on me. Why must we always be so irritable with each other? I'm not saying all of it's your fault. I'm responsible too. If I've been fresh, I apologize. I respect my elders—I do, though I suppose sometimes I say things that gives them the impression I'm conceited or think I know more about life than they do. I know you have experience and maturity, whereas I have only my idealism. Children can be pretty narrow sometimes. Look, I'm really very grateful to you. You took me into the Listening Post when I needed it very badly. I'll never forget that. Id really like very much for us to be friends."
"All right," Dick said, "so would I." It was true. He

375

had been uncertain of his ground with Richard from the first; even as he had baited him he felt himself in the wrong. And he had other things to worry about. "What have you been doing?" he asked.

"These two weeks have been wonderful," the boy said enthusiastically. "The Mail Baggers have been marvelous. You know, a lot of them just want to be cheered up, or if they do need something it's usually very small. There's a woman in Lakeland who's bedridden. Her TV picture tube blew out last month and she wrote to ask if I could let her have thirty-five dollars to replace it. Thirty-five dollars may not be much to you or me, but when you're trying to live on just your Social Security payments I guess it can seem like all the money in the world. I didn't replace the tube but I did get her a new color set."

"That was very kind of you, Richard."

"I hope she doesn't think I throw my money around to impress people. I thought she'd enjoy it."

"I'm certain she does."

"There's just one thing——"

"What's that?"

"Color sets require adjustment. That can be pretty hard on someone who's bedridden. The set can't be too close to the bed because of the radiation. I hope I didn't make a mistake."

"I don't think so."

"I bought three motorized wheelchairs last week and two hospital beds. I've arranged with several mothers who can't afford it for their children to have music lessons. They rent the instruments and the rental is applied toward the purchase if the kids are still taking lessons two years from now. I put the rest of the money in escrow for them. Another mother wanted dancing lessons for her little girl and I arranged for those too. I bought two gross of imported dashikis and distributed them throughout the inner city. I'm sponsoring a Little League team in the Sarasota ghetto. Everyone will have his own uniform, even the kids on the bench. I bought some bicycles for people who have no way to get to work in the morning. I'm having some people's plumbing fixed."

376

"That was very thoughtful, Richard."

"It robs people of their dignity when their toilets don't flush properly."

"You know, Richard, it sounds to me as though you've been spending a lot of money."

"Oh, well."

"No, I mean it," Dick said. "I know you want to help and I realize that three-quarters of a million dollars is a great deal of money, but that money has to last until you're twenty-one. At the rate you're spending it might be very close."

"That's not a problem," Richard said quietly.

"Oh?"

"It's not a problem."

"What is it, son? Has something happened?"

"Oh, Mr. Gibson," the boy sobbed, "I'd hoped this call would be a happy one, that we'd just chat about people's dreams coming true."

"Well, fine, Richard."

"No," the boy said manfully. "I have a duty. I was fooling myself when I thought this could be a happy call."

"What is it, Richard?"

"I really called to ask people not to write me any more. I won't be able to help them."

"I see."

"I'm sorry if I got their hopes up."

"What is it, Richard? Isn't there any three-quarters of a million dollars?"

"Yes," the boy said, suddenly fierce. "There is. It isn't that."

"I see. All right."

"I can't have them writing me any more, that's all. I won't be picking up my mail. They'd just be wasting their postage, and they can't afford it."

"All right," Dick Gibson said, "I see."

"I'm being adopted tomorrow," Richard cried. "When I gave out my real name, some people . . . They reported me. The courts stepped in. They had the juvenile authorities out here in two shakes of a lamb's tail."

"I'm sorry, Richard," Dick Gibson said.

"I shouldn't say this——"

"What, lad?"

"The people who reported me are the ones who'll be adopting me. I was like a . . . a finder's fee."

"Perhaps they're nice," Dick said encouragingly, "just the ones to give you guidance and security and love."

"They're pigs, Mr. Gibson." The boy was crying uncontrollably.

"Don't cry, Richard."

"They're greedy people, Mr. Gibson."

"Richard, you know if you really dislike them that much you don't have to stay with them. I'm sure the court would try to fix you up with parents who are more compatible. You don't have to go with them, son. There's no law that——"

"I've decided not to fight them."

"But why, Richard? Why, son?"

"It wouldn't make any difference. Anyone who'd want me now . . . It wouldn't make any difference." The boy blew his nose. He cleared his throat. Dick waited patiently while he got control of himself. "I won't be calling your program any more," he said at last. He spoke slowly, with great dignity.

"I see."

"They won't *let* me call the program."

"I understand."

"They're taking the phone out of my room. I won't have a radio."

"Oh, son," Dick said.

"I have to be in bed by eight-thirty every night."

"Oh, son," Dick Gibson said, "oh, Henry." But the boy was no longer on the line.

Then there was a string of calls from some of the unhappiest people in the world.

One man had been laid off for eight months and was unable to find work. His wife and eldest daughter had taken jobs as domestics. He would be a domestic himself, he said, but people were afraid to have a white man in their houses.

A woman called. She'd awakened two hours before. Her husband was not in the house. Her little boy's bed was empty. Their car was gone. A couple of suitcases were missing. They'd been having trouble lately. Her husband liked to listen to Dick's program. Perhaps he was listening now. She pleaded with him to return, to call and let her know where he was.

A man had lost his wife about four months ago. He couldn't sleep, and he was starting to drink, he said.

A high-school girl was having trouble with her stepfather. He had taken the locks off her bathroom and bedroom doors. She was afraid to be in the house alone with him.

Dick couldn't recognize any of their voices. They were not Mail Baggers.

Then a man called who said he was phoning from a booth just outside the emergency room of Miami Municipal Hospital. "I been listening to your program on this transistor radio in the waiting room," he said. "I called in to tell you about me. I take the cake. I thought you'd want to hear about it. If they gave out prizes they'd have to give me a big one. I take the cake."

"Oh," Dick said wearily.

"See, I live here. You understand me? In the emergency waiting room. This is where I live. I'm an emergency, do you follow?"

"They let you stay there?"

"Well, I'm an emergency, ain't I? Sure, the docs and nurses let me sleep here on the leather sofa. You should see the shape some of these clowns are in—their heads all unbuttoned and their blood upside down. Boy oh boy. They give you bad dreams on the leather sofa, some of them. I got my eye on one guy sitting outside this booth in a wheelchair right now. He ain't cut or burnt or nothing, but he looks pretty sick. Wife's more upset than he is. She's got this steel nigger comb, just keeps running it over and over through his hair and looking down at him

379

from behind the wheelchair. Yeah, you really see it in a place like this—second-degree burns, third-degree, the works. And accident cases. You know what's the worst accident case there is? Motorcycles. These kids come in, and I mean they'd *totaled*. Like they fell off the world. One time I seen a guy hold his eye in his hand like a marble. And raving maniacs—*they're* cute. You wouldn't believe the language comes out of their mouths—especially the women's. My God, what's on some people's minds!

"Tonight a little kid come in who'd worked one of these washers onto his finger and it wouldn't come off. They got a tool that cuts off rings and they used that. Imagine having a tool for something like that. That's what gets me. They got a tool for everything. For pulling beans out of people's noses and getting crud from their eye. There ain't an emergency they haven't worked out in advance.

"Most people couldn't take living in a place like this. I know what to avoid. If it's real bad, the ambulance driver comes running in first to tell the girl at the desk. Then I know it ain't something I want to see and I get out of the way."

"Why do you stay?"

"Why do I *stay*? In case something happens to me. I'm an epileptic, I got Grand Mal. That means the Big Bad. The Big Bad I got. But I'm right here, you follow? I'm Johnny on the spot. I'm never more than a minute from help."

Dick didn't know how he was going to get through the rest of the program. The man was waiting for him to say something, but he couldn't think of anything.

"I got a right," the man said abruptly. "Hell, I'm an emergency. I got Grand Mal."

"Where do you dress?" Dick finally managed. "What about your clothes?"

"Oh. Yeah. Well, that's interesting about that. I got this buddy in the hospital laundry. He throws my stuff into the hopper with the sheets and gowns. Everything on me is fresh every day. And there's this vegetable on the seventh floor—they let me use his electric razor."

"You've got it made," Dick said.

"How do I eat? You know how I eat?"

"How do you eat?"

"I take my meals off hospital trays! I eat what the sick leave!"

"Terrific."

"What, you don't believe me?"

"I believe you."

"Then what's wrong? You think I'm talking about garbage? Full-course meals! Full-course breakfast! Full-course lunch! Everything full course. I eat better than you do. It's balanced meals. A dietitian makes them up. I'm on a salt-free diet. My cholesterol's lower than yours is. I could *over*eat if I wanted—sick people don't have much appetite—but I watch myself, I don't gorge."

"Just push yourself away from the hospital cart, is that it? That's the best exercise."

"Yeah. Ha ha. Yeah."

"Yeah."

"Well, I do have this little staph infection. What's so terrible? It won't kill me. I can live with it. The residents have their eye on it. It's low grade, practically nothing."

Dick groaned.

"Well, where *should* I go, hot shot, where? I'm an emergency. My life's an emergency. Where's an emergency gonna go?"

"I'm not criticizing."

"Listen," the caller said, "I ain't stinted. I get everything I want. The chow's good. I get dessert, even. I already told you. Ha ha. *I take the cake.*"

He couldn't have taken any more calls. It was a good thing the show was almost over. He was tired. He did the commercials mechanically, announced the temperature and told his listeners the time, and then he reached forward, took the table microphone and brought it close to his mouth. He paused, not quite certain what he was going to say.

"I'm worried about Henry Harper," he said at last. "I'm thinking about Ingrid in the Buick. I don't even mention air pollution, foreign policy, or the terrible things that have been turning up in the artificial sweeteners. There's crime in the streets, and to tell you the truth, we've mucked up our fields and streams too. I hope the Sierra Club wins its battle against the Disney interests in California. I'm troubled about the whales, and I mourn for the death of Lake Erie. The pill has harmful side effects and not enough people wear their safety belts. We ought to have better gun laws. Everywhere the environment is as run down as a slum. Strontium 90 takes a generation to break down, but even that's faster than the non-biodegradable soaps. The young have chromosome damage from LSD and the old live without point. Our diet isn't any good. Where will the money come from for low-cost housing? Charcoal steaks cause irreversible lung damage; cancer is broiling in the barbecue. The pace is too fast and the noise level's too high, color TV makes you sterile and too much sunshine queers your skin. Speed kills and hot water from the factories raises the temperature of the river and murders the fish. Food preservatives poison our breakfast cereal. There's monosodium glutamate in the baby food and baldness in the hair spray. There's BHA in the white bread. Oh God, there's far too much nitrate in the soil, and unless the furriers become more responsible in five years the only leopards left alive will be in the zoos.

"I'm concerned about barium and arsenic in the drinking water of playground fountains, and about the carcinogenic wax on fruit like the bad queen's toxin on Snow White's apple. Jesus, friends, our bath water mustn't be too hot and the rubber from our tires dissolves into the air so that we're choking on our own tread. *Keep all medicines out of the reach of children,* I tell you. *If you drive, don't drink!* Coffee is bad for us and we don't know what aspirin does to our cells. We haven't figured out our priorities. Smoking stunts your growth, and I don't like the way they shunt the phosgene gas back and forth across the country on railroad cars. They're playing Russian roulette with our lives. The long straightaways on our freeways can hypnotize you and there's enough mercury in the eggs we consume to drive a thermometer.

Don't look directly into the eclipse. Only you can prevent forest fires. We're drowning in litter, shipmates. Jet lag upsets the circadian rhythms and plays holy hell with the stewardess's monthlies, and sonic boom is killing the gazelles. The air isn't clean. Mark my words, the population explodes even as we drop dead. A thermal inversion melts the icebergs and our coastlines are drowning. An underground nuclear explosion can set off an earthquake, and I'm not so well myself.

"There's too much obsession. I'm worried about Henry Harper. I wonder what happened to that man in Knoxville. To the lady with the pierced ears. I wish Angela and Robert would get out of the house. There's nothing they can do about the baby. What will be will be. They mustn't feel guilty. If they want, I'll go up to Tallahassee myself and sit with the kid so they can go to the movies. It would do them good to get out once in a while. What does that old man mean, everything's connected? That guy who called tonight should move out of the emergency room and rent an apartment. There's too much obsession. I'm guilty as the next guy. I can't stop thinking about Behr-Bleibtreau. He's a man I knew in Hartford one time, and I think he holds a grudge against me. He might be trying to force some crazy showdown between us, and I can't say I mind because I think it may be in the cards. Only . . . only . . .

"All those calls tonight. What's happening to my program? What's the matter with everybody? Why are we all so obsessed? I tell you, I'm sick of obsession. I've eaten my ton of it and I can't swallow another bite. Where are my Mail Baggers, the ones who used to call with their good news and their recipes for Brunswick stew and their tips about speed traps between here and Chicago? How do your gardens grow, for Christ's sake? What's with the crabgrass? What'll it be this summer, the sea or the mountains? Have the kids heard from the colleges of their choice? *What's happening?*"

6

It was time for the Dick Gibson Picnic.

To promote the event the station had been playing a series of spot announcements, one or two a night at the beginning of the campaign but gradually reaching saturation a week before the picnic. As in the previous year, it was decided that it would be held in Gainesville, Florida, a city about three hundred miles northwest of Miami. The management felt that though this worked a hardship on the heavy listenership concentrated in the Miami area, Gainesville was more accessible to the villagers and farm families of central and southern Georgia, southeastern Alabama and the great midlands of Florida itself than Miami proper, which would have been expensive and crowded even in the off-season. Although Miami contributed far and away the largest audience to the program, its participation in Listening Posts was disproportionately small. The backbone of the show was still the rural areas. Nevertheless, there were indications that an adjustment was taking place, the country people frightened perhaps by the increasing bluntness of the calls. All shows seek the level of the demands made upon them, but there was something alarming, as much to the management as to Dick Gibson, about the stridency of these demands, the way solipsism was gradually drowning out the inquiry, deference and courtesy that had set the show's original tone. As long, however, as the sponsors showed no alarm, no one made any serious effort to force the show back to its original instincts. Perhaps they had not *been* instincts.

WMIA picked up the tab for feeding the thousand or so Dick Gibson Picnickers expected to turn out, but all the work of preparing the fried chicken, potato salad, roast corn, iced tea and Jellomold fell to the picnic's official hosts, the Listening Post from Cordelle County, Georgia, who arranged, too, for the entertainment. Last year's Entertainment Committee had been too ambitious, and while they had put together a first-rate show of singers, bands, groups and chorus lines from the local dancing schools, everyone agreed afterward that they had come to meet and mix with each other, not to sit for three hours in a hot tent. Hence, this year the Committee had decided to emphasize various games and comical races in which all the Mail Baggers might participate. In fact, the Entertainment Committee suggested that this year there be *no* structured activity. It was Dick Gibson who reminded them that people would be coming from all over the Southeast and that since most of them would be strangers to each other there ought to be at least some minimal group activity. He had also insisted that an effort be made to keep people belonging to the same Listening Post from sitting together at the picnic tables.

On the day before the picnic Dick drove to Gainesville in his convertible with the top down, taking along his director and his engineer, the only people from WMIA to attend. The station manager and several other of the station's executives had planned to come, but Dick had discouraged this, pointing out that it would be better for the program if the Mail Baggers did not see him as just another employee of the station, and that the presence of a hierarchy would detract from their sense that the program belonged to them. The management conceded the point and so he went up to Gainesville accompanied only by his crew, Bob Orchard and Lawrence Leprese, who were already familiar to his audience. Particularly in the early days of the program, his listeners had become used to Dick's good-natured kidding of the two men. "Bob," he might suddenly complain to his engineer, "where are my Kentucky calls? You're not giving me a strong enough Kentucky signal. Turn this station around and get me blue grass." Invariably his little hint would inspire some Kentuckian to phone in, and then he would compliment the engineer on his improvement, building the conceit that the station was a sort of airplane which could be pointed in any direction they chose. He also commented on Lawrence Leprese's wild sports shirts, painting a lurid picture for his audience of the director's terrible taste. Actually, the man usually wore an ordinary dark business suit with a white shirt and plain tie, and so before going to Gainesville Dick had had to buy him the loudest shirt and Bermuda shorts he could find in the Deauville specialty shop.

There was a large sign taped to the long side of the convertible with Dick Gibson's name painted on it in bold red letters, so that as he drove along he looked like the grand marshal of his own parade. In DeLand, Florida, where they stopped for gas, he forgot it was there and tore the sign in half when he opened the door on the driver's side. They repaired it with scotch tape and drove the rest of the way up to Gainesville.

The station had booked three rooms for them at the Hotel Pick-Gainesville and they checked in at about six thirty on Friday evening. Tired from the long drive, Dick decided to have dinner sent to his room and then go to bed until it was time to do the show that night.

They had rented the facilities of WGSV, using the phone company's carrier line to take the signal back to Miami. This affected the sound quality, but worse was that the station didn't have the sophisticated phone setup

WMIA did, so the program's mechanics that night were very clumsy. All the incoming calls had to be handled through the receptionist's switchboard and shunted by extension phone to the studio. Since the station ran an all-night record request show, naturally the girl at the switchboard fell behind and when Dick finished a conversation there was not always another caller on the line. Nor did he have any notion where a call was coming from and found it difficult to recognize his listeners' voices. The occasion of the picnic and its publicity had reassured many of the old Mail Baggers that the program was being returned to them, inspiring them to call the show again, but it must have been clear to even the least astute that they'd been forgotten. Much air time was wasted in sly maneuvering between Dick and his callers, the caller wanting Dick to say his name and Dick trying to get the caller to do it for him. Though it was a dull program, it was a very hard night's work for him. It was dull, hard work, but there was something pleasant about it too. It was like the old days, the *very* old days, before they knew each other too well, and had had to take everything slowly and carefully, offering each other gentle, civilized banalities.

Still, by sign-off, he was exhausted. This may have been one reason he was so unresponsive at the picnic the next morning. He had not actually slept before Friday's show. From promotional considerations given the Pick-Gainesville in return for free accommodations, many Mail Baggers knew what hotel Dick was at, and at least half a dozen had called the room to invite him for drinks. By the time he told the desk to put no more calls through, he wasn't sleepy, and he watched television until it was time to go down to the station. Even afterward, tired though he was, he found it difficult to sleep, finally dropping off for two hours before he was awakened for the picnic. Those people who wrote the management afterward to complain of his "distance" either were poor readers of mood or had never been exhausted. After all, he was no chicken, he was pushing fifty. This, at any rate, was what he told the station manager when asked to explain the large amount of critical mail that had poured into the station following the picnic. And if these explanations were not frank, it was not the first time he had not been entirely open with the management about the picnic. Good as they were, his reasons for not wanting the station executives in Gainesville had nothing to do with anything as remote as the program's "image."

It was Behr-Bleibtreau. He was convinced that something savage would happen. The man had once tried to strangle him. He hadn't known his reasons then and he didn't know them now, and though he felt the Mail Baggers would protect him from violence, he really believed the savagery would take some other form. He needed strength and concentration; the presence of his employers would have been deflective. If he was to put on a show—*The Dick Gibson Show*—it must be for his poor callers.

At 10 A.M. they entered Gainesville's Emma Shulding Memorial Park and drove onto the broad expanse of contiguous athletic fields in the open convertible. The motorcycle policeman escorting them turned onto a green outfield and guided them past second base toward home plate. They toured slowly, giving as many of the Mail Baggers as felt like it an opportunity to approach the car. Dick, perched on the back seat, leaned down to shake their hands, scrutinizing their nametags in the few seconds they walked along beside the car, and whispered questions to them about their families. It surprised him that he knew so little about them. A man extended condolences on the death of Mrs. Dormer. It was the first confirmation he'd had of this.

"Then she *is* dead," he said sadly.

Bob Orchard drove around behind the screen at home plate and the three of them got out. There was some difficulty with the public-address equipment, so Dick dispatched Bob Orchard to look at it. When his engineer got it working there were a few remarks and announcements by the president of the Cordelle County, Georgia, Listening Post. Then she introduced Bob Orchard and Lawrence Leprese, who both said a few words to the crowd.

388

Leprese did little more than stand before them in the Bermuda shorts and loud sports shirt that Dick Gibson had bought. "How do you like 'em?" he asked. The Mail Baggers laughed and applauded.

Dick was introduced. He told them how glad he was to be there and that it looked like an even bigger turnout than last year's. It wasn't—the cop who conducted them across the playing field said later that there couldn't be more than six or seven hundred people there—but Dick wasn't trying to con them. He'd been looking for Behr-Bleibtreau, not sure he would recognize him—it had been ten years—studying each face, doubling back over groups he had already considered, losing track, beginning again, like someone trying to count spilled pennies on a rug. It was partly his distracted air that made him seem absent to the people who wrote the station to criticize him. Actually, he had never felt so keen, and though his words may have seemed bland, he experienced a genuine affection for his listeners, his special knowledge feeding his tenderness and making him protective as a statesman, fond as a champion. His ordeal would be theirs as well.

He publicly thanked the wonderful men and women of the Cordelle County, Georgia, Listening Post for the marvelous work they had done—he meant this sincerely, but our words are sometimes flattest when we are most deeply moved—and told the crowd that he would be out to meet as many of them personally as time would permit. Then he walked out to the raised pitcher's mound, and there he remained for most of the day, choosing the spot not as the malcontents had it because he was showboating but because he wanted always to be within clear view of the crowd. Until lunchtime there were always four or five Mail Baggers around him, but after eating with the Cordelle County chapter, when he returned to the pitcher's mound few people followed, and those who came up soon walked off. He continued to watch out for Behr-Bleibtreau, of course, and not until he had left the park did he begin to have doubts that it was Behr-Bleibtreau's voice he had heard that night.

On the whole it was a pleasant day. The food was

excellent and plentiful and they had good weather. His enemy never came.

If he failed to participate in the games it wasn't because he felt superior or was a bad sport, but because he was worn out. After all, he was pushing fifty.

7

There was time for one more call.

"Night Letters—go ahead please."

It was a woman, earnest and angry. "Well, thank God," she said. "I thought the program would be over and done with before I reached you."

"As a matter of fact, we *haven't* much time. What did you want to talk about?"

"Listen, I'm a little flustered. I really didn't think I was going to get through to you. I've never called one of these shows before."

"I'd like to tell you to take your time, but the old clock on the wall—"

"I'm sorry. Well." She took a deep breath. "I saw something today which makes me hopping mad. All I have to do is think about it and I can't see straight."

"What's it all about, ma'm?"

"I called the Better Business Bureau and they say there's nothing they can do about it, and I called the postal authorities and they tell me it has nothing to do with *them,* so I thought the only thing left was to try to arouse public opinion."

"That's what we're here for," Dick Gibson said cheerfully.

"I have a twelve-year-old boy. I was cleaning his room today—well yesterday afternoon now—and I found something in one of his drawers. I tell you, I was never so shocked in my life."

"Pornography," Dick said.

"No, not pornography. I'm not a narrow-minded woman, Mr. Gibson. My son's almost thirteen and I suppose he has a natural curiosity about the opposite sex. We don't take *Playboy,* but I suppose he sees it often enough, and a lot of those other so-called men's magazines too, probably. That's just part of growing up and I accept it, but this is something else. No, not pornography. More obscene than pornography."

"Look, ma'm, I hate to rush you, but this sounds like it might be something with a lot of pros and cons to it, and right now we just haven't the time to—"

"I'm sorry. I'm a little nervous, and as I say, this thing has upset me so I guess I'm not really making much sense. Somebody's got to do something about it. Somebody's *got* to."

"Well, you know, ma'm, *Night Letters* isn't really that kind of talk show. We're not a controversy program."

"It was in a comic book."

"We were off the track there for a while, but we've been trying to—"

"There was this *ad.*"

"Look, if it's a commercial product, the FCC won't—"

"Oh, for God's *sake,* Mr. Gibson!"

"We're not allowed to—"

"Listen to me, will you? Something's got to be done about this. Children mustn't—"

"Even if this is a war-toys thing I couldn't—"

"It's an *ad.* You mail in two dollars. They send pamphlets. They tell you how to do things. How to put together a zip gun and make your own bullets. 'How to coat the blade of an ordinary pocket knife with one of the deadliest poisons known to man.' I'm quoting from the ad. This is intended for children, Mr. Gibson. Do you have children? Just listen to this part. 'Our instruction booklet—' "

"I have no chil—"

" '—teaches you the secret of preparing an acid from ingredients normally available on your own front lawn. This acid, commonly known as *eye acid,* is from a formula long known only to the Seminole Indians, the only tribe in the United States never to sign a peace treaty with the American government. If so much as a single drop of this potent substance were to come into contact with the eye, vision would be permanently destroyed. *Seeks out and destroys the optic nerve on contact!* The fumes alone can impair vision for periods of up to ten years. Only your *enemies* need worry! Included in the booklet are simple directions for the mild antidote which completely protects you from the acid yourself. This is but one of the many exciting poisons described in our simple-to-follow manual. Never an offer like it! The directions are so clear that if you have ever baked a cake or even read a recipe you can make any one of the thirty deadly acids and poisons thoroughly and completely explained in this guide. Be as powerful as the cruelest murderers in history! *The secrets of the Borgias!* Know nature's other face, unlock the awful powers of chemistry! For mere pennies we can show you how to concoct a poison so toxic that just one cupful thrown into the water supply is enough to debilitate a community of 100,000 persons. *The powers of epidemic in your hands!* Useful for the destruction of pesky animals! Protect your loved ones!' That's only part of it. Shall I go on? There's worse, if you can imagine."

Dick was, excited, but something urged him to be prudent; he had to seem detached. He understood that his discretion had nothing at all to do with the new policy of the program, that it was important and useful to him personally.

He had to hear more, however. "Well, you know, dear," he said mildly, "that's kind of a wild ad, but I don't really think our kids will be very interested in that sort of thing. They're a pretty sensible bunch, most of them. Gosh, for every kid who goes wrong that you read about in the papers there must be ten thousand minding their own business and trying to get good grades."

"Mr. Gibson, this is *vicious*. I've never heard of anything so vicious."

"Oh, well," he said, "we've got another few minutes, I suppose. If you want to tell us some of the rest, I guess we can cut a minute or so out of the theme music." He spoke lazily and blandly, conscious that a tape recorder was taking down everything he said.

"Listen to this," she said, "tell me there's nothing wrong with a world where this sort of thing can get printed. I'm quoting: 'In addition to the pamphlet on poisons we have prepared a useful handbook on the assembly of handguns, small bombs and the infamous Molotov Cocktail, together with a section on how to make volatile powders and explosives in the privacy of your own home from chemicals sold over the counter for pennies. For those who send in their money now we will include at no extra charge an additional booklet, the top-secret *Commandos' Bible,* an indispensable guide to the deadly methods of the heroic commandos of World War II. *Be prepared! Available nowhere else! Fully illustrated, as are all the pamphets in this exciting new series!* THE VIOLENT DEVICES THAT HELPED TO WIN THE WAR REVEALED AND EXPLAINED: the garrote, napalm, the plastic bomb, along with *the new silent time bomb* impossible to detect. This light (two pounds), lethal instrument can be slipped into the luggage of an unsuspecting traveler and preset to go off anywhere from forty-five minutes to three hours after his plane has taken off or his train has left the station. *No ticking! Totally silent!* When you discover the secret of how it's done you'll laugh that no one ever thought of it before.' It's *all* like that, Mr. Gibson. It makes me sick just to read it. And it's so anonymous. You don't even know who's behind it. They just give a post-office box number."

"I've got to admit," Dick Gibson said, "it sounds a lot worse than the B-B guns they used to advertise in those books when *I* was a kid. I'm no expert, and this is just a lay opinion, mind you, but off the top of my head I don't see how it can be legal."

"They've got this disclaimer."

"Oh? They've got a disclaimer, do they?"

"At the bottom of the ad."

"Oh?"

" 'For educational purposes only. Not responsible for any bodily injury which may occur.' "

"Say," Dick said, "that's pretty clever. That's how they get around it, is it? Whoops, I see we've just about run out of time."

His director put the theme music on, and while the first few bars were playing Dick took her off the air and spoke casually into the phone. "Say," he said, "I'd like to see a copy of that ad. Why don't you send it to me? I've got this friend on the Attorney General's staff in Tallahassee. I'll look it over and if it seems as bad as you make it sound I'll see that he gets a copy of it with my personal letter. What do you say?" His hands were trembling. "Will you send it to me?"

"Yes," she said, "that's a good idea. I'll put it in the mail today."

"Good deal," he said. "Got to run now. Got to sign this ole program off the air."

His thought was that here at last was something he could do. There was too much suffering. Too much went wrong; victims were everywhere. *That* was your real population explosion. There was mindless obsession, concentration without point, offs and ups, long life's niggling fractions, its Dow-Jones concern with itself. What had his own life been, his interminable apprenticeship which he saw now he could never end? And everyone blameless as himself, everyone doing his best but maddened at last, all, all zealous, all with explanations ready at hand and serving an ideal of truth or beauty or health or grace. Everyone—everyone. It did no good to change policy or fiddle with format. The world pressed in. It opened your windows. All one could hope for was to find his scapegoat, to wait for him, lurking in alleys, pressed flat against walls, crouched behind doors while the key jiggles in the lock, taking all the melodramatic postures of revenge. To be there in closets when the enemy comes for his hat, or to surprise him with guns in swivel chairs, your legs dapperly crossed when you turn to face him, to pin him down on hillsides or pounce on him from trees as he rides by, to meet him on the roofs of trains roaring on trestles, or leap at him while he stops at red lights, to struggle with him on the smooth faces of cliffs, national monuments, chasing him round Liberty's torch, or up girders of bridges, or across the enormous features of stone presidents. To pitch him from ski lifts and roller coasters, to Normandy his ass and guerrilla his soul. To be always in ambush at the turnings in tunnels, or wrestle him under the tides of the seas. Gestures, gestures, saving gestures, life-giving and meaningless and sweet as appetite, delivered by gestures and redeemed by symbols, by necessities of your own making and a destiny dreamed in a dream. To be free—yes, existential and generous.

To feed him his own poisons, to blind him with his acids, pickle him in his vicious, zany juices, catch him in his traps and explode him with his bombs.

He made up his mind to kill the man responsible for the ad.

The earnest woman was as good as her word. In two days the comic book was in his hands. As she had said, there was no way to identify who had placed the ad; all he had to go on was the name of the company—"Top Secret!"—and the address, a post office box number in Latrobe, Pennsylvania. He clipped the coupon, signed it with a false name and sent it in with his two dollars. For a return address he gave a post office box of his own which he rented for the purpose.

In his dealings with the post office he learned that while the government would not rent a box to anyone unwilling to furnish proper identification, neither would it reveal the identity of a boxholder to anyone other than the representative of an authorized law-enforcement agency. He had no real fear for himself. He was confident that when the time came he would get away with the murder, but these conditions made it difficult to find out the name of the man in Latrobe. He was not discouraged. He remembered the caller from Georgia, the old man who found connections in everything. Surely if there were ways to delve behind the anonymity of a Pepsi-Cola bottle, there were ways to discover who was responsible for placing the ad. (It was a long shot, of course, but he couldn't help hoping it would turn out to be Behr-Bleibtreau.) Actually, he didn't have to start with the post office box at all. He could get the man's name from the agency that had accepted the advertisement. With his connections in radio and his knowledge of the media, that wouldn't be difficult; a couple of phone calls would do it. There were many ways. If all else failed he could go to Latrobe—he had a vacation coming—rent a box there himself and simply wait for whoever came to pick up the mail for "Top Secret!" Nothing was more simple.

Meanwhile, he waited for the pamphlets, checking the box every other day for three weeks. Then he began to wonder which would be worse, if the man who placed the ad sent the material or if he were running a swindle. Once or twice he was tempted to write a letter complaining about the delay, but each time he decided against it. To prevent the postal authorities from becoming suspicious, every so often he addressed an envelope to himself, always writing these notes on Deauville stationery but mailing them in plain envelopes.

A month passed, and still he had had no response from Latrobe. He decided to write the followup letter after all, but the very day after he mailed it the pamphlets arrived. Ain't that always the way, he thought as he opened the box and removed the manilla envelope.

He returned to the Deauville and pored over what he'd been sent. It was all there, everything that had been promised: the formulas for poisons, the instructions for assembling guns and bombs—everything. There was one item that hadn't been mentioned in the ad, a single sheet of greasy paper like the stock used in fortune cookies, the inked letters on the cheap paper like frazzled cultures under magnification. The sheet contained tips for growing and recognizing marijuana. The pamphlets had been run off on a mimeograph machine from abused stencils, and the illustrations were crude and vaguely pornographic like the backgrounds in ancient eight-pagers. The staples that held them together were at odd angles to the page; several were rusty. He shook his head sadly at the poverty of being that was revealed by the author/illustrator of the pamphlets. It was too shabby—basement evil, the awry free enterprise of a madman. Would the devices even work? How could he kill *him?* Nothing would change.

He scrawled a note to Robert Sohnshild at the Attorney General's Office in Tallahassee. "Dear Bob," he wrote, "the enclosed material has recently come to my attention. Is there anything your office can do?" He added a brief postscript. "You know what my hopes are for you and for Angela and for the baby. We are powerless in these things. What more can I say?" He placed the note on top of the pamphlets, shoved everything back into the manilla envelope, resealed and readdressed it. Maybe I would have killed him, he thought, if the mails had been faster. Maybe if I ever find out the man's name and happen to run into him I'll still kill him. But probably not.

He left the envelope with the woman at the information desk of the Deauville to mail for him. Surrendering it, he thought, ah, the cliché, the relinquisher, the man who walks away from triumph, who renounces revenge.

He asked the doorman to bring his car. Perhaps it was Behr-Bleibtreau who had permitted him his destiny after all, Behr-Bleibtreau who *would* have been his enemy, who would have focused the great unfocused struggle of his life but who had failed to show up, who had left him standing high up on the pitcher's mound in the Gainesville park, unheeded and alone and with an unobstructed view of the corny convertible with its top down and the mended Dick Gibson sign taped to its sides. On the mound there, silhouetted, a target of sorts but abandoned, with his arms at his sides, his shoulders slumped and only his eye still moving, darting this way and that, searching desperately for the man who would bring the mortal combat with him that would save his life. And then even his eyes stilled, mute as his character, everything stilled at last except for the potato and wheelbarrow racers, the oddly coupled men and women tied together at the ankles or locked back to back or joined in gunnysacks or squeezed in barrels or pressed facing each other and scrabbling sideways in the crab's oblique drift.

He drove down Collins Boulevard to the radio station and gave his car to the man in the Fontainebleau parking lot. He crossed the street at the light and rode up in the elevator to his studio. He waved wearily to the men in the control booth and took his place at his desk. The engineer asked for a voice level and Dick, confused for a moment, turned to see where the sound had come from.

"Give us a level, Dick," Orchard repeated.

He looked at the microphone. "Please stand by," he said softly. "One moment please."

"Too low, Dick," Lawrence Leprese said. "Can you move a little closer to the mike? We've got about a minute."

"Oh," he said.

"That's better," Leprese said.

"What I wanted," he said slowly, "was to be a leading man, my life to *define* life, my name a condition—like Louis Quatorze."

"A household word, is that it, Dick?" Leprese said over the loudspeaker. "The level's good."

"Not glory, not even fame." The buttons on the phone were already lit. "Not a hero, not even very dependable—"

"Thirty seconds, Dick."

"—but to be *excited*. To live at the kindling point, oh God, *at the sound barrier*."

The On the Air sign came on. It flared behind its red glass, bright as blood on a smear on a slide. He leaned forward and spoke to the microphone. "This is Dick Gibson," he said, "WMIA. The scrambled I Am's of Miami Beach."

He picked up the phone and jabbed one of the lighted buttons. "Good evening, Night Letters."

"I'm this man's mistress," a woman said. "His wife is dying and he has to take her to a different climate. He's asked me to—"

"Wrong number," he said, and punched another button. "Night Letters."

"My doggy was run over."

"Line's busy." He took another call. "Night Letters."

"I'm a peeping Tom. I think I'm going blind."

"It's a bad connection." All the buttons on the phone panel were lit. He pressed one again. "Good evening, Night Letters."

"If only, if only, if only—"

"Wrong number, bad connection, line's busy, he ain't in. *This number isn't in service!*" He wiped his face and poked another button. "Hello, Night Letters. Who's there?"

"The President of the United States. Dick, Bebe Rebozo and I are terribly concerned about what's been going on in Vietnam . . ."